THE CRAVING

AN AWARD-WINNING INSPIRATIONAL YA ROMANCE.

J F SAXBY

IRONSTONE PRESS

First published November 2021 by Ironstone Press
Second Edition May 2022
Sydney NSW Australia 2074
ABN 56 996 948 676

https://ironstonepress.com.au/
Email: info@ironstonepress.com.au

ISBN: 978-1-922820-02-0

Cover design © Brandi Doane McCann
Map © J F Saxby

Internal design by Impressum

A catalogue record for this book is available from the National Library of Australia

Brilliant!

Inspiring.

Story remained in my mind long after reading.

—CALEB Award judges' comments.

Mind boggling!

Exquisite, multi-layered book.

Un-put-downable!

What is hidden in these pages may impact your life forever.

Both an allegory and herald for our times.

—Amazon reviews

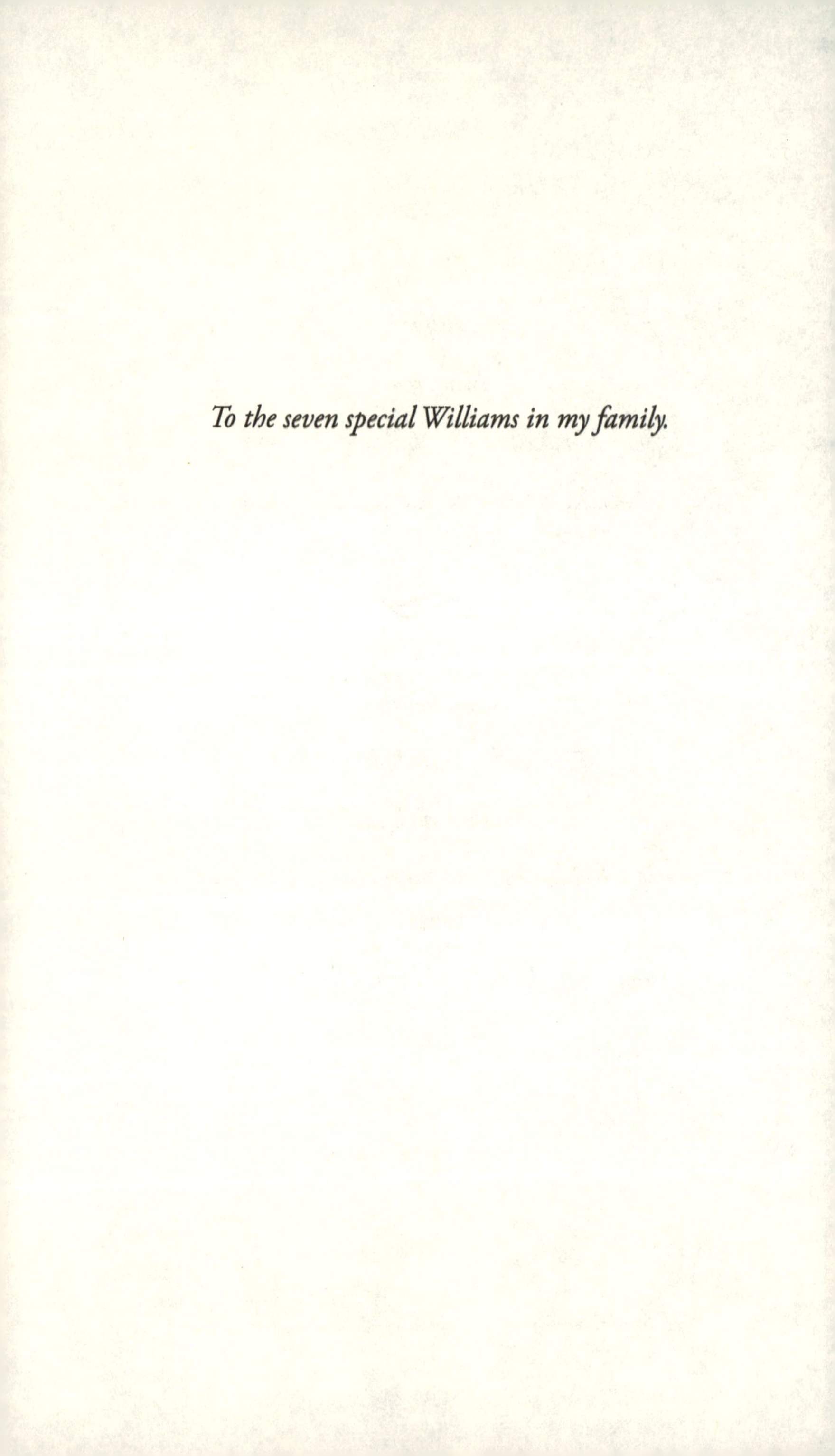

To the seven special Williams in my family.

THE ISLAND OF ELDRAD

Table of Contents

They were promised the world,
So shiny, so bright.
But they skittered and slid
On the mirror of life,
Until they cracked and burned.

J F Saxby

PART ONE

THE ISLAND

Chapter 1

Will Sutherland clanked up the stadium steps of the Maddock Arena. He clutched enough cartons of popcorn to last a week. The smell of fried food and sweaty bodies wafted through the air, and the setting sun bathed the arena in a wash of liquid red-gold.

Will flicked back his hair, still salty from a morning surf, and glanced up at the Aporto Bay News helicopter piloted by his father. It swung in from the coast and thundered toward the arena. It was an unwelcome reminder of how his family had imploded. How his father had cheated on them.

A cold emptiness seeped into Will's gut. This sold-out concert should have been the top event of the year for him. Ryder, his favorite singer, was about to perform. Will gritted his teeth and joined Mitch, Chen, and the other guys in the middle of the stand and handed out the popcorn.

The crowd shouted in time with the beat of the music played by the supporting act. "Ry-der, Ry-der." It sounded lame, but nothing else was going to spoil this concert. Everyone stomped their feet in time to the bass pumping through the main stage amplifiers.

Three girls pushed along the row to the empty seats in front of him.

"Wow." Will nudged Mitch and gave a low whistle, pointing at the girl in the middle.

Stunning. Honey-streaked hair, almost to her waist, swept around as she moved. But he couldn't see her face.

"Pull your jaw off the ground and get her attention," Mitch said.

"Ha. Why don't you?"

The grating on the metal floor shifted and creaked, and the girl's denim jacket slipped off the back of her seat. Will laid it over her chair uneasy about the floor's odd movement, but no one else seemed to notice.

"Hey Will, there's Ben Maddock." Mitch pointed toward the front of the stadium. "You won't want to see who he's with."

Will searched the crowd. Ben had his arm wrapped around a girl with auburn hair and purple streaks. *Stella.* That explained the unanswered calls. No wonder Stella didn't want to see him now she was with Ben, the girl-friend-snatcher. He choked on a mouthful of popcorn and crushed the carton until his fingers went numb. Life was the pits. He needed a drink.

"You have to do something about that jerk." Chen yanked at his black-brush hair. "He trashed your car, and now this."

Mitch shouted over the music with a screwed-up face. "I bet Stella just wanted to ride around in Ben's Ferrari."

"And let's face it, the Maddock family's in the spotlight because they built the new stadium." Chen thumped his feet on the steel floor. "It's not exactly top quality. How many millions did the bay fork out?"

Will shrugged. "Stella wasn't my type, anyway." But jealousy and a new resolve throbbed in his neck and throat.

Reverberations pulsed through the venue as the frenzy reached fever pitch. Ryder leaped onto the stage. His studded vest flashed in the laser lights, and his dreadlocks whipped around his head as he opened the set with "Ride or Die." The crowd was a sea, surging and swaying. Will allowed the deep-toned thud of beats reverberate through his body and numb his pain.

A harsh, wrenching screech cut through the music. The stadium shuddered and cracked in staccato bangs. Will's stomach did a dive. Something was wrong.

Mitch gripped his arm. "What's going on?"

Before he could answer, the grating at their feet split open. Rivets sprang out and scattered. The girls in front of him shrieked as their row of chairs swung away. Will leaned over and tried to pull them back, every muscle and ligament of his body stretched to its limit. Skin scraped off his fingers.

The seats wrenched out of his hands and tipped over. The girls disappeared into the void in a volley of anguished voices. The floor bent and slanted down. Heartbeats replaced drumbeats pounding in his head. He gripped his chair, but was slipping.

Falling.

Every organ in his body heaved toward his throat as he dropped underneath the stadium, arms and legs flailing.

Like the bungee jump at Valley Springs.

Without a harness.

And nothing to bounce him back.

He slammed into the ground, his body in a spasm of pain. The edges of his vision distorted. The stand above fractured and swayed in slow motion, like a scene in an apocalyptic movie. A girl lay nearby, crumpled like a broken mannequin, dust-filled hair tangled over her face.

The girl with the honey hair.

The entire stadium was imploding now. A long beam dangled from a swaying row of chairs. It dislodged and dropped toward the girl.

Shock spread in a bolt through Will's body.

He ignored the agony in his back and grabbed a sheet of metal lying nearby. He launched toward the girl, shielding her body with his, and pulled the metal on top of them. The falling beam hit the side of his head.

A bone-dry crack sounded inside his skull.

Chapter 2

Will forced his eyes open. They were gritty with sand. He lifted his aching head to look around and took a sharp breath at the barren landscape. Not a blade of grass in sight, and nothing but sparse bushes and the occasional light-colored boulder.

Where was he? He dropped his head back to the ground, light-headed. Had he missed the concert? Where were Mitch and Chen and the others? An agonizing pain flashed through his skull. Something trickled down his face and into his mouth. A coppery taste.

Birds screeched in the sky above, huge and circling. Vultures. Heat seared his skin. Mountains spread out in the distance under a purple haze. An expanse of still water lay in the other direction, reflecting the mauve-tinged sky. Panic hollowed out his stomach. He rolled over and tried to stand, but his legs crumpled. Why was he in this hellhole?

An odd squeaking noise came from the left. Two thin men walked toward him. One pushed a wooden trolley carrying a man who looked like Jabba the Hutt. He wore a grubby cloth stretched under his stomach to his upper thighs. His flesh flapped over the edges of the trolley, almost scraping the dirt.

The gaunt men cursed as they approached. Their torn, stitched-together clothing looked as if it hadn't been washed in months. He could smell them already.

"It's our lucky day." The shorter man jabbed Will with a stick. He had three fingers missing from his left hand. One long bone earring hung from an earlobe and his beard dangled in a long plait down to his waist.

Will struggled to stand again, but fell.

"Got anything to eat?" The man on the trolley puffed out the words. "First things first, Striker." His chins hung in folds onto his stomach. He took a long sip from a curled tube stuck in a pottery jug tied to his body.

The plaited-beard guy, Striker, gestured to the taller man. "Search his pockets, Flack."

A freshly stitched wound ran across Flack's cheek and into the back of his neck. He had a tattoo of a blackbird with outstretched wings on his arm and wore a necklace of assorted teeth. Will writhed as the man ripped off his jacket and rummaged through his pockets. The man pulled out a wallet, Chen's empty cigarette packet, and a squashed chocolate bar. He stuffed the wallet into his trousers.

The man on the trolley spat the tube out of his mouth. "The sweetie's mine."

"We can't have our little Grunter fading away to a shadow." Flack threw the chocolate to him, then dragged Will's phone out of the other jacket pocket.

"Give me my phone." Will croaked through the sand in his throat.

Flack sneered at him and threw the phone on the ground, then smashed it with a rock. Will's heartbeat pounded in his ears. He dug his nails into the dirt, trying to hoist himself upright.

"Where's your gold, scum?" Striker wiped drool from the side of his mouth with his plait.

"Don't have any."

The man kicked him in the ribs. Will recoiled. He could only imagine the super-punch he could have given him. Was he at some sort of dystopian reality movie set?

"What's the blood from?" Striker asked.

"I was in an . . . an accident."

Flack bared stained gums and black front teeth stumps in a sneer. "Another little one won't make any difference then. Good time to add to my tooth collection." He gestured to Striker, who stood on Will's arms, crushing them. Flack pulled a pair of pliers from his belt and leaned over Will, forcing his mouth open. A waft of putrid breath hit Will's face as the man stuffed the filthy pair of pliers through his lips. He jerked his head away.

A wind gusted across the arid plains. A tall man strode toward them from the other direction. The three men froze.

"It's him again," Striker said. "Hurry up, losers. Have to get to Stony Ridge for our supplies."

Flack yanked the tool out of Will's mouth. It cracked against his front teeth. "Till next time." The man straightened and pushed the pliers into his belt before Will could lash out. Striker rolled the trolley away, dodging rocks as though being chased. Flack followed. They headed toward an outcrop of red-ochre rocks in pillar formations.

Stony Ridge? Where was it, and why did they leave so quickly? A bronzed man in a light khaki shirt, trousers, and a hat walked toward him. A shaggy gray wolfhound with a torn ear loped at his side, and the vultures flapped away.

The man crouched on the sand next to Will. His eyes were a hypnotic steel gray, and his clothes smelled of pine and wood smoke. The dog sniffed at the blood on Will's clothes, snorted, moved away, and watched them. The bronzed man pulled a leather satchel from his shoulder.

"You must reach the hills before nightfall. Nighttime in Cawl Desert is not a place for humans." The man frowned and pulled a jar out of his pack. He applied cream to Will's head and tied a strip of cloth around it, then gave him water from the pottery jar.

"Who are you?" Will drained the last of the water.

"I'm the Counselor." The man helped him stand.

Will breathed a sigh of relief. "I think I can walk now."

"Your legs should get you to the mountains. You need to leave now, Will."

How did this guy know his name? The man passed him a skin bladder full of liquid and a cloth-wrapped package and draped his shoulders with a shawl. He looped the provisions into the shawl and tied the ends around Will's waist. "Keep your arms covered. You don't have the raven mark, which means you could be in danger."

When Will looked around, he'd disappeared.

Will staggered toward the mountains. The pain in his head had dulled, and although exhausted, his legs carried him well enough. He scanned the alien-looking landscape and sky. Something was wrong with this place. The sky had unusual tinges of purple. The sand and rocks were a different color and texture than anything he'd seen before.

A huge red-tinged moon, filling a third of the sky, rose in the distance as the sun set in a strange rainbow of hues. The whole place was weird. He kept a nervous watch for the men who threatened him earlier, searching the plains ahead and behind. How did he get here from Aporto Bay? Mom and Jess would worry about him. What happened to the girl with the honey hair, and to her friends?

Dusk fell. A sweeping constellation of stars and galaxies was overwhelmingly close. Too close. His lungs burned, and his head pounded with every step. The menacing vultures were back. If he didn't get to the hills soon, he'd be cactus. Foreboding raked through his stomach at the sound of their flapping wings. The birds were huge and looked like some kind of demonic creature from a video game. Maybe they weren't vultures after all.

Will struggled on. An eerie dark magenta clothed the desert. The trees on the mountains were visible now, even in the dim light. Weary with the exertion, his foot caught on a rock. He stumbled and fell. Three of the creatures plunged from the sky, screeching. Claws ripped at his flesh and clothes and their feathered wings whipped his face. He grabbed a stick lying nearby and slashed at them, then scrambled to his feet and ran like a crazed animal toward the mountains.

Trees. At last.

He crashed through the undergrowth until there was no sign of the birds and threw himself under the thickest vegetation he could find. Dead tired. Every heartbeat exploded the pain in his head. He tore some bread and pushed it into his mouth, hoping it might revive him, but every mouthful was an effort. At least he still had his teeth. He sipped the water with chapped lips, but it wasn't the sort of drink he craved at the moment.

Next time he opened his eyes, dry leaves half-buried him. Insects with zig-zagged orange markings crawled over his body. Pain still hammered his brain. Brushing away the insects, he rolled over and grabbed the lower branches of a tree, trying to stand, but without success.

His head was still resounding with the screaming of the crowds and the screeching and the crashing of the stadium as it went down. He wanted Mom and Jess. They'd be beside themselves with worry. His Mom would be bouncing off the walls by now. As if she didn't have enough problems. Will gritted his teeth. If he went missing, would his father have any regrets about leaving them for home-wrecker, fancy pants Maureen?

He checked his sand-filled pockets, wishing he had his phone.

The sun's rays waned, and a soft-breeze whisper rustled leaves. Will jumped as a shadow fell across him. A man as tall as a giant, with hair to his shoulders and eyes as bright as torchlights, loomed over him and scooped him up. Will yelled and struggled, but the man's muscles felt like rock.

His breath caught in his throat at the sight of the man's face, luminous in the dim twilight. Was he even human? Things were getting more bizarre by the minute. Like reality had fractured, and he'd fallen through a crack. He'd never believed in the supernatural, but maybe the rift in the stadium had been a portal into another world.

He must have slept because the land around was different now. The giant carried him up a mountain of boulders and caves.

"Who are you?" Will called out, but the stranger didn't answer. They came to a rocky outcrop with a couple of sparse trees outside. The man bent low and carried him into a cave smelling of burned logs, then lowered him onto a soft bed of furs and left.

Will ran his hands over the seams of what looked like a pile of rabbit pelts sewn together and flecked with white and gray. An oil lamp, dark-colored fruits, and a rough clay container of water lay on the sandy stone floor next to him. There was also a makeshift metal oven with a flat top, with a flue pushing through the roof of the cave.

Will stumbled to the entrance and peered outside at a rocky terrain. The cave was on a hill that loomed high above a forest of trees which spread out like a choppy green ocean. Wispy smoke floated from a village below and the smell blended with the waft of a salty ocean. A jagged snow-capped mountain range stretched out in the distance, like the one on the calendar back in his kitchen.

He sat outside, listening to the soft rushing gusts of wind in the forest and the bleating of goats on the peak of the hill. A mix of foreboding and homesickness formed a lump in his throat. He wouldn't make it to his shift at White Sands Cafe. Rob would be depending on him to help with their psychology assignment. He grimaced. It would be a dog's breakfast without his input. Rob was great with ideas, but he didn't have a way with words. Also, he'd miss the grading test for his black belt at Belmont Martial Arts. Being here was a waste of precious time.

He reached for a drink, but there was nothing. He was certain it had been there a moment earlier. His hands and feet tingled. Stomach cramps racked his body and a wash of desperation poured through him. If he didn't get a drink soon, he'd probably die. Thanks to his father's betrayal, he'd got used to dulling his pain with alcohol. Now he couldn't manage without it.

After a fitful sleep, he woke the next morning to find fresh water in a pottery jar and a pile of apples. The last thing he felt like was eating. He ran his fingers over the scabs of congealed blood on his head and crawled to the sandy entrance to relieve himself.

There was a sound. A girl singing. The enthralling sound drifted up from the valley. Notes resonated and filtered into his consciousness. They wrapped a silver thread through his thoughts. It was spine-tingling.

He had to meet this girl.

The singing stopped, and memories from the day of the concert came crowding back. They raced through his mind like a parade of mice on a treadmill. After an early morning surf, he'd finished his overdue English assignment and met the guys at his place. Lenny gave him a bag of drinks, which he'd sneaked through the dining room and into his bedroom for them to have later. After that, they'd walked to the Maddock Arena.

Then the disaster. It played in his head, over and over. How could the best day of his life have become the worst day of his life?

Chapter 3

Aporto Bay Hospital: Coma Ward.

Erin maneuvered her wheelchair to the front doors of C Block at Aporto Bay General Hospital. Balmy air swept in from the bay. She took a deep breath, enjoying the freedom after being in suffocating A Block. If she could call it freedom when both of her legs were plastered from ankle to thigh.

She had a plan, and needed to carry it out before the staff on her ward discovered she'd gone. She lifted her arms to tie her hair into a thick ponytail and winced at the pain in her bruised pelvis.

The glass entry doors swished open and cool air washed over her body. She rolled through and searched the directory on the left-hand wall.

"Need help?" A guy with freckles, wiry brown hair and a bandage wrapped around his head leaned on crutches nearby. His gaze lingered too long on parts of her thin hospital gown.

"I'm visiting someone in the coma ward."

"It's on the right, next to ICU. Pretty full at the moment. Hi, I'm Mitch."

"Were you injured in the stadium collapse?" she asked.

"Just going in for my electric shock therapy and lobotomy."

She gave him a crunched-up smile.

"Shame we're out of action. It's ace weather for a surf," he said. The lift opened, and he stepped in.

Her wheelchair made a zinging noise on the polished vinyl floor as she followed his directions. She pressed a red button on the wall. The doors to the ward swung open, and she peered inside, holding her breath.

Morning light flooded the room, accentuating the whiteness of the cotton blankets on the beds. Breathing apparatus, an extensive plumbing of cords and drips, linked to the ghostly bodies of the patients. The disinfectant didn't mask an unpleasant stench in the air.

A nurse approached. She had pulled her brown hair back so tightly that her face had a cling-wrapped look. "Can I help you?"

"I'm looking for Will Sutherland." Erin checked the name badge on the nurse's lapel. Skye Baxter.

"Are you family?" Nurse Baxter asked in an impatient tone. She lacked the bedside manner Erin had expected.

"No, an acquaintance."

The nurse pressed her lips into an invisible line. "You aren't permitted in this ward. Does the staff in your ward know you're here?"

"I slipped out. Can I see Will, just for a minute?" Erin bit her lip.

The nurse glanced toward a bed with a patient attached to a wall of machines. His lanky frame lay dead still. A knife-sharp spasm flashed through Erin. So he was the guy who'd saved her.

"Entry's not permitted. It's a matter of privacy."

"Okay. Sorry." Erin wheeled herself down the corridor. Her stomach clenched as hard as the plaster casts on her aching legs. The painkillers were wearing off. But she'd see Will Sutherland, no matter what anyone said.

***

Two days later, Erin returned to the coma ward. She pushed through the swinging doors to the nurses' station.

"Who are you looking for, dear?" A nurse with short gray hair looked up from the observation desk. "Do you have a pass?"

"My name's Erin O'Connell. Here's a letter from Susan Sutherland, Will's mother. I was in the stadium accident, and she'd like me to visit him."

The nurse looked at the letter and Erin's plastered legs. She nodded and pointed to Will's bed.

"I'll organize a pass for you. We're doing all we can for him." She sighed.

Will's sun-bleached brown hair spilled onto the pillow. Stubble covered his chiseled jaw. A sheet draped his body. Erin gripped the handles of her wheelchair, struggling to breathe. Various drips and tubes pierced his muscled arms. There were enough machines and screens around his bed to run a spaceship.

Good-looking guy. Shame he was out of action. She touched his hand, avoiding the lacerations. It was unresponsive and cold. Hot tears sprang to her eyes. She blinked them away, pulled a laptop from a bag hanging on her wheelchair, and flipped it open. She set it to play soft music while she typed, checking him regularly for any movement. But there was nothing.

An hour later, she pulled out her water bottle and gulped two smuggled pills from her bag. The staff in A Block would be looking for her, but she wanted to stay.

"Can you hear the music, Will?" she whispered. "I'm so, so sorry. It should have been me in this ward. I'll make it up to you. Promise."

Did his eyelids flicker? Erin held her breath, wondering if she'd imagined it. A nurse tapped her shoulder. It was Nurse Baxter, with two hypodermic needles on a tray.

"You need to go now. It's time for Will's next treatment."

Before she left, Erin leaned over him and whispered in his ear. "Please wake up, Will. Please."

Chapter 4

Daggers of pain punched at Will's skull, and his lips were as dry as the sticks strewn on the ground of his cave. Wisps of early morning mist filtered in.

A man stood at the entrance. "Are ye awake?" He looked like a bearded Viking warrior who'd seen better days. Will rolled over and sat up, rubbing his aching eyes with his fists.

"Can I enter?" The man shuffled in. Deep lines furrowed the man's face, and his eyes were green with tinges of brown, like a forest. Tattoos of Celtic knot work covered his arms. "I'm Roland. I live in a wee cave further up the mountain."

Will gaped as Roland unloaded corncobs, nuts, water, and a large cork with fishing line wound around it and stuck with hooks.

"How are ye today, son?"

"Like I've been in a dumpster bin for a month." This guy might show him the way home and get him what he needed.

The man threw a woolly coat to him. "Ye'll need this tonight. It's going to be a cold one."

Will pulled himself up. "I really need a drink. I'd give my right arm for one."

"Ye'll need to go to Shannon, the wee village, for that."

Will clenched his jaw. "That sucks. Where am I anyway? Some sort of TV reality show?"

"This is the Island of Eldrad." Roland stuffed sticks and branches into the metal cooker and lit it with a flint.

Island? "I was in a desert, attacked by evil zombies and killer vultures, then brought here by a giant guy with torch eyes. I need you to show me the way home." Will scratched at the stubble on his face.

"Ye need to ask the Counselor."

The flames in the stove crackled and Will ground his teeth with impatience.

"This place isnae yer earth," Roland said. "But is another part of the Earthlands. Another dimension, if you like. The Earthlands consists of yer world and mine. There isnae a way back to yer world that I ken."

"Has anyone else come here from my earth?"

"Aye, many years ago, but she dinnae return. She wrote the Earth Chronicles. They're kept in a library in Eladia. That's how we ken about earth."

Will slumped against the wall of the cave. He'd expected better news. "Are there any girls living nearby?"

"Two wee girls, about yer age and Jadyn. Ye are bound to meet them soon. Rest and wait. When ye feel stronger, ye can find fresh water at Fernhill Gully in Emerald Forest, and fish in the river." Roland pointed into the valley. "But dinnae enter Wyld Wood, the dark forest to the north."

After Roland left, Will punched the rock wall of the cave in frustration, bruising his knuckles. Getting back to the bay wouldn't be easy. At this rate, he could fail his first year of college. The need to fill the tormenting emptiness and the craving for a drink—sent his mood plummeting even lower.

***

After a hasty breakfast of berries the next morning, Will set off down the terrain. He had to find more water and would try walking, at least as far as the forest. By the time he reached bushland near a gully, his legs shook from the exertion, but the sound of rushing water called to him.

A canopy of trees soared high above and sheltered the area. The pungent smell of damp moss and fragrant orchids filled his nostrils. A spring trickled near the descending path into a hollow in a rock. He drank. Exhilaration washed through his body. Revived, he continued toward the sounds of gushing water. Lush plants and feathery ferns hugged the track. Iridescent butterflies fluttered lazily around the vines.

A beautiful girl kneeled at the edge of an azure pool.

He stopped. Transfixed.

She wore a tan top and skirt. A bow and arrow lay in the sand. Long sandy-colored hair dangled over one of her shoulders and trailed into the pool as she scooped water into a clamshell and drank.

He stepped forward and watched her through the dangling vines. The gray wolfhound, with the torn ear he'd seen in the desert, crouched beside her. It looked up and sniffed in his direction and growled. A twig under Will's foot snapped. The girl straightened up, grabbed her bow and arrow, and slipped into the bushes, giving the wolfhound a low whistle.

That night, the cave was as cold as a fridge. He stuffed more wood into the metal stove and threw himself onto his bed, tossing and turning as his mind raced. Who was the girl in the gully? Would his disappearance be on the news? By now Mom would be slamming the kitchen cupboard doors and crashing the dishes in the sink, even more than usual.

Will ran his hand over the rough stone wall, so different to the smooth, cream plaster of his bedroom at home. What would Ryder say about what had happened at the concert? Would he care? And why wasn't he missing Stella?

When he returned home, he'd confront his father and Maureen. He couldn't do that while trapped on the island. Letting down all the tires on Maureen's car last month was lame compared to what he was thinking now. When he returned, Ben would pay, too. Big time.

Will spent the next few hours of the night planning retaliation. Perhaps something could happen to the windscreen of Ben's flash Ferrari. For starters. Tit for tat.

Revenge would be sweet. He wasn't usually this angry, but times like these called for desperate measures.

A song drifted into his cave from the valley early the next morning. It was the singing girl again. The melody calmed the tension tormenting him. As long as she sang, he could forget. Forget about the bay. Forget about wanting something to deaden the pain. He finally fell into a slumber.

A fizzing and spitting and a smell of burning wood wafted in the air. Will crawled to the entrance. A striking guy was building a fire outside. He had straight black hair hanging over part of his face, and could have stepped straight out of an anime movie.

The guy threw off his calf-length coat. "I'm Jadyn, from up the hill. Roland sent me. Feeling better?" Knives and metal tools hung from his belt and clanked as he moved. "I've got rabbit meat for you."

Perhaps this guy would have answers. He had plenty of questions. "Where can I get supplies?"

"Down in the village." Jadyn pointed to the valley below, where the roofs of cottages poked through the trees and wisps of smoke curled into the air from the chimneys. "If you want milk and cheese, see Rosie up at Scraggy Rock. That's at the top of Caves Hill. She lives there with her son, Felix."

"Sure, but I'm all out of cash."

"I have gold. If you help on market days, you can earn gold as well. We sell berries, mushrooms, corn, and herbs."

"What currency do you use here?"

"Gold coins in different sizes." Jadyn tossed him a handful from his pocket. "They're yours." Will flipped a coin over, shaking his head at what he saw—a man's face on one side and a raven on the other. He dropped them in his pocket. The gold would be worth a fortune back at the bay.

"Why are the moon and stars so close to the island?" Will pointed at the sky. "Why is it that weird mauve color? And even the trees and plants are strange here."

"That's the way Eldrad is. Some parts are scenic. Other parts are to be avoided and are dangerous, especially near Nevara, where President Lorn lives. That's him on the coins."

Jadyn pushed the hair from his forehead. Will tried not to stare. The guy's left eye was missing. A thick scar streaked over where the eye should have been. Jadyn flicked his hair back over the scar and turned away. "Old eye injury."

Will nodded, not knowing what to say. But this guy's one good eye was so magnetic and intense, it made up for the other eye. "Do you know a way to get back to Earth? That's where I'm from."

"There's no way I know of. Do you want to come with me to the Shannon village fair? It's only a few days away."

Will agreed, and after they'd eaten, Jadyn left. Will settled against a boulder and watched the clouds race across the dark-purple-tinged sky, and the stars so close. Almost claustrophobic. He wondered about Jadyn with the missing eye and all the things he had said. He wouldn't wait for Jadyn to take him to the village fair. He'd go to the village himself now he could walk the distance, get a drink and some answers.

***

The day was cloudless, and the air crisp. Will breathed in the calming scent of the pine trees and a faint tang of salt spray from the ocean as he headed toward the village. On the way, he'd wash in the river. He could see the sliver of a river near the forest from his cave, so he followed a narrow path in its general direction. A rustling in the bushes stopped him in his tracks.

The girl from the gully.

This time, he came face to face with her. Only a few branches separated them. Her matted hair was full of dried leaves, as if she had been crawling in the undergrowth. He stopped breathing when their eyes met and his heart rate doubled at the sight of her. No girls back at the bay were a match.

Her eyes widened with surprise. "What happened to your face?"

What did she mean? He ran his fingers over the caked dirt, hair and dried blood on his head and cheeks. "A m-metal beam hit my head."

She stared at him, then disappeared into the thicket.

He took a bracing swim in the river, and washed his face and body as well as he could, disappointed by the girl's reaction to him. When he returned to the path leading toward the village, a group of thin men with ragged clothes walked ahead. Two of them looked like Flack and Striker, the men who'd attacked him in the desert. He didn't need that complication, so he turned back. On the way, he discovered a patch of fresh mushrooms and picked as many as he could carry.

If only he could see the girl again.

***

As he piled the mushrooms into a dented pan that he'd found on the stove, footsteps sounded at the entry of the cave.

"Are ye feeling better?" Roland called.

"I wouldn't turn down a hamburger with the lot."

"I've brought a container of fresh youngberries from Rosie."

Will popped a handful of them into his mouth. His tongue ached at the burst of the sweet-sour juice. "Roland, I'm going down to the village. Do you have any contacts who could help me get home?"

Roland placed his hand on his shoulder. "Sorry, son. I dinnae. The Counselor or the King of the Earthlands are the ones to ask."

"I don't know what king you're talking about, and who is that Counselor guy?

"The Counselor belongs to the King."

Will kicked at the sand under his feet. Roland stood up to leave.

"What about the girl? The one with the long sandy hair?" Will asked.

"We call her the princess," Roland said. "Her real name's Eleonora, but Jadyn started calling her Princess, and it stuck. She lives in a wee cave down toward the forest. She's had a tough life and is away a lot. Laurien, the other girl, lives up at Scraggy Rock."

"What happened to Jadyn's eye?

"Don't ye ask him about his eye," Roland said. "He clams up if ye bring up the subject. He works with Cadwyn at Yapton Forge. Have ye met Senka yet? She's a curious character. She uses the cave across from ye for making her potions."

"Not yet." But he would look out for her.

Will offered Roland some mushrooms as he turned to leave.

"Come and visit me. My cave's always open." Roland chuckled.

Chapter 5

Will cooked and ate the rest of the mushrooms, then headed up to Roland's cave. His body ached like he'd been punching bag, and he knew he'd never make it to the village. But Roland might have some ideas. When he arrived, Roland put aside the book he was reading and offered him tea. Will settled his back against the rock wall. Roland took an earthenware mug and dipped it into the pot of boiling water on the metal stove. Rustic chairs and a table stood next to a goatskin mat spread on the floor. Pots hung over the stove area, and a long shelf of books lined the wall above a wooden bed. It had a cozy atmosphere.

A brown bottle sat at the end of a shelf. Alcohol? Will became fidgety. It reminded him how much he needed a drink.

"Tell me about your past life, Roland."

"A-hah." The aroma of steeping leaves permeated the air. "I was always in trouble. But I was cunning. I peddled illegal goods, and I had a fierce temper."

"Did you get caught?"

"Five years in prison."

"Did you ever marry?" He wanted the brown bottle on the shelf. How could he convince Roland to give it to him?

"I had a girl once, Darcelle. What she saw in me—I dinnae. We were together for three years." He stirred the herbs in his mug with a stick. "It's hard to climb out when ye are in a deep hole." He paused and rubbed his forehead. "Sometimes ye lose your grip and fall back in, but the King gets me out. I'll always be grateful for that."

Will shook his head. Why would a king do that? "So why do you live in a cave and not down in the village?"

"Same reason as all of us here—except for ye. We like our freedom, and dinnae want to wear the raven mark. But I've firm friends in the village—Cadwyn, Merek, Dorian, and others."

A wolfhound bounded into the cave and licked Roland's hands, its tongue dripping. It was the same animal he'd seen with the Counselor and the girl. Will called to it, but it hitched its lips above its teeth and snarled.

"Dinnae worry. Wolfie willnae make friends on the spur of the moment, but he's adopted us here at Caves Hill. Ye are a smart rabbit hunter, aren't ye wee pup?" Roland ruffled its fur.

Will jerked his knee with impatience. He wanted the bottle. "Does the princess have the mark?"

"King followers dinnae have it. We're called Drifters."

"Roland, what's in that brown bottle?" Will kept his tone casual.

"It's mead. My friend Merek brews it."

"Would you mind giving it to me? I'll replace it as soon as I get to the village tomorrow."

"Ye are welcome." Roland reached up, then paused. "Drink a wee bit at a time, won't ye? Merek makes a potent brew."

"Of course," Will said with a twinge of guilt. Strong brew or not, it wouldn't be rationed.

Evening sent its soft violet light into the cave. Will left Roland and walked back down the hill, enjoying the mead and gazing at the glowing moon filling the sky. By the time he reached the cave, the bottle was empty.

***

The next day, thunder rumbled and crashed like an avalanche at Caves Hill, shaking the ground and stone walls of Will's cave. Even the metal oven rattled. Then miserable, driving rain blew in. Jadyn poked his head through the entrance to tell him the fair was canceled, then clomped away.

Will stamped around his cave. How long had he waited? He would go anyway. The village must have an inn where he could get another drink. The mead didn't make a dent in his need for alcohol. He had to distract his mind from the agony of being trapped in limbo.

He pulled on his coat and boots, and headed into the drenching downpour, slipping on the sodden ground. It was as if the ocean was sending tsunami waves over the valley. The path was ankle-deep in brown water, but the thought of a drink kept him going.

He finally arrived at the village, soaked to his skin, and his legs ached like they'd been hit with a truck. Puddles the size of small ponds covered the deserted main street. He slid along the slippery road, straining to look for any signs.

A woman sloshed through the lashing rain toward him. "Can you point me to an inn?" He gestured down the road.

"Goat's Horn Inn. Keep going and turn left at the circus sign." Even her voice sounded waterlogged.

The inn had a leaking veranda at the front. Will pushed open the swinging doors and dumped enough water on the floor to fill a small bucket. A few patrons with a variety of bushy beards huddled over playing cards on scratched wooden tables. A log fire crackled and spat, sending a thin warmth into the room. Will nodded at the men and held his numbed hands over the fire while he checked the drinks menu: ale, mead, and corn spirits.

He ordered a glass of corn spirits and settled on a stool at the counter, still dripping onto the floor. The barmaid polished a glass and poured a measure of golden liquid from a flagon.

"From these parts?" she asked.

Will savored the maple vanilla taste of the spirits. "Caves Hill." It hit his throat and flared through his veins.

He ordered a bottle of mead for him and Roland and two more glasses of the spirits. It would keep him fueled for the trip back.

Rain, branches, and debris rushed past the windows. Daylight was fading early. He wanted to ask questions, but her expression darkened along with the atmosphere outside. She packed the glasses away in a hurry. Concern about the weather and the effect of the alcohol shut down Will's resolve to talk to her.

"Time to batten down the hatches. Finish your drinks and get home," she said with a tone of annoyance.

Will dragged himself to the door of the inn, but his leg muscles weren't cooperating with his thoughts. Maybe he'd overdone the drinking session. He slumped on the verandah. There was no way he could walk back to the hill.

He remembered nothing more until he woke to a gray dawn and a light pattering of rain on the inn roof. A hammering pain battered his head, and nausea gripped his stomach. He crawled to the edge of the veranda and spewed.

It wasn't until the barmaid pushed him down the steps with her boots that he remembered where he was. He limped back to the Hill, thinking he would never arrive. He hoped Roland hadn't noticed his absence.

Later, Will woke in his cave, disoriented. The air reeked of a concoction of vomit and herbal tea. Roland was looking down at him with one eyebrow cocked and a mixed expression of amusement and concern. He ladled tea and passed him a mug.

"Back in the land of the living?"

"I'd hardly call it that." Will's mouth tasted foul.

"Wolfie alerted us. He was barking at the bottom of the hill. We found ye lying there, soaked to the skin."

"How did you get me back?" Will checked his bag. He must have left the bottles of mead behind.

"The princess and I dragged you back on this." Roland held up a mud-covered coat. "You might need a new one."

"Aargh." Will gritted his teeth. If only he could erase the last few hours. The corn spirits must have had some kick to leave him comatose after only three glasses.

Roland left and Will sat up, then tried to sharpen the blunt knife he'd found in one of the caves, against the rock wall. What would the guys think if they could see him now?

Mitch would say *wish I was living in a cave.*

Phil would say *sorry mate, can't talk right now. New game—have to wipe out the bloodsucking aliens.*

Chen would tell him about the latest rear spoiler or quad exhaust system for his dream car.

Lenny would say *I'll find a way to get you home.*

Jordan would say *rotten luck, mate.*

And Spud would say *make sure you get the girl, block-head.*

Will ambled down to the river. He needed food. Perhaps he'd catch a fish—or at least find a patch of mushrooms. He tried to ignore the pounding headache. Halfway down the mountain, he skidded on a loose pile of pebbles. Crashing like a falling boulder, he cursed and lay sprawled on the ground with blood oozing from scrapes on his legs and arms.

A shadow loomed over him. "Are you all right?" It was that singsong voice he'd heard in the forest.

Eleonora. Not her. Not now. He wiped the dirt from his mouth and smirked and then heaved himself to a standing position, willing himself not to sway.

"Anything to get your attention," he said.

Her partially braided hair spilled around her lovely face. The sight of her threw him as much as the fall—her flawless skin, with bright eyes the aqua color of the pool in the gully. She carried a bow and arrow and two dead rabbits.

She stared at his bleeding knees and thrust a rabbit at him. "Have one of these rabbits."

"But don't you need it for yourself?"

"It's yours." She gave him a lopsided smile with a hint of uncertainty.

Will mumbled his thanks, turned, and took the limp rabbit back to the cave. He wouldn't be going to the forest today, and needed to nurse his new wounds and mull over all the things he should have said. He ran his fingers over his protruding ribs. The thought of biting into roast meat, no matter how many tiny bones a rabbit had, was beyond tempting.

He piled wood onto the outdoor fireplace, took the carcass, and drove a knife into its skin, trying to rip off the matted fur. Pulling at the skin, he made no headway and soon blood spread into the sand. Should he cook it fur and all or get help? He headed up to Roland's cave with the dripping carcass, keeping a furtive lookout for the princess. He had enough embarrassment for a year.

"Where did ye get that?" Roland laid down the book he was reading. When Will told him what happened, he roared with laughter.

"It's not that funny." Will's grazes stung, and his stomach wrenched with hunger.

"Let me show ye how to prepare a rabbit and cook it. We'll eat together tonight. In return, I'll catch ye a sweet-fleshed fish from the river, and we'll have it another night."

"I live at a bay, remember. I'm an expert at catching fish and filleting them."

"Put some wood on the fire and light it for me." Roland sharpened the knife. "Ye needn't cut deep into the skin." "This is one of Jadyn's knives—he makes the best on the island. Watch. Ye slice around each leg, cut up the back, and pull away the hide. Then ye cut open the abdomen and gut it. Don't cut through the intestines—otherwise, it'll stink."

Roland skinned the rabbit in a few deft moves, despite its condition. While the rabbit roasted, he passed Will a calico bag of what looked like coarse yellow flour. "Here's some cornmeal mix ye can take home and cook on your stove for corncakes. All ye add is water."

They were soon munching on crisp, tasty meat. Will smiled. If anyone in Aporto Bay had predicted he'd be eating roast rabbit skewered on spicebush sticks over a crackling fire with an old homeless guy, he would have laughed them out of the room.

Night fell. Time flew by like the birds swooping down to the forest, searching for their roosts. Will and Roland huddled close to the flickering flames, shared stories, and munched on honeycomb into the late hours.

Chapter 6

Aporto Bay Hospital

Erin stared at Will's empty bed in the coma ward. It was stripped of linen. The wall of machinery was silent. No flashing lights. No sound. No sign of life. Her body contracted into a frozen block of fear. Where was he? All the other patients were still in the room, with three nurses attending to them. Surely he hadn't . . . she shouldn't . . . she couldn't think the worst.

The entrance door opened. Susan walked woodenly toward Will's bed, with a pallid face and blue circles under her eyes. Erin opened her mouth to ask about Will, but emitted an incomprehensible, strangled sound. Susan plonked down in a chair near the empty bed.

"Will's had emergency surgery." Her tone sounded like a recorded voice. "He'll be back soon."

Not dead. Emergency surgery. Erin wanted to grab her and dance around the room.

"How is he?" she asked in a measured tone, fighting the urge to bounce in her chair. Why did she care about this guy so much?

"He deteriorated, so they took him for a CT scan and MRI." Susan paused and took a long, shuddering breath. "They found he had bleeding on the brain."

Nurse Baxter hurried to them. "I've had a call from recovery. Will's in a critical but stable condition and will be back in a few minutes." She flicked a switch on a machine and set up an intravenous drip. "A subdural hematoma is common in people with head injuries. If there's a leakage of blood, it can put pressure on the delicate tissue of the brain. There isn't much room for extra blood between the brain and skull."

"Thanks for letting us know," Susan said. The entrance doors swung open. Two attendants wheeled Will toward them on a stretcher. Erin stared at Will's battered face in horror. Dozens of staples pinned an extensive cut across his forehead.

"Sixty staples," Nurse Baxter said in a grim voice. "You need to leave while we reattach the equipment and drips."

Chapter 7

The next afternoon, a sniffing and a scuffle outside the cave interrupted Will's dinner preparations. He stopped stirring the bowl of cornbread mix. A child sang in a high-pitched voice.

"Ride on the dragons
When there are ravens.
Ride on the dragons
And hide from the Cravers."

Will hastened out of the cave. A small boy with a runny nose and brown shoulder-length hair crouched in the dirt. He used charcoal from the outside fire to draw a dragon on a flat rock.

"What's your name?"

The boy shook his head.

"Where's your family?"

He shook his head again and added another wing to the dragon.

"Would you like some honeycomb?"

The boy wiped his nose with his sleeve. Will went into the cave, broke off a piece of honeycomb from his supply, and gave it to the boy. The boy snatched it and gobbled it with hardly a chew, then his words tumbled out. "Mom's with the goats. Coming back soon. Have you got more honeycombs?"

"So you're Felix."

The boy scrawled in silence. He drew a bird attacking the dragon. Will gave him more honeycomb.

Felix drew elongated claws on the bird. "Do you think ravens would attack a dragon?"

"Perhaps." Will stood up. "You're a master dragon artist, but now it's time to go home." "Tell me, Felix, why did you sing that song—the one about the ravens?"

"Mom taught it to me. It's to make me safe. If I see a raven, I hide."

"What's wrong with ravens?"

"Didn't your mom tell you?"

"Not really. Can you show me where you live?"

The boy took his hand and led him to the top of the hill. A woman with hair like a bird's nest and dressed in a long gray shift and a calico apron waited for them.

"There you are, you little rascal."

"He's fine."

"You must be Will." The woman smiled and scooped the boy into her arms. "Felix, it's time for your dinner."

"Thanks for the berries you sent, Rosie," Will said. She beamed at him.

He trudged back to his cave, wondering why Felix was afraid of ravens. What would Mom and Jess be doing back at the bay? He was desperate to see them again. Further across the peak of the hill, smoke drifted from a fire. Perhaps it was Laurien, the other girl. But a wave of depression washed over him. He couldn't talk to anyone. His heart was breaking for home.

***

After a midday trip back from the forest, Will halted at the sight of a plump woman hurrying up the incline of the hill. She wore an assortment of clothes that looked like a walking jumble sale. The woman tossed a bundle of long sticks near a cave on the village side of the hill.

Senka? He hurried closer and called to her. She may have answers.

Stained string and crystals clinked in the breeze at the entrance. An odor of burning leaves and charcoal wafted toward him.

"Come in, strange cave boy," she said. A large pot on her stove hissed and billowed steam to the roof, and rivulets of moisture trickled down the walls.

"What are you cooking?"

"I've heard about you, curious boy. I'm making my special elixir. I bottle it and sell it in the village." She added a powder to the pot and stirred. "Hand me that jar labeled burdock root, would you? And the juniper berry above you on the shelf. The berry brings luck. Perhaps you need some?" Will sorted through the array of containers on the shelves.

"Can you help me get off this island and back to Aporto Bay?"

Her crinkled eyes watered in the hot steam. "Come and see me at the next village fair. I'll be at my fortune-teller tent. I can look into your future and find a way. My abilities are greatly sought after."

"But I need your help now. It's urgent."

"Like I said, you'll have to wait until the fair. I can't do it here."

"Is there someone else at Shannon who could give me advice?"

"No one, boy. I can tell you that for a fact."

"Do you know the king they keep talking about here?"

"Yes. Why do you ask?" She reached for a bowl from a rock shelf and scraped the contents into the pot. Will stepped back at the pungent odor.

"Do you follow him, like Roland and the others?"

"The ex-crim and the fake Princess? You aren't listening to them, are you? I don't follow their King. I made that decision long ago."

She took a handful of dried leaves from a branch hanging from the roof of the cave and tossed them into the mixture. "I show my allegiance to the Dark Prince and his angels. They rule the Earthlands. That's our island and your earth."

"I thought President Lorn was in charge."

"He's just a man." She snorted. "The Prince has the greater power."

"Why do you follow this prince?" Will asked.

Senka laughed. Her gold bangles jangled, and her black hair clung in damp ringlets on her forehead.

"He gives me the power I need. I make my own destiny."

"What about the demonic creatures?" The memory of them dropped a chill like a stone into his stomach.

"You mean the dark angels and the demons. The King banished them from his realm a long time ago, because they wanted to rule the cosmos. Why shouldn't they have a chance?"

He peered into her eyes. Something in their depths drew him into enticing but shadowy pools.

"I'll see you at the fair." He stumbled outside and blinked in the dazzling sunlight. Her promise of help gave him hope.

***

That evening, a glowing fire swirled its smoke into a cloud around the top of Caves Hill at Scraggy Rock. A girl sat outside a cave. It would be Laurien. At last he might get to meet the other girl. He sprinted up the rocky terrain.

She sat by the fire, turning a corncob on a stick over the flames. Her hair hung in dull, stringy clumps and she glared at him with a dirt-smeared face and a don't-mess-with-me expression.

"What do you want?" She grabbed a large stick and pointed it at him. Faint scars crisscrossed the skin on her arms.

He stopped in his tracks. "Just thought I-I'd come and introduce myself. I'm Will."

"Where're you from?"

"Aporto Bay. But I live in a cave down the hill at the moment." He perched on a rock nearby.

She chewed on a nail. "I only have visitors if I invite them. And there's no such place as Aporto Bay. I know all of the island." She hit a log in the fire with the stick, making sparks spiral into the darkness.

"Sorry. I'll leave if I'm making you uncomfortable."

She stared at the knife hanging on his belt and jabbed her finger at it.

"Where d'you get that knife?"

"I found it in a cave."

"Give it here."

Will passed it to her, tension building up in his shoulders.

"You stole it! See this L engraving. It's mine." She reminded him of a mangy cat springing out its claws.

"Really? It was lying in the dirt." A sinking feeling settled in his stomach.

She pushed the knife into her belt.

"OK, just keep it. I'll find another." Somewhere. Now he'd have nothing to cut his food with, or clean fish. Just great. If only he had access to all the knives back at home in the kitchen drawer.

"Who said you could move to Caves Hill?" she asked.

"A guy with eyes like beacons brought me here. Don't know his name."

"So you're a king follower?"

"No." She turned the charred corn over in the coals. His mouth watered at the smoky aroma.

"Are you?" Will asked.

"Of course not." She picked up the cob, blew on it and took a bite. "Bye now. I need to eat. I have to go down to the village."

"What's on at night?"

She scowled at him. "None of your business."

"Enjoy yourself." He raised his eyebrows at her. She was one person he'd be happy never to see again.

He kicked at the stones all the way down the hill.

***

The morning mist dissipated from the mountain range. Only one more day until the village fair. It seemed like ages since he'd had a drink. He'd look forward to visiting the inn and would pace himself better next time. He longed to see Eleonora. He gulped the last of the toasted cornbread and wandered to her cave. As he stepped down the hill, thin wisps of smoke from fires in the village drifted up into the air like wool from a spindle.

Unlike the other caves on the hill, Eleonora's cave had a wooden door with metal hinges, and it was open. "Hello. Eleonora," he called. But all he could hear were birds of prey screeching across the valley.

He stepped into the low entry. A potpourri of spicy fragrances filled his nostrils. A flickering light inside the passage drew him in. A large cavern beyond branched off into two caves. An oil lamp bathed the walls in fluctuating patterns. He walked in further, breathing in the perfume and ambience.

All the nooks and crannies around the sandy walls displayed rows of amber and green bottles. Woody stems of dried herbs hung from a higher section of the ceiling from a square rack. Books lined a wall. A bed of soft gray furs rested on an elevated flat rock in one of the caves at the rear. Behind the bed, a glistening white curtain sparkled in the glow of another lamp. Will walked to the curtain and touched it, but it wasn't soft fabric. It was a type of quartz rock.

The sound of light footsteps behind startled him. His stomach contents lurched. It was like the time he was caught wagging school, but this was worse.

"What are you doing here?"

He swung around, his face flooding with heat. Bust it.

"Well?" Eleonora's eyes flashed enough fire to light the cave.

"I came to see you."

"Do you always just barge into someone's home with no invitation?"

"No. I didn't mean to."

"Then why are you here?"

The closeness of her sent his mind off-kilter and his legs to jelly. "I'm sorry. You need not be—so precious about it."

"Would I come into your place without asking?"

"I wouldn't mind . . ." He bit his lip. She stood aside and motioned for him to leave.

"I promise it won't happen again."

He left. Embarrassment saturated every cell of his body.

***

An endless deluge hit Caves Hill again. It stranded Will in his cave. At least he could spend the time planning and plotting revenge on Ben. He could think up a strategy for the showdown with his father and new partner as well. The anger would incinerate him if he didn't follow through. But most of all, he needed to come up with a way to make things right with Eleonora. It was depressing he couldn't think of a solution yet. Maybe there was none, and she'd never speak to him again.

The dampness seeped into the rocky walls, his clothes and the furs on his bed. The wood sizzled and steamed but wouldn't light. He checked his scrappy supply of food: two wizened plums, three moldy mushrooms, and a slimy corn cob. What he wouldn't give for a hamburger and fries at White Sands Cafe, and a drink from Goat's Horn Inn wouldn't go astray. He ached with hunger and frustration to the very core of his bones.

At last, a feeble sun shone through the clouds. Will took his pack and ventured into the sodden forest to forage for a meal. The berries were good after the rain. He found a crop of plump purple ones and picked his fill. On the way home, he left a bulging cloth of the berries outside Eleonora's door.

That afternoon, a familiar voice boomed into the cave. "Can I enter, son?"

The Counselor. The guy from the desert.

The man bent low as he looked through the opening. His tanned face creased into a wide smile. He looked younger than Will remembered.

"How's my traveler?" This time he wore a white over-shirt and ochre-colored pants.

"Maybe my travels will be over now you're here. Roland said you could help me get home."

"My son, there are things I can't do right now." The Counselor took items from a cloth bag and went outside to light the fire. "You'll understand one day, either in this life or the next." He lit dried leaf kindling under the logs in the ring of stones.

"As well as enjoyment, there'll always be difficulties in life," he said. "Sometimes you'll be rescued from the pain. Sometimes you won't. There's a journey you must take to find the truth. Your destiny depends on it, and in the King's realm your destiny is always good."

The truth? Destiny? Will added sticks to the fire. What did that mean for him?

The Counselor wrapped a piece of fish with vegetables in a large leaf, and they chatted until glowing embers replaced the flames. The man placed the bundle in the embers.

"Why does life have to be so difficult? For me, anyway," Will asked.

"There's always a bigger picture." The Counselor prodded the wrapped bundle in the coals. "A world with evil in it can never bode well for the inhabitants."

Evil? This place was getting stranger by the minute. Will closed his eyes for a moment, breathing in the delicious aroma. It reminded him of the nights around the fire with Mitch and the guys on White Sands Beach back at Aporto Bay as they cooked the fish they'd caught from Mitch's boat.

The Counselor sprinkled the meal with fine salt crystals, and they both ate with gusto. The wolfhound, dripping with mud, came bounding up the hill from the forest to greet the Counselor. But the dog fixed hostile amber eyes on Will.

"Soon I'll explore the island and find a way home." Will savored every mouthful of fish as he spoke.

"It's not a large island, but there are other mountain ranges, a picturesque countryside, intriguing cities and perilous seas," the Counselor said. "You can't swim in the ocean here because of dangerous currents and sea creatures. Also, be on the lookout for the President's combatants and the demons and the Cravers."

The Counselor put his half-finished dinner on the ground, lowered his head, and kneaded his forehead with his hand.

"The men who attacked you in the desert were Cravers. My heart pains at the deception that crushes them." The Counselor closed his eyes. The wolfhound whined and eyed his food.

Will waited, fidgeting at the Counselor's lengthy silence. "And the big one on the trolley? Grunter?" he asked.

The Counselor peered at him through clouded eyes. "He's not a Craver. He's a madecia dealer. Cravers are thin, they have little appetite for food." He scraped the leftovers onto a flat rock for the wolfhound, who ate it in two gulps. "A scientist called Malory, who works for the President, formulated the drug. Although originally manufactured as a healing drug, it has sinister side effects."

The Counselor piled fresh logs at the cave's entrance before leaving. Will took shelter inside the cave, still shivering in the cool night air that blew in. He added more wood to the fire in the metal stove and drew his legs to his chin, soaking in the warmth. Could this place get any stranger and could the bay get any further away from this new reality he was trapped in? If only there was a button he could press to launch him back home.

Chapter 8

"Come to my place tonight, Will. We're playing mancala." Jadyn leaned into Will's cave. "Bring some fish or mushrooms."

Will took his pan of freshly fried cornbread off the stove and offered Jadyn a piece. "Never heard of mancala. I'll come, but I can't cut bait or clean fish until I get a knife. Laurien took the knife I found. Said it was hers." Something bitter headed into Will's throat.

"Ha, did she now? You can have one of mine." Jadyn pulled a medium-sized knife from the assortment hanging on his belt.

"Thanks. Anyone else coming to your dinner?"

"Roland and Laurien."

"Laurien?" Will kicked at the stones on the floor of his cave.

"She has her reasons for the way she behaves, but there's something else going on with her. I can feel it in my bones." Jadyn crunched on a piece of the crispy cornbread.

Later that afternoon, Will walked to Jadyn's with a bag of mushrooms. It had taken him over two hours to find a good patch. He slashed a stick at the sparse bushes. Who would have thought he'd be scavenging for food. It was like he was destitute. Way below the poverty line.

Laurien and Jadyn were already outside the cave, busy preparing the dinner. Laurien ignored him, her lips curled in disdain. Jadyn greeted him and continued to chop and throw various vegetables into the pot hanging over the fire. Laurien's eyes darted around as if she was expecting someone else to arrive.

"Add the mushrooms. We're having a throw-in-every-thing dish." Jadyn sprinkled dried leaves into the pot. The steam soon filled the air with a mouth-watering savory smell.

"Roland, where's the princess?" Jadyn asked, laying out pottery plates and keeping an eye on the bubbling food. The metal implements on his leather belt jangled a tune every time he moved.

"The princess. The princess. Always Princess Eleonora," Laurien said under her breath.

"She's at the Potters' Caves with Sanelder," Roland said.

Jadyn tasted the stew and gave a satisfied nod. "Let's eat."

After the meal, Laurien licked her plate and stood up. "I have to go now. I'll see you at the next village fair when I help at the soup stall," she said, turning to Jadyn.

Roland put down his plate. "I'll walk you back."

Laurien's eyes flashed toward Jadyn. Perhaps she wanted him to walk her back, not Roland. As Roland led her away, she stared at Will and whispered under her breath. "Thief."

"She treated me as if I was invisible—until her polite parting comment," Will said to Jadyn after she left.

"Give it time." Jadyn ground the blade of one of his knives. "You seem to be settling into Caves Hill?"

"Sometimes I feel like I'm in limbo. I miss bits of the day and lose track of time." He focused on Jadyn's open eye, trying not to stare at the scar over the empty socket. "Do you know about the king and the truth the Counselor told me about?" He hadn't wanted to ask the question with Laurien around.

"The King's the one who made all this and the Earthlands—and us." Jadyn gestured to the valley and the sky. "He has the key to the truth."

"How can you believe in a king who allows so much suffering? Why can't we be happy and have what we want?"

"Good question, and it needs an involved answer. The King isn't the only one who rules the Earthlands. To answer your question about wanting happiness—at present, the Earthlands are ruled by an evil Prince. His aim is to destroy. We can't expect all to go our way."

Jadyn took a stick and made two rows of six holes with a small trench at either end, then tipped a pile of pebbles on the ground. "We pretend each stone is a combatant. It makes the game more entertaining. There are forty-eight altogether."

"How can you be so sure—about the evil guy?" Will poked at the embers in the fire and stretched his numbed feet toward the warmth.

"Not everything in our world is as it seems—in your world or ours. Even back on your earth, the supernatural is as powerful as it is here, but you may not be aware of it." Jadyn piled two more logs on the fire. Sparks swirled upward, as though chasing one another into the night air. "But those back at your bay or here on the island who live in the realm of the King or practice the rituals of the Darkness—they understand."

"Like Senka?"

Jadyn nodded. Roland joined them again.

"You can watch while Roland and I play the game, then I'll give you a turn Will," Jadyn said. "The aim is to capture as many combatants as you can. I'll show you how to sow the stones." He took a handful of the pebbles and dropped one into each hole as he moved around the set. "The last stone is dropped in the mancala, the trough at the end of the row. You can steal the other player's stones." He demonstrated. "When there are no moves left, the one with the most stones in their mancala is the winner."

After several games, many loud interjections and much laughter, Jadyn won the majority. They packed up while making plans for fishing the next day.

Will stood and stretched. A long howl echoed around the hills. Black shapes sped across the night sky as if on a mission. Did the talk of truth and evil help to add another piece to the solution of the island puzzle? It needed more thought.

***

Will stared at his wizened berries and meagre food supplies. He couldn't believe how much work it was to keep his hunger at bay. Hopefully, he would catch something edible and find out why Jadyn lived at Caves Hill when they went fishing.

Jadyn arrived, and they strolled down the steep incline toward the river. The icy mountain range nearby had a recent heavy blanket of snow and it spilled down into the tree-filled areas below the peaks, but the sun was out and warmed their faces.

When they reached the forest, Jadyn grabbed Will without warning, and spun him through the air. Will landed hard on the ground. A flock of birds screeched and darted into the birch trees at Will's shout of surprise.

"What was that about?" Will's heart jackhammered.

Jadyn laughed and pulled him to his feet. "It's the start of your combat training. I'll meet you tomorrow for your first lesson. We'll make you a pro in no time. Do you understand why?

Will brushed twigs and damp leaves from his clothing. "Because of the Cravers?"

"Not just the Cravers. You and I may need to defend Caves Hill one day. Some people wish us ill."

"I hate the stinking Cravers." Will hacked at a bush with his knife.

"They're human, just like us," Jadyn said. "We might need to avoid them for our own safety, but we also need to think of ways to help them. Once madecia rewires their brains, it's hard for them to backtrack."

Will kicked the nearest tree. Didn't he know it? The need for a drink was killing him. "So what are you doing about the madecia problem?"

"We have ideas, but it's not that simple. It'll take time."

They walked on in silence. But Will had a plan. Jadyn didn't know he'd spent the last four years training at the Belmont Martial Arts Center. Will whistled a couple of Beatles songs as a distraction. After ambling for another few minutes, he swung toward Jadyn, and with a deft maneuver of his arm and body, he also landed Jadyn on the ground.

Jadyn lay winded, staring up at him with a bewildered expression.

"Maybe I can teach you something," Will said. They laughed and continued glancing at one another. On guard.

"I'll give you a warning next time, if you do the same," Jadyn said.

"No promises."

"Bet you can't beat me at knife throwing," Jadyn said.

"Try me. Tomorrow." Will chuckled. "You'll have to supply the throwing knives."

Jadyn turned from the regular track, whistling to Wolfie to follow him, then parted the bushes to reveal a large rock jutting out over the shimmering river. Nearby, ferns clung to glistening rocks around a surging waterfall. They unloaded their packs, and then threaded junks of foul-smelling rabbit meat on the hooks.

"Do you ever take Laurien fishing?" Will asked.

"Don't believe she's the fishing type."

"I think she has the hots for you."

"Laurien's okay. If you knew what she's been through, you'd understand her better. But she's too screwed up for me."

"Let me see that knife you're using."

"Made it at the forge." Jadyn passed it to him.

"It's heavy but has a good balance in the hand—different from the ones I have at home," Will said. "How'd you make it?"

"From a single bar of steel. I heat it and pound it into shape. The bolster balances the blade and serves as a finger guard. Has a full tang." Jadyn pulled in his first catch of the day. He gutted the large trout with his knife and threw it in a container. "I sell the knives at the village fair for Cadwyn, the best metalworker in the island."

He threw in his line again. "Cadwyn's training me in metalwork at the forge. He and a group of others are planning to overthrow President Lorn. They want me involved. My father died in mysterious circumstances after he discovered Lorn was embezzling the taxes." Jadyn took a shaky breath. "Lorn's stockpiling the gold for himself.

He was like an uncle to me when I was younger, but the desire for control changed him into a monster."

"That's really tough for you." Will chopped at the stinking rabbit meat. So that explained why Jadyn lived at Caves Hill.

Two hours passed, and Will was sick of pulling in long strands of slippery reeds instead of a fish. Jadyn already had three silver trout thrashing around in his container.

"I wish I had a genie in a bottle and three wishes," Will said. "Then everything would be sweet."

"So what are the wishes—catch more fish and . . . ?"

"To get back to earth alive, to get revenge on Ben and my father, and have an unlimited supply of whatever I wanted. What else could I desire?"

Jadyn chuckled. "An unlimited supply of what exactly? Spell it out."

"Just a few of the simple things in life. Money, girl-friends, alcohol . . . the list goes on." He yanked the fishing line. "Got one. Hand me that knife, will you? Another thing I'd like, is to see the forge where you work. Could I go with you sometime?"

"We'll make a time."

When they reached Will's cave, Jadyn set down the container of fish. "I'll prepare the fish if you collect the wood."

The eerie night sky threw an amethyst light over the distant glistening peaks, which were illuminated by a vast floating moon. Will placed dry bracken and sticks on the outside fire, then fanned it alight. He loved the smell of the sweet wood smoke. If only Eleonora was with them then he'd actually feel happy and tonight, Jadyn could tell him about how he lost his eye. It probably happened in a fight.

"Have you done anything you've regretted, Jadyn?"

"Lots. Who hasn't?" Jadyn skewered the trout and waited for the flames to die down. "Why do you ask?"

"You seem to have your life together."

"I guess I've a few things in place, thanks to the King. But no one's perfect." Jadyn laid the fish over hot rocks in the coals.

"What's the king got to do with anything?"

"He can give us a clean slate." Jadyn added sprigs of thyme to the fish. "The judicial system works differently in his realm. The King took the punishment for all the wrong things we've done in our life."

"This King has no rules in his kingdom? Where do I sign up?"

"You have to have remorse, though. I think our dinner's cooked."

Will blew on the steaming flesh before taking a mouthful. Wolfie flopped beside him, watching with wide eyes. After the meal Wolfie bolted the leftover fish, and they wandered back to the hill.

"Where's this so-called king now?" Will asked.

"At his home in another realm." Jadyn pointed to the stars pulsing their fire in the haze of the velvet sky. "But he's here with us as well." Will stopped and gazed at the sky and the vast misty spray of galaxies. So close, yet so far. How could a king be up there, and also with them? He didn't believe it.

Later that night he heard voices at the foot of the hill. Thin figures huddled around a fire. He could tell they were Cravers. He ground his teeth and sat at the entrance of his cave, plotting what he'd do if they went anywhere near Eleonora's cave. He sat watching them for hours, knowing he wouldn't sleep a wink while they hung around. He needed to protect Eleonora—and Laurien. If Flack was one of the group and made a move, the guy would be losing more than the string of teeth around his neck. And if Striker showed his ugly face, he'd lose his plaited beard in a flash.

***

A salt-laden breeze blew memories of Aporto Bay into Will's mind. A dull ache of disappointment panged in his stomach every time he thought of the princess and the cave fiasco. He sprinted to Rosie's for goats' milk. Roland was already there, collecting his favorite soft cheese.

"Do you want to come and help in the corn patch tomorrow, Will?" Roland asked. "You can earn good money. The princess is coming."

"I'll see." Humiliation mixed with longing grabbed at him. He bent over Felix, who was drawing on a rock with a thin stick of charcoal.

"More dragons?"

Felix's charcoal-smudged face lit up. "Have you ever seen one?"

"We have loads of books and games about them, back where I come from."

"Can you take me there?"

"Wish I could. Having trouble getting back."

"Tell me all about them."

"He's obsessed." Rosie laughed.

"So was I, at his age. How about I visit after dinner and tell Felix some dragon stories?"

Felix leaped up and launched his small body at Will's chest like a catapult. "Please?"

Will grabbed him and swung him around in the air. He squealed.

"Come when you like," Rosie said.

Chapter 9

Will pulled his coat up to his chin and stayed in bed the following morning. His mind was still full of Felix, who'd pressed his little body to his, and listened with thumb in mouth, eyes wide, while Will told his best dragon stories. The evening left him homesick for his mother and Jess, and more lonely than ever. But when he heard Eleonora calling to Wolfie, he bolted out of his bed and pulled on his coat. If he saw her at the corn patch, he might find a way to rebuild the bridge he'd so stupidly demolished.

Eleonora, Roland and Jadyn were already working in the garden. The laden green plants towered over them, swaying in the breeze.

"Sleep in?" Jadyn asked.

Will muttered under his breath.

The princess worked at the rear of the garden, barely visible in the leaves. She would be avoiding him. He hated his life.

"The crop's good this year," Roland said.

"Back home we buy it from the supermarket, all prepared in packets." Will hacked at the corn, not caring when his knife slipped, and he cut himself.

"The easiest way to pick them is for ye to grasp the ear and pull down, then twist and pull." Roland demonstrated.

When the princess approached him about an hour later, Will's raw emotions went into meltdown. He bent over and threw a corncob in the bag so she couldn't see his face.

"Did you leave those berries for me?" she asked.

He mumbled into the sack. "Found a good patch just off the path to the river. I left them to apologize for—you know." He was too mortified to say the words.

She tied her full hessian bag, then pinned back a strand of golden hair that dangled over her cheek and pointed to the ooze of blood running down his fingers. "Here, let me check that cut." She took his hand, washed it with a liquid from a small bottle that hung from her belt. Her touch and the balm she applied soothed the memory of every angry word she'd said to him in her cave.

Roland heaved his bag along the ground and stretched. "We can have a bag each to sell at the fair. It will fetch good money for ye, Will. I've kept leaves for Rosie's wee goats as well. Dinner at my place tonight, everyone?"

The Princess and Jadyn agreed, and Will nodded. He couldn't speak over the lump in his throat.

Will spent extra time in the river that afternoon washing off the dirt from the garden and took ages to shave with one of Jadyn's blades. He buckled his tan belt around the cotton overshirt Jadyn had given him and then clambered up to Roland's cave. His heart raced at the scuttle of stones behind him.

He turned and tried not to stare at the mesmerizing vision of Eleonora. Her blouse was pulled in tightly at the waist. It accentuated the alluring shape of her body, and her skirt skimmed above her knees. A silver pendant, decorated with scrollwork, hung around her neck. They walked together, and Will glanced at her profile glowing in the golden light of the sunset as they chatted.

"Where are the others, Roland?" she asked when they arrived at his cave.

"Cadwyn called Jadyn to the forge for an urgent village fair order. I huvnae seen Laurien for a few days," Roland said.

Eleonora sat on the hessian rug Roland had laid beside the fire and stirred the fragrant stew. Will edged closer to her, but she shifted away. The move was almost imperceptible, but enough to leave a small hollow of disappointment in Will. But he still felt a charge in the air between them.

"I saw Laurien in the village, but—" The princess clutched her pendant.

"Is anything wrong?" Roland said.

"She was with some Cravers."

"That's surprising." Roland frowned. "They dinnae mix with Drifters."

"I'll ask her about it when she comes back. It may mean nothing."

"Are ye missing everyone back at your bay, Will?" Roland asked.

"Some, but not all. Like Ben Maddock."

"What was the problem with him?" the princess asked.

"He'll never be my friend. Our families don't see eye to eye. The Maddocks are troublemakers."

"Did he take yer girlfriend?" Roland's eyes twinkled.

Will tensed for a moment. "He takes everything. His father built the stadium that collapsed. He even trashed my car."

"Was he caught?" the princess asked.

"No. I'd parked down the road from the café where I was working and went to drive home at the end of my shift. The car was a write-off. He smashed the windscreen and dented the doors." Will dug at the dirt with the heel of his boot. "Chen said he saw Ben and his mates in the street near the car earlier that afternoon. They had a cricket bat."

Will picked up a stick and snapped it over his knee. "I don't have enough proof for the police to charge him, but I know he did it. I hate him. I'm planning to get revenge when I get back to the bay." He stabbed the fragments of the stick into the embers. At least Ben wasn't on the island. If Ben met Eleonora, there'd be more than fireworks.

They stared at him, faces shadowed with concern.

"What started this family conflict?" the princess asked.

"It's a long story, and it began ages ago. A jilted Maddock—and a dead body."

"Revenge isnae what it's made out to be," Roland said.

"But it makes me feel better. As though I'm doing something constructive." But the only thing that would make him feel better at the moment would be a drink.

"The truth will free you from the desire for retaliation," Eleonora said.

"What truth?"

"Ye can find it at the House of Wisdom at Eladia.

Ye'll find the answers there," Roland said.

The princess passed around small plums. "Will, could you help Laurien and me take the bags of corn and pot of soup to the Shannon village fair and help at the stall?"

"Sure." He hoped his tone of voice didn't reveal his eagerness too much. The village fair. At last. And Eleonora's company.

A scraping of stones on the hill interrupted his thoughts.

"Laurien," they all exclaimed together.

She panted, her eyes wild. "I've got news from Nevara. There are rumors Lorn is going to take control of the south of the island—and that means Shannon and Caves Hill."

A prickle of apprehension crept down Will's spine at the look on their faces. He should increase his training regime and be ready.

***

Will threw off his fur bedding and checked the weather. Mist nestled into the valley like drifts of goose down. Smoke spiraled from the chimneys of the distant shingled roofs of the Shannon cottages. The village fair was on, and the temperature was mild. He'd pay Goat's Horn Inn an all-important visit, call on Senka, and find a way back to Aporto Bay. A streak of elation shot through him at the thought.

An hour later, Eleonora and Laurien walked with him along the well-worn path through Emerald Forest, and then past Wyld Wood. A heavy, dank smell wafted from the undergrowth. Will carried the pot of soup, and had a bag of corn on his back. The princess and Laurien also carried sacks of vegetables and plums.

"I haven't heard you singing lately," he said to the princess.

"I still do, but sometimes in my cave. Cravers have been hanging around, so I don't want to attract attention."

"Sensible." Will ground his teeth at the thought of Cravers near her cave.

"Keep your arms covered," the princess said. "The President may have his combatants checking for Drifters at the village. There will also be Cravers around. They'll make any excuse to start a fight—especially if they remember you from Cawl Desert."

A faint jingle of lively tunes drifted on the breeze. "Where do the Cravers get the madecia?" Will ducked under a low-hanging tree, hoping he wouldn't spill the soup.

"It's readily available. The President makes sure of that," Eleonora said.

"But why would he?"

"I guess he uses it to keep people under his control, as a reward for loyalty. And he makes a huge profit from proceeds."

"Why does he force people to take the raven mark?" Will glanced back at the Hill. A sudden feeling of belonging surprised him.

"To show allegiance to him. But we live in an isolated community here, with the mountain ranges as protection," she said. "We don't see many of the President's combatants, and most people around here keep to themselves."

"That's why we live here, stupid," Laurien said. But she looked around furtively every few steps.

"Why do you take soup to the village? Does it bring much money?" he asked.

"There're a lot of poor people in the village. We don't ask for payment."

"Most can't be bothered to help themselves." Laurien twisted her lips into a grimace.

"We like to help them," the princess said. "It was Roland's idea, and most are not like that, Laurien."

The smell of toffee and honey biscuits wafted in the air. A bustling fair with a motley crowd milled around the stalls and fairground, chatting or shouting, as though trying to outdo one other. It was like the annual medieval fair back at Aporto Bay, but this one looked real, even without a castle. The Celtic clothing and accessories and assorted piercings added to the atmosphere. Tiny rat-like squirrels scurried around the tents, chattering amongst themselves as they searched for morsels of food.

"What are they?" Will pointed to one hurtling across the track with a piece of bread in its claws. "I sometimes see them in the forest."

"Ha, that's a mirren." The princess dodged one as it ran under her feet. "They look cute but have a painful bite."

Bony dogs, screeching chickens, and other livestock added to the cacophony. Colorful wooden caravans, faded striped tents, and canvas stalls were set up haphazardly in the village park. Stallholders shouted to the surging crowds advertising their wares. Others performed contortions and tricks for gold. People gathered around a man with a feathered, peaked cap while he conducted a tin whistle workshop.

"Will, would you build the fire so I can heat the soup?" the princess asked.

Laurien placed several bowls of fresh forest plums on a makeshift wooden table Jadyn had lent them and covered it with a crochet-edged tablecloth.

"I'll see you later." She disappeared into the crowds.

The princess stroked the fabric. "Aunt Nora hand-crocheted this tablecloth."

Will nodded. As if he wanted to know about crochet. His mouth watered at the hot savory aroma of the vegetable and onion soup steaming into the air, but it only made him crave a drink more. He ladled soup into a pottery mug for a child dressed in tattered clothing, and then for a lady in a yellowed blouse and patched skirt. The soup pot was soon half-empty, and the crowds thinned.

"Can you manage while I have a look around?" Will said to the princess. He couldn't wait any longer. She waved him away.

He wandered along the dusty main street, littered with discarded cabbage leaves, until he found the inn. He pushed through the rowdy crowd and ordered a bottle of corn spirits for himself and a bottle of mead to take back to Roland. He also ordered two glasses of corn spirits. He gulped them down and rushed back to the soup stall, placing the two clinking bottles under the table. The next stop would be Senka's fortune-teller tent.

A man with wide-set eyes, wearing a coat with a shaggy neck fur, strode to the soup table. He leaned over it toward the princess. "There's talk of trouble in the village. Be ready to pack up and go." He turned away and joined the surge of people passing by.

Eleonora's face tightened. "That's Dorian, Roland's friend."

Unease seeped into Will's guts. Two men slunk by. A chill shivered down Will's spine as he recognized them. The skinny Cravers—Flack and Striker.

"Don't make eye contact," Eleonora said under her breath.

The men passed by, then were swallowed by the crowd.

"Do you know where Senka has her tent?" Will asked. "I promised to see her."

The princess folded her arms and frowned at him. "Why would you want to visit a fortune teller? Especially Senka."

"She invited me. I'll go after the soup's finished."

They served the soup until only a few dregs lined the bowl. Several customers gave them small gifts in return: a woven cloth, apples, and mandon nuts. The familiar squeaking of Grunter's trolley cut through the noises of the crowd in an unwelcome intrusion to Will's ears. That was a memory he could do without. A muscled man Will had never seen before wheeled Grunter through the crowd. Grunter peered at Will through narrowed eyes and pointed at their table.

"Plums," he called. The muscled man swung the trolley toward them.

Grunter took a whole plate of plums, tipped them into his lap, and sniggered.

"Hey," Will said, "leave some for the others." Grunter signaled to his companion to go.

Will clenched his fists. Flack and Striker were back. They shouted at a curly-haired boy standing behind a table of jewelry and beads.

"Pack up. We leave now." The princess threw everything except the soup pot into the packs and dragged off the tablecloth.

Chapter 10

Striker pounced on the curly-haired boy. A shrill scream from the boy split the air.

"You little fiend. You took our stuff," Striker shouted. "We have proof."

A mirren-sized spotted dog leaped at Striker's leg and latched its teeth into his calf. The man swore, reached down and plucked off the dog. He hurled it against a caravan window, splintering the glass. Flack grabbed fistfuls of the boy's hair while Striker punched his face.

The boy's cries cut through Will. He gripped his knife and stepped toward them.

The princess grabbed his arm. "No. They could kill you."

But rage pulsed through Will's veins. The boy was silent now, but they still kicked. A crowd gathered. Will pulled away from Eleonora's grip and strode out, his knife ready, wishing the alcohol wasn't in his bloodstream. It addled his thoughts and doubled his vision.

Flack jerked his head up and Will met his hollow, olive-brown eyes. The man thrust the boy aside, leaving the boy's left leg bent sideways and twisted.

"Fresh meat." Flack's eyes glinted. "I remember you."

"Pick on someone your own size." Will hoped he wasn't slurring his words.

"We have."

Flack lunged behind him, grabbed Will's right arm, and yanked. The cartilage and muscle of his right shoulder stretched in nauseating agony as Flack pulled the bone from its socket. Will swung around, his arm dangling and useless. He swallowed the urgent need to retch.

Will used his other arm to trade blows in a series of eye-watering thumps and guttural grunts. His eyes watered with the exertion, blurring his vision even more. Striker grabbed a wooden paling lying nearby, then lunged toward Will.

He struck Will's face. Blood streamed out of his nose and across his lips. He doubled over, his dislocated shoulder burned with a searing pain. Flack kicked him to the ground. A dull crack sounded in his ribcage. Will squirmed in the dirt, blood oozing down his cheek.

The princess stepped toward them.

Will lurched upright. *No, Princess.*

She drew a sword. Its blade flashed as though it had its own light. Low murmurs rippled from the crowd. Where had the sword come from?

"The King's sword won't work against us, scum," Striker said in a scornful tone. They stalked toward her. Will's stomach twisted into a double knot. She looked small and vulnerable, but she stood tall without flinching.

Clouds raced over the sun. A gust of wind blew leaves and dust into Will's eyes. The crowd peered up at the sky. The fair music stopped, and everything froze in time. A tall giant of a man with the blackest skin Will had ever seen strode toward them from the clump of trees next to the circus tent. His feet barely touched the ground.

The two men paused. Flack growled, Striker shrugged, and they slunk away in the opposite direction. The moment passed, and the crowd gaped. Will struggled to his feet.

"We need to get you and the boy to Dr. Wells—and quickly," the princess said.

The sword had disappeared.

***

An enormous full moon had risen by the time they arrived back at Will's cave. Roland came to see what the fuss was about, and Will gave him the replacement bottle of mead. The princess helped make a stove fire and boiled water for tea, while they talked animatedly about everything that had happened.

"Fortunately, Will only has one broken rib, and a dislocated right shoulder. It could have been worse. They broke the little boy's leg." The princess turned and glared at Will. "By the way, you were very foolish."

"So were you. Just as well I'm left-handed." He twisted to a more comfortable position, recoiling at the pain. But somehow the pain didn't matter as much because Eleonora was with him. Everything was better when she was around. "Who was that guy who made the mysterious arrival, and where did you get the sword?"

"One of the King's angels," Eleonora said.

"I thought angels had wings." Will leaned back against the wall and ran his fingers over his nose. It wasn't broken but had swollen to twice the normal size, like his puzzlement about everything that happened.

"Angels come in many forms."

"I wish that sort of thing happened on Earth."

"It does," Eleonora said. "But you may not see it. Like the sword. All King followers have the King's sword, but it is invisible."

Roland and the princess left his cave. A long silver streak lit the dark velvet sky, and their voices carried towards him on the nightfall breeze.

"Do you think the angel came to save ye, or Will, or both of ye?"

"I'm not sure, but it appears Will is under the protection of . . . he's not a King follower, perhaps he has a . . . ."

The hooting of an owl in the forest below muffled her words. Will wished he could have filled in the blanks. He dragged his fur bed outside, pain mixed with adrenaline still coursing through his body. What happened in the village had blown his mind. Sleep would not come easily this night.

But he needed to heal quickly. He had scores to settle, not only on Eldrad, but with his father, Maureen and Ben.

***

After a short time of recuperation, Will trained most days, despite his lingering injuries. He often shared roast rabbit, stews, or fish with the others in the evening. Wolfie joined them when he wasn't hunting. Jadyn kept them up-to-date with the latest rumors about President Lorn's moves and revealed Cadwyn's plans to gather support to save the island.

That evening, Will and Eleonora walked back together to their caves after having dinner with Roland. Spending time with her and the others was the one thing that distracted Will from the homesickness and fear of the unknown which threatened to engulf him.

But the princess still kept him at arm's length. Why was he so upset about that? He couldn't develop feelings for her. She'd be a distraction to his all-important goal of getting back home. It was a no-brainer.

"How do you think the President will take over the south of the island?" Will asked, breaking the silence. Wolfie trotted beside him, and he reached down and ruffled the hound's fur.

"He'll most likely send his combatants. There are also rumors he has a plan to attack us at Caves Hill. We can only speculate how he plans to do that. Did you know Jadyn and Laurien are both on his 'wanted' list?"

"No. That's news to me." Will gripped the handle of his knife and kicked at the stones at the thought.

"I'll be leaving soon for my next trip," she said. "By the way, what did you do to befriend Wolfie?"

"I made him run a month's worth of marathons with me. It broke the ice."

"Ha."

"Can I help you get ready for your next trip?" What was he doing, making excuses to spend time with her? He needed to keep his feelings under control.

"You can help me collect the supplies I need from Silver Brook tomorrow if you like."

"How do you know about all these flowers and herbs, and which ones to gather?"

"It's a passion of mine. Dr. Wells is teaching me about the therapeutic benefits of the plants. He's an expert. We have a wealth of supplies in Emerald Forest. It's my ambition to have my own stall in the village one day."

Her face glowed with enthusiasm in the soft moonlight. Admiration for her, and the things she did, flipped something in his heart.

This girl and her beauty could launch a thousand ships.

And these ships would not be taking him home.

This girl could be his downfall.

***

The air was crisp and bracing. Will and Eleonora sprinted to Silver Brook Glade's wild floral garden. He spent the entire morning helping the princess pick bunches of dandelion, rosemary, sage, thyme and plants he'd never heard of, like hypericum and borage. She explained how to identify marigold and chamomile.

That afternoon, back at her cave, they stripped leaves from branches and filled bags with dried herbs and seeds. His hand brushed against hers as she passed him a handful of the small calico bags for the lavender. His skin burned at her touch. His heart thumped in his chest. What was wrong with him?

"Where are you going this time?" He wished he could ease the ache in his heart at the thought of her leaving. As soon as she left, he'd go down to the inn and get a drink.

"To the Potters' Caves." She packed a leather box in her bag.

"What's in the brown box?" He picked seeds from the last dried pods and dropped them into a cloth bag.

"Lift the lid and have a look." She took it from her pack and passed it to him.

He read the faded words engraved into the surface with gold embossing. "The King's Sword. It must be a tiny sword." He lifted the lid and exclaimed. "It's really a book."

"The title of the book is 'The King's Word.' You're right—it's like a treasure box."

Will peered at the small print. "This looks boring. What's so special about it?"

"You need the key to understand it."

"How do you get the key?"

"The King gives the key to the people in his kingdom. The door it opens leads them to the truth."

"Then it's no use to me."

"That's not entirely true. It may help you understand why you're here on the island."

Will shrugged.

She took the book and packed it in her bag with her clothes.

"Who printed it?"

"We have printers in Eladia. I know Caves Hill seems backward, but Eldrad is quite a civilized island."

Will left Eleonora and scanned the Hill for suitable firewood to cook his dinner. A key and the truth? Could there be a connection between them in his quest to get home? He'd find out more tomorrow, at the village fair. Tomorrow he would see Senka. This time, nothing would stop him.

***

Distant melodies of minstrel music filtered up the hill from the village fair. Anticipation bolted through Will's body in a rush. He hurried through his usual set of early morning exercises, then strode toward the village. He longed to see the boy and small dog the Cravers attacked during his last visit.

An enticing mix of roasted meat and wood smoke from the stall fires drifted toward him. Odd-looking vegetables and fruits piled the tables in the food market. Hungry, he used one of his smaller gold coins to buy slices of roast pork from the spit dripping over a slow-burning fire. While he chewed on the succulent meat, he poked his head into the circus tent. Dogs dressed in tiny vests tottered on tightropes and leaped over impossibly high jumps. The boy with the curly hair and the little spotted dog the Cravers had attacked were nowhere to be seen.

A long queue of people waited in front of a painted sign: *Meet Mayor Ranker.* The imposing man, dressed in a long russet cloak and wearing a gold chain, sat under a canvas shelter. Impatience twisted the mayor's features as a woman with no teeth and a sunken face shouted at him.

Will walked past toward the knife and axe-throwing competitions. He wanted to enter the knife-throwing contest, but his heart sank at the long queue. He asked the woman with a laced bodice selling tickets. "Who runs the show here?"

"Odin. That's him handin' out the axes."

Odin wore a goatee beard, a snakelike face, and eyes which threw their own daggers. Will lined up with the others, torn whether he should wait in the line, go to the inn or visit Senka. But this was his chance to see how far his self-imposed training and sessions with and without Jadyn had taken him.

After half an hour, it was his turn at the knife-throwing. He struck all the targets. It had been worth the wait, and Odin presented him with a small knife for his skill. He tucked the knife into his belt and continued to the metalwork stall, keen to show Jadyn his prize and get directions to Senka's tent.

Dorian was serving at the stall. "Is Jadyn around?" Will asked, picking up one of the ornate swords on the table. "I wanted to ask him where the fortune tellers are."

"Ah, William Sutherland." The man spoke in a deep and resonating voice and stared at him from head to toe through squinted eyes. "Jadyn's at the forge. Just keep going down the path, and you'll find the soothsayer."

Will headed in the direction Dorian had indicated. Why had the man reacted so strangely toward him? Boisterous singing and shouting rang out from Goat's Horn Inn. Groups of men and women sat at round tables with green checked tablecloths. Will counted his coins and ordered two glasses of corn spirits inside at the bar. The familiar fire-scorch of the amber liquid burned a track into his stomach and flared into his veins. He also bought a bottle to take back to his cave.

He hastened toward circular striped tents further down the path, light-headed and hot in the midday sun. He pushed up his sleeves to cool off. A red-headed girl with a yellow skirt edged with bells and muddy tassels stopped him and pointed to his arm.

"No raven mark." She rolled her eyes. "I'm sure the mayor would be interested to see that."

Will dragged his sleeve back over his wrist, wrinkled his nose at her body odor, and walked on. A stone of unease settled in his stomach.

"Come and have your fortune read, then I won't tell anyone." Her hair bounced around her head as she caught up with him.

"I'm looking for Senka."

"It's your lucky day." She pointed to a tent with stripes of red and blue. "And it's only one medium gold coin. I'll ask for extra time—especially for you." She smiled a toothy grin of broken teeth and led him to a tattered tent. She poked her head through the entry flap, spoke with words Will didn't understand, and then thrust out her grimy hand for the gold coin.

Chapter 11

An acrid incense odor filled the stuffy tent. A woman sat in a shadowed corner at a round table and pointed a gold-ringed finger at the empty stool opposite. A shiver of recognition and nervousness slicked down his back.

"Senka?"

"Will Sutherland," she said in a husky voice. "So you decided to come?"

He nodded. His eyes grew accustomed to the smoky dimness of the tent. The silver stitching on her dress and shawl glistened in the candlelight. A crystal ball, a pile of bleached bones, and a small-scale statue of a naked woman sat on the table. Senka picked up a pack of cards.

Will perched on the stool. "Can you help me?"

"You know I can read futures, boy. Listen to everything I tell you. You won't be sorry. You'll say—why didn't I come to Senka sooner?"

She shuffled the cards on her table as fast as the flutter of a butterfly's wings, then peered at them. She frowned, paused, cut the deck, and then reshuffled. Will gripped the legs of the stool.

"Interesting." She pursed her lips. Damp curls clung to her neck and chest. "What are you doing on our island, Will Sutherland?"

"That's what I want you to tell me."

"You haven't answered my question."

"I don't have a clue." Will shrugged. "I just want to go back to my world."

She peered at him for a long moment, caressing the bones on the table. "I can organize that, but you must trust me." She rolled her hands around the crystal ball and sucked in a breath. "You have so many desires, impulsive boy, and so many hurts."

He leaned toward her, not wanting to miss anything. She reached out, took his hand, and traced the lines on his skin. "We can change your destiny." Her coal-dark eyes glowed.

"What do you mean?" He pulled his hand away. "I may not want my future tampered with."

"What did I say about trust? I can tap into great powers." She chanted over the crystal ball. A movement inside the sphere raised the hairs on the back of his neck. His lungs were leaden in the stifling air.

"Have to go." He staggered off the stool, but reeled when the interior of the tent lurched at an alarming angle.

"Wait. I haven't finished, doubting boy," she said. "Don't you want to go back to your real home? To be close to your family again?" She reached up and took a small bottle from a bag hanging on a hook. "Take this once a day for three days. It will take you home. I guarantee it."

"What is it?"

"It's a therapeutic mix handed down through the generations." She held out her hand. "That'll be another gold coin. This is a special favor. It's worth much more."

He'd do anything to get out of the suffocating tent. He fumbled in his coin pouch, struggling to focus, and dropped a coin on the table.

"Now look into my eyes."

He couldn't focus.

She clapped. "You aren't concentrating. Distracted boy."

He wanted to escape. A fire danced in her eyes. He was a helpless moth fluttering toward the flame. Surely it was only the reflection of the candle. But a fire raged in his head.

He forced his body to stand, but swayed. Lunging to the canvas opening of the tent, he ripped it open and landed on his knees in the daylight. Gulping fresh air.

"Come back to Senka. Come back to Senka." The tent walls muffled her shouts.

He dodged through the streaming crowds until he found a bale of hay to collapse on at the far edge of the fairground. When his heart had stopped pounding, he went back and continued to search for the boy and the spotted dog, avoiding the fortune teller tents. But they were nowhere to be seen.

The crowds thinned, and the stallholders packed their wares. The crimson setting sun painted the fair in soft gold. He needed to get back to Caves Hill, but he was having trouble concentrating. He wasn't sure if it was the effects of the corn spirits or his emotional state. Once he found the pathway back, shadows closed around him. Cobweb gray clouds streaked the moon. Something or someone was watching him, he was sure of it. Confused thoughts spun havoc in his mind.

"Come to Senka . . . Senka." Voices hissed in his ears. "You are one of us now. Welcome to our realm. We can take you home."

Dusk fell too quickly. He'd taken a path into Wyld Wood by mistake. An irrational dread gripped him with its talons. He pushed back through the bushes toward the Caves Hill track. Exposed roots tripped him, and brittle branches scraped his arms. Plump, velvet-bodied spiders with glowing eyes swung into his face from dense webs. He hit at them with a stick, shuddering. Then he fell, sucked into a swirling vortex of horror.

***

Will woke. A small furry body, heavy and warm, hugged around his neck. He lurched up in a panic, flinging it off. The thing leaped away into the undergrowth. *A mirren.* He breathed again. Better than a giant spider. Bracken on the forest floor chafed his skin. Patches of lilac sky shone through the dense canopy of the Wyld Wood trees. Spirited birdsong filled the early dawn. He stretched his stiff limbs and rubbed his aching head, then wrenched his bag open to check the contents. He seized the amber jar of potion Senka had given him and sniffed the bitter odor.

"Take it. Take it," voices crooned. But he wanted to ask Eleonora about it first. He sipped a few mouthfuls from the bottle of spirits, then pushed through the undergrowth until he found a track out of the woods toward Caves Hill, which loomed above him.

***

Later the next night, Will woke to a rustle in his cave. A shape morphed in the dim moonlight. It half-slithered, half-stalked toward him with a low hiss. Will froze as a wash of icy fear slicked down his back. It was one of those demonic birds again. Will drew back from the gargoyle head. Its red eyes, full of hate, were like two laser beams pointed at his face.

"They won't miss you now you're dead and buried." The demon's voice made a hollow sound, like a shattered echo. "And Ben Maddock is spreading rumors about you. All over the bay. And you can't stop him."

Will picked up the biggest stone he could reach and threw it at the creature. The stone hit its forehead. The beast snarled, reached out a thin clawed hand to Will's neck, and dug sharp claws into his throat. Will writhed and grappled with the creature, but couldn't wrench it off.

More of the creatures gathered in the cave, making chittering noises. He didn't have a chance. He shouted for help and then reached down, grabbed his fur bedding, and flung it over the demon's head, but the claws still burrowed. Barks echoed through the valley, and just before Will thought it would shred his neck beyond repair, the demons swept out of the cave, and Wolfie bounded in.

Wolfie sniffed him all over and Will stroked the dog's ears. "Thanks, pup." Will ran his fingers over his stinging neck. But the skin where the claws had been a moment before was smooth. No blood covered his hands. No blood dripped from his neck.

As he often did, Will tossed back and forth on his stony fur bed until morning, his thoughts trapped an unsolvable maze.

***

The scent of rain hung in the air. Clouds misted the mountains into oblivion, and soon a driving torrent washed over Caves Hill, matching Will's gray mood. He checked his neck again for injuries. Nothing. Visiting Senka was a let-down. He didn't trust her. He drank more of the corn spirits and slept all morning.

That afternoon, Will pulled on his thick skin coat and headed toward Roland's cave. He needed to leave Caves Hill and find the way home. More than ever.

He entered Roland's cave, dribbling water on the stone floor. Roland set his book aside and gave him a searching look.

"How about a wee cup of tea?"

What was it about being with Roland that made him feel safe and happy? Will thawed his hands at the heat radiating from the oven and pointed to the book Roland was reading. "So you have the King's Word like the princess."

"Aye." Roland filled two mugs with steaming tea.

"Tell me about the king's key. Does it open other doors as well?" Will asked.

"Aye."

"What will it open?"

"It opens many doors, and there are other keys. There are keys to the truth like the keys to the seven doors of the House of Wisdom in the city of Eladia."

"Have you been there?"

Roland nodded and gestured with excitement, spilling his tea. "But it's quite a journey from here. Many days."

"I want to explore the island now I've recovered. I'm going to find out why I'm here and how to get home."

"I wudnae get yer hopes up." Roland stirred the herbs in his tea. "But if ye go to the House of Wisdom ye could learn the truth about why you're here."

Will walked back to the entrance of the cave and peered out at the cold gray drizzle washing down the mountain in a torrent, and returned to Roland's crackling oven fire.

"The lady of the house, Sophia, is at the entrance gate of Eladia most days speaking to passers-by," Roland said. "It's an experience not to be missed. I'll never forget the spread she gave us for dinner."

Will leaned back against the cold rock wall and flicked through the book.

Roland turned toward him, his eyes lighting up like a forest fire. "The words of that book ye are holding are more powerful than any other book in the Earthlands. The words can transform yer life. There are words that can call vast armies of angels and protect ye against demonic forces."

Will gripped the small book. He peered at the words in the dim light, mystified.

***

The rain blew out to sea after two days of deluge. Will needed more money for food and drinks, so he worked with Roland in the vegetable garden, and he also hoped Roland would tell him more about the mysterious Eleonora.

"Don't you find life tedious here, living in a cave? What do you do with your life?" Will asked.

"I garden. I spend time with my friends—like ye—and I spend time petitioning the King to save the island. That's my passion at the present time."

"You really think petitioning a king will make a difference?" Will asked, crunching on a carrot. "Where is this king, anyway?"

"You can't see him, but he's with us. I wudnae waste my time if I dinnae believe it. Have ye been to Silver Brook Glade yet?"

"Yes, the princess showed me. A floral wonderland, with a fresh spring."

Roland smiled. "Did she now."

Will piled the corn in a bag. "How well do you know the princess?"

"She originally came from the Napier Mountains. She's had much hardship in her life." Roland wiped his forehead as they headed back to his cave "Are ye keen on her? I see the way ye look at her."

"Do you blame me?"

Roland shook his head. "It won't be easy for ye."

"Why do you say that? Is there someone else?"

"What I meant is—she's most likely driven by her own plans. A relationship may not be what she wants at the moment. Would ye like some soup? All I have to do is warm it on the stove."

Will nodded, and they wandered back. Roland added wood to the oven and placed a pot of soup and a container of water and leaves on the stovetop.

Once the tea was steaming, Roland poured him a mug. "Mint and rosehip from Silver Brook."

Will swirled the leaves around in the hot tea, mirroring the spin of thoughts in his head. "What do you mean— she's had hardship?"

"She lost both parents when the President Lorn flooded the Napier Mountains valley. The diverted water swallowed many homes without enough warning for the families to evacuate."

"That's awful." Will kneaded his creased forehead. "Why is she called a princess? Was her father a king?"

"Her Eldrad father wasn't a king, but our King is a father to her and us. She's like a princess, don't you think?"

Will nodded, wishing he could see her again. There was something about her that took his breath away. It wasn't only she was beautiful. She had a presence about her that sent his mind into a crazy carousel spin. It scared the life out of him that she didn't feel the same way. And it scared the life out of him that he may not want to go back to Aporto Bay, because of her.

Chapter 12

A few evenings later, they huddled around the fire outside Roland's cave. Only Laurien was missing. Roland ladled thick rabbit stew into their bowls, and the princess tore pieces of cornbread and handed it around. They chatted about the day's events and the rumors circulating around the village about the President. Jadyn left to find more wood to top up the fire.

Will stood and collected their empty bowls, then swished them around in a large basin of clean water.

"Where's the detergent?"

They looked at him blankly.

"The soap."

"On the wee shelf." Roland pointed into his cave.

"Why are you king followers?" Will asked. "So many kings in the past were power-hungry and ruthless—in our world, anyway."

"Our King isn't like that," Jadyn said.

"How do you know?"

"His kingdom is an upside-down kingdom."

"Upside-down?"

"He cares about minorities, the poor and broken people," Eleonora said. "When he came to the Earthlands to rescue us, he didn't arrive as a royal person would, in all his wealth and finery. He knew he'd be tortured and murdered. It was the only way he could save us from the Darkness."

Will looked at her with raised eyebrows. "You guys believe that? You're living in a fairy tale."

"It's like a fairy tale." The princess nodded. "I guess the difference is that it's a true story. It's part of the Earthland's history—his story."

Will held one of the dripping plates midair. "So you're claiming he doesn't like wealth and power?"

"No. Plenty of rich and powerful people are King followers," she said.

Someone yelled nearby, into the night air. "Felix. Felix!"

"That sounds like Rosie." Jadyn frowned as he piled more wood on the fire.

"Felix is out late," Eleonora said.

Will finished washing the last bowl. There was a crunch of footsteps on the hill.

"Rosie," Roland said.

"Have you lost Felix?" Eleonora asked.

"He went outside in the afternoon." Rosie's voice quavered. "He wanders, but usually comes when he's called. He's never out this late."

"I saw him near Senka's cave this afternoon," Will said.

"That's a concern." Roland staggered to his feet.

"Why do you say that?" Rosie wrung her hands.

Roland stepped to his bookshelf and took down a book with a maroon-colored cover. He flicked through the pages, brown with age. "It's just as I thought. Ye should get yer coats, Jadyn and Eleonora." Roland had a tone of urgency in his voice. "It's Samhain. I've heard talk in the village there's a coven meeting in Wyld Wood. I can't say for sure, but wee Felix could be in danger. Life-threatening danger." He pointed to the woods. "See the glow down there."

Will peered through the darkness at pinpricks of yellow light through the trees.

"Jadyn, we need to leave," Eleonora called, already striding down toward the valley.

Jadyn leaped up and tightened his belt. "Roland and Will, you stay with Rosie."

Rosie's eyes darted from side to side in terror, and then she slumped to the ground. Roland held her as her entire body shook.

Will compressed his lips and checked for his knife. That Felix was in danger was more than he could take—and that Eleonora was going to Wyld Wood without his protection was unthinkable.

Will scrabbled around for his coat. "I'm going with them."

"It's too dangerous for ye, son. It's the King's business."

"I have my knife and my wits." No matter what they said, he was going.

"Ye may need more than that for the Darkness."

"Don't worry, Rosie. We'll find Felix." He sprinted down the hill, skidding on the stones.

The hairs on his arms bristled at the faint chanting in Wyld Wood. He pushed his way through the forest of trees. There was no way he'd find a track. An unnerving energy permeated the dank and clammy atmosphere. He slipped on mossy logs and shuddered when spiderwebs as strong as mosquito netting dragged at his skin and clothes. He tried not to think of the fat spiders that were sure to be waiting in the webs.

Yellow lights flickered like a warning through the foliage. The rhythmic incantations were louder now. A burning wax odor filled his nostrils, and the trees swayed oddly in the breeze. He sensed an oppressive presence, as he always did when the Darkness was near. He pulled out his knife. Ready.

In a clearing, a fire flared in a shining brass container placed next to a stone altar. Six flaming candles were arranged around the clearing. Three people walked with measured steps around the altar. Will's breath seized in his throat.

Senka. Ranker, the village mayor. And Odin—the one with the mean face and goatee beard.

He crept closer. His heartbeat suspended for one terror-filled moment. A tiny, trembling figure tied with thick ropes lay on the altar.

Felix.

The child whimpered, and his hands clawed at the stone.

Senka, the mayor and Odin, chanted and paced around the altar in a trance-like state. Their faces were eerie in the reflected glow of the flames.

Senka took a candle and dripped it into a shallow bowl of water, then peered into it, her lips moving. A pungent, smoky stench seared Will's throat and nose, and he stifled a cough. The woman swung around, staring at the bushes where Will was hiding, as if distracted for a moment. He drew back.

Odin paused at the altar, chanting in a monotone. He closed his eyes, slipped his sword out of the sheath and held it point down. He touched the ground three times, then resumed the march around the altar.

A hand landed heavily on Will's shoulder. An icy chill pooled in his stomach, and he jerked away.

"It's me." Jadyn muttered through clenched teeth. "What are you doing here?"

"Came to help. Where's the princess?"

"She's over on the other side." He pointed. "Getting ready to free Felix. We're in huge danger. Odin's an assassin. He works undercover for the President."

The chanting increased in intensity. Jadyn spoke in a low tone. "Time's short. Be ready. I'll take Odin. He's the only one with a sword. You deal with Ranker. Watch out—he's fast for a heavy guy. We'll both keep an eye on

Senka. She has one of my best double-edged knives. Eleonora will rescue Felix. Wait until she signals. And—we're not here to kill."

Jadyn unhooked ropes from his belt. "Use these if you need to. I'll let you know when it's time."

Will threw off his coat. The clearing resonated with spine-chilling incantations. The coven's ceremonial dance gradually drew closer to the white-faced Felix on the altar.

Will drew a quaking breath at the ominous whispers in his mind. *Leave this place. Leave this place.*

The princess burst from the other side of the clearing. Jadyn nudged him, and they charged toward their targets. Will caught a flicker of surprise on Eleonora's face when she saw him. The chanting stopped. The coven froze. The assassin swept his long, thin sword into the air and gave an enraged shout. Curses and cries echoed through the woods.

Will spun at the mayor, sweeping him off his feet with one of his best throws, then whipped the rope around the man's beefy arms. The man snarled in rage and kicked him in the face with his boot. Will reeled back, his lip torn.

"You'll pay for this, Drifter deserter." Odin shouted at Jadyn in a high-pitched cry.

A rush of bodies, shouts, and dull thumps filled the clearing. Weapons clashed and reflected the flames in flashes of searing red. The princess sawed and sawed at the rope binding Felix.

"Watch out, Will," Jadyn yelled.

Will swung around. Senka was behind him with the knife. He ducked, but it was too late. The knife lodged in his upper arm. She wrenched it out and stabbed again.

"Aargh." The pain blinded him.

The mayor kicked Will in the kneecap, and he buckled to the ground. Will staggered to his feet again, grinding his teeth at the sharp pain in his knee. Sidestepping the mayor's lunge, Will threw the man onto the ground once more. The mayor hit the back of his head on the stone altar with a thud, and his broad frame lay spread-eagled and motionless.

"Come to me, earth boy." Senka beckoned to Will and spoke in a sneering tone. She wiped her bloodied, slippery knife on her coat.

Will launched toward her, gripped her wrist and wrenched the knife from her, and then flung it into the bushes. She ran to find it, scrabbling around in the undergrowth. His arm wound hung open, pouring blood, splattering his boots.

He ground his teeth. His vision blurred. Everything in the clearing faded, except for one horrifying sight. The princess was still sawing back and forth at the ropes on the altar. Desperation etched her face.

Will sprang toward her. Hadn't he spent years unknotting fishing nets at the bay? Now was the time to put his skills into action. He dug into the knots and untied the ropes, then scooped Felix up and threw the whimpering boy into the princess's open arms.

"Go!" Will caught a flash of two anguished faces pressed together as they dashed away.

The mayor stirred and hoisted himself up, rubbing the back of his head. He lumbered into the woods after the princess. Odin looked around to see what was happening, but he had Jadyn pinned, writhing and grunting under his boot and the point of his sword.

"Like father, like son," he said to Jadyn. "Traitor."

Senka found her knife in the undergrowth and rushed back into the clearing, shouting. "Come back, Ranker. Don't worry about the boy." Senka jabbed her finger in the air at Will. "He's the one I told you about. He's the one we want. Tonight is a night of great fortune."

The mayor turned back, panting and staring.

Will wiped at the tracks of sweat running down his face and braced himself. Senka and the mayor stalked toward him. Two sets of eyes bored into him, blazing from the firelight and glowing with triumph.

Will ducked and lurched away, but the mayor blocked him. Senka charged. Her expression a fierce, dark madness. Will now had his back pressed against the altar, and was also trapped by them and the burning brazier.

Will slashed out at them with his knife. Ranker kicked the knife out of his hand, sniggering. The flames seared Will's clothes and skin. The odor of burned cloth filled the air. He was about to be roasted. The mayor's dagger dug into his throat.

Jadyn shouted from the ground, still under the tip of the assassin's sword. "Stop, in the name of the King!"

Odin laughed in derision. "A witch, a wizard, and an assassin against two clumsy weaklings. Whose power is greater? Where are your angels now?"

Senka and the mayor threw a rope around Will's neck and yanked him to the ground.

"It's a lucky night to have you visit Wyld Wood." Senka's tone was grim. "You didn't take your medicine, did you? Foolish boy. Never mind. We have a most coveted prize for the Dark Prince."

The mayor tightened the noose around Will's neck.

A clanging of metal filled the air. Jadyn was on his feet again, sparing against Odin's sword with his knife. Senka and the mayor ignored them.

"This filth, Will Sutherland, jeopardizes the future of Eldrad," Senka shouted in a tone of victory. "I read it in the cards. We will end the threat. We will finish him on the altar."

They threw Will onto the slab. His back and head slammed on the hard stone. The leaves of the trees above him whirled in a fury. The mayor bound him with more rope. He tried to draw in air through the constriction. He was suffocating.

"The Great One will be most pleased," the mayor said in a booming voice.

The image of the knife held above Will's chest fragmented. He clenched his eyes shut. Eleonora and Felix were safe now. That was all that mattered. He sank into green depths. He was back at the bay, drowning. A shark circled him, blood streaming from its wide jaw of perfect white teeth.

Senka's voice gurgled through the water. "It's time."

Shouting and crashing streamed into the shadows of his waning thoughts and bubbled into his now almost-beyond-hope longing for air. A clatter of metal on the altar stones jolted his senses. Someone unwound the rope from his neck, and he inhaled fresh air. He propelled out of the dark water dream.

A group of masked and hooded men tied up the three coven members. Another pulled him off the stone platform. All Will could see of his rescuer's face were wide set brown eyes, almost swallowed by heavy eyebrows. Will lifted his uninjured arm and rubbed his chafed neck, coughing.

Senka wailed at the top of her husky voice. The mayor and Odin stood silent, glowering.

"Where did you all come from?" Will asked in a hoarse voice, gripping his cut arm to stem the tide of blood.

"That I can't tell you." A man with wide-set eyes and calloused hands bound his arm with a cloth. The rest of the masked group hauled the mayor, Odin, and Senka into the forest.

Will and Jadyn dragged themselves back toward the hill, shoulders hunched.

"Who were those guys who rescued us, and why were they so secretive?"

"I'm almost positive it was Cadwyn, Merek, Dorian, and some other men. It wouldn't be in their best interests for the coven to recognize them. Let's hope they didn't. I'd say it was Roland who got help. He moves fast for an old codger."

"It was close," Will said with his still strained voice. "I thought I was going to cook.

"Like a roast pig?"

"What do you mean—pig?" Will asked.

"Ha. Then you ended up garroted on the altar. We need more training."

"Thank goodness Senka didn't stab me in my knife-throwing arm, although I think they permanently crushed my Adam's apple." He winced with every swallow and every step as he labored up the hill.

***

They all gathered at Eleonora's cave, exchanged stories, and praised Roland for getting help from the village in time. A pallid Felix slept safely in Rosie's arms. She rocked him and kissed his cheeks every time he drew a quivering breath.

The princess passed Will a cup of sedating herbal tea and laid out a needle, thread and balm. Much of the angst melted away as he watched her captivating face and her lips pursed in concentration, so close to his as she treated his wounds. He would enjoy the moment.

"It's almost worth the pain to get all this attention," he said. But he couldn't help grimacing at every piercing prick of the needle in his skin.

She hit his unbandaged arm. "Let's hope it never happens again."

"Senka, Ranker and Odin are in detention, and Dr. Wells said he'd come to see ye all tomorrow," Roland said. "He husnae been to Caves Hill before."

"A big question is why does Senka want you dead, Will?" Jadyn asked.

"Not sure."

They all stared at him, silent.

"Have you still got her potion?" The princess packed away her needles, thread, and bandages in her bag.

"Yes, it's still sitting on my shelf."

"Bring it to me some time, and I'll try to find out what's in it."

It was well after midnight by the time they all returned to their caves. Will reclined on his furs, head too full for sleep. He needed to consider his situation.

A realization struck him like a bolt of lightning. As crystal-clear as day.

He couldn't go back to Aporto Bay. He'd stay on the island. For now, anyway.

What he'd suspected for some time was true.

He was in love with Eleonora.

He would fight for the island, he would find the truth of his life, and he would win over the entrancing princess.

PART TWO

THE QUEST

Chapter 13

Despite his injuries, Will continued training at dawn with his one good arm. Sweat slicked down his chest from the set of axe and knife throws at a tree in Emerald Forest. He ran to the river, threw down his bag and weapons and plunged in, gasping at the icy water. He swam to the far bank under the drooping willows, using his uninjured arm. Then he swam back to the Caves Hill side of the shore, exhilarated.

Bare-chested, he ran a lap up to Scraggy Rock, sending the goats into a frenzy. Then, as he dragged on his shirt, he sprinted to Eleonora's cave. To win her over meant he needed to spend time with her, and he had an excuse this time to visit—the bottle of potion Senka had given him.

But his stomach agitated, as if a colony of bugs was crawling around inside it. So this was what it was like to be in love.

The princess sat outside, stirring a mixture in a pottery bowl, her hair in a thick braid over her shoulder. She wore a linen shirt pulled in with a brown leather belt. A spicy apple aroma filled the air.

"Apple cake?" he asked.

"The best on the island."

"I knew there was a reason to visit."

She laughed and stepped into the cave, beckoning to him. Will paused for a moment, unpleasant memories flooding back from the last time he entered. He swallowed, then followed her, breathing in the herbal and spicy bouquet from the hanging dried branches of foliage. She poured the batter mix into a pan and pushed it into the tiny metal oven, then clicked the door shut.

"Where are you going next?" he asked.

"To Elgin Village, in the mountains. I have supplies for them. It's remote, and most of the people are elderly, including my Aunt Nora, who lives on her own."

"I have Senka's potion." Will pulled Senka's bottle out of his bag.

The princess pulled off the cork and sniffed the contents. "Atropa belladonna. It has some nasty side effects, including death."

"Glad I didn't take it then."

"I'll find a suitable place to get rid of it. People have mixed it with poppy, monkshood, and poison hemlock to bring on hallucinations of flying."

"Might give that a miss." Will turned and nearly tripped over two loaded packs on the floor. His thoughts took an unexpected turn.

"Can I go with you on your next trip?"

The princess jerked her head up. "Of course not."

"But why not?"

"It's a long way." Her cheeks flushed. "I'll be staying with Aunt Nora for three nights."

"Do you have to carry all that?" He pointed to the packs and tested their weight. "These are too heavy to carry on your own."

She frowned. "I don't have a choice. This is just the bare essentials of what Aunt Nora needs for herself and the others. Most of the people in Elgin are too old to come down to the village."

"I can help you. You'd be doing me a favor. It will give me something to do other than hanging around the hill."

The princess opened her mouth and closed it again.

"You can trust me. You know you can."

"Can you be ready early tomorrow?" She pulled the tin of apple cake out of the oven

"Of course."

"Maybe, just this once." She cut him a steaming slice of cake. "I leave at the crack of dawn. Make sure you pack warm clothes."

He ate the apple cake in a few gulps and resisted the urge to leap with elation on the way back to his cave. Now he understood what walking on air meant.

***

They left just as the dawn light tinged the mountains with a gleam of silver. Dewy dampness clung to the air, but by the time they reached the foothills, simmering clouds rolled in like green pea soup. The princess wound her red goat's hair scarf around her neck.

They quickened their pace, but the climb was arduous. Will led the way with instructions from the princess, occasionally helping her on the slopes. A feeling of unease filled him at the color of the sky. "What are the seasons on this island?"

"The weather's much the same all year. It depends where you go. Cawl Desert is hot, but in the mountains and hills it can be freezing—and we have fierce storms—as you know." Her forehead crinkled into a frown. "We're walking toward one right now. We must hurry."

Soon thunder rumbled and split the sky. The ground shook as if a giant was stomping on it, and driving rain washed across the slopes. Cold water coursed down Will's neck and onto his back, making him shiver. He continually wiped his coat sleeve over his eyes to clear his vision.

"We must find shelter." He yelled over the roar of the deluge. The princess's hair had turned to dripping ringlets, and the end of her nose had a blue tinge. They labored toward an overhanging ledge on the level above. It gave them shelter from the rain, but a chilling wind cut through his clothes to his skin. Will took off his coat and pulled it around Eleonora's shoulders.

"The weather's set in," he shouted over the pounding rain. "We need to find better protection. This looks like cave country. Wait here."

He left her with the packs and scurried into the torrent, scrambling up the mountain, peering through the gray curtain of water and slithering in the mud. After a fruitless search, he turned to go back. An icy fear settled into his body. How long could they last in this weather?

He slid back down the hill. But which way had he come? He should have noted landmarks. What if they were separated? No one would rescue them. His mind raced with lost-in-the mountains horror scenarios. It was all his fault for leaving her.

He skidded along the slope, searching for a rock or tree that looked familiar. A narrow opening in the bank caught his eye. He pushed through it and found it led to a dry cave big enough to shelter them both. Encouraged, he continued his search for Eleonora. This time, he noted any distinctive boulders or tree shapes to use as landmarks.

A flash of red from the princess's scarf under a ledge caught his eye. He rushed to her, his teeth chattering. He leaned down and kissed her. It was a soggy, full-on-the-mouth kiss, making her lurch back in surprise. Then he beckoned for her to follow. The rattle of his teeth stopped after the pleasurable shock of feeling her lips on his.

They crawled into the cave and threw down the soaked packs.

He pointed to the circle of stones. "I think there're enough sticks scattered around to build a fire. This cave's been used by someone before."

"Well spotted." Eleonora crouched beside him, shivering as he piled branches in the middle of the stones.

"I nearly lost you," he said. "I couldn't find my way back. Had a few tense minutes, that's for sure. Hence the kiss."

She grinned at him, but didn't answer. With numbed fingers, he placed a handful of dried moss under the sticks and, with soft breaths finally ignited them. Soon, the fire crackled into a small blaze. They sat as close as they could to the flames, soaking in the meager warmth.

"My clothes are wet through." She tried to wring the water out of her shawl at the entrance. "I'll have to dry them by the fire. Is there another cave out there you can go to while I strip some off?"

He laughed. "It's okay. I promise not to look—but only if I get some of that apple cake."

"I don't trust you."

He turned his back to her. "Like this . . . and then it's my turn. Can I trust you?"

"No." The princess shook her head with an unreadable expression. "Ha." She gave a shivering chuckle. "Time to avert your eyes, before I freeze to an icicle."

He turned toward the back wall, searching his pack for food until she called she was ready. He twisted around and glanced at her. She'd peeled off her outer clothes to her thin undergarments, and his pulse quickened at the sight.

He stripped off to his trousers and made a rough rack of sticks to put their clothes on. "We should heat some soup," he said. "It'll help warm us." And keep his distracted mind occupied.

He leaned outside and held his metal pannikin under a rivulet of water, rushing outside the cave. It brimmed in no time. He put the container of the water over the fire and threw in strips of dried meat and mushrooms, then rested it between sturdy sticks.

Eleonora added herbs from a sachet in her bag. They tore off dry bread, toasted it near the coals and ate the meal, ravenous. The mushrooms were plump and fragrant in the simmering, slightly mud-flavored soup. They finished the meal with leftover apple cake.

"We'll have to spend the night here," he said.

She nodded. "I know."

But what she didn't know was there was nowhere he'd rather be in the whole of the Earthlands. Thunder rumbled, the wind howled and the torrential rain continued.

"Tell me a story," the princess said.

"Would you like me to tell you about a hobbit?"

"What's that?"

Will sat cross-legged and stared into her eyes, which reflected the flames. He was drawn back to another time. Another world.

"Once upon a time, there was a hobbit called Bilbo Baggins. He was like us, but only half the size, and he lived in an underground home built into the side of a hill."

"Like back at Caves Hill?"

"Not as rocky, with grass over the roof and a lot more comfortable. A wizard called Gandalf asked Bilbo to help the dwarves reclaim their ancestral home and their treasure from a fierce dragon called Smaug."

***

Hours later, and half-way through the story, their eyes were drooping.

Will yawned. "I'll tell you the rest another time."

The princess settled into a crevice at the side of the cave. Will put the last sticks on the fire and laid on his still-damp bedding. He gazed at Eleonora's tousled hair, then rolled over. He tried not to think about what it would feel like to hold her body close. If he was in a wilderness cave back on earth with a girl, he wouldn't be turning away toward the stone wall and grinding his teeth. But this girl was different. Everything was different here.

He woke the next morning, with stiff limbs and hands and feet ice-cold. The fire was only a jumble of charcoal.

The princess stood at the entrance, rubbing her eyes. "At least the weather looks clear today." He joined her and surveyed the tall rocky peaks, with torrents of water rushing down the slopes in impromptu waterfalls.

"We should get to Elgin Village by the afternoon," she said, packing her bag.

They continued their journey. The sun shone and dried their clammy clothes in a cloud of steam as they hiked up the mountain. Will took a deep breath. It was time to ask her the question that was always on his mind. He paused his striding.

"Eleonora, have you ever been interested in someone?"

"What do you mean?"

"I mean someone you liked? A g-guy?"

"You mean a relationship? Not really. It would complicate my life too much."

"You mean, you would never?" Will held his breath.

"Perhaps one day."

A small flicker of hope spread its warmth through his body.

They reached the village after midday. Gray stone houses with rounded roofs clung like giant limpets on the face of the craggy mountain, glinting in the sun. As soon as someone caught sight of them, cries of welcome echoed across the valley. People rushed out of their houses to greet them as they strolled down a narrow pebbled road.

A man with a frizzy beard walked with them. "We dinnae see many from the outside these days."

Aunt Nora greeted them with hug and a wide smile that split her apple-round face. She ushered them into a modest courtyard. A brown sleeveless pinafore swathed her ample waist.

"Come, and I'll show ye around, braw Willy. I dinnae know ye were coming as well." Her one-room home had a kitchen, living area, and bedroom. The bathroom was a separate area outside, off the courtyard. "Tonight ye can share my bed, Eleonora. Willy sleeps on the couch."

"Off ye get, ye wee cat." She pulled the sleepy cat from a cushion. "Now my braw dearies, sit at yonder table, fill me in with all the news, and dinnae spare any detail."

After much talking, Aunt Nora bustled around the kitchen and Will helped Eleonora pull bottles and supplies out of the packs, checking them for dampness before laying them out by the fire.

"Ye've got a pot of goat meat and mountain turnips for dinner," Aunt Nora announced, carrying a simmering pot to the table.

***

They spent three days in Elgin village. Will had met all the residents by the third day. As they packed to leave, Aunt Nora reached to the top of her tall cupboard near the couch.

"I've knitted something for ye travels." She handed them three thin blankets.

The princess held one to her cheek. "They're as soft and light as thistledown."

"Aye. Millie, the spinner, sent me enough woolly balls to make three wee rugs. I dinna know why, so I asked the King how many ye needed, and he said three. The second rug is for Willy, our cheery braw duine. Ye'll have to wait and see who needs the third. Only the King knows. He always works ahead of time."

***

They returned from Elgin Village without incident, and the next day was warm with a deep ocean-blue sky. He spent the morning helping Roland in the garden.

"How was the wee trip?" Roland asked.

"The people at Elgin village were awesome." He yanked a bunch of plump carrots from the dirt. The pleasure of his Elgin Village visit, and the enjoyment of the time spent with Eleonora and Aunt Nora, filled every nook and cranny of his mind. "Next, I'm planning to explore the island. I might visit the House of Wisdom."

"Did you know the King gives true wisdom to those who ask him for it?" Roland threw another carrot in the sack and sat on a rock nearby to rest.

"Really? So how do I get to the house?"

"It's over two or three weeks' journey from here. Ye must cross Mordrach Mountains and Vertigo Pass."

"So there's no reason for me not to go?"

"Ye could go if ye were prepared with enough gold, a shelter, and food. But any travel on the island holds its perils. The President's combatants are always on the lookout for Drifters like us.

"I'm sure I can manage. What's this house like?"

"It's extraordinary in so many ways. I cannae really describe it and ye cannae tell the size by the exterior. It has a grand front entrance, and the whole building is supported by seven pillars. Behind each pillar is a door." Roland dug up a turnip from the soft earth, and then stretched. "The Head Gardener gave me keys which allowed me entry through each door. I took a journey through each door to find the truth of my life."

"That's what I want."

"Yes, but only King followers get the keys." Roland sprinkled carrot seeds onto the soil and pressed them in.

Will sighed. He didn't want to be a king follower just to get keys.

A sudden sharp cry from Laurien sounded out from Scraggy Rock. "Ravens! The ravens are coming!"

Heart pounding against his ribs, he stared up into the sky.

Chapter 14

In the distance, a flattened dark cloud approached at a surprising speed from the north. Will froze at the sight. This couldn't be happening.

The princess ran up the hill, panting. "Hurry. We need to get to Jadyn's cave."

"I'd rather stay and fight," Will said, adrenaline kicking in.

"Hundreds of Lorn's ravens? I don't think so," she said. "Jadyn's cave is the safest place."

They rushed to Jadyn's, and he ushered them inside when Will lagged at the entrance. Roland checked the others were all there: Rosie, Felix, Jadyn, Laurien, and Eleonora.

"Has anyone seen Senka? I heard she's already been released from detention," Eleonora said.

"Huvnae seen her since the rescue. I doubt she'll return to Caves Hill after what happened in Wyld Wood," Roland said.

"I've kept that poisonous potion as evidence against her if we need it, Will," Eleonora said.

Metal axes, cutters, and other tools hung from hooks on the rock wall. Jadyn's chubby gray cat lay camouflaged on the thick fur bed. Its eyes seesawed back and forth from them to a mouse perched up on a rock ledge. Jadyn showed them the three dark hollows at the rear of the cave to further caves and passages.

"How many ravens would there be?" Roland asked.

"Hundreds. Even more." Jadyn reached over and stroked the cat's head. It kneaded its paws into the fur bed.

"So the President sent them?" Will asked.

"I know he did," Laurien said.

"What makes you so sure?"

"You know nothing. Why don't you go back to your bay?" Laurien twisted her lips in disdain. Will clenched his teeth.

"I used to live in Nevara. So did Laurien," Jadyn said. "She's right, despite her rudeness. You can tell by the formation they're flying in."

"So what's the danger to us?" Will gripped his knife.

"We need to be concerned about surveillance and the possibility of an attack. Once the President has more information about us at Caves Hill, he may send his combatants to check we're toeing the line—or he might have something worse in mind."

"Surveillance? A backward island like Eldrad? You don't have the technology," Will said.

"That's where you're mistaken, dummy," Laurien said. "The President uses technology. We just don't have it here. He keeps it for his own uses."

They sat silently, listening to the cries of the birds.

"They're getting closer," Rosie said.

The cat padded to the entry of the cave, growling, and then stared back at them, its fur standing stiffly on end and its orange-flecked eyes full of questions. Will wondered if his hair was standing on end as well. It felt like it.

"Stay here, Blade," Jadyn warned. The cat ignored him, stepped outside, and made a sound like a distant rumble of thunder.

Laurien joined the cat, but she swung back. Will's gut clenched at her ashen face and dark-with-horror eyes.

"What is it?" The princess rushed to her side and looked out. She grabbed Laurien and pulled her into the cave and gulped. "It's w-worse. Much worse."

Laurien ran toward the passages at the rear. "I'm getting out of here."

"What did you see?" Jadyn said to Laurien.

"It's him," she said in a tight voice.

"I'll have a look." Will strode to the opening of the cave.

"Keep out of sight," the princess urged.

"Can I see?" Felix asked, clutching a ragged stuffed dragon to his chest.

"Not now, Felix." Rosie held him in her lap while Will, Roland, and Jadyn moved to the entrance.

Three monstrous airships hovered above Scraggy Rock. Each displayed the image of a raven with open wings on its bulging side. The airships cast shadows on the hill, and one was descending. The ravens milled around, crying overhead.

Will stared, awe-struck. Was this some sort of dystopic dream?

"It's landing at Scraggy Rock," the princess said.

"If it lands and they f-find u-us . . ." Rosie clutched Felix even tighter.

"Follow me." Jadyn sprinted to the back tunnels. "We'll keep out of sight until they leave. The fact is, we can't fight against hundreds."

Jadyn distributed lamps and food supplies. Will carried Felix on his back, and Felix perched his stuffed dragon on Will's shoulder. They followed Jadyn into the far left-hand passage. Orange reflections bounced on the walls from their flares.

"How far does this go into the mountain?" Will asked as they walked in single file through the tunnel, which snaked into the mountain. Blade followed behind with bulging eyes.

"I've only been as far as the large cavern. I never go into the other two passages anymore. Got lost once."

They stepped cautiously along the damp track, dodging the limestone formations hanging from the roof.

The route was getting narrower and more oppressive. After a few minutes, they reached a spacious cavern filled with white and cream rock formations and a stream. The formations looked like the soft serve ice creams at White Sands Café. Dripping water plopped and echoed.

"Here's our hiding place," Jadyn said. "We should be safe, but if anyone comes, we have an escape route. This tunnel leads to the coast and the ocean."

Will sat on what looked like a sandy beach. The air smelled fresh and slightly salty. Roland handed around pieces of honeycomb as they waited.

"I've always loved birds," Will said. "I nursed a young barn owl back to health a few years ago. I admire ravens as well. I know they have a cruel-looking beak and eat dead stuff, but they're a striking bird."

"Aye, they're smart creatures." Roland agreed. "When I was a boy, a wee raven would come to my window with a demanding warble. I fed it scraps of food. It talked in its language as if telling me the day's news and was a clever mimic. It could say 'wee bird' and make the sound of the window scraping open."

"I've seen a raven doing acrobatics with a stick in the air, dropping it, then doing somersaults to catch it," the princess said.

"Did you know they call a flock of ravens an 'unkindness' or a 'murder'?" Rosie's forehead was knotted into a frown.

"What's the problem with the President's ravens?" Will asked.

"The President trains them. To attack p-people." Laurien pulled her knees to her chin and hunched over them.

"How?"

"They peck your eyes," Rosie half-mouthed, half-whispered, stroking Felix's hair as he slept.

"What do you think happened to my eye?" Jadyn said in a voice that was as tight as a string on a bow. He hunched and gripped his hands between his knees. Rosie put her arm around his shoulders. A tug of shock mixed with sympathy pulled at Will's chest.

"And you don't want to end up in his prison, like I did," Laurien said, in a lowered voice. "He uses ravens to punish his prisoners." She rubbed her scarred arm.

Will squashed his hands under his armpits to stop himself from punching the wall. "How dare he? How did you escape, Laurien?"

"With the help of Pen. She's a Drifter spy who lives in his Nevara palace," Laurien said. "I'll never go back there again—even if my life depended on it."

"What happened to Michelia, the President's wife?" Eleonora asked.

"No one knows," Jadyn said. "Most believe she's no longer alive. There's suspicion about her disappearance."

"We should sleep now," Will said. "I'll keep watch first. Then Jadyn can take over."

***

Will leaned against the rock wall, his ears alert to a clinking noise in the distance. Everyone else slept. The clinks became metallic crashes and reverberated through the rock walls.

He shook Jadyn to wake him, then put his finger to his lips. "Something's going on at the surface. I'll see what's happening. Can you stay on watch here?"

Jadyn rubbed his eyes, then his hand swung to his knife. He nodded.

Will hurried toward Jadyn's cave, stepping with care in case he slipped on the damp path. A clattering mixed with shouts resonated through the rock walls and jarred his nerves. He crept to the end of the tunnel and glimpsed a scene that seized the air in his lungs.

Combatants were pulling Jadyn's implements from the wall and tossing them onto a pile in the middle of the cave in loud clanks. Other men stuffed them into large bags.

He drew back, hoping no one had spotted him, his body as tense as a wild boar ready to charge. He pulled out his knife. He knew he had to stop them. He'd take them by surprise and throw as many down as possible. But he hesitated as he thought about his chances of success and that he may put the others at risk.

A voice bellowed a muffled command over a loudspeaker from outside the cave. The crashing and shouting faded. The cave was silent. Will stepped out to inspect the damage. The wall where Jadyn hung his metal implements was bare. Everything else had been trashed. Will yelled in fury.

He stepped outside. The airships and ravens were heading north in menacing blots of horror against the sky. He hurried back down the passageway to tell the others. Everyone was awake and sitting in a huddle, concern etched on their faces. He broke the news, and they trudged up to the surface of the mountain without a word. When they saw Jadyn's cave, they vented their anger.

"I can replace those things," Jadyn said. "As long as we're OK, that's all that matters."

Felix held his arms up to Will. Will heaved him up, and the boy pressed his small face into his neck.

They stepped back outside, scanning the sky. All appeared calm over Mordrach Mountains and the forest.

"What's that over there?" The princess pointed to a dark shape on the ground near a stunted tree further down the mountain.

"A raven," Laurien said.

"Must be injured. It's lying on its side," Roland said.

"Could be dead." Jadyn joined them.

The bird squawked and flapped a wing.

"Jadyn, give me your largest knife, and I'll stab it through the heart." Laurien turned to him.

"It has an injured wing." The princess hurried toward the bird.

"Don't kill it," Will said.

Jadyn crouched next to the princess. "It might be a trap."

"Wait." Will put Felix down, pulled off his coat, and wrapped it around the raven. It cawed loudly, pecking at him with its pointed beak.

"What are you doing?" Laurien stamped her feet. "It's evil. It'll try to injure you."

"The bird isn't evil. But what they've trained it to do is evil."

"There's an old cage in the cave next to mine," Roland said to Will. "I'll fetch it for ye, but ye cannae expect to get much sleep at night."

Jadyn tried to release the bird's leg from the soft material of the coat. "Let me see that wire. It may be a surveillance band." After a struggle, he restrained its thrusting claw, then snipped off the band, ending up with bloodied fingers. "Just a marker. All Lorn's ravens have one. I'll get rid of it."

He shoved the bird back into Will's arms. "He's a big one. A male. Just a broken wing from what I can see."

Roland arrived back from his cave with a dusty wire cage. He dumped the cage on the ground, fuming. "Ye should all go back and check yer caves. Mine's ransacked. They even smashed my pickle preserves. Now hold onto that bird while I secure its broken wing." The bird thrashed and screeched in protest as Roland wrapped a cloth around the broken wing and feathers.

Laurien tossed her head and stomped up the mountain, throwing them a look of disgust.

"Give the wee bird food and water and cover the cage tonight," Roland called, as Will carried the raven back to his cave.

Will stood frozen at the disarray when he entered. Broken pottery covered the floor, his stove door had been wrenched off, and his best coat was nowhere to be seen.

***

Will woke at dawn after a fitful sleep. The raven was silent. Perhaps he'd died in the night. He lifted the rug hanging over the cage in slow motion. The bird lay unmoving, its eyes glazed. Will's throat closed.

Then the bird's eyes swiveled toward him. At least he was alive—but for how long? "I'm going to the forest to find you something tasty to eat and check on the others."

The President's combatants had ransacked all their caves. Some of Eleonora's gold had been stolen. They would have to wait until the next fair to purchase new kitchen utensils and knives. Jadyn promised to replace anything he could from the forge.

The raven barely moved for three days. He occasionally dragged his body around the base of the cage, which was now soiled with droppings and decayed food. He sometimes had a half-hearted peck at the food or water. Will moved his bedding to the entrance of the cave, away from the smell. Blade, Jadyn's cat, was hanging around at night so he couldn't risk putting the cage outside.

The next morning he lifted the cover and reeled at a sudden harsh squawking. The bird flung its body against the cage walls with a wild glare in its eyes.

"Settle, or you'll injure the other wing." Will sat down to watch it. All the food he'd left the night before was eaten. Perhaps the bird would recover.

***

Will's new companion kept him busy. There were six days of protest, and six nights of interrupted sleep. Will drank a bottle of spirits to get him through. By the seventh day, the raven had settled into its new environment. But it protested with raucous cries when anyone else came to see it.

"It stinks in here." The princess threw berries into the cage.

"I've been tempted to open the door and let him out. He's driven me crazy." Will stretched his aching shoulders and yawned. "I've spent hours a day hunting for small creatures to feed him, dead or alive. He particularly enjoyed the maggots, but I didn't enjoy having the escapees crawling around the floor of my cave and into my food."

"Eww." She shuddered. "He's giving me the evil eye. Have you named him yet?"

"Shadow."

"Do you think he can fly now? Should we let him out and see?" she asked.

"His wing's healing. I've taken off the cloth bandage, but some feathers still droop. We need to be careful. Blade's been paying us daily visits," Will said. "I'll give the bird another week."

Will dangled a small piece of meat in the cage, and Shadow snatched it with enthusiasm. Then he preened his sleek black feathers and made satisfied throaty sound. Will sighed. The bird's response filled him with contentment.

Chapter 15

Aporto Bay Hospital: Coma Ward

Erin entered and limped to Will's bed. A calm and ordered atmosphere filled the room. She balanced her crutches against the wall and sat on one of the spare chairs.

"I'll spend some time with you Will, in between my orthopedist and physio appointments." She sat and stared at his pale face and stapled head, then did a double take. Had his eyelids flickered again? Her heart raced. She checked again, trying not to blink, in case she missed the slightest movement. But there was nothing.

Erin pulled her laptop out of her backpack, occasionally checking Will's face and the activity in the room. Nurses moved from patient to patient. A woman, perched on a chair beside the adjacent bed, clutched at her scarf and twisted it around and around. She stared at a sleeping girl. A doctor stood with them, tapping his pen on the clipboard as if he was marking the passing of time.

"Lara is now responsive. We're moving her to the general ward tomorrow. If she continues to improve, we can release her into rehab, then home care. She can breathe on her own, has a normal heart rate, and can use her hands a little. There's a small chance she'll learn to walk again with intensive physio." The doctor closed his clipboard with a snap and left.

The woman hurried out. Erin wished she could follow her and hug her. But the weight of what the doctor had said crushed her down. She hunched in her chair as still as a stone.

Nurse Baxter unlocked a cupboard in the nurses' station and took out three small white boxes. She grabbed a russet-colored bag sitting on another shelf, glanced at the entrance doors to the ward, then put the packets inside and zipped the bag closed. Erin stiffened. Surely the medication was for patients, not nurses? Erin had problems concentrating on her computer screen after what she'd heard and seen.

The nurse wheeled a metal trolley toward Will's bed with a rattle of equipment. "You'll have to give me some space."

"I'll just move to the other side of the bed if that's OK."

Nurse Baxter pushed past before Erin could gather her belongings, knocking her books onto the floor. "Wouldn't it be better to do that work, whatever it is, at home?" she said, in a sharp tone.

"I have three hours between doctors' appointments," Erin said. "I'd rather spend the time with Will. Who knows what he can see while he's in the coma?"

A vein on the nurse's forehead swelled into an angry line. "His current Glascow Coma Scale indicates he can't see a thing. I don't think you realize the amount of care a coma patient requires. He needs to be moved every two hours to prevent bedsores, plus he needs regular sponge baths, feeding, and toilet care. And that's just the start. We can't have visitors here for long stretches of time."

"I appreciate what you're doing for him, Nurse Baxter." Erin cringed with embarrassment as she packed her things and headed toward the visitors' waiting room. She'd come back and see him before her appointment with the physio.

Chapter 16

Will called to Eleonora as she made her way toward the forest. "Do you want to come and watch while I free Shadow?"

She turned back and ran toward him, panting. "Wonder if he'll fly back to Nevara?"

"I doubt his wing will ever be strong enough for that." Will carried the cage outside. Shadow's feathers shone with deep navy hues in the sun.

"He's a magnificent bird," she said.

"Yes." But nothing could be as magnificent as Eleonora. Her hair cascaded in waves over her chest as she crouched down. Her floral fragrance reminded him of the glade's flower and herb garden.

Will untwisted the thick wire that secured the cage door. "I'm going to free you, Shadow." The raven cocked his head. He eyed them for a moment and made a soft sound, then strutted toward the opening. He paused.

"Come on."

Will held his breath. Shadow pushed through the door of the cage and tottered along the ground with a questioning warble. He flapped his wings and tripped.

"Keep trying."

A breeze blew across the hill. The raven flapped his wings for a moment with a low rumble in his throat. He flapped harder and rose in the air a short distance, then flew awkwardly onto the low branch of a stunted tree nearby.

He looked back at them and made a loud *cr-r-ruck*. Then he spread his wings and fluttered in a haphazard zigzag toward the forest, like a baby bird on its first flight. Will's stomach twisted with a mix of sadness and gratification.

"What now?" Eleonora asked. "Laurien may be right. The bird could pose a danger now it's free."

"It's a risk I decided to take."

***

The princess was away for five days, and it rained too heavily for Will to practice his knife throws or swim in the river. He threw on his coat and wandered up the hill to see if Roland was in his cave. Now Shadow was free and the visit from the airships was in the past, it was time to search for the truth the others had told him about. The truth about why he was stuck on the island. It drove him mad, not knowing.

Roland put down the book he was reading and poured steaming tea for Will from his new kettle on the stove.

As Will crouched on the ground with the mug, it slipped from his fingers and smashed on the rocky ground. The dark tea soaked into the soil.

"Blast." Will's fingernails dug into his palms.

"Don't worry, son. There's plenty more where that came from."

"But that was your new mug." Will picked up the pieces of pottery one by one and placed them in a bowl, then wiped the splashes from his pants. "That's what my life seems to be—broken pieces. It's slipping away. I've nothing to show for it. My life makes no sense. It's just a waste of time.

Roland looked at him, a deep line between his eyebrows. "None of us have it all together. We're all broken. The King understands. He knows what it's like."

Will shrugged and stomped to the entrance. As if a king would know. "I have to go and collect wood before dark."

"I'll take ye to the Potters' Caves in Yapton Mountains," Roland said. "There's something I'd like to show ye. It'll be a slow journey. My legs dinnae carry me like they used to."

"I'll go if it gives me answers."

"Aye. It will."

"When can we leave?"

***

A couple of days later, Will followed Roland on the path to the Potters' Caves. The morning sun spilled amber and burned orange over the jagged ridges of the Mordrach

Mountains. After an hour of walking, they skirted Black-thorn Woods and climbed a moderate ascent on a narrow rocky path. The early morning mist dissipated, and Will paused to look at the landscape below.

"Great view of the valley, with Shannon and Caves Hill in the distance."

"Aye, and take care. It's a long way down if ye stumble."

"Who runs the Potters' Caves?"

"Old Sanelder. The workers are mainly Drifters' families the princess helped relocate when the President flooded their village for his lake." Roland plonked himself onto a boulder, puffing. "Even though a huge surge of water inundated the land, some of the community had enough time to get to the hills."

Will kicked stones over the path into the deep ravine.

"That's how the wee Princess lost her parents. She was away when the valley filled with water. It's been difficult for her. When she first came to the hill, she barely spoke to anyone." Roland stood up and continued along the track.

"Where's this lake?"

"North-west of here. Thorburn Lake."

"How did she help the ones who escaped?"

"Sanelder was a family friend. He was always short of people to help in the Potters' Caves." He stopped, catching his breath. "She made the connection, and now most of them live there. It's a safer place for Drifters than many areas now."

They hiked toward a yawning cavity in the rock face up above them. A waterfall cascaded in a misty veil from a nearby cliff. They now shared the ascending track with braying donkeys. The stocky creatures trotted back and forth, carrying the potters, who were dressed in brown clothes and who clutched containers of wet clay.

Will dodged a lurching donkey as it rounded a hairpin bend. "This is mayhem. Hope they don't trample us."

"Aye, I cannae guarantee it." Roland squelched in strong-smelling manure and laughed. They reached a flat landing, which led into a large cavern. Will paused and gaped at its size. The opening was as high as the tallest tree in the forest. Stunted ferns and wispy vines clung to the rocks around the cavity.

"I'll take ye through the main cavern first." Roland leaned against a rock, gasping for air. "This place is a labyrinth, just like our Caves Hill, except the caves are larger."

Once inside, Will exclaimed at the unfolding scene. A myriad of potters' wheels whirred in a hypnotic harmony. Men and women focused on shaping the soft caramel-colored clay into pots and bowls.

An angry voice split the calm. "It's the clay from downstream," a woman said, with red-rimmed eyes. "It's not malleable. I won't use it anymore."

Two of the workers stopped spinning their wheels and hurried to her, examining the warped pot. Roland and Will moved closer. One man took the pot and threw it into a trough, where it squelched into a shapeless heap.

"Wait." A woman placed her own pot on a shelf and gathered the discarded clay and carried it to her bench. She deftly whirred the wheel, and the lump gradually took shape.

A stocky man dressed in a turquoise coat burst into the room.

Roland turned to the man. "Sanelder!"

"Roland." The two men embraced one another. Roland introduced Will, and Sanelder held out his hand to him in greeting.

"Follow me. Let me show you the kilns." Sanelder looked at Roland. "How's Eleonora?"

"Fine. She's at Horsham for a few days."

Sanelder led them through cave after cave filled with huge kilns and shelves laden with terracotta pots. The women wore loose shifts, and the men wore nothing but a type of loincloth. None of them displayed the raven mark on their arms. The heat seared Will's skin. He wiped the dripping sweat from his eyes and face.

"Too hot?" Sanelder laughed. "Let me take you to the glazed pots' cave." A cool breeze blew through the next passageway, which led back out toward the front of the cliffs. Men and women worked in recesses, applying colors and glazes. A few looked up and nodded as they passed. "The surface looks dull until we apply more heat." Sanelder took a bowl and let Will feel the texture.

They entered another cavernous room. Shining glazed pots and containers in an array of vivid turquoises, olives, and saffron filled every available space.

Will gazed around in awe. "Impressive. Where do you sell them?"

"All over the island. They are highly sought after."

Will pointed to a small pot decorated with two dragons breathing fire. "How much would this one be?"

"One medium gold piece.

"Felix back at Caves Hill would love this. Can I buy it?"

Sanelder nodded and passed it to a potter to wrap.

"Will, I have a small gift for you as well." Sanelder gave the potter a glazed jug with a wreath of leaves around the rim to wrap for him. Then he took them into the next room.

"Could we see the broken pots?" Roland asked.

Will followed Sanelder through another maze of passages smelling of damp clay. He'd rather not look at wrecked pots. They passed more shelves lined with containers in varying stages of completion until they came to a room with a door.

"Come. Here is our special room for the broken pottery." Sanelder creaked the door open.

Will glanced into the room. He'd seen enough pots to last him a lifetime, but he took a sharp intake of breath at the scene. A man with oiled skin and black plaited hair sat at a wooden table with fragmented pottery laid out on a woven mat. His body was tense with concentration as he placed the shards together with meticulous care. Shattered pieces of pots lined shelves.

Sanelder whispered. "After breakage, the service of the piece has not ended. We regard the cracking as an incident in its history."

The man was oblivious to them. A bowl of what appeared to be molten gold lay on the table.

"He takes the damaged pots, highlights the cracks and traces over them using lacquer mixed with powdered gold. The break and repair make it more magnificent and valuable than before. He's a master of the art. Come and see the completed pots in the next cave."

They walked past the man to the next room. Sanelder lit a lantern and held it up to rows of earthenware. Shimmering gold glowed richly on the laced surface of the containers.

He turned to Will and smiled. "This is what the King does for us if we are willing. He'll take our broken pieces and put them together to create something remarkable."

Will took a vase from the shelf, and ran his fingers over the seams of gold. Could the fractured, puzzle pieces of his life be put together? Like this?

***

The weather was clear but frosty. Will sat with the princess, Jadyn, and Roland around a crackling fire at Roland's cave two days later. Will warmed his hands on his mug and breathed in the delicious aroma of cornbread that Roland was browning in a pan. He rubbed at his old shoulder injury, sore from his latest workout in the forest, but he didn't care. The workouts kept him focused while he was protecting Caves Hill and planning to find out why he was on the island. He also needed to cut down on his trips to the inn to keep focused. And most of all, he needed to impress Eleonora. Being this close to her was sending his feelings into a meltdown.

"So how many bulls'-eyes did ye two manage this morning?" Roland asked.

"More than I could count. What's more, I have a graze from Jadyn's mean no-spin throws when he had me up against a tree." Will lifted his shirt to show a thin red incision along his side. "I believe you did it on purpose," he said to Jadyn.

"You moved."

"So it wasn't because of the double leg takedown I surprised you with earlier?"

They chuckled.

"By the way, there are combatants in the village." Jadyn spooned honey onto his bread. "We need to be careful. One checked out my display of metal wares. I had my coat on, fortunately, and he didn't ask to see the mark."

"They already know who you are, Jadyn," Eleonora said.

"Then why don't they arrest you?" Will asked him.

"He makes the best metalware in the island," Roland said. "It's not in their interest to take him away at the moment."

Jadyn threw his bread back on the plate. "That's a bleak thought—that they could use one of my knives against us. Like Senka did."

The princess frowned. "How many combatants were there?"

"Four. They arrested three people, chained them, and took them away. Roland, one was your friend Merek."

"I was hoping it wudnae come to this." Roland stroked his beard and the furrows on his face deepened. "Be ready for anything."

"I heard from Cadwyn that the President has already expanded settlements to the lower reaches of the Mordrach Mountains. He'll be here next," Eleonora said.

"What will your king do about the spread of evil?" Will asked. How would they answer a tricky question like that? What was their so-called king doing to help the island?

The princess took a stick and stirred around the embers of the fire.

"Our King sees evil as an unnatural state," she said. "He asks us, with his help, to battle against it. His plan will bring justice in the end."

"So you're saying the king's realm is here in the Earth-lands, right now?"

The princess passed around a bowl of gnarled red apples. "It's here in part but won't be fully present until the end of time as we know it. His is the only kingdom that will last forever. Other kingdoms always fail, and the Dark Prince's time is almost up."

"I'm going to the forge to pick up goods for the next village fair," Jadyn said. "Why don't you come with me, Will? You won't see Cadwyn—he's at Eladia. But you can see where we work."

"May as well." A restless anticipation filled Will's mind and thoughts. He ran his fingers over the knife Jadyn had given him. At last, he would get to see Yapton Forge.

Chapter 17

Will cleaned out his cave and added to his outside pile of firewood early that morning. A raven cawed loud and close. Then it swooped and grazed his head with its sharp beak. Will ducked and instinctively put his hands up for protection. Blood spattered his coat.

"Shadow!"

The bird dropped a mangled mouse on the ground and landed at his feet. He peered at Will, fluffing out his chest feathers.

"A mouse? Have you brought your dinner?" Will crouched beside the bird, letting out a breath of relief. The blood was mouse blood, not his. Shadow made a gurgling croak, looking from the mouse and then at Will.

So this was dinner for him, not the bird. How could he show his appreciation?

"I'll have it later." He put the mouse on a flat rock nearby and carried it into the cave, smiling. When he returned, Shadow flapped away, soaring on the air currents above the forest. Pleasure spread through Will as the bird dived into the valley.

Jadyn walked toward him. "Was that who I think it was?"

"Shadow brought me something tasty to eat."

Jadyn laughed when he heard the story. They took the path that bypassed the village, then strode toward the eastern hills. Will pulled his coat tightly around his body against the blustering wind.

"How far is the forge from Caves Hill?"

"It's near the Potters' Caves in Yapton Mountains, but not as far, and it's steep in parts."

"Why isn't it closer to Shannon?"

"Because Cadwyn needed somewhere isolated. He's on the President's wanted list. He used to work at Nevara. Cadwyn's a clever guy," he said as they hiked up the mountain track. "Also, there's a good route for horses to Eladia from the forge. Cadwyn travels all over the land, recruiting people ready for the overthrow of the President. It's our only hope for the island."

Will stopped to stare at the silvery stream snaking its way below into Blackthorn Forest. "So where are your parents now?"

Jadyn kicked at a rock. "My father's dead. Mom lives with her sister in Fawley Village."

"That's rough for you, with your Mom so far away."

"Yes. It's not by choice, but for her safety." Jadyn pointed to a small opening in a low cliff. "There's the entrance." The cave gaped like a dark mouth hanging open with a green horseshoe-shaped mustache. Three horses grazed nearby.

"We should stop to eat," Jadyn perched on a lichen-covered rock and gave Will an apple and a handful of nuts.

"Do you make many swords at the forge?"

"We do." Jadyn took three more apples from his pack and gave Will one. "For the horses."

"Why do the king's people have those special swords, like the one the princess has?"

"The King's sword is armor he provides his people against the Darkness. The King's words are also likened to a sword."

"How can that be?" The horses whinnied and pawed the ground as they approached with the apples.

"The words in The King's book can pierce like a sword, and aid us in the supernatural battle of life and death. But his sword doesn't maim human flesh or kill. The evil armies also have weapons—we need defense against them."

Jadyn headed toward the greenery-draped entry. "The King calls us to be warriors in his kingdom, but not like soldiers in the territories on the Earthlands, or like combatants here. And some fight because they're forced to, or because of necessity, cruelty, or profit."

"Or fear," Will added.

Jadyn nodded. "A true warrior doesn't fight for those reasons."

"Why do they fight?" They entered the passageway. A mixed scent of smoke from flickering torches on the wall and damp stone filled his nostrils.

"To be a warrior is a way of life. A true warrior fights for what's good. They are honor-bound to something greater than themselves." Jadyn led him down to a slight descent.

"Do you see yourself as a warrior, Jadyn?"

"Yes."

Jadyn paused at a landing, then descended a few stairs hewn out of rock to a heavy wooden door. Clanking and loud vibrations echoed from inside. Will placed a hand on the stone wall to steady himself in the dim light.

"This is it." Jadyn hauled the door open. Warm air mingled with an oily metal odor hit their faces.

Three men labored over a container. Steam rose toward an opening in the wall of rock. A fiery glow came from a receptacle to the right. There were diagrams of swords and weapons on tattered, yellowed paper clipped to a wooden stand. A medley of metal objects and weaponry hung on hooks on other walls.

Will walked over to check the swords lying in rows on a table. "I'd love to see the process of sword making."

"Perhaps you will one day. Did you know many physical things of the Earthlands are used by the King to show us a greater truth?" Jadyn said. "A sword is one. Making a sword is like the making of a life. It might help you understand why life isn't as easy as we expect it to be."

One of the blacksmiths picked up two jangling bags and passed them to Jadyn. "The order's ready."

"Before we leave, I've made you something, Will." Jadyn strode to a small set of shelves leaning against the rock wall. He picked up a parcel wrapped in a piece of thin leather and gave it to Will.

Will unwrapped it and exclaimed. "A throwing knife. I won't have to borrow yours anymore."

Jadyn grinned at his reaction. "I'll show you around. Then it'll be time to leave. We need to get back before nightfall. I'm on the metalwork stand at the village fair tomorrow. I should tell you I saw two Cravers near Eleonora's cave yesterday."

Unease spread through Will. "Do you think she's in danger?"

"Who knows? We're at a disadvantage. Cravers need gold. If they turn in a Drifter, it may mean a reward."

***

The next morning, while his eggs fried in the pan until they were sizzling, Will counted his gold coins. There'd be enough gold for the supplies he needed for his trip to Eladia, a couple of bottles of mead, with enough left over. He'd also visit Jadyn at the metalwork stall.

The air was still, and a weak sun streamed through the trees on the track to the village. Will paused. A short sharp scream and raised angry voices came from nearby in the forest. The princess? He ran toward the sound, trying not to crack twigs underfoot.

"Leave me alone, you putrid-smelling bully!"

A mocking voice replied. "Too late—and keep your nails to yourself."

"Let me go!" she shouted.

Will stopped. A thin man with a tattooed head leaned toward a towering oak trunk. A streak of fiery anger flashed through Will.

Striker the Craver.

Striker had pinned the princess against the tree. Rope encircled her body and the trunk. One of his hands wrapped around her neck, and the other rested above her head. His two stumpy fingers spread out on the bark.

The princess's eyes widened when she saw Will over the man's shoulder.

Will pulled his throwing knife from his belt. Sucking in a quick breath, he held it and aimed at the man's hand on the tree. What if he hit her face? He balanced the cold steel. Ready. He shifted his weight forward and let the knife fly.

Bull's-eye.

The Craver swiveled his head toward Will, cursing, his finger impaled in the trunk. He stared at Will with crazed, wild pig eyes.

"Lost your knife?" Striker asked in a mocking tone. He yanked the knife out of his hand, then slashed the princess's blouse from the neck to the waist before she could move.

"I've seen the way you look at him in the village," Striker said to the princess in a snarling voice. "But you're mine now."

She mumbled a response Will couldn't hear. A blush worked its way up her neck.

Will hesitated, trying to decide on the next move. His thoughts were completely scrambled at her open blouse, revealing more than he should see, and from the shock at what the Craver said. And why was he so stupid—giving the Craver the only knife he was carrying?

A dog barked nearby.

Wolfie. Will blew his best piercing whistle, and the dog came streaking through the undergrowth and barely skidded to a stop before taking a flying leap at Striker's thigh, plunging his teeth deep. He twisted the man to the ground with a shake of his head.

Will covered Eleonora's half-exposed breasts, untied her, snatched his knife, and they fled.

"Good throw," she gasped. She still trembled. "Been practicing?"

"Just naturally multi-talented. But it wasn't good enough, unfortunately."

"It stalled him, though. I couldn't bear the thought of him kissing me or . . ."

He avoided her eyes, knowing his face was burning a deep shade of red after what he'd seen and heard. "Keep Wolfie with you and call if you need me."

The Craver's comment about the way the princess looked at him was puzzling. He'd seen no interest from her. There'd been plenty of exasperated glances, even friendly ones—but attraction? No.

He'd give his trip to the village a miss this time. Eleonora needed protection.

***

Will needed to leave Caves Hill and find the answers to his questions about Eladia. Find the truth the others talked about. Eleonora was at the Potters' Caves, and Roland was in the village. Will left a message addressed to everyone in Roland's cave, wedged under a bowl, and headed north. He had enough provisions packed, including Aunt Nora's blanket.

The Mordrach Mountains, iced with white, shone in the morning sun. He walked all day, getting as far as the second mountain, then lay under an elm tree for the night. He tried to ignore the pang of unease every time he thought of Striker's attack on Eleonora. Would she be safe while he was away?

As he was drinking from a stream the next dawn, a raven rustled around in the leaves nearby. One wing hung at an awkward angle. *Shadow.*

"Did you follow me, you crazy bird?" The raven warbled and strutted around like a peacock.

Will soon reached Vertigo Pass. It was worse than he had imagined, a gut-wrenching dirt track just wide enough for a single person or donkey, with a cliff on one side and a sheer drop into a deep ravine on the other. He stepped sideways, his back to the cliff, hoping he wouldn't meet anyone. A rockfall ahead had sheered the path away, and an old wooden bridge provided passage to the other side. The wind whistled upwards from the valley. He exhaled with relief when the pass led into a broad path between two mountains.

After two days of walking, he arrived at a bustling town. Dusty donkeys, overfed pigs, whining children and carts, hustled together. He joined the surge until the crowds thinned past the next town. A rocky path meandered at the side of the road in the shade of tall oak trees. He paused for a moment to rest and checked a rough map a stallholder had drawn for him.

A boy who looked a similar age to him called a greeting. "Where're you headed? I'm Sam."

"Eladia." Will brushed the dirt from his own coat when he saw the boy's smart shirt and slicked-back hair. A raven mark darkened the boy's wrist.

"Mind if I join you? It's a steep climb ahead." Sam pointed north. Thick cloud blanketed the peaks.

"Sure."

They chatted until they reached the top. Will exclaimed at the expanse of plains and glistening rivers beyond. In the distance, a sprawling city lay spread on a low-sloped hill with a shallow valley on the right-hand side.

He squinted into the distance. "So that's Eladia?"

"No. That's Idella. Eladia is over on the east coast. You must have taken the wrong path," Sam said. "Why don't you come with me to Idella."

"That's not where I'm headed." There was no Idella on his map.

"It's a must-see on your way to Eladia. I'll take you."

Will quizzed Sam about his life as they worked their way up and down mountain paths. It was a surprise to hear Sam lived at Idella without his family.

***

They reached a clearing with a suspension bridge over a rushing river. Idella was close now and an extravaganza of colored buildings in the shape of fruits and flowers spread across the land. Skyscrapers with stamen-shaped towers soared into the sky and a myriad of statues sprawled into a valley.

"Awesome?" Sam asked.

"Seen nothing like it. Ever."

"It's a place that fulfills your every desire. You can do whatever you like there, let me tell you."

"Anything?" Will asked.

"Anything. Are you hungry? What's your favorite food?"

"I haven't eaten for hours. Do they have chocolate? And I wouldn't mind a drink."

"Idella offers both," Sam said.

Will's stomach rumbled. "I'll take a quick look."

Chapter 18

"See the rides?" Sam said as they approached. "There's the Ride of Demise, the Ride of Doom, and the Ride of Delight. I'll take you to them. People race around on them all day. It takes their mind off things."

A sweet waffles' aroma filled the air and fairground music intermingled with screams from the thrill rides. The roller coaster's multiple rotating wheels made it look like a giant wagon plowing toward them. Long contorted water slide tubes reminded Will of the Carnival Fair that came to Aporto Bay every year. But this one was ten times bigger—if only Mitch and the guys could see this.

A sign suspended over the entry gate flashed.

WELCOME TO IDELLA.
Come and play. You'll want to stay.

The place bustled with commotion. A raven, perched on top of the sign with its head on one side, peered at him.

Shadow. Will smiled and waved at the bird. Several girls in shiny blue dresses passed striped bags to each person as they entered.

Will searched his pockets. "I don't have much gold. How much is the entry?"

"It's free, compliments of the President." She passed him a bag with a raven image on it. "You have a map and coupons in your bag. They'll keep you going for a while."

"I won't be staying." He couldn't squash the feeling of unease. But hadn't he taken this trip to find the truth, meet people and explore the island? What was the harm?

"Long live the President," the girls chorused, then giggled. "If you play, you'll always stay."

"You can use the ticket to travel whenever and wherever you like, except to the white complex on the hill." The girl who'd handed him the bag turned and pointed at a flat-roofed building in the distance with pyramid-shaped columns at the entrance.

"Why didn't they give you vouchers?" Will asked Sam.

"I don't need them—I have a part-time job. I'll take you to see where I work tomorrow."

"Your pleasure is our desire." A man in a satin pantsuit, with legs pumping up and down on a monocycle, called in a sing-song voice. "Let us know what you require."

"Let's eat first." Sam hurried toward an orange building that looked like an ornate iced cake. "Have you had a pie with fifteen ingredients? Have you ever tried salted caramel cake with burned sugar frosting so delicious that you can't stop eating it, or a sweet that pops in your mouth?"

"That's not like the usual Eldrad food." It sounded like something from a storybook.

"It isn't. It's all thanks to the generosity of the President." Sam ran ahead.

Will sprinted along beside him, gawking at the odd-shaped buildings and milling crowds.

"There are floors of food," Sam shouted back to him "Savory food on the ground floor, and desserts on the top—if you make it that far."

A man dressed in a striped blue and white coat and white pants met them at the door of the iced-cake building. He bowed to them. "Eat all you want, stay as long as you want."

They took the glass elevator, which gave a clear view of each level. The lift attendant, in the same striped outfit, announced the offerings of each floor as they ascended. The experience made Will light-headed. Eating might make him feel better.

"Hors d'oeuvres, starters, entrees, themed mains, cakes," the lift attendant said as he munched on a layer cake. "And desserts."

"Take us back down to themed mains," Sam said.

The lift descended. The attendant stuffed the last mouthful of cake into his mouth and wiped his hands on a napkin just before the door opened. "One perk of the job." The man smiled.

"Come and check out the menu," Sam said. "You sit on a stool and eat at the counter."

Will looked at the array of selections in more glass cabinets than he could count. He'd never had so many choices. Jess would go crazy here. Mom would be in seventh heaven.

A girl pointed to a sign above the counter. "We can't have everything on display, so look at the menu if you like."

Will ordered a towering hamburger with so many fillings it toppled before the first mouthful. There was no way he could finish it.

"Eat all you want, stay as long as you want," the man beside him wheezed. He spread himself over two stools.

Sam led Will back to the lift when they couldn't face another mouthful. "Time for dessert."

Will peered around the desserts floor. It was all so out of character from what he knew of Eladia. He couldn't wait to visit the rest of Idella. His mouth watered with anticipation at the huge counters of cakes, creamy-looking mousse and a ten-flavor fairy-floss machine. Best of all were the towering mounds of chocolates shaped into white and brown pyramids.

"Let's join those people over there." Sam pointed to spare stools at a counter full of trays of cupcakes decorated with swirls of rainbow icing and dotted with confectionery. The three large people nearby ignored them and kept eating.

"I'll have that salted caramel cake—the one you said you couldn't stop eating," Will said.

"Ha—and I'll have the triple chocolate mousse cake and the green mint garnish."

The girl behind the counter hummed as she served the sweets. Will added a handful of the chocolates from a pyramid and devoured the whole plate of food as if he hadn't eaten for a week, until a wave of nausea swept over him.

"I'm not used to rich food anymore. I can't manage another slice." Will checked the map in his bag and read the list of attractions. "Let's explore. Do they have a bar?"

"You should stay, come what may," the doorman said in an insulted tone as they left.

"We'll come back later," Will said.

"They prefer their customers to stay longer," Sam said. "So where do you want to start?"

Will scanned the brochure. "Paradise Retreat, Fame for a Day, Crime Den, Inner Sanctum, Pain Haven, Horror Haunt . . . too many to take in. I'd like to see as many as I can. What's your favorite place, Sam?"

"I'll show you soon. We all need something to make us feel better or help us forget, don't we? Which place do you think would give you the satisfaction you are looking for?"

Will hesitated. None of them would likely lead him to the elusive truth he was searching for. He wasn't that stupid.

"I'm not sure."

"What is it you desire most in life. That special thing that will make you happy?"

Will shrugged. How did he know? He knew he wanted the princess. Maybe it was her he needed more than anything. Sam stared at him. Will said nothing. He wouldn't tell a stranger his private thoughts.

"Whatever it is, you can find it here. Or find something to take its place." Sam led him toward a tram station. "I'll take you to the Casino. That's where I work, and they have the best bar. We can catch transport and get an overview of the city, and then you can decide. Then, if you still can't find what you want, I have the ultimate place. It's where most people go."

"You mean The Madecia Center?" Will couldn't hide the sarcastic tone in his voice.

"No, not there. This is much better."

A tram slid into the station, and a man with a bright blue cap and a pudgy potato face collected the tickets. The tram whooshed away. Will peered left and right, not wanting to miss anything. Impressive building complexes, people with ravens printed on their clothes, queues to attractions, and flashing lights streaked past them

"Are Cravers a problem here?" Will asked.

"Not so much. If they're a problem, the Catchers take them to the white building on the hill. It's quite safe here. We have good security."

"The more you play. The longer you stay," a man said to them, yanking at a mirren he had on a leash. Will stood at a safe distance from the animal.

They hopped off the tram, and Sam led him down the road. "Come and I'll show you Casino Central." A man greeted them with a sweeping bow at the entrance of an opulent, cream-colored building.

"This is my favorite place in Idella."

"Once you play, you'll always stay." A man bobbed his head at them and flicked a pack of cards through his fingers.

Rows of slot machines lined a carpeted room the size of a large theater. Tiny star lights dotted the ceiling. In the middle of the room, a statue of a woman towered over them, with water spouting from her hands into a circular pool.

"Sit at the bar and order a drink." Sam said. "I'm going to play the slots for a while. 'Rolling Treasure' owes me. You can join me if you like."

Will waved him away and perched on a barstool, eyeing the array of bottles on dozens of mirrored shelves. This place made Goat's Horn Inn look like a backwater.

A croupier whispered in Will's ear. "You can overstay, and you don't have to pay." Sam's gold coins clinked into the machine nearby.

Will ignored the man, but thoughts spun in his mind like the symbols on the slot machines. One day wasn't enough time in this place. He pointed to a row of bottles sitting on the counter labeled Pleasure City Spirits, when the bar attendant asked him for his order. It had been too long since his last drink. How had he survived?

"Coming right up." The barman poured a generous glass.

Will sipped the spirits until the fire in his veins lessened the unease about his detour to Idella.

"Let me refill your glass." The barman had the bottle poised. Will nodded.

Sam made most of his money back after an hour of clinking, clanking, and swearing, Will lurched from his stool, still holding onto the glass counter.

Sam pocketed his coins. "I'll get the rest tomorrow."

Will left the bar with a stagger. "I should go now."

"But you've seen so little of the city. Why don't you rest up for the night at The Cardella Hotel?"

"How much does it cost?"

"Look in your bag. You have two accommodation coupons. What about the free passes you haven't used yet? This place is the President's gift to the people. Why do you think he's so popular? If it weren't for him, Idella wouldn't exist."

Will searched for the accommodation coupons, fumbled, and dropped the bag. "What's his motive?"

"You have to obey him, of course, and have his mark to show you belong."

"What if I don't?"

"You wouldn't get a pass." Sam's head shot around. "Don't tell me." Sam wrenched back Will's sleeve and gave a low whistle. "I should have guessed. How did you get in?"

Will pulled back his sleeve over his bare arm. "They didn't check."

"That's because you were with me." Sam dragged him into a side street.

A sinking, sick feeling gripped Will's stomach.

"Why didn't you tell me you were a Drifter?" Sam asked. "I could be in a lot of trouble for bringing you here."

Will scratched his spinning head. "I didn't know. How would I?"

"Look, I'll stick with you and show you around, but do what I say, and keep your eyes skinned."

"Okay. I'll stay a couple of nights." A night in a comfortable hotel was not an opportunity to pass up. He also had to admit, the spirits had left him too muzzy in the head to leave right now.

***

Will and Sam waited on another platform until a ten-carriage tram arrived. The seats were full, so they clung to a pole inside, swinging from one side of the carriage to the other as it took the corners. A mirren in a tiny knitted coat sat on a girl's lap, its eyes bulging with importance.

"You'll get a glimpse of Idol Valley from the tram as we head up the mountain." Sam pointed. "Look down there."

Will gawked at the lower section of the broad valley. Hundreds of statues of all types of creatures, in various shapes and sizes, filled the area. Bicycles pulling covered carts wove around the figures on narrow roads.

"That's the favorite place I was telling you about. It will blow your mind."

"I'd like to go there. What are all the people doing?"

"Offering gifts to their chosen gods. I'll take you there soon."

"The Cardella Hotel," the tram driver announced. They screeched to a stop in front of a massive building, in the shape of a giant flower with thick petals in a whirl formation. Every surface reflected the colors of the rainbow.

"See how the petals have windows on them? That's where the rooms are."

Will followed Sam to the double glass entry doors. Men in white uniforms, helmets, and reflective orange glasses stood at the door.

"Who are those guys?"

"The Catchers. Keep away from them."

A drip of fear trickled down Will's back. "What if they stop and check me for the mark?"

"Just walk in, don't look at them, and try to walk in a straight line."

A well-groomed woman in a tailored suit greeted them in a velvety, monotone voice. "Welcome to the Cardella Resort. Your comfort is our satisfaction, but if you would like to stay, then you must play."

Will's already churning stomach gave a complete flip as a super-fast travellator whisked them up a forty-five degree angle to the sixteenth floor.

"Room 1506," Sam announced.

"Have you stayed here before?"

"Heaps of times." He strode into a room that was as big as Will's house back in Aporto Bay.

Will flopped onto a couch near two king-sized beds. "Why are you helping me?"

"I like you. And . . . I get lonely sometimes, despite the crowds."

"What happens when the coupons run out?"

"You leave, pay, or go to Casino Central and win some gold back to buy more."

"But how can you play without coins?"

"They give you credit and keep a tab."

"A tab?" Will said.

"That's how I can live here." Sam picked up the remote control. "Let's play Cosmic Terminator. It's ace."

"What happens to the Cravers here if they take too much madecia?"

"If you take it for too long, you waste away. I've seen them all wizened and bent. Then they die. They're taken to the Catchers building if necessary."

"I have seen no one like that around here."

"Like I said. They're taken away," Sam said. "They live the fast life. That's their choice."

***

Will woke late the following morning. Playing Cosmic Terminator had kept them going until three in the morning. They ate a room service breakfast. It was motel style, like the one at the motels back at the bay. Then they headed out towards the Idella attractions, and into the hustle of the crowds.

"We'll go to the rides first. If you like them, you can stay all day while I go to the Casino for my bar shift in the afternoon. Or you can explore on your own, if you want a break from the rides," Sam said.

"Sounds great."

"I'll take you to Jungle Drop first. You plunge over a waterfall, then white-water raft in a fake canyon. Afterwards we'll do Pipe Pursuit." Sam pointed to the contorted maze of tubing in the distance.

***

Will spent an adrenaline-filled and stomach-in-mouth morning with Sam.

"That's enough for one day." Will curled over with his hands on his knees, gasping. "You go on your shift, and I'll explore."

Will checked some of the other attractions on the map: Madecia Central, Fashion Reno, Killer Street, Shoppers' Mania, Velocity Highway, and Depression Buster. He'd pay a quick visit to a few and find a favorite. The place was unbelievable.

His first stop was Fame for a Day. The staff dressed him in a pop star outfit and he sang to a crowd of hundreds in a cringe-worthy performance. The audience still gave him a standing ovation. He chuckled after he left the concert. Phony but fun. He stumbled back into the street. Now he had a headache coming on.

He hurried past Madecia Central. He didn't need a complication like that in his life—fast-tracked pleasure or not. Keeping up with his need for alcohol was enough to deal with.

He approached an arena where an enthusiastic team was handing out free tickets to the horse races at the front gate. Will spent two hours at the grand affair. Most of the crowd were dressed like royalty. He removed his stained coat, dusted down his clothes, and then used the offered Idella credit to bet on three horses: Much Maligned, Corkscrew and Mud Flinger.

He watched the races and lost the bets. The Betting Station gave him a note stating he owed ten gold pieces. How would he pay that back? He stomped down the road to the next attraction, putting the thought out of his mind.

By late afternoon, after trying various venues, his head spun like the fairground rides. The flashing lights pulsed in his vision and made his head ache as he walked along the street. He needed to get back to the hotel and find Sam.

Chapter 19

That night, Will and Sam played Cosmic Terminator until the early hours of the morning. At midday, they caught the train to the Valley of Idols. Crowds of people streamed toward the area. A smoky incense wafted through the air, and tinkling bells reminded Will of the goats at Caves Hill. He sighed when another pang of longing for Eleonora struck him without warning.

"How many idols are there?" he asked as they joined the queue.

"Hundreds. Some people visit them every day. Many come from the villages around Idella. They petition their god for the things they need and make offerings to it—to keep their god happy."

"What offerings?"

"It depends on the god. It could be gold or food or candles. Don't worry. You can buy what you need when you get there, at the stalls, or from the driver. When we arrive, you choose your preferred god by filling in a form at the Idol Station, and a driver will take you to the god. Easy."

Will gawked at the impressive statues, the crowds and cart-bikes spilling down the hill. Chants, music, and drum beats echoed around the valley.

Will pointed down the hill. "What's that one—with the biggest queue?"

"That's for the people who want to be the god. It's just a mirror, but they all like it."

"Strange."

"Not so strange. They like to be in charge. To have all the power and attention. Why don't you choose that one?"

"Stand in front of a mirror, offering wilted flowers?" Will laughed. "Would you?"

"I go to Sumba," Sam said. "He's awesome—you should see him. He is one of the biggest."

They queued at the Idol Register Station

An attendant dressed in the shiny plastic uniform called in a sincere tone. "Let your idol make you whole." People who had already registered pushed through the gate to the carts.

"Let your idol have your soul." An attendant led Will and Sam to screens and keyboards. "Fill in your form here," she said.

Will nearly burst with excitement at the sight of the computers. "I'll send an email back to the bay."

"You can't do that on Eldrad. It's forbidden. Anyway, it wouldn't work," Sam said.

Will groaned, gritted his teeth, and read the screen:

> *Idol Register.*
> *Idol Preference Survey.*
> *Terms and Conditions: The idols are under the rule*
> *of the esteemed President Lorn and must not take*
> *any precedence over his jurisdiction.*

Will looked at the questions and typed an answer for each one.

1. What outward form do you prefer in an idol?

A god who looks human.

2. What gift are you giving? If you are giving in gold coins, please pay at the Idol Register Station before proceeding to the Idol Precinct.

Nothing. Just me.

3. What essential characteristic you require your idol to have?

That he's good and always looks out for me.

4. What do you expect your idol to do for you?

To accept me and not give up on me.

5. Any other requirements?

Be available to me personally 24/7 and is the most powerful of all the gods.

He pressed enter, but an instruction flashed in red text.

A gift must be purchased for your idol.

"Hurry up," Sam said. "The form doesn't take that long to fill in." He peered over Will's shoulder at the screen.

"There aren't any gods like that. It's impossible. You're not conforming. These answers go straight to administration. Delete everything and fill in the form again. Hurry before it's noticed."

A siren pierced the air. A streak of unease flashed through Will. He swung around to check the entrance. Three Catchers hurried toward the Idol Register Station from the street.

Sam clenched his arm. "I think you're in trouble." He dragged Will through the entry gate, thrusting his pass at the guard. The guard was staring at the Catchers with his mouth gaping and let them through without checking for Will's ticket.

"Stop!" A Catcher pointed through the entry gates. "Grab him. He's a King follower."

Sam hauled Will into a bicycle cart. "Hurry," Sam said to the driver. "We must get to Sumba for an urgent request." The driver nodded to them, then lurched down the hill. Floral garlands and bells swung back and forth from the roof of the cart.

Will glanced back, heart pumping and his nerves on a knife-edge. The Catchers were following, but twelve carts tore down the mountain. It might give them a chance to escape.

"What happens to the people they arrest?" Will asked. The Catchers gave him the creeps.

"You don't want to know. Listen to me and do what I say. You're lucky I didn't leave you behind." The statues blurred as they sped along the road. Crackling bags of sweets swung from the roof of the canopy.

"Here's Sumba. Jump out and hide in the garden." Sam's terse tone multiplied Will's fears.

"Let your idol have your gold," the driver said. Sam thrust a coin at the driver and grabbed a bag of sweets. The driver cycled back up the hill to collect his next customer. "Sumba loves sweets. Hide behind those low palms while I give him my requests," Sam said. "If they catch you, then I don't know you."

Will crouched low in the undergrowth, gaping at the massive stone carving of Sumba. Its eyes seemed to look at him. People in the queue leading to the statue placed gifts on the step in front of it and some kneeled, calling their requests.

Will flinched at a poke on his shoulder.

"All done," Sam said. "Now we have to get you out of here. I have an idea. Give me a small coin." Sam ducked toward a stall across the track and bought a hat. "Put this on your head and tuck your hair out of sight. It's better than nothing."

The Catchers had gone when they returned to the Idol Register Station.

"Phew," Sam said. "We'll head back to Food Heaven, spend a couple of hours at Casino Central, then go back to the hotel and play Cosmic Terminator again. Tell me—are you really a King follower?"

"No, I'm not."

***

Sam leaned back on his stool at Food Heaven and rubbed his stomach. "I'll have another slice of lemon pie."

Will bit into the rich sweetness of his own berry pie. "Why did you bring me here, Sam? I want the truth."

"I guess I can tell you. I don't usually. But I trust you. My other job is to bring people here, to encourage them to find what they are looking for in life, and to promote the generosity of President Lorn."

Sam put his piece of pie back on the plate, leaned toward Will, and whispered. "A lot of people on the island are critical of the President's rule. But I'm happy, as long as I have easy access to Casino Central and get paid."

"Why don't they like King followers?" Will finished his dessert and piled a pyramid of dark chocolates on his plate.

"King followers don't conform. They aren't interested in madecia and their belief in the King is a threat to the President's overarching rule."

Sam grabbed a handful of chocolates from Will's plate. "Why don't you get the raven mark? That way, you'd be safe. You wouldn't be accused of being a Drifter anymore."

"No way," Will said.

***

Nausea swept over Will as he stood on the travellator on the way back to their room. He yawned. "Forget about Cosmic Terminator. I can't wait to go to bed."

Sam peered out the window and cursed.

"What's up?"

He closed the blinds. "I think we have a problem." Sam had an irritated edge to his voice. "The Catchers are waiting down below." He beckoned Will to the window and lifted a slat on the blind. "Over twenty of them. I overheard someone say the Catchers were searching for a Drifter who went to Idol Valley."

"Why didn't you tell me?"

"I wasn't sure it was you until now. They'll be swarming the hotel any minute. I'll have to go. I can't risk being associated with you."

"Can you help me get out of Idella?"

"You can't get out."

"Why not?"

"There's only one exit out of the city, and it will be crawling with Catchers. It always is when they get a whiff there's a Drifter around. They'll capture you, for sure."

"You still haven't told me what happens in that Catchers' building."

"Let me tell you, no one sees you again." He drew his hand in a cutting motion across his neck.

"What will I do then?" Will's nausea ratcheted up a notch.

"You'll have to work it out. You don't have the mark, and you aren't conforming. I gave you the chance. You didn't take it." Sam stuffed his clothes into his pack, went to the door, and then paused. "Been good having your company, Will."

Will stood at the door, debating his next move. He'd rather be a Drifter than rot in this place. He grabbed his pack, slipped out of the room, and dashed along the corridor to the fire escape. Muffled footsteps pounded on the carpet in the hall, and he pulled the exit door closed just in time. Darkness. His stomach churned like a blender. Running down sixteen floors without light was not his ideal getaway. He ran his hands over the wall to feel for a switch.

After several frantic moments, he found a square-shaped switch on the wall and turned the lights on. He hurtled down the stairs until his knees shook. When he reached the ground floor, he thrust the door open. Sunset threw its waning light over the luminescent city. People jostled in the streets below, and blinking night signs flashed.

There were two Catchers around thirty paces away. Will hid behind a column at the back of the hotel, prickles of alarm spiking through him at the sight of the white Catchers' building. It was too close for his liking and surrounded by the same high wire fence as the boundary fence of the Idella. Like a prison. He exhaled in disgust and sank to the ground, head in his hands. He had to think fast.

A raven circled above, giving guttural cries. Shadow? Will waved to the bird. The bird plummeted toward Will, soaring so close to his face the wing feathers brushed his cheek. Shadow then landed on a nearby branch and let out a caw in a tone Will hadn't heard him make before. The bird bounced his head up and down as though telling him something important.

Will wished he could speak raven. The bird took off again with his usual ungainly flight, flew up the hill to the fence around the Catchers' Building, then swooped back to the tree nearby, then he flapped back to the same location again. Will let out an exasperated huff. Was Shadow asking him to go to the fence? Why was he leading him to the most dangerous place in the entire city? Will wasn't sure he could trust the bird.

Will labored up the hill, keeping behind the trees on the hotel side of the road. Catchers would most likely watch from the flat roof of the white building.

Shadow peered down at him from the top of the wire fence. Will crept closer, still under the cover of the trees. The two Catchers were even closer now. The heavier man handed a package from his pocket to the other.

"Have you got any more?"

"Plenty where that came from."

"Why do you think I work in this hole of a place?" He spat on the ground.

"When did you start working here?"

"A month ago."

A blood-curdling howl emanated from the building. Will forced himself to repress the urge to run back down into the city.

"How many Drifters did they take last week?"

"Three."

Shadow didn't move, and Will waited and watched.

***

It was getting dark, and Shadow was still perched on the wire enclosure. The bird kept his beady eye on the tree where Will was hiding.

The two Catchers left, but others stood on the top of the flat-roofed building, like tiny white plastic figures. Will chewed on his nails. Then he saw a sight that blew his mind. He'd missed the most important thing.

A tear in the fence.

A section of the wire in the Catchers' building enclosure had torn from the base at the back of the complex.

And there was another tear. At the base of the rear boundary fence. It was barely noticeable, and if Will hadn't stared in that direction for so long, he would have missed it. Someone else must have ripped the mesh and made an escape. Two openings. One escape route. He could enlarge the hole in the Catchers' prison enclosure, then crawl a few steps to the rift in the back fence, and bolt into the woods. But entering the Catchers' complex would be the least favorite part of the escape plan.

Will waited until the evening light faded. The muscles in his head and neck ached with tension. Shadow had gone. Two burly guards stood at a side door into the white building and checked the badge of each Catcher as they entered. Will counted fifteen. But more left for the night shift.

When night fell, searchlights methodically panned back and forth over the area, bathing it every couple of minutes in a blinding light. Will cursed. He'd have to risk being seen if he wasn't fast enough.

As the floodlights panned the lower part of the hill, Will crept to the gap in the white Catchers' building enclosure. He shoved his pack through first, then pulled off his coat and used it to protect his hands as he pushed at the steel mesh. But the hole was too small. Every time the floodlights swung toward him, he ran for the cover of the trees.

After three tries, he was back again at the opening. He pushed and pulled. At last, the hole was large enough for him to crawl underneath. The wire ripped his clothes and pack. But he had broken through and was now in the most dangerous place in the whole of Idella. He crouched low as he edged through the grounds toward the other gap in the city's back fence. He stood up momentarily to throw his pack over the fence.

But floodlights lit the area.

A siren pierced the air.

Shouts rang through the valley.

The Catchers were coming.

Doors slammed.

He tried to push through the jagged hole, but the opening was once again too small. He wrenched at the stiff wire, ripping his skin. Footsteps sounded closer. His body jammed in the spikes of metal. A Catcher grabbed his coat and wrenched him back. A bloodcurdling cry pierced his ears.

Shadow.

The bird swooped out of the darkness. He screeched at the men, and pecked at the face of the Catcher who gripped his coat. Will yanked himself out of the man's clutches and launched his pack and his body through the break in the fence, losing his shoes. He collapsed on the ground outside the complex, then he grabbed his pack, jumped up, and sprinted for his life.

He dashed into the forest, leaping over rocks and slippery fallen branches, dodging spiny cones and thorny weeds, bruising and pricking his bare feet. The light of the moon was the only thing that kept him going. When he could no longer hear shouting and crashing in the bushes, he stopped to rest for a moment. Then he continued, gasping for breath, with his lungs on fire.

His running turned into limping. After what seemed like hours, he collapsed under a moss-covered tree-trunk and slept. When he woke, all he could hear was the chirping of birds and the rustle and scraping of leaves above. Will let out an audible sigh of relief. All he wanted was to go back to Caves Hill to see Eleonora and the others.

His trip to Eladia would have to be postponed.

Next time he traveled to Eladia, he wouldn't get lost in a city of pleasure and empty dreams. And next time he might even go, not only as a Drifter but as a King follower. If he was a King follower, he would have the keys to the House of Wisdom. The key to the truth.

Chapter 20

Will settled back into life at Caves Hill. As they sat around the fire in the evenings, he told the stories of his adventures at Idella. Everyone's favorite story was Shadow's rescue. Some nights, Roland read to them from The King's Word. Will listened, but was restless after his experience. Eleonora treated the lacerations on his feet, and he enjoyed every minute of her attention. She always sat with him now, and they always hugged when they parted at the end of the evening. But it wasn't enough. However, he planned to leave for Eladia as soon as his feet had healed.

The sun shone, and a pine-scented breeze wafted from Emerald Forest. Will planned to go fishing with Jadyn to catch salmon and have a bracing swim in the river. Spending time in the woods was like surfing back at the bay. It filled him with a sense of well-being and helped him think.

"Have you seen Laurien?" Jadyn asked.

"Not for days."

"She isn't in her cave. I've checked."

"Should we worry?"

Jadyn cut the bait. "She isn't usually away this long. I'll ask around when I go to the village." They threw in their fishing lines and secured them with a rock, hoping to catch a fish while they swam.

"I have a question." Will shook the water out of his hair and sat on a rock while he dried in the sun. "In The King's Book, the king is sometimes a father, sometimes a son, and he's the Counselor as well. How can you make sense of that?"

"The son is the King, and his father is God and the counselor is one with them as well," Jadyn said. "Yes, there are three, but also one. It isn't an easy concept to get your head around. I can take you to Severin Peak tomorrow and show you something that may help you understand."

Will nodded as he sharpened his knife on a flat stone.

"I'll meet you at Bare Rock before dawn tomorrow," Jadyn said. "Then I'm heading up to the forge. I have an important meeting with Cadwyn and Dorian. Hand me your knife, and I'll show you how to polish it."

Jadyn pulled off his belt and ran the sharp edge of the blade back and forth along the grain side of the leather. He passed the belt and knife to Will. "Try it now."

***

Early the next morning, in the dim pre-dawn light, Jadyn led the way up the mountain. They scrambled on the slope, slipping on the loose rocks as a breeze blew around them. An overpowering scent of fish-laced sea spray from the gray Cardina Sea blew towards them.

They followed the wild goats, who galloped ahead on the rocky terrain. "I still haven't seen Shadow around."

"I haven't seen him since my escape from Idella. It's a concern. I hope the Catchers didn't get him."

They climbed around a spur and rested. The wind dropped as if the earth and sea had paused its breath, ready for daybreak. Jadyn pointed to the horizon. The tip of the burning orange sun emerged and lit the vast shimmering ocean, streaking color into the sky. Then the fiery cauldron burst upwards, spreading its light and heat in a golden trail to the shore far below.

The sun warmed Will's face and penetrated his thick coat to his skin. It blinded him but filled him with a promise of good. Another day of life. He shielded his eyes and loosened his scarf. "Spectacular."

"Yes, the sun is like the King." The flaming sphere slipped above the horizon and coasted higher on its inevitable journey, up into the sky. "And there's more to see." Jadyn pointed across the ocean. "Look at the islands near the horizon."

Will squinted into the distance. "Three islands."

"Follow me." Jadyn took him further up the mountain. They stepped over isolated drifts of snow left from a recent fall until they reached Severin's Peak.

"What do you see now?" Jadyn stood tall, his calf-length coat flapping in a sudden gust of wind.

"The three islands are really one island when you look at them at this level." Will rested on a lichen-covered boulder.

"It's called The Trinidad Isle and is bound by land bridges. It's connected even in violent seas." Jadyn ran his fingers through his windswept hair. "The three are one."

"So the Counselor is that important?"

"There's a lot more to him than meets the eye."

***

The next day, Will was walking into the forest with Wolfie when he heard Laurien screaming from Shaggy Rock. It wrenched his gut and shattered the usual peace of the valley.

The princess was already halfway up the mountain. He sprinted after her. Laurien was inside her cave. Eleonora motioned for him and Wolfie to stay outside. Will stopped. He'd likely be the last person Laurien wanted to see.

"Leave me alone," Laurien shouted at the princess. Eleonora spoke to her in a soothing tone.

After a few minutes, Laurien's yelling diminished, but Will could still hear sobbing in between hollow dry-retching. He sat outside with Wolfie's hairy body pressed against his. The hound whimpered in unison with Laurien's intermittent sobs.

A while later Eleonora came out of the cave, her face pinched with worry. "Can you collect wood so we can make a fire? Laurien needs a wash." She patted a pouch hanging from her belt. "I'll make her some soup with healing herbs."

"What's wrong with her?" he asked in a low voice.

"They won't give her any more madecia."

"I didn't know she was taking it."

Eleonora nodded. "I didn't either, but I had my suspicions. She's always so secretive."

"Why has her supply dried up?"

"She won't take the mark, and she's run out of gold. I'll spend the night with her."

"How serious is this?"

"Very. She's stopped eating. We'll need to get Dr. Well's advice."

Wolfie crept to the entrance of the cave, shivering, then tried to enter.

Eleonora pushed him back. "No, Wolfie."

The dog whined, turned away with his tail between his legs and sat dejected outside.

"All right, in you go. Laurien will send you away if she doesn't want you."

"I'll bring up wood and food—and get the doctor to come and visit." Will strode down the hill, his stomach churning. The trip to Eladia would not happen while Laurien was sick. Also, he still didn't have the key he needed to find the truth.

***

Dr. Wells visited Laurien, and Will took supplies up to her cave every day. In the meantime, he became more edgy about his trip to Eladia. It wasn't just the worry of Laurien's illness, or even that he hadn't told Eleonora how he felt about her. His last trip had failed and now he was having doubts about becoming a King follower. He certainly wasn't a suitable candidate for the realm of a King. Not like Roland or Eleonora or Jadyn.

But how could he get access to the House of Wisdom without the keys? How could he discover the truth of his life if he didn't become part of this kingdom? He trusted their advice. He wanted those keys.

That night, once again, thoughts and misgivings raced through his mind like the frantic rides at Idella. He tossed and turned on his fur bed until half the night was over. He had a dream that Roland was walking toward him with a key, but a demonic creature blocked his way.

The sun was riding high in the sky by the time he ate breakfast and his eyes were heavy from exhaustion. He cleaned out his cave, planned the next hunting trip, and then strolled into the forest, drawn toward Silver Brook.

He strode over the bracken. Birds twittered and searched for nectar in the blossoms, and fragrant jasmine scented the air. He pushed aside the vine draping over an arbor at the entrance of the glade, then walked through the rambling flower garden. It brought back pleasurable memories of the time he and Eleonora had gathered herbs and supplies for Aunt Nora.

He rested under a birch tree on a carpet of spongy green moss beside the clear stream. He wanted to fill the emptiness in his life with something greater, something more meaningful. Would the keys be the answer?

He cupped his hands and drank from the stream.

"I can give you living water." Will jumped at the sound of the voice.

The Counselor leaned against an aspen tree with a gray-feathered owl perched on his shoulder. "If you drink the living water, you'll never thirst again." The Counselor moved to sit with him on the mossy bank, and the owl flew to a branch nearby, its golden-orb eyes staring.

Will dried his mouth on his sleeve. "That's impossible."

"If you drink it, it will make you new," the Counselor said. "It will satisfy and open your eyes to the spiritual realm. The more you drink, the more you'll see. The more you will understand."

Will took a pebble and skimmed it across the surface of the stream, the eddies in the water reflecting his turbulent thoughts.

"You mean this supernatural living water will make me a King follower? But I think that following a king may not be for me."

The Counselor sat, silent.

Will stood to leave. "I'm not good enough. The king won't want someone like me in his realm."

The Counselor turned and looked up at him with his fathomless silver-gray eyes.

"Did you know," Will said, "that I went to the Holsworth's Marine Engine Factory with my friend Mitch and smashed his windows with broken pavers? All the windows. Did you know I want Ben dead? The King's Book says you're supposed to love your enemies. And there are other things." They were humiliating things he would never reveal to anyone.

The Counselor's face showed no surprise. No anger. "I know all about your struggles."

"Can I ever find this truth you and the others have told me about?" Will asked.

The Counselor smiled. "Of course. But you need to make the choice. The King's way or your way. Remember, the King's not focused on your past, he's focused on your destiny." The owl hooted softly and inclined its head, still staring at them.

Will settled on the mossy bank beside the Counselor and ran a hand over the soft green surface. He could see in his mind's eye beams of light streaming through the cracks around the edges of a door. There was a key in the lock. Could he open this door to his true destiny?

He wanted to be like Roland, Jadyn and Eleonora. He could walk away and never know—or he could unlock the door. What if this was the only chance he had to find the truth? What if he missed out on something that could be the greatest adventure of his life?

"Where is the water?" Will asked.

"I see your heart is willing. Just say you want it and you will have it—and all its benefits."

"Then I'll take the way of the King. I am sorry for the things I've done. I'll open the door to your realm and I'll drink the water."

In his mind, the door opened. Warmth and brilliance streamed through, and he sensed a new wholeness that filled him to bursting. Nothing in his life came close to this new feeling. Ever.

***

The next morning, Will threw back his bedding and rushed outside and breathed in the bracing pine-scented air. Pleasure fizzed through him like a soda stream. He was different. Everything was different. It was as though his view of life had been blurry before. He wished he could tell the whole island that he was now a follower of the King. He couldn't wait to tell the others.

The Counselor strode up the hill toward him, with a spring in his step and a carved wooden chest under his arm. He put the box on the ground and embraced Will.

"You live in a whole new world of possibilities now you're a King follower. You have access to his realm and his promises. In this chest I have gifts for you."

Will bent down beside the Counselor as he opened the chest. "Do all the King's followers get gifts?"

"Yes, but they vary from individual to individual. It depends on what you need for your unique journey and what you request. Also, in times of need, we may give you additional power and insight."

"Like Pandora's box—but with good things?" Will asked.

The Counselor laughed. "The gifts in this chest are available to all the King's followers. It's up to you how much you make use of them. It contains the armor you'll need to defend yourself against the Darkness. Wear it daily. Now you belong to the King's realm, you'll be a target, but you also have the great power of the King and his angels to call on."

The Counselor took a belt from the chest and passed it to him. "This is the Belt of truth. It will protect you against evil and help to show you what is truth—and what is not."

Will examined the ornate buckle and exclaimed, "Remarkable."

The Counselor pulled a breastplate from the wooden box. "This is to protect your heart—your emotions, your self-worth, your trust. And here is the footwear which will help you tell what of the King has done for the Earthlands."

Will pulled on the sandals. They were precisely his fit.

"Next is the shield. This shield will protect you when tempted to do damaging things. The Dark Prince will put obstacles in your way. Be on guard."

Will tilted the shield in the sun to catch the glitter of the metal and gemstones.

The Counselor pulled a ringlet of burnished gold from the box. He placed it on Will's head. "This will help you trust the King and protect you from doubt." He reached into the chest again and pulled out a sword. "And here's something I know will please you."

"The King's sword." Will pulled it out of the sheath and drew a sharp breath of awe. "This is priceless."

The Counselor nodded.

"I've seen the princess with this sword."

"Yes, you may occasionally see this spiritual armor on the island, but it is normally an invisible armor. The King followers on your earth can't see it either, however most use it regularly because they know its power and protection.

"I have a question."

The Counselor nodded.

"Are you the King?"

"If you have my presence, then you have the King's presence. We are one."

Will sprang up and held the sword to the sky. He belonged to the forever kingdom. Everything else he'd ever known, everything else he'd ever believed, everything else, paled into insignificance.

Chapter 21

Aporto Bay Hospital: Erin's uncertainty.

Erin walked on crutches toward the hospital entrance from the parking lot. A balmy day scent of salt and sunscreen hung in the air. Families walked dogs and some meandered along East Street toward the beach.

Inside, the coma ward was silent, apart from the electronic pings of the life support machines and the rhythmic, artificial sucking of breath from the three coma patients left in the ward. Erin glanced at Nurse Baxter typing in the nurses' station, then hurried to Will's bed. They had removed the staples from his head and the scar was healing, but he'd lost more weight, and his arms that had bulged with muscle were bony and wasted. Her stomach cramped in concern.

"Please wake up, Will. I need you to wake up. It's been too long." Her eyes filled. She'd spent hours researching on the internet. The longer a patient was in a coma, the less likely they were to make a good recovery. She held Will's hand and felt a slight pressure on hers. Her heart somersaulted. Had he moved his fingers, or had she imagined it?

Nurse Baxter glanced at her from the nurses' station with pursed lips.

What was wrong with the woman? Was she plotting to steal more medication? Surely not. Erin sighed. It was possible the PTSD she had after the stadium accident was making her overly anxious and protective of Will. Her desire for him to wake was becoming an obsession. She longed to keep holding his hand. Her heart still pounded from the sensation of his fingers moving, but she settled in the chair, opened her laptop and checked what occupational therapy courses were on offer. The medical treatment she'd received had sparked an interest. It might lead her on a career path.

An hour later, the distinctive squelch of Dr. Max Cooper's rubber-soled shoes came from the outside corridor. Erin looked towards the entrance with a surge of expectancy. She'd been looking forward to talking with him.

But something strange was happening at the desk. Nurse Baxter lurched out of her chair, smoothed her hair, and tightened her belt, then grabbed a folder from a shelf nearby, spilling files over the floor. She scrambled to pick them up.

The doctor entered the nurse's station and nodded at the nurse. He reached up to pull a file from the shelf. "I can't find the Somerset file," he said.

"It's here. You should look at these results." Nurse Baxter's cheeks flushed. He leaned over her to peer at the notes. Erin smiled. Had the nurse deliberately put them in a strategic spot to bring the doctor closer? He nodded his thanks and walked toward Will's bed.

"I hear you've been talking to my comatose patient," he said to Erin. He drew his hands through his graying hair. Even with his unshaven face, he looked distinguished, like a middle-aged film star who'd kept his looks.

"Feel a bit responsible for his state."

"What do you mean?"

"He tried to protect me from a falling steel beam in the stadium accident. Unfortunately, he suffered the blow instead."

"Your knight in shining armor. It's a shame he's out of action." He glanced at her legs. "I see you've had your own challenges as well. Who's your doctor?"

"Dr. Lindsay."

"Well, you're in expert hands."

The doctor flipped through a readout from a machine wired to Will's body. The doctor's trousers were crumpled, and he wore odd socks. Poor guy. He must be struggling to cope with the overtime.

"I see you've noticed my odd socks." He gave her a rueful smile. "I've been a bit sloppy with my clothes since Pat passed away. She was always so particular."

The doctor checked the notes on his clipboard. "We have an interesting readout. It shows the extent of Will's brain activity using a tool called electroencephalography or EEG. There are hopeful results."

"I also thought his fingers twitched."

"Good. Keep up the visits."

It was as if all Erin's birthdays had come at once. She sat down, fighting tears. Tears of unexpected hope. The doctor left without speaking again to Nurse Baxter, apart from a brief nod. The nurse's red face turned to thunder. She snapped four pills from a piece of foil and swallowed them with a bottle of water.

Erin checked her watch. Mom would be waiting to pick her up at the parking lot. She straightened Will's sheets, then gently pushed back the new growth of hair from the scar on his head.

"Have to go now, handsome, but I'll be back." Tonight she'd celebrate. She couldn't wait to see him again.

***

A few days later, Erin made her way toward Will's bed. Her pink flowery dress swung around her legs. She squeezed his hand, then flicked through the folder on the table beside his bed.

Nurse Baxter threw down her pen and strutted stiffly toward her.

"You don't have permission to look at a patient's readout or files. It's private information."

"Sorry. Has Will shown any improvement?"

"No change. You're wasting your time here. Do you know that?"

"Not according to his doctor."

"The doctor?"

"Dr. Cooper said Will's readout shows he may be responding. I've seen him flicker his eyelids, and his fingers have moved a little."

The nurse leaned over and adjusted the height of Will's bed and winced as she straightened. "What's your name?"

"Erin."

The woman took the clipboard and looked through the pages. "There's a slight response, which means nothing significant. Many coma patients open their eyes and make movements. Even patients in a vegetative or a deceased state can move. At this stage, it means nothing." A nervous spasm twitched the nurse's face, and she strutted back to her desk.

Erin sat for a while, deflated. Then she took some notes from her bag and read them aloud, hoping to get a response from Will. She couldn't resist keeping an eye on Nurse Baxter as well. This time, the nurse took three pills with her bottled water, while two of the other nurses attended to the other patients.

Susan and Jess Sutherland arrived, which added to the excitement. Susan dropped her bag on the floor and hugged her. "Thanks for coming to see Will. How are your injuries?"

"The bones are knitting. But they're taking their time." She wouldn't tell them how often she visited Will. They might think she was infatuated. Maybe she was.

Susan adjusted Will's pillow, and sat staring at him with a drawn face. Jess pulled another chair closer to his bed, pinned the brown curls of her fringe back, and chewed on a piece of hair hanging over her face.

Susan took Will's hand. "Can you hear me, Will? Dad said he's coming to see you this weekend." She turned to her daughter without loosening her grip on Will's hand. "Hopefully without that awful woman."

Jess's eyes narrowed.

"I'll go now," Erin said. Her crutches and shoes made a rhythmic, clunk-hopping noise on the polished floor as she left.

Chapter 22

Roland organized dinner at his cave the next night because Will said he had important news to tell them. Even Laurien and Wolfie came. He wondered why Laurien had come. Laurien hadn't joined them for dinners around the fire since she became ill. And she looked so thin that even a puff of wind could blow her away.

"Are you going to hurry up and tell us your news?" Laurien demanded once everyone had arrived.

Will turned the fish over on the grating with a fork before answering. He was glad Eleonora could be there. She looked stunning in her forest-green laced vest and soft suede boots.

He stood and faced them. "I've decided to become a King follower."

"We actually already know." The princess smiled and smoothed down her skirt. "News travels fast."

Will beamed at them. "I've gone from a dead end to the-sky's-no-longer-the-limit."

Roland pulled him into a hug. "May the King bless yer new life's journey."

The princess walked to him, took both his hands and held them with a firm grip. She gazed into his eyes with her brimming ones. Then she pressed one of his cheeks with a kiss, then the other. Something in her expression sent his heart into overdrive.

"My turn." Felix leaped up, his body stiff with eagerness and importance. He clutched an object in his fist.

"This is for you, Mr. Wills." He stood still for a moment with his fist closed.

"What is it?"

Felix opened his fingers and held out a small red dragon carved in wood.

"Thanks, Felix. I might have a special story for you about this one." Will dropped the wooden dragon into his top pocket, grinning.

Jadyn leaped up and beckoned to him. No words were needed. They paused, facing one another. The others tensed. They gave a shout in unison that rang through the valley. Then they gave an impromptu display of their well-practised combat prowess with a background of exclamation and a mix of noisy howling and barking from Wolfie.

Jadyn stepped back, doubled over and panting. "We needed to let off steam."

Will laughed. "It's been building up for a while."

A charred aroma filled the air, and Will bounded to the fire and removed the fish.

Laurien raked around in her bag. "Will. I've got something for you too."

He swung his head around, surprised at the tone in her voice. He expected nothing from her. She passed him a package wrapped with calico and string. He pulled on the string, intrigued. Inside was the knife she'd accused him of stealing. But the L engraving was now carved neatly into a W.

"I can't take it, Laurien."

"Yes, you can. It's a gift from me to you."

Will smiled and nodded.

Wolfie lumbered over, rested his saliva-streaked chin on Will's thigh, and gazed up at him. Eleonora poured steaming tea into mugs, humming to herself. Will let out a long breath, barely able to contain his overflowing emotions.

He placed the fish on a pottery platter. "So Roland, how do I get to the House of Wisdom? I want to leave as soon as possible and I don't want to get lost this time."

"Ye may get a ride with someone on a horse or wagon, but most of it will be on foot. Ye'll need to get across the mountain range as you did before. Once ye are down on the Cerith plains, ye head northeast. Take enough food to last ye the first leg of the trip, and enough gold." Roland drew a map of the island in the sand with a stick. "We're here. Eladia is on the eastern coast of the island." He marked an area on his rough map with a stone.

Laurien drew an N on a stone and placed it at the northern end of the map toward the eastern coast. "Keep away from Nevara."

"Ye'll find the road forks when you come to Clayden," Roland said. "Take the right fork, and you only have another three days to walk. A woman called Sophia will be at the gate of the city. She's there most days. Ask her to take ye to the House of Eladia and tell her I sent you. She'll ken."

"How will I know I'm in the right place?"

"Ye'll know. The house has seven columns. Ye cannae miss it."

"Why seven?"

"Seven's the number of perfection, and columns give the impression of stability and strength. There's a door behind each column, and ye can go into each one."

"What's inside?"

Eleonora smiled. "Prepare to be surprised. The King's realm is greater than any of us can imagine. Don't go with any preconceived notions."

***

Will prepared mindfully for his next journey. The torn skin on his feet had almost healed, and he planned to leave for Eladia in three days. He had everything he needed, except for fresh food—but he had one more thing to do. He had to tell Eleonora about his feelings for her.

Only one day to go before he departed. He packed a bag of dried mushrooms, red apples, mandon nuts, and various sachets of herbs for seasoning and healing that Eleonora had suggested. How would he broach the subject of his feelings with her? He stuffed in Aunt Nora's blanket, a makeshift shelter, and a copy of The King's Word. A container for cooking, a thin pottery mug, and eating implements went in next.

He swallowed the homesickness which coursed through him and then laughed at the irony of his emotions. How could he be homesick for Caves Hill? He should be more homesick for the bay. He still was but it had lessened. Mom would be shocked if she knew. A reason was walking up the hill toward him. As magnificent as a shooting star on a velvet night.

"I have something for you." Eleonora panted from the climb. She took a goat's hair scarf and a pair of gloves from her basket. "Roland gave me the gloves, but they're too big for me."

He squashed the feeling of longing threatening to undo him when she came near him. "I'm leaving tomorrow before dawn." It was as if his throat had a handful of gravel in it.

"May the King go with you," Eleonora said.

"Will you and the others be OK without me?"

She laughed. "We managed—"

"Before I arrived. I know. But I'm concerned about Roland. He tires easily these days. And what if Striker tries to grab you again?"

"Don't worry. For you to find the truth is the most important thing and you are now already on the path."

Will nodded and then clenched his teeth. It would have to be now—or never. "Princess, I need to tell you something."

"Fire away." She sat crossed-legged on the threadbare mat and a violet and rose fragrance wafted through the cave. He crouched beside her, gazed into her ocean-blue eyes and looked away. He'd drown if he didn't.

"I'll miss you," he said.

She flicked a stray piece of hair from her cheek. "You'll be back."

He reached over and touched her hand. "I mean, I'll miss you a lot. I may not be back. Who knows how long I have here on the island? I have feelings for you. Did you know that?"

"You do?" Her voice was barely a whisper.

"I need to know if you have any for me. I don't think you feel the same way. But is there anything?"

She stroked the fur on her coat. "I'm not in the position to have an emotional attachment. You mustn't think like that."

Will's insides churned with disappointment.

She leaned toward him and gave him a light hug. "Have a safe journey. I'll think of you and petition the King for your safety every day."

His body heated at her touch. He wished it could have been longer.

She made her way back to her cave. Will's earlier excitement dissipated. The last of his trip preparations were now a tedious chore. He pressed the scarf and gloves to his face, smelling her lingering fragrance, then placed them into the top of his pack. Did he really believe she'd say she felt the same way? What was he thinking?

He heaved a sigh. He was going on this trip to find the truth and the answers he so desperately needed. The King would be with him. What could be more important?

***

Just as the dawn light seeped into the purple night sky and the spread of stars faded, Will swung his pack over his shoulder and headed toward Shannon, his breath fogging in the crisp air. He gave Caves Hill a last longing glance. A woody fragrance drifted lazily upwards from the curling smoke of the early morning village fires.

A scuttle of stones behind him made him freeze.

Eleonora had followed him, without her coat, barefoot and with disheveled hair.

Will's heart thumped in his chest. "What's wrong?"

"I needed to tell you something."

He threw his pack down and faced her.

She hesitated. "I haven't been entirely open with you. I do have feelings for you."

"What sort?" he asked, his throat closing over.

"I am attracted to you."

His already aching heart squeezed so tightly his chest hurt.

She wrapped her arms around her body against the frosty morning air.

"You're not the sort of guy I thought would interest me. I've always fought it. But now you're going . . . I needed to tell you before you went."

"How long? When did you start feeling this way?" Striker may have been right after all. Something inside him did a crazy dance.

"Don't even ask."

He stood facing her. What should he do? There was only one thing. An irresistible current of energy drew them closer. He walked toward her. She lifted her head and looked up at him. The faint sweep of dawn stars reflected in her eyes. Daybreak brushed her skin. He reached out to her and wrapped his arms around her slender waist, and pulled her soft body to his.

He closed his eyes and bent his head. His heartbeat roared in his head. His lips were on her full ones. The sensation transported him to a new and secret place. A place he never wanted to leave. He was riding on cloud nine, a cloud nine made only for them.

She pulled away.

He heaved a shaky breath. "I'm so happy you told me." His voice still constricted with emotion.

She cooled her burning cheeks with her hands. "An attraction doesn't mean we're together, though. I'm not ready for a relationship. Not yet. She turned to leave, then half-turned back, holding one hand out to him. He grasped it for one emotion-charged moment, then they parted.

The fire of her touch stayed with him all day.

***

Will spent the first night in the Mordrach Mountains. He slept under his drafty makeshift cover, using Aunt Nora's blanket to keep warm. He left around dawn as soon as birdsong woke him. A sense of the King's presence and thankfulness that Eleonora was interested in him invigorated his every step. But his emotions fluctuated between thrills of hope and pangs of doubt. She said—attraction, not commitment, but she'd admitted her attraction for him. And she'd kissed him. A kiss to keep him fired up for a lifetime.

He reached the other side of the Mordrach Mountains and paused to admire the vast panorama of the Cerith Plains, before starting the long walk down. By the time he finally reached the plains, the muscles in his legs were cramping. He stopped to drink from a mountain spring, then strode across the lowlands, leaving the grandeur of the jagged mountains behind him.

His trip had been smooth so far. He wouldn't get distracted by anyone like Sam this time. But danger could lie ahead. He kept his eyes open for a village market, longing for a hot pie to fill his growling stomach. Soon, a muddle of people, carts, and animals thronged on the road. Will wrinkled his nose at the overpowering stench.

Chickens squawked and squabbled in metal cages, and flocks of goats bleated as they tore at the weeds in the ditches. Dusty donkeys waddled past, laboring under wicker baskets filled with wilting vegetables. Occasionally Cravers or combatants slinked by with wary eyes. He bought a steaming apple pie from a stall and bit into the hot, crusty pastry. It reminded him of his Granny Meg's pies back at the bay.

"How far to Eladia?" he asked the woman at the stall.

"Over three day's walk from here," she said. She rolled out a piece of pastry the size of a small table, and cut it up with a knife so fast her hands were a blur.

***

Will continued for three days until he came to a sign pointing to Eladia. The roads were bustling with even more crowds. Anticipation quickened his pace. He'd waited so long for this.

The towering granite walls of the city soon came into view. Will headed toward the crowd on one side of a massive open gate in the stone boundary walls. The people stood facing a woman who towered over them all. She wore a flowing lavender gown.

"Who's that woman?" he asked a man in a brass-buck-led hat.

"Sophia. She's the one who speaks in riddles and verse every day at the gates of the city."

Will pushed through the engrossed crowd, who had pressed in to hear what she was saying.

She spoke in a heartfelt tone. *Wisdom and understanding are more profitable than silver and more precious than rubies. They are incomparable to anything else.*

He listened, riveted at her words, he had read them before in the King's Word. She paused and walked into the crowd and placed her hand on a child's head, then turned to leave. "Come to my house and join me for dinner and more instruction."

Most of the crowd followed her. Will pushed his way through until he reached her side. She beamed at him as though she recognized him. "William Sutherland, I've been expecting you."

"I'm here to find the truth."

"The King always rewards those who seek such things. Follow me."

Chapter 23

Will walked next to Sophia, trying to absorb all the sights of the city on the way while listening to her words. They finally reached an immense mansion with seven imposing columns. *The House of Wisdom.* A surreal, light-headed feeling overtook him at the realization that he was finally at the house. A man in a coat with two rows of gold buttons swung open iron gates, decorated with elaborate swirls. The house, surrounded by extensive gardens, loomed at the end of a long driveway.

"We have a splendid feast for you tonight," Sophia said to the crowd. "Roast meats, fresh local vegetables, and delicious platters. Food for the soul and food for the body. Food is part of life's celebration, is it not?"

Will nodded. His jaw hung open. The exterior of the house appeared to be white marble. The front doors were open, and each as big as his garage door back at the bay.

She turned to him. "I'll introduce you to Aiden, who will assist you on your journey. You must stay with us in the house, William of Aporto Bay."

A man dressed in what appeared to be a ship captain's outfit greeted the crowd. "Dinner will be served at six." He turned to William. "Follow me, and I will take you to your room. How is my friend Roland?"

"Not well. He struggles now with everyday chores."

"Age overcomes us all, does it not? Hopefully, it is accompanied by greater wisdom," Aiden said. "Let me relieve you of the burden of your pack."

The entrance hallway had a magnificent two-story ceiling, ornately carved in geometric patterns. Will sank into the thick floral carpet with each step. Framed portraits, as big as the wall of a small room back home, hung on the walls of the corridor. The people in the portraits appeared to speak.

Will pointed at the portraits. "Who are they, Aiden?"

"They're some of the King's people and part of my family and yours. Everyone in the realm of the King is part of our family."

"What are they talking about?"

"They're speaking of what the King did for them. It's just a simulation. They are with the King now. You'll meet them all in person one day, when you have your immortal body." Will's heart raced. Eldrad had always been a place of surprises, and now the surprises were ramping up.

Aiden beckoned to him to follow. Upholstered chairs with gold-painted woodwork sat at intervals along the hall. One of the open doors led into a substantial library, where three floors of books lined the walls.

Aiden waved toward the room with his hand. "Eladia Library."

At the end of the hall, two sweeping staircases led upstairs—one to the right and one to the left, curving around and joining the next landing. Will and Aiden climbed the stairs and walked along a corridor. Their footsteps were silent on the thick lilac carpet.

Aiden stopped at a door. "Your room."

The scents of cedar and sandalwood filled the air inside the room. Aiden pulled aside apple-green curtains, and light streamed across a quilt of patchwork leaves covering the bed. A detailed map of Eldrad filled the wall above a desk.

"You can see the gardens from your window," Aiden said. "The head gardener's pruning the roses. He's often pruning. You'll meet him tomorrow when you start your first journey."

"This place is mind-blowing," Will said. He wouldn't have missed it for anything. If only Mom could see it. If only she could be here with him.

"Now, it's time to wash and get dressed for dinner." Aiden threw the wardrobe open with a flourish. Inside were enough clothes to dress all the actors in a medieval-themed play.

Aiden whisked away Will's traveling clothes, muttering that they stank like a pigsty. Will washed and dressed in an outfit that made him feel like Legolas from Lord of the Rings.

***

Roland had been right about the dinner at the house. It was everything Will had imagined and more. Sophia ushered in the sizeable crowd that had followed her from the city. She'd changed into a rustling ivory gown covered with another sheer coat of the same color, and a band of gold on her head.

"Welcome, cherished sons and daughters of the King. Please enjoy his abundant provision and let us not forget to look forward to celebrating with him in our next life. It will greatly surpass our offerings here tonight. Let's thank the King and begin our feast, enjoying his presence in the company of family and friends."

Fine lace tablecloths covered the long U-shaped dinner table. The laden serving table took up a quarter of the room. "Roasts of meat from our local farms," Sophia announced, "soft and hard cheeses from our goat herds, platters of freshly picked vegetables from Wicklow, crisp salad greens from our garden, delicacies from Woodburn Forest. The seafood is from the Caelan Sea, and the fish from the crystal rivers of Mordrach Mountains."

Will wandered from one end of the serving table to the other, not sure where to start. He'd feast his eyes first, then his stomach He filled his plate to overflowing and when he'd finished, he needed to loosen his belt.

Sophia wandered around the tables, chatting to the guests, at ease and graceful. Something about her mesmerized him. Then the man sitting next to him nudged his arm. "The desserts have arrived." He pointed to the far end of the room.

Will went to investigate. A crystal candelabra lit with candles hung over the table of desserts. Two of the biggest vases of white flowers and greenery he'd ever seen rested on either side. The fruit platters could have covered a billiard table. Bowls of clotted cream, parfaits and custards filled crystal bowls. Jellies glistened in multi-colored jeweled layers.

"Why isn't the whole city eating here?" Will asked the man next to him at the table. "I heard Sophia inviting people in the street to dinner as we walked to the house. This is the best food I've ever seen. It's even better than Food Heaven at Idella."

"Ah, yes. Many don't hear Lady Wisdom's call because other things distract them. Many are too busy. Many think they already know the way they should go."

"Lady Wisdom? Is that her other name?"

"Yes, that's who she is—and more." He took a gleaming plate and a silver spoon for the dessert. "Only the wise ones who are searching for the truth will come. They are the ones who will receive the reward."

"I'm here to get the keys for the seven doors of the house," Will said. "Have you been inside the rooms?"

"I have."

"What were they like?"

The man stopped spooning berry mousse onto his plate and set it on the table. He stared nowhere in particular, as if reminiscing. "It's not something I can describe in mere words."

He stroked his beard and shook his head. "There's nothing like it. The entire experience was extraordinary."

***

The following morning, Will chose a light breakfast of oatmeal and sliced fruits in The Conservatory, a smaller area than the main dining room. He sat at a table looking over the garden, without eating. His stomach felt as if a swarm of bees had taken up residence.

"Not hungry?" Aiden called to him.

"Hardly. Still recovering from dinner last night." And he was nervous.

"But are you hungry for your adventures? Let me take you to meet the Head Gardener. He has the keys you need to enter each door."

Will followed him. "How long will I be inside the first room?"

"Every journey is different. Just as you are unique, so are the King's plans for you."

"Are the journeys difficult?"

"Some are.

"I'm here to find the truth of my life and why I'm here, on the island."

"May the journeys take you closer to the answer," Aiden said.

Chapter 24

The First Door

Will strolled into the gardens of the House. Dew still glistened on the lawn. A heavy scent of roses and lavender hung in the air. The fragrance reminded him of Granny Meg's cottage garden behind his house in Sanderson Street, and a pang of homesickness hit him in a rush.

The garden stretched into the distance. Clipped hedges hugged trees, fashioned like upended cones. Painted garden benches rested under shady trees, small arched bridges spanned water-lily-covered ponds, and soft rustling grasses and statues of various animals added to the effect.

Behind the towering columns of the house, a wide portico led to the doors. The seven doors were in various designs and crafted from different timbers, glass, or metal. The last door was timber, and half the height of the others.

"Welcome to our house and your next path of learning." The Head Gardener, dressed in overalls and a long leather apron, placed a bunch of roses into a wheelbarrow.

Will leaned down to smell the fragrance. "We have these in our garden at home."

The Head Gardener nodded and passed Will an iron ring of keys. The keys were of various sizes, but even the smallest was three times as large as the key to Will's house back at the bay. "Here are the seven keys to the seven doors."

"What should I expect from the journeys? Will I discover the truth?"

"You are already on the path to truth. Your next journeys will take you closer to a real understanding. But you'll be the one to decide how far you'll go on the truth journey and how abundant your destiny will be."

When Will reached the landing of the wide porch, he stroked the cold marble column. The First Door was actually two ornate wooden doors. When he pressed the key in the lock, firey words appeared on one of the doors. Astonished, he drew back to read them.

The honor of the King is the beginning of wisdom.

The doors swung open, and Will stepped into a huge entrance to a place like a museum and even bigger than an aircraft hangar. Apart from his echoing footsteps, it was so quiet he could hear his heart pounding in his head. He took a deep breath to calm his nerves. Ahead of him was a tower of multiple levels. Each story had many doors. An ornate skylight at the top streamed light into the building.

An angel as tall as a giant stood, waiting. The angel's eyes blazed red, and his skin was the color of burnished copper. Will bowed and clenched his teeth to control his jaw from a sudden tremor. The angel was awesome, but unsettling.

"Do not bow to me, young earthling. Only bow to the King of Kings."

Will straightened, but avoided the angel's fire eyes.

"You are on your path to wisdom," the angel said, "but you cannot discover this path without knowledge. Without the knowledge of who the King is, and without the honor of the King in your heart, you will not know him deeply or understand your destiny."

Will peered up at a high wall on his right hand side, engraved with text. "What are those words?"

"The words are the promises of the King."

"How many promises are there?"

"Thousands."

Will moved closer to the wall to read it.

For I know the plans I have for you, plans to prosper you and not to harm you, plans to give you a hope and a future. Reassurance spread through his mind. That's what he wanted.

The angel beckoned to him. "Come."

"Can I read more of the promises first?"

"They are all in The King's Book. You can read them whenever you want."

The angel led Will toward a hallway. "You have entered the ground floor of The First Door of the house, but there are many other doors on this particular journey. See the corridor ahead and above? I want you to choose one door to enter," the angel said.

"But I don't know what's inside them."

"Ask the King to direct you. He knows your interests and your heart's desire."

"So there's a different experience inside each room in the honor-of-the-King journey?" Will said as they walked along the corridor.

"Yes. But there's a limit to the time you spend here. It would take more than a lifetime to see all the places that each door leads to, and even longer to truly comprehend the greatness of the King."

Will wandered along further. Which door should he choose? He paused as he sensed a pull of interest toward one door. "I'll try this one."

"When we enter this room, hold tightly to me," the angel said. "Don't fear what you see. Marvel in it. It's what the King has made for us." The angel took his hand. The door opened onto a ledge.

Beyond it was—a black night.

Will's stomach contracted. In a split second, the angel pulled him out into the void. They dropped. The bungee jump at Valley Springs and his plummet at the Maddock

Stadium was nothing compared to this. Here they were in free-fall. No ground underneath. Falling, falling, falling. His organs were about to explode.

Then the terrifying descent slowed. The angel tugged at his hand, and they catapulted forward at breakneck speed. In a split second, they were rushing past a myriad of far-reaching galaxies. Will screamed, but there was no noise. They accelerated into a constellation of blinding planets and stars, dodging comets and asteroids. His eyeballs felt like they were plastered into the back of his skull.

Swirling galaxies were so close now that Will shouted with a mix of horror and awe. It was as if someone had transported him into a virtual reality cosmic computer game.

"Take me back. I'm going to die!" he yelled at the angel. But he glimpsed an ecstatic look on the angel's face. He wasn't listening.

Then the angel pointed to a stellar cloud in a pillar of gas and dust.

"I know it," Will called. "The Trifid Nebula."

"A stellar nursery full of embryonic stars." The angel's words whipped back at him.

They sped deeper into space, past exploding stars and ice planets, swirling supernovas, and gigantic galaxies. A massive star gushed fire at them with no heat. No sound. But Will's eardrums were close to bursting. His throat and stomach felt as if he'd swallowed an entire bag of dry ice. But if he was going to die, he should make the most of it.

"See Pismis-1." The angel pointed out a star to their left. "Look at the bright young star blowing a stellar bubble inside the nebula." They raced further into the black velvet, and then the angel slowed their pace to show him a place that looked like magical mountains from Lord of the Rings.

"That's the intensely turbulent Mystic Mountain in the Carina Nebula with its glowing colors. Did you know neutron stars can spin at a rate of over seven hundred rotations a second?"

Will stared at it all in astonishment.

"And here's the Messier 101 in Ursa Major. We are now twenty-three million light-years away from the Earthlands. An exquisite pinwheel galaxy flung its sparkling jeweled arms into the blackness, and something in the deep recesses of Will's mind shifted at the immensity of it all.

The angel tugged on his arm. "We must turn back now."

"No. I want to see more," Will called. His fear and discomfort had switched to wonder. "I don't want this to end."

The angel flashed his blazing eyes at him. "I can only show you a minute section of the universe the King has created. It would take many lifetimes to show it all to you."

The angel dragged him back through the dark cosmos. Will clamped his eyes to shut out the dizziness and nausea that was overcoming him from the extreme velocity. When he opened them, he could see the solar system in the distance, like the perfect miniature model hanging back in his old school lab. In the next breath, he was back in the passageway with the angel, outside the door they'd entered.

The floor swayed back and forth like the deck of a ship in a storm. His legs gave way, and he crumpled to the floor, panting. He peeled his tongue from the bottom of his mouth. "Was that t-trip for real?"

"Give yourself a minute to adjust," the angel said. "Your journey was an example—no human could survive those conditions. But one day, you will no longer have the limitations of the physical realm."

"How many stars are out there?"

"Only the King knows. There's around 70,000 million million million, and he knows every one, and calls each one by name."

The angel reached out his hand. "Now I must take you back to the garden."

The angel sang as they strolled toward The First Door. Will followed, enthralled by the sound. It was like a whole choir of astonishing harmonizing voices.

"Will we sing like that one day?"

"Oh yes—and much more," the angel said.

"Please don't take me back yet." Will's mind was spinning with astonishment . Why hadn't the others told him how phenomenal this place was?

Will paused at another door leading from the passageway. "What's inside this one?" If the angel hadn't been with him, he would have opened it himself.

"That's the door to the anatomy room. In that room you can observe a surgeon and this team operating on a patient. They teach the wonders of the human body. Do you know how many atoms and cells make up the average body?"

"Not exactly."

"One typical cell is a Lilliputian world and consists of ten million million atoms. The cell operates like a high-tech factory that is beyond a human's capacity to fully understand."

The door swung open, and a nurse in a white cap and uniform wheeled a trolley of rattling metal implements down the corridor.

"The body has seven octillion atoms, making up the 37 trillion cells in our body. Some can regenerate themselves over time. But your body is not designed to last forever. When the heart stops beating, human decomposition begins around four minutes after death. The good news is that in the supernatural world, your immortal body will last forever."

Will followed the angel back along the hall, but lagged. He pointed to another door. "What journey is inside here?"

The angel turned back. "It shows how your earth is uniquely designed for the existence of humans and your needs. There's no other place like the Earthlands in the entire cosmos. That journey is one of my favorites, but takes longer than you have time for."

"I'd like to see it."

The angel shook his head and beckoned for him to follow. "Your time here is over, but look forward to what you will learn on your next six journeys and in your life ahead."

"Above all, read the King's Word. It will instruct and teach you much you need to know. The more you read it, the more you will discover. Tomorrow you will enter The Second Door."

Chapter 25

The Second Door

Will woke the next morning, sprawled on his green-leaved quilt, exhausted but exhilarated. How could such an awesome King be interested in him? Everything he understood about life would be altered from now on. The journey inside The First Door had lifted him out of the ordinary, out of the triviality and into a new understanding.

After a quick breakfast, he pulled the ring of keys from his pocket and he strode out to the garden. He spoke to the Head Gardener on the way to the portico. "Is The Second Door like The First Door?"

"Every door will lead you to a different place," the Head Gardener said, pruning the hedge and cutting above a bud on each branch with precision. "From now on you may have two journeys when you enter each door, and some journeys may be in unexpected locations."

The man put down his secateurs and stared at him, his eyes clouded and sad. "May the King be with you in the next journey. May you have strength and courage, my son."

Will's gut clenched with unease at the gardener's words and expression. Heavy metal paneling decorated The Second Door. He placed the key into the lock. Four words lit up in fiery writing.

The Door of Love.

The door creaked open. As he stepped inside, a stifling hot wind swirled dust into his face. The door slammed closed behind him. A towering angel dressed in a sweeping robe and sandals stood waiting.

"You may hold my arm for comfort if you need to."

Will glanced at the angel and shook his head. "I'm fine."

The sky was simmering with gray clouds. Thunder rumbled all around them. The angel led the way up a narrow cobblestone road. People dressed in ankle-length clothes and sandals hurried past with panicked faces. Some herded sheep, while others carried loads of bread or dates. The potent mix of odors from dust, sweat, and animals overpowered Will's senses. Soldiers dressed in impressive armor and holding long spears marched through the streets with stern faces. The place reeked of fear.

This wasn't Eldrad. He'd been transported somewhere else, and no one was looking at the angel or him. Maybe they were invisible. Will dodged a cart and toppled. His vision dissolved into blackness.

***

When Will opened his eyes, he found himself lying on a hill overlooking flat buildings. He raised his head out of the dust and brushed away a swarm of flies buzzing around his face. A dark reddish stain pooled on the earth near his hand. The smell of death hung in the air, infusing his nose and throat. The atmosphere pressed down like a heavy blanket. Bleached skulls and human bones scattered over the earth nearby. A drawn-out wail echoed across the hill.

Foreboding bored into Will's very core. He'd read about this place in The King's Book, and it was the last place he wanted to be. There was only so much he could take. Nothing would convince him to look up. Of course, it would have to be part of his experience. Wasn't it the most important part of the King's book? Reading the story was one thing, but the physical and raw reality would be too much to bear.

He ground his teeth, swallowing back nausea. Perhaps he could escape. Go back through the town, back to the safety of the garden at the house. He rolled over and sat up, and then drew up his legs and pressed his forehead into his knees.

He brushed dust from his clothes to pass the time and plan his next move. But this was part of his journey. Going back wasn't an option. Will braced himself, turned his head and raised his eyes.

A man hung on a giant wooden sword, plunged into the ground.

Thick metal nails as long as fingers impaled the dead man's feet. It held them in an agonizing contortion. Red trickled from the ripped skin at the nail holes. Blood-smeared marks streaked the body above him. A seepage oozed from a gash in his flank. Flies swarmed around the torn skin.

The man's head had slumped. Hands nailed. Arms flung wide open.

In welcome.

It was the King.

An invisible fist reached into Will's chest and squeezed his heart. A tornado of emotion slammed into his consciousness. Another missing puzzle piece fell into place.

Did the King love him—that much?

He reached out and touched the man's feet and then lay under the corpse, ignoring the smell and the crawling flies. He remembered the stained glass image of this scene back at Granny Meg's funeral, four years ago. He could never understand why everyone talked so much about life when death was all around them. But now he knew what it meant. He would stay with the King and keep watch on the hill as long as he could. But finally sleep overcame him.

When he woke, the wooden stake and body had gone. The angel in the robe bent over him, his face shining. "He died, but now he lives again. You'll be with him when it's your time."

"I know," Will said. This would be a place he would come back to in his thoughts. Whenever he doubted. Whenever he needed the King.

This story had the best ending of all stories.

***

Will staggered back through the town with the angel. The overcast sky threw a gloomy pall, although still daytime.

The ground rumbled and shook. Upturned stones lay on the road, and fearful expressions painted the faces of the people who hurried through the streets.

The angel took him into a corridor of an ochre-colored building. "You haven't finished this journey yet. You must take the next one alone," he said, pointing down a dark passage.

The passage had no doors and no windows, only lamps on the walls. Will continued until he came to rough-hewn double doors with a tree trunk on either side, like the Doors of Durin from the Lord of the Rings. He pulled on the round iron handle and stepped into a rustling forest.

Mystified, he followed the path through the trees, still engulfed in emotion and still overwhelmed by the experience on the hill. He rested on a mossy rock to eat a slice of bread he'd stuffed in his pocket from breakfast, then continued down the track.

An anguished cry followed by moaning interrupted Will's thoughts. He hesitated. The sounds came from the woods to his left. With a tight throat, he pushed through the bushes and gasped.

Flack, the Craver, lay writhing on the ground. The trunk of a young oak pinned his lower legs. The man looked up at Will with glazed eyes, his black gums and tooth stumps bared in distress. Will reacted with a conflict of feelings.

He should leave Flack to rot. The Craver was helpless at the moment, but if released, he could attack. And what if Striker was nearby?

A pang of pity pushed the thoughts aside. He was a King follower now, and he should love his enemies. He sighed. "I'll lift the log off your legs, Flack."

Flack moaned and closed his eyes. Will heaved and pulled without success. The trunk was heavier than he expected. Splinters pierced his hands. "Have to try something else, mate."

"Hurry." Flack's head rolled back and forth, his eyes wild now. Saliva foamed around his lips.

Will found a small log and pushed it in the space between Flack's legs and the fallen trunk. With one push, he levered and rolled the weight off the man's shins. Flack lay still while Will checked his scrawny legs. No sign of broken bones.

"Can you walk?"

Flack growled and rolled over. Will tried to help him up, but Flack pushed him away. Instead, the Craver crawled to the stump of the broken tree and used it to pull himself upright.

He hobbled through the trees without turning back.

Will stood gaping as the man disappeared into the forest, stupefied at his own lack of anger, and dumbfounded at how much he cared about the guy.

He turned back and retraced his footsteps to the double tree-trunk doors. This time, the dark passage led straight to The Second Door and out into the garden of the house.

His second journey was over.

Chapter 26

The Third Door

Will rose early, but exhausted from his experience the day before. Today he'd enter The Third Door. Aiden had already told him it was The Door of Truth. This would have to be the door of all doors for him. This was the door that would show him why he was on the island, and show him the truth of his life. He rushed his breakfast and strode outside into the early rays of sun. Fresh drops of dew glittered on the grass. Will waved to the Head Gardener, who was still pruning the never-ending beds of rose bushes.

"Don't you ever tire of pruning?"

"I sometimes find it painful, despite my gloves." The man chuckled, then removed a glove to show Will several thorn scars. "But it's an essential job, and we look forward to seeing the results when the bushes yield abundant blooms."

Will strolled to The Third Door, which was built with a cypress wood frame and inlaid with glass. It displayed etched images of trees bordering a river. As Will unlocked the door, the words "The Door of Truth" burned their fire.

He entered. An apple orchard with rows of trees loaded with ripe fruit stretched to low hills in the distance. An apple scent filled the grove. Groups of pickers, some on ladders, and some singing, plucked fruit and placed them in baskets. A girl with a mass of curls and a pink dress with a ruffled edge lay under a tree, reading a book. She reminded him of an illustration in his old *Alice in Wonderland* book.

"What are you reading?" he asked.

"The King's Word, the last chapter."

"So you've nearly finished the book?"

"Oh, no." She laughed. "You never finish this book." She closed it, jumped up, and shook the trunk of the tree. Several apples fell to the ground, and one landed on Will's head.

"Hey!" He hollered as he ducked the falling fruit.

She stopped shaking the trunk and reached up to a large branch and shook it. More apples fell on the grass. He leaped further away from the tree. "What are you doing?"

She took a small branch and shook again, reaching for her basket underneath to catch the falling apples. "Would you like one?" She threw it to him. He crunched into the white flesh, savoring the sweetness, but kept his distance. She put the basket on the grass and pulled down a twig, then examined each leaf, including the underside.

She sat down and picked up the book again. "A great man once said that studying this book is like examining a tree. First, you shake the trunk, then you shake the limb, then you shake the twig, after that you examine every leaf.

She patted the ground next to her. "There's no book in the Earthlands like this one. Its meaning is a deep treasure of truth waiting to be discovered."

He hesitated for a moment, then joined her. "How do you discover its meaning and find the truth?"

She flicked through the book and read:

"'Consider carefully what you hear, with the measure you use, it will be measured to you—and even more.'" She closed the book and walked away with her basket of fruit.

He chewed on the apple. How was this going to help him find the truth? He picked up the book, flipped it open, and his eyes alighted on the words:

'I am the way, the truth and the life.'

Did this mean the King was the truth? It was a puzzle that would take time and thought to solve. Will looked around, disappointed there wasn't an easier answer.

The workers in the apple orchard left, and he returned to the entrance door. Instead of etched glass, there was now a tall wooden door with a heavy latch and a knocker like a miniature anchor. He swung around, disoriented.

Then he remembered that the Head Gardener said he may have two journeys once he entered the door. Perhaps it wasn't time for him to leave yet. Baffled, he reached for the anchor, but the door opened and a woman stood in the gray-walled foyer.

Sophia.

"Walk with me, William of Aporto Bay." She swished down the hall in a dress the colors of the ocean, then led him into a room. Four paintings of sailing ships hung on one wall, and various wooden oars hung on another. A glass cabinet with shells and sponges stood in one corner, next to an aquarium. A round mat with the image of a compass on it covered most of the flagstone floor.

She turned to him. "Will, tell me, what is your desire?"

Will hesitated, not sure how to answer. "Many things."

"Everyone longs for something," she said. "Some want meaning and significance, others want power and wealth, or that special person in their life. They might want endless pleasure or a way to dull their pain—the list goes on."

Will stared at a long wooden boat suspended from the ceiling by chains Would he ever find fulfilment? What if he wanted all those things?

"Desire is the deepest emotion of the human heart," she said. "It fuels a search for the life we prize and our destiny. We must all take the journey to find it. Sadly, some drink from the wrong source, while others get distracted by unimportant things. Others even crush their soul's longing."

Will ran his hand around the smooth circular shape of a ship's helm hanging on the wall. "When I found myself on this island, I had cravings for certain things, and I wanted to get home and get revenge on my father and Ben. That's not as important anymore because the King is part of my life. Now I want to take the path to the truth and to be happy. I still have cravings—but they've lessened—and there's a girl . . . I want."

"Sounds as though the truth is already having an impact." She gave him a Mona Lisa smile. "There's only one thing that will truly fulfill you. It's the real wellspring of life. If you find the desire you were made for, your life will be transformed. This is the truth." She walked to one of the porthole-shaped windows and beckoned for him to look outside.

Fishing boats tied up at long jetties, bobbed in the green water. Men shouted instructions to one another as they labored with barrels of squirming fish. A line of motionless ships languished on the horizon.

"The Port of Eladia and the picturesque Caelan Sea." She settled on a window seat under the porthole window and beckoned to him. "Come, I'll tell you a story."

"Once upon a time there was a Sea King. He ruled a glorious and powerful kingdom with vast oceans and verdant islands. He loved to survey his kingdom every day and admire its magnificence, but he longed for company. He wanted a family to love—a family of his own, to share his kingdom and riches."

"How did he do that?"

"With much planning and labor, the Sea King created a sea family in his own image, and he loved every single one—as one loves their own child. He gave each creature a special characteristic. Can you guess what it was?"

Will went to the aquarium and stared at the vibrant coral and jeweled fish dashing through the water in darts of silver. "Unique gifts?"

"Yes, but that's not the answer to this question. When he created each creature, he put a little of the seawater from his kingdom into each one."

"Why would he do that?"

"It gave them a thirst for their father, the Sea King, and his kingdom. If they strayed and lost contact with him, they would keep searching for that feeling of love and belonging only he could provide. Their desires for the things and experiences outside his realm never fully satisfied." She took a basket of shells from the floor and sorted through them, putting some aside. "They became homesick."

"So they found their satisfaction in being with him," Will said. "I'm beginning to understand this—as a King follower."

"If you thirst for the King and his realm, you will find what you long for. Will, you can take the things you need from the Earthlands, but don't let them possess you." She smiled at him. "You were made for another world."

Will swallowed. "You mean Earth and Eldrad aren't my real worlds?"

"That's correct. Your earth world and the Island of Eldrad, or the Earthlands as we call them, are temporary places in your forever life. They are where you prepare for your destiny and life in the King's realm now and in the future. You are in your testing ground right now. Your crucible.

"You're saying my experiences are life lessons? And that difficulties are a natural part of it?"

She nodded. "How can you function in your high calling as a royal subject of the King without training, without hardship, to hone your abilities?" She took her choice of shells from the basket, went to the cabinet and placed them on one of the glass shelves inside. "How can you help others in the world now and the world to come, without experience and understanding?"

Will yanked at a frayed edge on his coat. "But sometimes the suffering is too much."

"Do you remember how much the King has suffered for you?"

Will sighed. "True."

"You may expect perfection in life, but you can't understand and appreciate perfection if you've never experienced imperfection."

She closed the glass cabinet with a rattle. "This journey of truth is over for now. But have your heart open and ready to receive truth's gifts, which will be offered to you. Always."

She led him back to the hallway and took him outside to the Port of Eladia and the Caelan Sea. The bright afternoon sun streamed down, and a stiff sea breeze gusted around them. "Let's walk back to the House together and on the way I'll show you the wonderful sights of the Eladia Port shoreline."

Chapter 27

The Fourth Door

It was time for Will to enter The Fourth Door. Will's experiences on his truth journey had been thought-provoking yet perplexing. But it enabled him to place more pieces onto the jigsaw puzzle of his life. He was sure as he read the King's words and made a conscious decision to include the King more in his life he would progress further in his quest.

The Fourth Door had a meticulous wooden inlay of Celtic knot-shapes. When he turned the key labelled with the number four into the keylock, the words *The Peace Door* lit up in a blaze.

A swarthy man with leathery skin and a dark gray overshirt stood waiting for him inside. The man took two swords from a table near an ivy-covered wall and threw one to him. "Let me see what ye are made of." He faced Will with his sword and parried.

Will's heart raced as he dodged and ducked the oncoming attack. He wasn't expecting this. The area filled with the sound of clashing of steel blades. Will blundered, and the man soon had the point of his sword at Will's heart. He pressed in until the point dug into his skin.

Will stepped backwards with one hand up. "You have an unfair advantage. The last time I sparred with a sword was in the backyard with my friend Rob using a fake plastic one."

The man laughed, placed the swords back on the bench, and held out his hand.

"I'm Cadwyn, Will. Haven't seen ye since Wyld Wood."

Will stared at the familiar heavy eyebrows and wide set eyes. "

"So you were the masked man who rescued me from the altar?"

"Aye," Cadwyn said.

"I owe you a heartfelt thank you." Will rubbed his hand around the skin on his throat. The incident in Wyld Wood came into his thoughts too often. "Why would we spar with a sword on a Peace journey?"

"Just testing yer mettle, and I wanted to prepare ye for your next lesson. Sometimes ye have to fight for peace. Peace, like the truth, has many facets. There's a peace with and in ye, and a peace with others. Most importantly, there is peace with the King. Being a peacemaker is another aspect—but ye can't be a true peacemaker if ye are beset by turmoil and troubles yourself. I'm here to show ye how to have peace, even amid the trials of life."

"I'd like to see that," Will said in a dubious tone.

"Jadyn told me ye would like to see how a sword is made. I'll show ye how the making of a sword is like the making of a life."

"Cool."

"Come and visit my Eladia Forge. It's larger than the one near Shannon. We'll have to leave the House and walk an hour to reach it."

***

Will followed Cadwyn along a damp passageway. Cadwyn chatted about Caves Hill, Jadyn, and the village fairs. Will grinned to himself. Swords in a peace lesson? What next? Each lesson had been so unpredictable.

"Why do you think I'm on this island, and what do you think the truth of my life is?" Will asked.

"I'll tell ye one reason you're on the island, soon, but not on this visit. And aye, ye will learn something today that will help you understand the truth of your life."

They arrived at a cave similar to the one at the forge, but more spacious. Cadwyn took two leather aprons from hooks on the wall. "Ye should make yourself comfortable while I start the preparations." He pointed to a fur-covered bench.

"How many swords have you made in your lifetime, Cadwyn?"

"Many. I'll call on ye when I need help. I don't mind company."

Cadwyn walked to a barrel, picked out several bars of metal, and placed them together. "I heat the metal, then knock it into shape. It's called drawing out the sword. It lengthens and narrows it."

He compressed his lips with concentration and repeatedly heated and hammered the metal, sweating profusely. Sometimes he warmed and cooled it.

"Why didn't you hammer it this time?" Will asked, pressing closer.

"To make it strong and flexible enough." Cadwyn held up the metal and examined it.

"Have ye been in the fiery forge of life, Will?"

"I guess."

"We all have. It's painful, but if we have the right attitude, it can produce a fine result. We use fire, water, and pressure to make a sword. The King allows the process of hardship to refine us, to transform our weaknesses into strengths, our rigidity into flexibility."

Cadwyn smiled as he held the unfinished blade toward the fire's light. The crisscross of wrinkles on his face was the texture of the tan leather covers on the oak tables. "Aye, it's good. Now it's time to for tea."

Cadwyn made a pot of tea. The wooden board with strips of cheeses, dark berry jam, and crusty cornbread made Will's mouth water. It had been a long time since he'd eaten. Cadwyn threw a rug on the floor of the cavern and Will put the platter of food on it.

"If ye submit to the refinement of the King, he'll forge ye into the tempered steel of a true warrior, so ye are ready for responsibilities as a son of the King."

"Sounds painful." Will piled a slice of bread with the sticky jam and cheese.

"Aye. We live in a world overtaken by evil, but he can turn the bad into good. Remember—we aren't meant to fight battles on our own. The King is here to help."

"How does he help us?" Will rubbed at the scars on his forehead.

"All ye have to do is ask. You could let the hardship overwhelm ye, or ye could allow it to transform ye." Cadwyn smoothed his hand along the length of the weapon. "Next, I'll heat the sword again, then cool it gradually for its annealing, so it's soft enough to grind."

"Can I help with the grinding?"

"Perhaps. There's something I need to talk to you about, Will. Our plans to overthrow the government will be soon. We'll be calling on your help. We're hoping Jadyn Reeve will temporarily take the place of the President until things settle down."

"Jadyn? Do you mean Jadyn from Caves Hill? How could he be a president?

"Did ye know his father was our former President, Alexander Reeve? I worked with him at the palace until Lorn had him eliminated."

Will shook his head, dumbfounded. "He never told me. Isn't Jadyn too young? Would people think him capable enough?"

"Most know Jadyn. He has the integrity, the energy, and an understanding of Nevara matters. He can lead in the interim until the island is in a position to vote."

Will's thoughts reeled. What a dark horse Jadyn had been. "So where's the President's wife, Michelia? Did you know her when you lived at Nevara?"

"Aye. A most unusual woman, and one who had significant influence over the President. No one has seen her for years. Now have some rest."

Will sprawled on a rug laid out on the floor. He dozed, dreaming dark dreams of the president's wife. She flapped black wings, and screeched at him and Jadyn, with raven eyes, and menaced them with pointed claws. He recoiled as a hand gripped his shoulder.

"It's time for the grinding, Will."

Will threw off the coarse, gray blanket Cadwyn had thrown over him and stretched, wondering about the dream. "When will the sword be finished?"

"Quite a few more steps yet. Come and try the grinding. Ye use the wee grinder to make the edge and point of the blade."

Will gripped the heavy sword, savoring the cold metal. Then he followed Cadwyn's actions.

"Nae. Use yer body weight." Cadwyn demonstrated.

Will kept trying, but the weapon slipped and clanged on the stone floor.

"Aargh." Will picked up the sword and handed it to Cadwyn. "So the King causes our suffering?"

"We experience it because of the evil in our world, but the King has an uncanny ability to use the bad for good. If we depend on him, it's during hardship that a hero is made."

"I still don't understand why we aren't created perfect in the first place?"

"Ye are asking why the King didn't create us as puppets with no free will?"

Will hesitated. He couldn't think of an answer.

Cadwyn finished the grinding with his face set in concentration, and then gave a satisfied sigh. "The sword is ready for the hardening and tempering."

"I didn't know the process took so long."

"Next we'll heat the sword to a high temperature." Cadwyn placed the sword over the flame until it turned a hot blue-purple color. "Superb," he said, in a hushed tone. He plunged the sword into a container of liquid. Steam rose, and the liquid splattered and hissed. "The quenching will cool it fast and evenly, and harden the metal. Then there's more hammering, heating, and quenching."

Will craned his neck and moved closer as Cadwyn explained the process. "This makes the blade strong but not too brittle, and it's sharp but just flexible enough. Like we should be after some tempering."

Finally, he placed the blade of the sword on a bench and tidied his tools. "It's late. We'll sleep now. Tomorrow we'll crown the sword with the pommel, the guard, and the hilt."

***

Will woke to the smell of cornbread, toasted at the fire, and steaming tea. His mind reeled with disorientation after the long period in the forge.

"What time is it?"

"Around five in the morning, I would say. Time has no meaning when one is creating." Cadwyn polished the blade until it shone like a flaming arrow.

While he waited, Will read the words carved into the stained rock face wall nearby. *When you walk through the fire, you shall not be burned; the flame will not set you ablaze.*

"The King's words." Cadwyn pushed the sword into a sheath and handed it to him. Will eased the blade out of the casing, savoring the metallic notes. He tested its weight. Will chuckled. Mitch would say this was the coolest thing in the world if he was here.

"Now it's time to hand ye back to the Counselor." Cadwyn took the sword and pointed with it at the entrance to the passageway. The Counselor stood waiting, his eyes wide with interest. Will greeted him and shook Cadwyn's hand in farewell, but the man pulled him into an embrace.

"So is this all I have to learn about peace?" Will asked them.

"Let's walk back together and have a chat," the Counselor said. "What did you think of the sword making?"

"Riveting. I wish I could take one back to the bay and show my friends."

The Counselor lit the way with a flare. "Remember—the King's sword, not an earthly sword, is the one to covet. The most important battles have been and will be won, not with an earth sword but with the King's sword. What you have learned today will bring you another step closer to the truth."

***

Will and the Counselor arrived back at the ivy-covered wall opposite the Peace Door.

"Come into the house." The Counselor led Will to the lounge room of a country house. Soft music from a piano tinkled in another room, and snug couches hugged the walls. Expansive windows overlooked drifts of lavender and daisies. Subtle green hues blanketed distant hills. It was such a contrast to the stark Eladia forge.

"How do you feel toward your Father and Ben now you've had time to ponder your life?"

"I've tried to forgive them. But I have my moments of weakness."

"It is a difficult task." The Counselor beckoned to Will to sit with him. "Sometimes you have to forgive again and again. Unforgiveness hurts you more than the person you have anger toward. Forgiveness is a process. And forgiveness doesn't always mean you need to be close to that person if it's damaging to do so. Your rescue of Flack was a great demonstration of how far you've come on your journey."

"I'm not sure how I'd go if I came across Flack in a less compromised situation."

"Yes. You need the wisdom to make the right choices." The Counselor poured lemon juice from a jug into two glasses and passed one to Will.

"I know it's hard for you to have peace in your life at the moment," the Counselor continued. "You've been taken from your home, thrust into an unfamiliar place, and you can't make firm plans. But see it as an opportunity to grow in perseverance, maturity, and trust in me."

Will walked to the window and looked out at the vista. "Are these the King's words?"

"The King and I are always in agreement. Give me that heavy load of worries you carry—your uncertainties about Eleonora, the President, Ben, and why you are here on the Island of Eldrad. If you look at your problems for too long, you may sink under them. Choose the worry-free way."

"Ha," Will said, "I'd love to get rid of the troubles in my life. I'm not sure I can stick to remembering to give them all to you. Mom always called me a worrier—but I'll try."

As Will walked back out into the garden, he was sure of one thing. It was more than a random coincidence he was on this island.

Chapter 28

The Fifth Door

The following morning Will woke late, his body aching with tiredness and longing for Eleonora. A tray of tea and fresh fruits lay on his desk. Aiden knocked on his door and stuck his head in.

"Are you ready for the next door?"

Will nodded, grabbed his coat and a plum to eat on the way.

He took a detour past a splashing fountain that surrounded a circular bed of low shrubs in lilac and silver-green. The orange scent from the murrayas reminded him of the hedge he trimmed back at home. He took the ring of keys out of his pocket and flicked them around until he found the fifth one.

The Fifth Door featured ornate silver scrolls of ironwork attached over wood. He placed the key in the lock.

The words on the door appeared in fire on the wood behind the silverwork.

The Door of Humility.

Will's heart sank. Humility wasn't a trait he coveted. It was a weakness and a cop-out. He turned the key in the door, but it wouldn't open. He turned the key again. Nothing happened. He twisted the key the other way and jiggled it. Still the door remained closed. Embarrassed, he turned to check if anyone was watching, then laughed. His pride had already surfaced. He tried again, and the door flew open.

It opened into a long and empty ballroom with a polished parquet floor, which reflected the many chandeliers, creating the illusion of a sparkling pond. Soft orchestral music filled the room.

No one was around, so he waltzed out onto the shining floor, pretending he was back at the bay at a college ball. He would have missed the end-of-year ball. What a bummer. He imagined he held Eleonora in his arms, twirling her around the floor in abandon, while Ben glared from the sidelines. Jealous and alone.

Will paused when a flamboyant figure swept across the floor toward him. He wore a high turban and a flowing tunic over ballooning pants in bright orange and purple. Will gaped.

"William Sutherland. I've been looking forward to meeting you. Welcome to our adventure."

"Who are you?"

The man strutted toward him in a sashay, bowed and then spoke.

> "I am here, at your disposal,
> Smart and rich, with a proposal.
> I am yours, I am the way,
> Will show you riches come what may.
>
> I am your extravaganza,
> Will make you first, I'll give you power.
> I'm never weak, and never humble.
> You can guess, I never crumble.
>
> Narcissism is the fashion,
> I lead the way.
> I have the passion."

"Tempting." Will smirked. "Yeah. I like the idea of riches and power, but I'm supposed to be here to learn humility."

"But I have strategies." The man took Will's arm and twirled him around on the floor. "I'll teach you how to maneuver and win. Show your rivals you're the boss. Crush your enemies. The winner takes all."

"I'll have to decline your proposal," Will said. The guy was laughable.

The man stepped away with eyebrows raised and stomped back across the ballroom floor with a flourish of his loose sleeves. The fabric of his outfit flapped against his body with each step.

The Counselor entered from another door, chuckling. "I thought you might like some entertainment before we get to more serious matters. I noticed you had doubts about humility when you arrived. Come with me and tell me about it."

They strolled across the floor toward a row of white carved wooden chairs with cloth seats. "Humility isn't a characteristic I admire," Will said. "Why shouldn't I have pride in what I do? Surely, as the King's ambassador, I should be proud."

"Of course, but we are talking of a different humility. Did you know that true humility needs courage? It's not timidity. True humility means you're willing to take a lower place than you're entitled. True humility allows you to bear insults for a higher purpose."

The Counselor turned to him. "It doesn't make you think less of yourself. It makes you think of yourself less."

Will sat on a chair. "I'm still not convinced. If I ever get back to the bay, there's no way I'll be groveling to the Maddocks. I'm not as consumed by revenge as I was, and I'm not planning to trash Ben's Ferrari anymore—but if he antagonized me again . . . " Will kicked the leg of the chair. "How does a lesson in humility help me answer my questions? How does it explain why I'm here on the island?"

"Let's walk back to the main house together," the Counselor said. "There's something I want you to see.

They strolled through the garden in silence, towards the grand entrance and into the carpeted hall of portraits.

"The King's people are strong because they don't give in to earthly pressures. They don't take advantage of others or react forcefully. They trust the King to work everything for good and are at peace in their lives."

The Counselor stood in front of a portrait of a small, frail woman hunched over a walking stick. "See this woman, disabled from birth? Some people regarded her as a nobody, useless in society. But she enriched and transformed many lives because of her petitions to the King, not only for those she loved, but also for those who abused her."

The Counselor pointed at the other portraits. "See all these people? They are only a small selection of King's followers who made a substantial difference to the Earthlands. Some were important leaders, and others were quiet workers few had the privilege to meet. They were courageous, passionate, and hardworking—and what other characteristic did they all have?"

"Humility?"

"Yes. Without humility in ourselves, we can't show true respect to others. Think of all the leaders or acquaintances you trust and esteem the most on your earth. What characteristic do they all have?"

Will thought back to the people he'd admired most in his life: Granny Meg, some of his teachers, his best friend Rob, and Rob's father, his scout leader.

"Humility, I guess."

"You've taken this journey because you'll need what you have learned today in your future life," the Counselor said.

Will headed back to his room, thoughtful. So this was part of the truth? The truth was more complex than he'd thought. Humility was the better way. But when the time came, would he put it into practice—or not?

Chapter 29

The Sixth Door

Will walked to The Sixth Door with a mix of anticipation and sadness. His journeys were almost over. After this door, only one door remained. The Sixth Door was constructed of light paneled wood with a clear crystal door handle. He placed the key in the lock and writing appeared in fire.

The Door of Purity.

Will's stomach plummeted. He snatched the key out of the lock and hurried into the garden. He didn't want any lessons on purity. It had been different for the other doors. He'd found them all worthwhile. Even the Door of Humility had been okay, but this one? No. Purity. The very word made him recoil.

He walked down the lengthy, tree-lined driveway of the house and headed into the city streets towards the markets.

Now would be an opportunity to have a look around. He also needed a drink. It had been too long since he had one.

Carpets flapped in the breeze, and earthenware pots tottered on makeshift shelves, clothing and boots spilled from stalls onto the road.

"Quality silks, lapis lazuli, jewelry, and spices!"

A woman rushed to him and hung a cloth bag over his shoulder. "All double sewn with soft leather trim," she said in a crooning tone.

He waved her away and ambled past racks of goods and tethered animals for sale. Tortoises paddled in water-filled bowls, and baby mirrens scurried around in cages. Piglets tied to table legs, sniffed for food. He dodged a variety of strong smelling animal droppings and also a group of Cravers prowling along the road. He slipped behind a stall until the group passed. The old ache in his shoulder and ribs was enough of a reminder to avoid them.

He arrived at a T-section. Two people waited at the entrance of each road. A man sat in a chair on the pavement at the left-hand junction. One sleeve hung slack and empty by his side. A burn injury had scarred and deformed one side of his face and neck. Will turned his face away in case his expression showed discomfort.

On the right-hand side of the junction, a woman with wavy, light brown hair called to him. He stared in surprise. "Carly, what are you doing here?"

"Waiting for you," she said, spinning around in a top which revealed her hourglass figure and short fringed skirt. "Like my new outfit?"

"Not bad." She had always looked alluring.

"Come and see the girls," she said. "It's been too long."

He followed her down the street. Maddy, Bea, Kitty, Carmel, and others. He knew them all. They were on his computer back at the bay.

They gathered around him, giggling.

"Where've you been, Will?

"Choose me, Will. You won't be disappointed."

Tempting. He'd love to spend time with them. Yes, it had been so long. But he thought of Eleonora. She was the one he wanted. Anyway, they weren't actually real, but he knew enough now to understand that staying with them was a mistake that would lead to his downfall.

"Girls, I'm sorry. Took the wrong street."

"But this is the best way." Bea flung off her coat to reveal the ample expanse of her breasts.

"You know you want to stay." Carmel grabbed him.

He wrenched himself away and turned back to the main road. They all pleaded with him to turn back. It was weird that they'd turned up here—in Eldrad.

The disabled man was still sitting on the chair at the entrance to the other street.

"Where do you live?" Will asked the man.

The man gestured with his head. "Down the alley. I'm Sol. Why don't you come and see?"

Will followed Sol into a sheltered lane with a row of white and blue painted buildings on both sides. People with various disabilities sat on the pavement. Will's heart wrenched at the sight. One couple stared at the road and took no notice of him. Others worked on crafts and chatted. Sol introduced some of them: Orik, Ryla, John, Brent, Fleur, Desi and a small boy called Tobin. Tobin's hair and eyebrows were snow-white, and his legs hung from his chair, wasted and deformed.

The blind woman, Ryla, reached out to him. "Let me feel your face," she said.

Will hesitated. It was the last thing he wanted. But he couldn't say no. He leaned over and took her smooth hands up to his face, and she caressed his cheeks and hair.

"Where do you all live?" he asked.

"We all have a place to live here," Sutton said. "Aiden from the House makes sure of that. Why don't you stay with us until dinner."

"Do you like dragon stories?" Will asked Tobin, who looked around Felix's age. He pulled up a stool next to the boy. "Did you know that once there was a fierce red dragon which was so small it could fit in a pocket?"

The boy's jaw dropped, his eyes as big as saucers in his tiny face. Will pulled out the miniature wooden dragon Felix had given him and pressed it into Tobin's hand. Will told him his best dragon stories, and many of the others drew closer to hear them.

It was soon early evening. Two men brought platters of food for dinner and Will helped hand around the bowls and fed the people who needed help. After dinner, Will said his farewells. Tobin thrust the wooden dragon toward him with soulful eyes.

"It's yours, Tobin."

As he strolled back to the House, an inexplicable happiness soaked deep, filling him to the brim. He'd got through the day without a drink. And he had an idea.

***

Will skipped breakfast and wandered into the garden. The reasons he couldn't enter the Purity Door came flooding back. He'd started to forget the temptations he had back at the bay until he met Carly and the others again. Without technology and his phone, he'd been distanced from his sexual cravings. But should he opt out now? He'd disappoint the Counselor and Roland if he missed a door.

He stood at the sixth column, leaning his heated face on the cold marble. Only two doors left. He had no right to enter the purity door. He gripped the keys in his pocket, gritted his teeth, and forced himself to unlock it.

Inside was a shady woodland clearing, with two paths with two signs pointing down a fine gravel track. One path led to the left and one to the right, with a stone bench in between. One sign displayed the words 'The King's Way', and the other 'My Way'.

It was no easy decision. This experience was by far the biggest stumbling block on his journey. What did being pure mean for him? He'd have to be strong against any temptations the Dark Prince put in his path. He wasn't sure he could commit to purity in his state of mind. He sat hunched on the stone bench. The footsteps of the Counselor crunched on the fine gravel, and he joined Will.

Will heaved a sigh. "What is purity, anyway?"

"It's from the Greek word *katharos*, which means inner moral cleanliness in all areas of your life, including lying, stealing, and hurting others."

"That's a tough call. How can anyone manage that?"

"Don't despair. Everyone has challenges in different aspects of their lives. You can ask for help."

"I know I shouldn't say this, but what's in it for me?"

"Ha. There are many advantages. You'll be less likely to stray onto the destructive path the evil one has planned for you. Immorality can corrupt character. The corruption will filter down into your life and others around you and all you touch. Morality is part of the very nature of the King. Purity will enable you to see the King more clearly."

"If I take this path, I'm not sure I can keep on it. I have my weaknesses."

The Counselor turned to him. "I understand your dilemma. Passion and sex are both good gifts from the King—but for the right time and in the right context. Sometimes you need to wait. Holding back gratification is a sign of maturity."

Will rubbed his forehead. "I did something back at the bay. Spud told me about a new internet site 'Core Passion'. I couldn't sleep, so I threw on my dressing gown, opened the laptop, and had a look."

Will gripped the stone seat. "I glued my eyes to the screen. I gorged on everything I saw. Then I heard a car door slam next door. My neighbor was leaving for his early shift at four in the morning. I'd been watching for hours."

Will stood up and paced the gravel pathway, then hit his forehead against the nearest tree trunk. "The stuff I viewed was like a black oil slick mixed with cheap sequins. It's still sitting in the back of my mind, and it left me craving to see more. At times, I gave in." He laughed without smiling.

"The Dark Prince wants us to believe we'll never move on from our human weaknesses, our failures and the consequences," the Counselor said. "This is a lie. But it's an effective strategy, because it distracts us from experiencing the grace of the King."

Will knew the Counselor well enough to trust what he said. The tension in his body eased. The Counselor made him feel safe and whole.

"Then I guess I'll choose the King's way."

"Would you like to bathe in the Spring of Purity?" the Counselor asked. "It will give you time to meditate on your choice."

Will nodded, and the Counselor led him along a stone path to a grotto.

"Yes, another cave. This time with a hot spring." They both laughed. Two people already floated in the clear pool toward the rear of a subterranean cavern. Steam drifted from the surface into the cool air above. Will took off his outer clothes and entered the crystal pool. He lowered himself into the tepid water to his shoulders. It enveloped him like a balm.

"Will, your level of morality is not your identity." The Counselor's voice resonated softly in the grotto. "Your identity is that you are a much loved son of the King. May you be cleansed and purified."

Will slicked the water from his hair and sat on the rocky edge of the spring while he dried. Then he climbed the stone steps and sprinted along the path toward the front door. The streaming sunshine and the Counselor's promises rejuvenated him.

He had a brand new start.

***

The Seventh Door

Aiden greeted Will the next morning with a somber face. "I need to see you in my office after breakfast. The butler will bring you."

An hour later, Will walked with the butler through the hall, disquiet clouding his thoughts because of Aiden's expression. He still had The Seventh Door to enter—the intriguing low door.

Aiden's office was the most crowded room he'd seen in the mansion. Yellowed maps, a stuffed owl, and family portraits cluttered every available surface. Patterned boxes and books buried the velvet sofa.

"How have you found your journeys so far, my son?"

"Mind-boggling, to tell you the truth."

"And they are just a small part of your journey in life. There will be others, in keeping with your growth and your progress."

"I still have one door left," Will said.

Aiden pushed aside the china cups on his desk, and drew out two chairs. "You won't enter that door."

"Why not?"

Aiden's brow furrowed. "It's not your time."

"What do you mean?"

"You had a visitor yesterday." Aiden unfolded a small piece of paper.

"A visitor?" Will raised his eyebrows.

"A carrier pigeon from Shannon village. It brought a message." He passed the scrap of paper to Will.

Will's gut tightened as he read the neat writing.

Greetings from Caves Hill.
Roland is injured and very sick. Please tell Will.
Eleonora.

Will gripped the handles of his chair. "I must leave."

Will packed and said his farewells to Sophia, the Head Gardener, Aiden, and the other people he'd got to know at the house. But before he left, he had two more questions for Aiden.

"What is behind The Seventh Door?"

"The journey of trials," Aiden said.

"If I miss that door, does that mean I won't have trials?"

Aiden stroked his short beard and shook his head. "No. Your journey of trials will start soon. May the King go with you."

Will frowned. It wasn't the best news. "There's one more thing I need to ask of you."

Aiden nodded.

Will took twelve large gold coins from the pouch hanging from his belt and tipped them onto Aiden's desk. He put three coins back in the pouch for the trip home. "This is for Sol and his friends. Could you ask the Head Gardener if he could plant a garden and shady trees for the end of their street?"

Aiden beamed at him. "Why didn't I think of such a thing?"

Chapter 30

Will rushed back to the hill, dodging increasing numbers of Nevara combatants on the roads. He barely stopped to eat, grabbing whatever he could find in the forest, and buying bread and fresh produce at village market stalls. At night, he threw his rough bedding onto the ground and collapsed under the closest sheltering tree he could find.

Each morning, as soon as the amethyst dawn spread its light, he grabbed his pack and continued. He kept the note from Eleonora in his front pocket. His heart twisted every time he looked at it. He couldn't wait to see her again, and he couldn't wait to tell Roland everything about the House. But would it be too late?

After an exhausting pace, he finally reached Shannon. Caves Hill loomed high and rugged behind the village, like a beacon. The village fair was in full swing, so he walked via Jadyn's metalwork stall. Out-of-character worry lines etched Jadyn's forehead. He stood behind the leather-covered trestle table with its impressive array of metal goods and tools. Would Jadyn be President one day? Will would be proud to support him if he was.

Jadyn embraced him. "Welcome back, stranger." He smelled of leather and smoky metal.

"How's Roland? What happened to him?" Will held his breath for the answer.

Jadyn arranged his knives in a straight row before replying. "Not good. The princess is with him. Combatants assaulted him near the village."

Anger poured through Will like molten iron. "We have to do something. How could they attack a defenseless old man like Roland?"

"I know. Cadwyn has contacts all over the island now. Plans are in motion. Be ready." He handed Will a bulging bag from under his table. "Can you take these supplies back for Eleonora and Roland? I won't be back for a couple of days. They're struggling, but they'll be pleased to see you."

***

Eleonora was outside Roland's cave, washing plates in a bowl. She leaped up and reached out for him. He clung to her, breathing in her fragrance, drinking in her beauty, He never wanted to let her go. Ever again.

"I think seeing you again is the only thing that's keeping Roland alive," she said.

"What did they do to him?"

"Beat him up for not having the mark. They left him lying on the track, bleeding. Said he wasn't worth taking back to Nevara. Dr. Wells said he has internal injuries."

She led him into Roland's cave, which was dimly lit by the fading embers of the oven fire. A strong aroma from an infusion of leaves on the stove wafted in the air. Bruised skin on Roland's face and limbs hung like loose parchment. Deep shadows gouged the hollows under his eyes and cheekbones. Will's throat contracted. He couldn't speak.

Roland raised a gaunt hand. "What a fine kettle of fish I'm in," he said in a scratchy voice.

Will went to him, bent down and wrapped his arms around the old man and hugged him gently. The man's body felt like Shadow's metal cage.

A constricting lump grew in Will's chest. "Missed you dreadfully."

"Did ye find the truth of yer life?"

"I think finding the truth is a process, but the puzzle is coming together."

"Ha. Now ye sit here and tell me about the journey. Every wee detail."

Eleonora added wood to the stove fire, gave them tea, and left them to talk. Will sat cross-legged on the goatskin rug and began.

Roland smiled as he talked, his mouth stretched tight over his teeth. He gave an occasional nod, and his weary eyes glinted in the fire's light. When Will started to tell him about The Truth Door, Roland fell asleep and his breath came in irregular, wheezing gasps. Will left him, stood outside and stretched, inhaling the forest scent and the faint whiff of ocean spray, then turned back to check on Roland.

Roland opened his eyes. "I'm dying, Will. I huvnae much more time with ye."

The lump of sorrow spread from Will's chest to his throat. He held a cup of Eleonora's herbal tea to Roland's lips. Roland shook his head.

"Dinnae grieve for me for long, my son. Ken where I'm going." He closed his eyes. "Get me the wee brown-covered book from the shelf." Will passed it to Roland, who took it and flicked through the pages with trembling hands. "This book is like the story of my life. I've been favored to be part of the King's story."

Roland turned to the last page.

"When I bought this book at the village, someone had ripped off the back cover. It's like my life. My story doesn't end here." He pointed at the last page with his quivering finger. "No book can give justice to the next part of my story. The best part is about to begin, and I know it will be magnificent."

The book slipped from his hands onto his chest. A shiver of excitement surged through Will at Roland's words.

***

Eleonora shook Will awake just after dawn. He blinked into the thin rays of light filtering into Roland's cave.

The look on her face pierced him. "He's gone."

"I slept. I didn't mean to." Will turned to Roland. His chiseled face looked still and peaceful.

A wave of loss swept over him. "What do we do now?"

"We'll ask Dr. Wells. He'll know."

***

A day later, all of the cave dwellers and a few villagers met at Roland's burial plot. It was a small piece of land kept aside for the cave dwellers. They wrapped Roland in his favorite rug. Eleonora placed a bunch of wild violets on his chest. Jadyn read about the gift of eternal life from The King's Word.

Later, Will and Eleonora warmed thin vegetable soup on the fire outside Will's cave. He sipped without enthusiasm. Eleonora sat with her shoulders slumped. Will moved closer to her and enveloped her in his arms. Velvet skin rested against his cheek, and her sigh caressed his neck. He held her for a long moment, stroked her hair, and then let her go. They sat, shoulders pressed together as the glowing coals faded. The reassurance of her presence, mingled with the sense the King was with them, was like a comforting rug wrapping him up and giving him peace.

***

Three days later, Will met Jadyn for a day of fishing. Before they left, Felix ran toward them and skidded to a stop, gasping.

"Guess what Mom and I saw in the forest? Mom said I could come down and show you."

"A gigantic dragon?" Will asked, chuckling.

"Smaller than that, but nearly as fierce."

"A huge mirren with razor teeth." Jadyn said.

"You'll never guess," Felix said. "I heard raven sounds in the tree. I was wondering. It might be Shadow. There was a nest. When I got closer, I saw Shadow looking for dinner on the ground. He didn't fly away."

Felix jumped up and down, his hair flopping around his face. "He's had babies!"

Will punched the air with elation. "That's why I haven't seen him. Show us, Felix. But wait a moment." He headed back into the cave and came out with one of his pockets bulging.

They followed Felix to a tree in Emerald Forest near the river. Felix pointed to a bunch of rough sticks that Will had to admit was the untidiest bird's nest he'd ever seen. Urgent cries came from the nest. A raven swooped down and landed on Will's head. The bird's body was heavy, and he scratched Will's scalp with sharp claws.

Will ducked. "Get off."

Jadyn laughed. "He's pleased to see you." Shadow glided to the ground and pranced around, cawing.

"Shadow, I've brought you something. You'll need extra food now you have a family to feed." Will extracted a duck's egg and a piece of rabbit meat from his pocket and placed them on the ground.

Felix crouched to watch.

Shadow pranced to the egg and pulled it away from them with his beak, checking around to make sure all was safe. He pecked the egg open, ate the contents with gusto, and then flew back to the nest with the meat, to a chorus of pleading cries.

"Can't wait to see what you'll do when you have an entire family of ravens hanging around your cave," Jadyn said.

"Yeah, can't wait." If it was Shadow's family, he didn't mind.

***

The next morning, Will woke to a call from Jadyn.

"Meet at my cave. I need you now."

Will threw on his clothes and sprinted up the hill. A grim-faced Jadyn, Eleonora, Laurien, and Cadwyn sat in a tight circle. A bedraggled man with a bushy beard with a single streak of gray and mud to his knees sat with them. Laurien's appearance was a surprise. Her cheeks and body had a healthy plumpness, and she'd combed the knots out of her hair. It was the first time he'd seen her face and hands without streaks of dirt on them.

"This is Kelvyn, my cousin," Cadwyn said. "He lives up north, in Fawley village. He's traveled here by horse and on foot, and had little sleep."

Kelvyn scratched at the whiskers on his face. "The madecia scourge has spread out of control. Even the lab can't keep up with the increased demand." He took a piece of cornbread and gulped it with barely a chew. "Cadwyn has gathered a sizable group for the overthrow of the President and his government—but it can't happen until the successful destruction of the madecia lab at Hoarfrost Keep."

"Why not overthrow the government first?" the princess asked.

"Once the people know the madecia is no longer readily available, many will support the overthrow. They won't have reason to support the President's rule anymore and it will stop the flow of gold to his stockpile. All is ready for the dismantling of the lab." Kelvyn cleared his throat and then took a sip of water from the mug. "We have tasks for all of you."

"What do you need us to do?" Eleonora asked.

"Firstly, Jadyn, as we've discussed already, you'll take over the rule of Eldrad. You've displayed integrity, and knowledge of the island governance when you lived at Nevara with your parents," Cadwyn said. "Most remember your father, our beloved former President, with great favor, and will agree to have you in the interim, until we're in the position to organize a formal vote."

"I'll do my utmost." Jadyn nodded.

Laurien yanked and twisted a strand of her hair, staring at Jadyn with sad eyes.

Kelvyn stopped talking for a moment and scrutinized Will. "So this is the visitor from the Earthlands?"

Cadwyn nodded.

"You may be a vital part of the plan, Will," Kelvyn said.

"I'm ready and willing."

"Kelvyn is saying that you may be on the island for a reason. There's a prophecy in the Earth Chronicles." Cadwyn's eyes glinted in the fire-light as he related a riddle in a deep, hushed tone.

> "From lands afar,
> A falling star,
> Will change the course,
> Of the island's curse."

Will sat, stunned. Was this why Senka wanted him dead?

"Will, Eleonora and Laurien, we know of your allegiance to the King," Kelvyn said. "We're asking you to make the journey to Hoarfrost Keep, to infiltrate it and destroy the madecia lab."

"Why choose me?" Laurien asked. Will squirmed. She'd cause trouble for sure.

"Laurien, you have useful knowledge of the island and know the best routes to take to Hoarfrost Keep." Kelvyn reached for more bread.

"I know the island, but I'm not going anywhere near Nevara," she said.

"You'll bypass it. Can I have your agreement?"

Laurien gave a slight incline of her head.

Eleonora leaned towards Will and whispered in his ear. "Now we know who Aunt Nora's third blanket is for."

"We'll all go," she said.

"This is a dangerous mission." Kelvyn drew the route on the map. "I'll be leaving in a day and will be back in Fawley Village by the time you get there. I'll meet you at Wingate Inn in the village, where I'll give you final instructions from Amber. She's working undercover at Hoarfrost Keep. My brother works at the Wingate Inn. Let him know when you've arrived, and he'll call for me. I can't guarantee your safety, but the best strategy is strong and regular petitioning of the King.

"When do we leave?" Will fidgeted with his knife, restless to leave and dumbfounded at the prophecy.

"As soon as possible. I can spend a day assisting you with plans and preparations, and then I must return," Kelvyn said. "Wear the King's armor for protection and strength."

"What happens to the people addicted to madecia after we dismantle the lab?" Will asked.

"We already have places all over the island to help those who are suffering from withdrawal symptoms," Cadwyn said.

"You think you'll die, but you get over it," Laurien said. "The first two weeks are the worst."

Jadyn moved to Laurien and put his arm around her shoulders. Her eyes sparkled and her cheeks flushed.

Chapter 31

Will, Eleonora and Laurien set off under the cover of darkness three days later, having spent the time in a frenzy of preparation. They packed enough food to last them a few days, a selection of Eleonora's herbal mixes, Aunt Nora's blankets, three shelters, and a change of warm clothes each. They trusted only a handful of people with their plans. Jadyn had already left for Eladia with Cadwyn to finalize their strategies for the takeover of Lorn's leadership.

They shivered in the early morning mist, detoured around the village, and then started the long climb over the Mordrach Mountains. After three days of arduous hiking, they reached the Cerith Plains. They rested while they ate cornbread and apples whilst admiring the plains surrounded by waves of undulating mountains, clothed in a mauve haze.

Two days later, they could see the tiny dot of Napier Village at the base of the Napier Mountains, in the distance. That night they slept in a barn at Wicklow. The next morning, Will opened the barn door and checked the weather. Gold mingled with ribbons of violet painted the morning sky. He and the princess packed their bags.

"Where's Laurien?" he asked.

"She got up before dawn—wanted to get supplies in Burford village before we left. Can you help me fix the tie on my bag?" The way she looked at him made his breath seize in his throat.

Will sat beside her on the bale of hay, threaded the tie, and then put the bag aside. He drew closer to her, put his arm around her waist, and held her. She pushed the hair out of his eyes and stroked his stubbled face. Her fingers left a trail of fire. He leaned down and kissed her cheek and neck, breathing in her scent. His pulse pounded.

Laurien's footsteps sounded on the track outside. Will released Eleonora and sighed.

They walked through Corwen Valley until midday. "Can we visit Thorburn Lake in Napier Mountains?" Eleonora pulled and twisted the pendant on the silver chain around her neck. "I-it's where I lived with my family."

"Sure," Will said. "You show us the way."

"Let's have the pumpkin muffins I bought at the markets first," Laurien said.

Eleonora took one bite, shook her head, and gave it to Will. "I can't eat."

She led them along a woodland track and up a steep incline until they reached the peak. The mountain range stretched to the coast, and a dull gray lake filled the hushed valley. The only sounds were distant bird cries. There was no sign of settlement around the shores.

Eleonora sat on a rock, hunched over, and sobs shook her body. Will and Laurien crouched either side of her with their arms wrapped around her. Will longed to rip away her grief and throw it into the wind.

"If the King's so powerful, why doesn't he just raze the President's Palace and get rid of the evil once and for all?" Laurien asked as they descended the mountain. "What chance have we got to save Eldrad from Lorn?"

Eleonora dried her eyes. "The King could destroy Nevara Palace and the lab in the blink of a raven's eye. But there's always a good reason for what he does and doesn't do."

"And we must rely on him to make things right—in the end," Will said.

"So we'll succeed no matter what?" Laurien said, hunching her shoulders.

Eleonora threw her pack onto a grassy patch of ground near a brook. "Not necessarily—he may have other plans. We may not survive this, but death isn't the end."

She drank from the brook and washed her face. "In the process, the King will teach us to depend on him. Then we'll experience his power and be transformed." She handed them the leftover muffins. "Laurien, how long will it take to get to Hoarfrost Keep from here?"

"It depends on whether we can get horses at Hoarfrost Gate. It also depends on the weather. I spent two weeks sheltering in Woodburn Forest while it poured in a flood. I've never been so waterlogged in my life."

"How did you end up at Caves Hill, Laurien?" Will asked.

"Pen, my friend at the palace, said Jadyn had found it safer to live there. Pen was from Shannon originally," she said.

"So you already knew Jadyn."

"Most people know who Jadyn Reeve is." She flushed.

Laurien laid out her bed and blanket under a tree a short distance away and settled for the night. Will sat by the fire with Eleonora, toasting cornbread and strips of dried pork. "I'm not exactly over the moon about Laurien coming with us," he whispered.

She chuckled. "As if I couldn't guess."

"You know what she's like. She grates on my nerves. We're not the best of buddies—to put it mildly."

"Laurien's changed. Did you know she's a King follower now?"

Will gaped at her. "No. When did that happen?"

"We had long talks about it when she was sick. She hated her life and was looking for happiness. She has a lot to learn, like all of us. But haven't you noticed how different she is—and her interest when I read The King's Book?"

"That's true."

Eleonora threw another log onto the fire, making it hiss and crackle. "Anyway, you know I wouldn't be going on this trip if it was just the two of us." She poured honey over her toast.

"You mean we need a chaperone? I think I have enough control to be trusted. But on that note, I would love to kiss you. Just once. We may not get through this. I would die happy."

"Sounds like the kiss of death."

"Whatever it is, if it's the last one, it has to be good," he said.

"Are you saying my kissing isn't already good?"

"I haven't had enough exposure to be sure." He twisted around, drew her into his arms and looked down at her inviting lips glowing in the fire's light. She lifted her head, and he leaned down and kissed her. Her lips tasted of toast and honey. His heart tumbled in his chest, as hot as a furnace.

He pulled her closer, and they kissed again. Her velvet lips molded to his. The outside world dissolved for one long, exquisite moment.

Eleonora turned her face away "We have to stop."

He pressed his lips to her cheek and her neck. "Can't we stay here, like this, another day? Another week?" His voice muffled against her skin.

She giggled and took his hand.

He stroked her arm as they listened to the chatter of mirren mingling with the rustling of other small animals in the undergrowth. Despite the dangers they faced, no words could describe how happy he felt.

And the kiss of death had been dynamite.

***

A couple of days later, they approached the Nevara bypass. They paused for a few minutes to catch their breath and drink at a gushing spring. Will pulled Kelvyn's creased map from his pocket and laid it out on a rock. He traced his finger over the directions on the map. "We're heading toward Hoarfrost Gate." The Gate would be sure to have an inn, and he'd finally get a drink.

They resumed the journey but looked for a nighttime shelter once the sky threw its splashes of purple and yellow light, and dusk set in.

"There's a large oak over there with dry ferns underneath," Will said.

"What's that foul smell?" Laurien pulled her scarf over her nose as they settled under the tree.

"Have no idea, but I'm too tired to care," Eleonora said. "Just hope it isn't something dead."

They chewed on sour plums they'd picked earlier, then sprawled under the branches. Will covered his mouth and nose with Aunt Nora's blanket to cut down on the offensive odor. He kept watch on Eleonora until she'd settled into the rhythmic breathing of slumber. He'd be lost if anything happened to her.

Later that night, Will woke in a panic. A hand shook his shoulder. He snatched his knife.

"Put the knife away," Laurien whispered. "It's us. Me and Eleonora." Despite the late hour, there was no sign of sleepiness in their eyes.

"You've got to see this." Eleonora dragged off his blanket, and they led him down a track. The putrid smell became even more rotten.

Will pinched his nose. "This had better be good." But his complaining changed to an awestruck exclamation.

A glowing fairyland of fungi spread out on the forest floor, abundant with luminescent toadstools in brilliant greens on delicate stalks. Others were in ghostly creams and a mix of iridescent blues and oranges. Will took Eleonora's hand and pressed it to his lips as they stared in a flabbergasted silence at the magical scene.

"Fried fungi for breakfast, anyone?" Will chuckled.

"And violent abdominal pain, vomiting, and other symptoms you don't want to hear about at this late hour," Eleonora said.

***

They left later the next morning, stepping around the now dull, no longer magical, but still-stinking fungi. Will spotted combatants on the main road, so they took a detour. Thick undergrowth and soggy marshes hampered their progress, and the detour took the rest of the day. In the evening, they found an abandoned barn with dry hay bales in one corner. After eating a quick meal, they unrolled their bedding and settled for the night.

"We leave at dawn," Eleonora reminded them.

The rustling of leaves on the barn roof lulled Will to sleep. A while later, he woke. His limbs hurt with a deep-bone ache, and a bitter chemical taste filled his mouth and throat. His lungs burned. He gasped for breath.

An intense white light blinded him. Muffled voices sifted into his ears, and a blur of strange faces came into focus. People leaned over him as though he was a specimen under a microscope. Parts of his body had an assortment of tubing attached to them. A streak of horror flashed through him. Was he in some sort of sci-fi experiment?

White coats. Stethoscopes. A needle, poised and ready to strike. Something like a plastic cup was stuffed into his throat.

He couldn't breathe and gagged.

"He's coming to. Hand me the syringe," a voice said.

"Will, can you hear me?"

The faces came into focus. Unfamiliar faces. A psychiatric ward? A hospital? Thoughts flashed back and forth like traffic on an expressway. He fought a rising sense of dread. Air whistled through his too-tight trachea.

He must be back. At the bay. But he couldn't go back now.

With all his strength, he wrenched at the implanted needles and tubes and wires attached to his body, shocked at his weakness.

Blood poured onto the sheets. He yanked at the suffocating plastic blocking his airway. Panicked shouts rang in his ears. Sets of horrified eyes stared at him. Hands pressed him down. A stinging needle jabbed his arm.

His body jerked and convulsed.

No air.

Chapter 32

Aporto Bay: Erin's fears.

Erin limped into the ward with one leg in a walking brace.

"Out of plaster at last?" Maddie, one of the nurses on duty, stood up from the desk in the nurse's station and adjusted her cap.

Erin grimaced. "About to train for the next triathlon."

"Will's Dad's here."

"Oh." Erin hesitated. Nurse Baxter was attaching a bag of intravenous fluid on the stand at Will's bed, and a man with a likeness to Will sat on a chair watching her.

"Go on in," Maddie said.

Nurse Baxter took the clipboard from Will's bed and made notes. She glanced up without a smile as Erin approached.

Pete leaped up and shook her hand. "It's Erin, isn't it? I get to meet you at last. Sorry to hear you were injured as well." His eyes were red-rimmed. He offered his chair to her and sat on the bed, resting his hand on one of Will's legs.

"How is he?" she asked.

"Not so g-good."

Erin's gut twisted in a sharp pang.

"Perhaps you should tell Erin, Nurse Baxter," he said.

"He came out of the coma five days ago," the nurse said. "The doctors took him off life support, but he became agitated and stopped breathing."

"Will he still be all right?" Erin chewed a nail and held her breath, waiting for the answer. What if he suffered brain damage?

"He's stable now. We are taking it a day at a time." The nurse tore a readout from a machine next to Will's bed and took it to the nurses' station. Erin sat staring at Will. This was terrible news.

"I went to see Bruce Maddock on Thursday about the stadium accident," Pete said, breaking the silence.

"At his four-story business in Main Street?"

Pete nodded.

"What happened?"

"Not a memory I'll keep foremost in my mind. It was Andy's idea. He's my brother and business partner." Pete laid his hand on Will's arm. "You can practically smell the money in the fancy foyer at Maddock Construction. He's obviously doing very well for himself. Bruce made it clear we were the last people he wanted to see. He wipes his hands of the disaster. Blames the steel supplier. Still, he agreed to see us."

Nurse Baxter returned to dress and bandage a pressure sore under Will's heel. Dr. Cooper strode into the ward, his shoes squelching on the floor. Nurse Baxter dropped the treatment cream into Erin's lap. Erin passed the tube back to her. Dr. Cooper approached, smiled at them and checked one of the monitors behind Will's bed.

Nurse Baxter fumbled with her tray and it fell on the floor in a clatter. A red tide traveled up her neck and face as she bent over and grabbed the tube of cream and used bandages.

Dr. Cooper leaned over to help her. "Will's been in a coma for five weeks now—apart from the recent incident. I want another full set of bloods and a CT scan. Could you organize it, Skye?"

"No problem, Doctor." Beads of sweat shone on the nurse's forehead.

Erin squirmed in her chair, baffled. What was wrong with the woman? Was Will getting the best care?

***

Erin visited Will again the next day, on her way to her physio session. Dr. Cooper was back in the ward.

"All appears to be in order." Dr. Cooper jammed a folder into a filing cabinet in the nurses' station. Despite his lowered voice, Erin could hear the conversation between him and the nurse.

"We're concerned about the extent of potential damage to Will's brain. When he woke from the coma, he behaved violently. According to his family, this was out of character for him."

The nurse nodded as he spoke. Erin pretended to be absorbed in her computer screen.

"He may have an aggressive personality if he ever regains consciousness. We could need extra resources, even help from security and his family may need special assistance on his discharge, if he ever gets to that stage."

Cold fingers reached into Erin's chest, chilling her heart until it iced over. Erin gazed around the room trying to find distraction from the haze of fear clouding her thoughts.

Nurse Baxter's face oozed admiration as she looked at Dr. Cooper. Maybe the woman had a crush on him. That would explain some of her behavior. Dr. Cooper touched his heels together and stared at the nurse with a serious expression. Erin listened in case they said any more about Will's condition.

"Could I see you in my office after your shift, Skye?"

The nurse nodded and frowned.

As soon as the doctor left the ward, the nurse walked to Will's bed. She looked as if she'd heard the worst news of her life. She changed Will's urine bag without pulling the curtain or asking Erin to leave, and then returned to her desk. She leaned over the computer with her fists wedged hard into her cheeks. Perhaps the nurse was in trouble? Even Dr. Cooper's usual relaxed body language had been tense.

The nurse grabbed her russet bag and left the ward. Erin typed for a while, straightened Will's top sheet, packed up her things and walked down a corridor past the Physiotherapy Rooms and toward the carpark. Nurse Baxter brushed past her and dashed in the opposite direction. Her makeup was streaked and smudged, as if she'd been crying. Whatever happened in Dr. Cooper's office must have been serious. Perhaps they'd caught her taking the hospital's medication. Perhaps she'd even lost her job.

Chapter 33

Will woke in the barn just as the first soft rays of sun sifted through the dust-coated windows. He reached out to feel brittle hay on the floor. The blinding lights, the strange people in white uniforms, had vanished. The choking had eased, but his throat still stung as if it had been scraped with a razor. Eleonora rolled up her bedding, and Laurien packed her bag as if nothing had happened.

But something had happened. Everything had changed. It shook and unnerved Will to the core of his being, and it brought back the myriad of questions that had plagued him ever since he found himself on the island. Had he gone mad? Could this all be a dream? But it couldn't be. How could he experience something he had no knowledge of before, like sword-making? He shook his head in confusion, and groaned. The slightest movement of his neck was agony.

Laurien passed him a bowl of oats and honey, warmed with hot water. He put it aside after the first painful swallow.

"You're quiet this morning, Will," Eleonora said as she braided her hair.

"Just thinking." His voice came out in a croak.

She gave him a quizzical look, and as she did every morning, opened The King's Book to read aloud. Will remembered nothing of what she read. He barely concentrated on the path they took through the woods that day, tormented with endless questions. What if his body was at the bay, but his mind was here in Eldrad? What would happen if he actually died back at the bay?

He staggered on, reeling with what-ifs-and-whys, his legs barely held him upright. Eldrad was the best of places, because Eleonora was here and because he was on an astonishing and important journey, but it was also the worst of places. It wasn't home, and he was on a deadly mission. His mind hauled back and forth in a tug-of-war of indecision.

Eleonora watched him, her eyes full of concern. But he couldn't tell her.

***

They continued north, keeping under cover in the woodlands when possible and stocking up on food at farms and small markets in the villages. Will swallowed with less pain now, and he tried to put the weird experience at the barn out of his mind. Protecting Eleonora and Laurien and finishing his mission was paramount.

Laurien offered endless warnings about the dangers of Nevara. Will gritted his teeth in exasperation as he held back low bushes for them to pass.

"It wouldn't hurt to pay our President a quick courtesy visit on the way," Will said.

Laurien narrowed her eyes at him and lagged for the next hour of walking in protest.

Then Eleonora pointed to a jet black cloud heading toward them from the north at an alarming rate. "Is that what I think it is?"

"Ravens!" Laurien screamed. "Drop your packs and run." As they sprinted toward the woods, at least ten of the birds swooped toward them. The ravens pecked at their heads and bare arms until they reached cover under the oaks. They peered up at them through the foliage, panting.

"This isn't sheltered enough. We need to go further into the woods," Laurien said.

"Is anyone hurt?" Eleonora asked, feeling her head for cuts as they moved to a thicker tree canopy.

"I've had much worse," Laurien said.

Finally the birds flew away.

"Get your packs, and we'll keep close to the cover of trees for the rest of the day." Will said. He pulled his coat around Laurien and held her around the shoulders until her shaking subsided.

Eleonora dragged her fingers through her knotted hair. Dirt coated her drawn face. "We'll take turns to guard the camp tonight."

Despite blistered feet, they continued for three more days, stopping only for quick meals or shelter when the rain was too heavy. They read aloud from The King's Book each morning and discussed their plans as they travelled.

***

Crisp frost covered the grass the following morning. Eleonora and Laurien hurried to a stream in a nearby gully to wash and fetch fresh water. Will sharpened his knife and wrapped mushrooms and bread in a cloth for their lunch later that day.

A muffled sob from Laurien startled him. She came running through the bushes, eyes dark and wild with fear. "Eleonora. They took her."

Everything in Will's stomach turned to water. He leaped up. "Who took her? Where?"

She heaved another sob. "Combatants. They grabbed her further downstream from where I was standing, behind the trees. They covered her mouth and dragged her away."

"We'll get her back."

"They'll take her to Nevara. We'll be sitting ducks there. And it's the annual festival. A stallholder at Burford told me."

"Do you know the way?"

Her lips disappeared into an invisible line for a moment. "I'll show you. That's all."

They climbed the Nevara Mountains, taking a path to the east. Every minute counted. Visions of Eleonora being tortured by the President's men and attacked by ravens gave Will new impetus with every footstep. They reached the top of the mountain and looked onto the plain to the north.

"Nevara Province," Laurien said in a tight voice.

Will drew a breath of surprise. An expansive city lay below them in the distance. It was nothing like Idella, with its haphazard fairgrounds, ornate buildings, and the towering maze of rides. Nevara looked like a miniature board game, all set up, ready to play, with nothing out of place. Four airships hung suspended over it like tiny toys, each displaying the raven insignia.

Four black and silver pyramids sat on the corners of a square-shaped design with a larger pyramid in the middle, all gleaming like glass in the sunlight. Dark-olive palms surrounded the building and dotted the avenues.

"See the pyramid in the middle? That's the President's Palace," Laurien said.

Will shifted his legs with impatience. "We must hurry."

"How will you keep from being noticed once you get to the gates? They have checkpoints."

"Don't know yet. I'll think of something." They reached the bottom of the hill and crouched behind a thicket, away from the road. A mix of people walked toward the city, including Cravers and Nevara combatants. Many carried flags with the raven symbol, and a few were on horses. Will stared at the combatants' distinctive blue-gray uniform. The coat extended below the buttocks and had dull bronze buttons down the front. It gave him an idea.

"If I capture a combatant, we could take his clothes and I could use the disguise to enter the checkpoint," he said in a low voice.

Laurien threw him a skeptical look. "How could you do that? And don't forget they have special combat training you don't have, if there's trouble."

"I'm not as incapable as you think. Do you have any brilliant ideas?"

Laurien shook her head.

"We can't leave Eleonora. If it's the King's plan for us to succeed, he'll make a way," he said, watching for a combatant walking alone.

After a frustrating wait, Will sighed. "We're wasting time. Let's head down the road and look for an opportunity. At least we'll be getting closer to the city."

As they waded out of the bushes, four Cravers slunk along the road. Will's skin prickled, but they passed, too busy arguing amongst themselves to notice them. Another combatant strode past them, giving them a cursory glance.

Will leaned down to Laurien and said in a fierce whisper. "Now's our chance. I'll knock him out, and then we'll drag him into the bushes."

Laurien frowned and shrugged.

Will turned around and checked the road behind them. "The coast's clear. It's now or never." They sneaked up behind the combatant, but the man turned around. Will struck him and the combatant slumped to the ground.

Laurien tried to gag him with her scarf, and Will grabbed his legs.

The combatant opened his eyes and cursed. "Get off." He lashed out with bruising kicks, and then rolled over, trying to stand. Will braced himself, clenched his fists, and hit him hard enough to knock him out.

They dragged him into the bushes and stripped off his trousers and coat. Laurien tied him up like a trussed duck while Will dressed in the blue-gray uniform. The man opened his eyes again and writhed around like a wild bear. A clopping of horses thundered on the road.

"We'll come back and deal with you later," Will said to him. "Please come with me to the city, Laurien. We should get into Nevara, now I'm wearing the uniform."

"You have no idea what you're asking." She reached and pulled down the sleeves of the combatant's coat Will wore, trying to cover his bare wrist, then heaved a sigh. "I'll come—for the sake of Eleonora."

Will squeezed one of her shoulders and led her out of the bushes onto the road. He slowed down into a typical combatant-style swagger and put on his best scowl expression.

She smirked at him and pointed to his ankles. "There's too much sock showing."

The road became thick with a jostling crowd. Faint cheering drifted toward them. The walls of the palace, built with smooth ebony and white stones in a tessellated pattern, loomed ahead. Flocks of ravens circled above the city, crying like agonized victims.

Combatants guarded the entrance. They checked people's bags randomly at the checkpoint. Soon it was their turn in the jam-packed queue. They ignored Will, but a combatant grabbed Laurien's pack and sifted through the contents. He took out her knife and a piece of cheese and put it on a table, then waved them through.

"How will we find Eleonora?" Will asked.

"She'll be in the palace under guard. We'll have to find a way in." Laurien struggled to walk beside him as the throng shoved them along the main avenue.

The gigantic pyramids and the dark palms gave the place a surreal atmosphere. The hard ball of anxiety in the pit of Will's stomach grew as they approached. What if they were too late? He scanned the sunken arena at the end of the avenue, directly in front of the central towering pyramid of the Presidential Palace. All the seats were taken, so the audience spilled into an area in front of a podium.

"Long live the President," the crowd shouted in unison. A sea of raven insignia flags fluttered in the breeze. On the podium above the crowd, a line of people stood on one side of the stage with their ankles chained.

The princess was with them. A fist squeezed Will's heart in a bruising grip. President Lorn perched on a towering throne carved in the form of a giant raven. The black wings were tight against its body and its head towered above him. The President's bony hands rested on carved bird claws. A live raven perched on his shoulder and inclined its head toward his stony but striking face, as if waiting for the next instruction. A thin, demonic-looking giant in a cloak stood on one side of the throne.

"Hurry, it's about to start," someone called. The crowd hushed, and an atmosphere of anticipation filled the air. A line of security guards in belted brown uniforms and high black boots stood to attention along the base of the stage. They wore a cap in the same color as the uniform.

The President unfolded his thin frame from the throne. Long plaits of white hair dangled over his chest, and a bronze circular ring settled around his forehead. The crowd cheered as he stood.

"Honored guests and residents." The President's voice boomed across the arena like a foghorn. "I have great pleasure in opening the annual Nevara Festival. Your presence here is a validation of your allegiance to the rule of Nevara. We have stalls and markets to visit for your pleasure. Our accomplished combatants will show their prowess in a series of displays of courage and skill during the next three days."

A girl wearing a close-fitting coat in the same brown color as the guards' uniform wedged her body between Laurien and Will. She spoke to Laurien. Will tried to move away from her, but the crowd pressed in.

"I've done much to ensure this island is a pleasant place for you to live, and as you know, I've worked hard to provide an unrivaled quality of life." The President's voice droned. "I'm sure you will all agree my rule has ushered in a new and golden age for the Island of Eldrad. I ask you to ensure you have the mark of the raven. It is the mark of belonging and the mark of loyalty. You all know what I am asking. There are no exceptions."

The crowd rippled an agreement.

The girl in the coat hardly turned her head as she spoke to Will. "A combatant without the mark? How odd." Will glared at her, and she withdrew into the crowd.

"I know her," Laurien said in his ear. "She's Pen, the sister of the boy who the Cravers attacked in the village. She said you need to stand with the other combatants or you'll be noticed." Will nodded, and they pushed toward a group of combatants.

President Lorn marched across the stage. "Friends and comrades, for those few people who do not have the mark, I am asking you to move to the front. Right here. Right now. Form a line. We have a space for you in front of the stage and we have markers skilled in the application. They are waiting for you in our marking tents. There will be an amnesty for the next three days. Think of it as a privilege."

Will clenched his fists, his eyes riveted on Eleonora.

Several people pushed toward tents erected near the arena.

"Is there anyone else? You all know our new decree. Any subject without the raven mark will suffer the consequences." He made the announcement in a short and sharp tone, like the cutting of a guillotine.

Will's heart constricted at Laurien's frozen profile of fear. More people joined the queue. The President stalked back and forth along the stage with his marionette gait and settled on his throne again and compressed his lips. He turned to the group standing with Eleonora. "Now for your punishment—unless you would like to join the marking line." He thrust his right arm into the air. "Look at me. I bear the seal of Nevara with pride!"

Four of the people on the stage stepped forward. A combatant removed their chains and led them to the lengthening queue near the marking tents. The princess did not move. She gazed at the crowd, her pinched white face defiant. A middle-aged woman wearing a gray woven shawl with a boy in a faded coat stood stiffly with the princess.

"No more takers?" The President tapped the bird's claws on the arms of his throne. "Bring the boy." He lurched from his throne again. Two men yanked the boy toward the President. Panic swept over Will in waves of heat and ice. The giant standing guard at the throne held the distraught woman.

"My dear boy, what a waste." A murmur ran through the crowd as the President bared his glittering teeth. He grasped the boy's neck and made a jerking movement. The crowd gasped. Will turned away. The boy lay motionless.

"Next traitor," the President called in a deep monotone. "Bring me the girl."

Chapter 34

The President's words punched a hole in Will's chest. It was too late. He needed to be up there on the stage. At least to let her know he'd come for her. To tell her he loved her. He pushed through the crowd, with Laurien close behind. People elbowed and shoved them back. It was impossible to move in the crowd's crush.

"I know you," the President said to Eleonora as the guards dragged her toward him. "I know you better than you know me. I've been watching you in your little caveland. No one is beyond my surveillance. You are a special prize who requires a special punishment."

He stood over her. "Who are the clever ones who found this girl for me just in time for a public showing?"

Two men came forward.

Odin and Striker.

The guard threw them each a purse, clanking and heavy. The arena was silent, apart from the sharp raven cries above. The dark giant next to the throne bent and whispered to the President.

"We have plans for you." The President turned to Eleonora. "They are slow and excruciating. Reserved only for the deserving." He gestured to two guards, who grabbed her arms and dragged her through a door at the back of the stage. Will swayed. It was as though someone had nicked an artery, and he was losing blood fast.

The President stood and straightened his hunched shoulders. "We have two more defiant individuals who do not have the interests of the island in their hearts and have not come forward. My assistants, as always, have been vigilant. Come, come, stand with me on the stage."

The ravens screeched, sending a spasm of pain through Will's head.

"You know who you are. Will Sutherland and his companion. That girl—the Nevara deserter." Will's insides gyrated in a nauseating churn. Two guards from the stage headed straight for them. The crowd opened a passageway. There was no escape.

"Come. Stand with me and let everyone see who the traitors are. It's too late to ask for forgiveness." Rough hands pulled them toward the stage. Will felt more for Laurien than himself. If a demon had dug its teeth into his neck, it wouldn't have felt this bad. He shouldn't have brought Laurien with him.

"What do you have to say now?" President Lorn spat on the podium. The raven on his shoulder cawed at them in disapproval.

Will turned to the tense crowd and filled his lungs with a deep breath. He was calm and in control now. "My name is Will Sutherland." His voice rang out over the crowd, loud and sure. "Born at Aporto Bay, a loyal son of the true King. I stand for the good of the people of this island."

The crowd murmured.

"The good?" The President spat his words. "Spying, capturing my combatants, stealing Nevara property, and questioning the supreme rule of your Prince and President?"

Venomous anger twisted the President's face. His voice rose in a high-pitched shriek. "I charge you with treason." The guards chained him and Laurien and dragged them into a corridor in the Palace. They were flung against one of the ebony-colored walls.

"This place is so evil," Will said to Laurien, who was curled up and pressed against the wall. Up above, ornate light fittings were fashioned with crisscrossed sticks. They looked like bones and reflected multiple times in the mirror-white floor and ceiling. It was like being trapped in a tomb, but with the lights on. Will longed to see Eleonora.

"What did I tell you?" was all Laurien said, her face as white as the tiles on the floor. A combatant ordered the guards to move them to the throne room, and they walked down several passages until they reached it.

Eleonora lay sprawled on the tiles in front of another raised podium. Her legs bled from the cutting chains. Will winced at her state. Eleonora's initial shocked expression when they entered the room turned into a steely, don't-give-in-to-them expression.

Will scanned the throne room. A light fitting, similar to the ones in the hall, hung above them, but it was three times as large and even more ostentatious. It would kill them all if it dropped. White curtains hung behind the throne, and a crow's eye decorated the wall above the curtains. Lorn sat on another throne similar to the one overlooking the arena.

A whiff of a cloying, decayed smell drifted from the President's body, like the fungi in the woods. The raven on the man's shoulder cawed in a whining tone, "Why? Why? Why?" He tapped it hard on the beak. The curtains behind the throne moved and parted in a flicker of movement. Will glimpsed a tiny, bird-like creature through the slit.

The President tapped the arm of his throne with his nails. "We've enjoyed watching you all in your little mountain hideout. Biding our time. Now that time has passed, for time waits for no traitor." He gave a mocking laugh as he stroked the wing of his raven, whispered to it, then turned to them.

"My Prince has been impatient for you to arrive at Nevara. As you know, I have several charges to bring against you, including the kidnapping of one of my prized birds."

Shadow. He knew about Shadow.

"The Dark Prince has no power over us," Will said. "We belong to the King of the entire Earthlands."

The President's eyes were dark cauldrons of venom. "You question the power of the Prince?"

"We know of his power, but the power we have is greater, and the power we have is for good, not evil. We stand for life, not death."

"Ah, but I hold the power of death over you all." Lorn's nostrils flared as he gave a sinister smile.

"Death is not the end for us." The princess clanked her chains on the floor as she scrambled to a standing position. "The King has defeated death. He paid a costly price for it."

The President's face contorted into a stare of fury. He gripped the clawed armrests of the throne so tightly they made a cracking sound.

"So let us see who has the power? Don't you know I own and rule the whole of Eldrad? I have untold riches. You are nothing. I can torture you until you confess. I can coax your mind into an irresistible craving. I can send you into a dark abyss where you will beg for death."

They all stood as still as figures in a wax museum.

The President strode down the steps, bent over, and caressed the princess's hair. "What a waste. So charming. But this girl does not bear my mark. Therefore, she's worthless." The princess pulled away from him, but he placed one hand on her head and reached his other to her neck.

"Everyone is equal," Will shouted. "No person is less than another." *We need you now, Counselor.*

An ear-splitting sound filled the room, echoing off the walls and floor. The President sprang back. Everyone covered their ears at the agonizing drilling noise, faces contorted in pain and panic. Will's brain felt pulverized as the sound penetrated every cell in his body. He had an uncontrollable urge to throw himself on the ground.

Through the haze of anguish, Will remembered the girl in the crowd. Pen. This may be their chance to escape.

Will took his hands from his ears, kicked his confused guard to the ground, and leaped toward Eleonora. He grabbed her, beckoned to Laurien, and they staggered toward the entrance of the throne room. Eleonora tripped on her chains and slid along the polished floor, leaving a long smear of red. Will scooped her off the ground and carried her into the corridor. He slammed the two entry doors closed.

"Tie the door handles together with your belt," he yelled to Laurien. She whipped the belt off, wound it through the handles, and tied a knot.

As they ran along the hall, the deafening sound suddenly ceased. A door at the side of the hall flew open. Pen leaned out and beckoned to them, her face puckered with strain. They hurled themselves into a small storeroom. A few seconds later, they heard the doors of the throne room crash open, followed by an uproar of commotion. Pen pressed her finger to her lips. Will held his breath. He expected the storeroom door to be yanked open any second, but the yelling of the guards and the footsteps continued down the hallway.

The room they had crammed into was not much larger than a cupboard full of cleaning aids, mops, and buckets.

Pen threw open another door on a side wall next to an array of hanging brooms.

"Quickly. They may guess where we're hiding," she said, gasping. They tumbled into another passage, and she took a bundle of keys and locked the door behind them.

"I'm the only one with the key to this door, as far as I know." She tucked the keys into a bag she was carrying.

"Was it you who caused that ear-piercing noise?" the princess asked.

"Used the President's sound room, where I work. Have a few tricks up my sleeve."

"Clever ploy, but I'm not sure my eardrums are still intact," Will said, as he helped Eleonora remove her chains.

"Ha. This passage will lead us outside the walls of the palace," Pen said. "I'm leaving with you. Going back home to Shannon. Can't stay here anymore. They're checking all palace workers for the mark as soon as the Festival's over, and I don't have one."

"What happened to your brother and the little dog after the Cravers attacked them in the village?" Will asked.

"Ollie's all right, but he's scared to go anywhere now. Spark, won't leave his side unless he's performing at the circus."

Will heaved a sigh. As soon as he got back to Shannon, he'd visit them.

"We're on our way to stop the production of the madecia at Hoarfrost Keep," Eleonora said.

"The drug lab? No one can get in there."

"We have a contact."

"In that case, may the King be with you." After a tense walk along the underground passage, Pen led them outside to a forest. "This place is the north of the palace and outside its walls, so we part here."

"Before you go, why did the Cravers attack Ollie?" Will asked.

"He buried their supply of madecia and word got out."

***

Unnerved after the ordeal at Nevara, they continued toward Fawley Village, even more aware of the danger they faced. Fatigue from the traveling, and the worry of capture took its toll.

Laurien threw her pack down and collapsed into a heap. "If I don't have a rest, you'll have to leave me behind."

"And I can't go without food much longer," Eleonora sighed. "I guess we won't be able to hire horses at Hoarfrost Gate now."

"They'll be looking out for us. We'll have to go through the marshes instead," Laurien said, still panting.

"How did Kelvyn get down to Caves Hill?" Will asked.

"By horse, mainly. He would have traveled up along the north coast and back down the side of Zenith Peaks on the western coast, past Napier Mountains, and into the Cerith Plains," Laurien said.

A twinge of concern hit Will at the dark circles under Laurien's eyes. He searched in his pack and handed her and Eleonora his last two pieces of cheese. "Let me carry your pack for a while to give you a breather," he said to Laurien. "And I haven't thanked you for everything you did to save Eleonora. Because of your bravery we're free."

Laurien beamed at him.

"You should try smiling like that more often, Jadyn wouldn't be able to resist you," he said, impressed how it transformed her face, despite her tiredness. She punched his arm, but kept smiling.

The next morning, Laurien stopped on the track and held up her hand. "We can't risk taking the road near Hoarfrost Gate. We'll go across the marshes. Some take the Woodburn Forest way, but not everyone who enters the forest comes out again. It's worse than Wyld Wood. The marshes are safer."

A sinking feeling spread into Will's gut at the sight of the wetlands area. How could anyone get across that? A series of flat, grassed, circular shapes dotted extensive areas of water like irregular mats of plush green carpet. Strange water hens and birds flocked above, and the air reverberated with their deafening calls.

"The trick is finding safe passage on the grassed islands and not sinking into the mud or ending up in the water," Laurien said.

"I think I'd rather brave the forest." The muddy stench made Will feel queasy. "To be sucked into a sulfurous-smelling swamp surely isn't part of the plan."

Laurien threw him a disapproving glance. "Follow me. I've done this before." She leaped onto the first grassy island, scattering waterhen in a mayhem of flapping and screeching. Eleonora followed with a distinct look of displeasure on her face. Will also leaped, but landed in a stinking quagmire. Mud seeped into his boots.

After a couple of hours of painstaking follow-the-leader and a few more dunks in the mud, they made it to firm ground on the other side. Muck coated them and chilled them to the bone.

Will flicked sludge from his pants. "My favorite part of the trip so far."

Laurien tied her matted hair away from her spattered face. "Better than getting lost in the forest—and it cut a day off our trip, at least."

They continued, only stopping for a brief wash in a stream, a rest or a quick meal from their dwindling reserve of apples and nuts. They were always on the lookout for edible food in the forest. There were no farms in this part of the country to buy eggs or homegrown produce.

Eleonora and Laurien dragged their feet, eyes dull with exhaustion. Will insisted they eat the last apples, but he'd never been so hungry in his life. Bedraggled and bone tired, soon they were bickering over minor things. Night fell, and they searched for a place to settle for the night.

"I see lights," Will said. They quickened their pace. A village up ahead had an evening market lit with swinging lanterns, twinkling like a haven.

"At last," Eleonora said. "I could eat a whole goat, hooves and all."

"I'll buy the food while you girls keep out of sight."

"Hurry, I'm starving," Laurien said. "Be careful."

Will pulled up his coat hood to partially cover his face and approached the food stalls. His mouth watered at the rich aroma of the cooked meats steaming into the frosty evening air. He nodded at a bearded stall keeper, whose ample belly hung over the table, and pointed to strips of roasted meat on sticks.

"Show me your mark," the bearded man said.

Will's empty stomach flipped. "I d-don't have one."

"If you don't have the mark, you don't get served. Move on." He turned to the next customer. Will staggered to another stall selling baked corn cobs. His body shook with weakness and hunger. He asked for three.

"I need to see your mark," the woman said, balancing a crying baby on her hip.

"Sorry, I don't have one. I'm a visitor to these parts."

"You can't buy food or goods at any stall here without it. President's latest orders."

"Look, I'm famished—can't you give me anything? I have the gold. My two companions have had nothing to eat for a day and a half." A sudden spasm of regret gripped him. He shouldn't have told her there were two others. If she'd heard about their escape, she might make the connection.

The woman stared at his bare wrist and shook her head.

Will dragged his feet back to the tree where the girls waited. He told them everything.

Laurien sank to the ground. "Then I'm going to starve to death."

"We might find something in the forest in the morning," Will said.

"If we last that long." Laurien heaved a sigh.

Will froze. A figure walked toward them in the shadowy darkness.

"Let's run." The princess grabbed her pack.

"Wait," Will said. "It's the woman from the corn stall."

The woman put a finger to her mouth, then handed them a warm parcel. A hot, savory aroma wafted from the paper wrapping. The woman turned to go, then paused. "We don't all follow President Lorn," she said. "He's a scourge on our land."

They offered her gold coins, but she shook her head. They exclaimed their thanks and then settled at the edge of the forest to eat.

"Soft buns and corncobs. Enough for all of us. We must thank the King," Eleonora said. Will sank his teeth into the yeasty bread, then took a bite of the cob which was bursting with sweetness. This would have to be one of the best meals of his life.

Chapter 35

Will woke the next morning to Laurien's warning cry. Dark shadows swirled in the sky above. *Demons.* The three of them cowered, gathered their bedding and packs, and moved together into a tight huddle.

"I had ominous dreams last night," Will said in a low voice.

"Me too," Laurien said. "The demons were clawing at me and telling me to go back to Caves Hill."

"I'll ask the King to protect us with his armor," Eleonora said. "It means the demons see us as a threat if they're targeting us. They know our quest is a danger to their plans." They sat together, held hands and made their request, then packed their bags and waited. After wild chattering, the demons left.

Eleonora took three small calico bags with drawstrings out of her pack. She cut bunches of dried grasses growing nearby and stuffed them full.

"What are they for?" Laurien asked.

"Trust me, we may need them at Hoarfrost Keep." They continued until they reached Fawley village at midday. Eleonora pointed to a rustic building with the head of a deer on the sign. "There's Wingate Inn, on the right. Hope it's safe to go into such a public place."

They walked warily to the counter. The smoky inn reeked of eggs and fried onions. A man with the same gray-streaked beard as Kelvyn stared at them with suspicious eyes, and then his jaw dropped. The group playing cards in the far corner glanced up, stopped their game, and whispered. Will kept one eye on them. He also glanced at the rows of spirits and meads. He wrenched his eyes away. Drinking at this stage of their trip could spell disaster.

"There are no lodgings here for you lot," the man at the counter said in a loud, unfriendly tone. Then, under his breath with his mouth barely moving, he whispered, "Get out. Now. Meet Kelvyn at Oakford Lane. End of street."

They left the inn and walked along the main street, checking no one had followed, and waited under a beech tree near the lane. Kelvyn met them a few minutes later with a relieved expression. "You three are on the President's wanted list. Stay under cover on your way to Hoarfrost Keep. The good news is, you have only one day's journey left." He handed Laurien a bag. "Some supplies to keep you going. There's not much around after you leave Fawley."

"What are the plans?" Laurien asked.

"Amber works undercover, in the kitchen. She'll put a sleeping herb in the dinner at the keep the night you plan to access the lab."

"So how do we let her know when we've arrived?"

"With this." Kelvyn handed Eleonora a hand-sized mirror. "Flash the last rays of sun three times into the window above the entrance doors. Do this at least twice. Amber will be watching for the sign and will flash back with a flare three times from the window as soon as night falls to show she received the message. Send your sign before sunset on a fine day. It must be the day before you plan to enter. This will give her time to carry out the plan. If it's cloudy, you'll have to wait."

"How do we destroy the lab with the scientist there?" Will asked.

"Amber will advise you."

***

They walked east from Fawley Village with the Hoarfrost Mountains on their right. Soft green vegetation covered the lower parts of the mountains, but ochre cones of rock stood above the green bases, like sentinels.

A box-shaped granite building came into view mid-afternoon.

"Hoarfrost Keep. At last." Laurien dropped onto a log to rest.

"Nothing special to look at." Will expected a much more imposing building.

"Most of the building is beneath the ground," she said.

They set up a makeshift shelter under a grove of elms in Hackthorn Wood, a safe distance away, but close enough to watch the keep. Men in gray uniforms patrolled the perimeter of the building.

Late afternoon Eleonora pulled the mirror from her pocket. "Stay here. I need to move closer to signal Amber." She slipped into the bushes, and Will kept watch. She returned around two hours later. "I flashed the mirror and Amber returned the signal. We need a good sleep tonight, so we're rested for tomorrow night."

***

The following morning, large plops of rain dripped through the trees and chilled Will's skin. He stretched his stiff limbs and chewed on an unappetizing dried mushroom. They sat hunched together, pulling their coats and scarves tightly around them.

"What I wouldn't give for a blazing fire and hot tea," Laurien said.

"Or a burger with the lot, from the cafe," Will said under his breath.

"I'll make apple cake when we get back to Caves Hill," Eleonora said. Will slipped his arm around her waist and pulled her close. Would they ever be back there just the way it used to be? He wasn't sure about anything. He grasped her hand and held it to his lips.

That evening, they peered through the gloom of nightfall at the keep. The guards changed their watch.

"They don't look drowsy." Laurien frowned as she pulled her coat hood over her head. "I wonder if they've eaten the food with the potion in it yet?"

"They may eat later," Eleonora said. "If that's the case, we'll have to wait. Let's move closer."

Will could no longer feel his toes or the ends of his fingers. "Apart from the cold, the weather's on our side tonight. The clouds are covering the moon."

Eleonora shivered. "Have you got the ropes ready, Will? We'll need them to tie up Malory."

Will patted his pack and put his arms around both girls. They clung to each other's warmth.

"I'll watch the keep," he said, after a few minutes. "You girls get some rest." Will shook the raindrops from his coat and settled under a tree closer to the keep. At last, four people arrived with trays of steaming bowls for the outside guards. After they'd eaten, Will sneaked back and woke the girls. "Let's hope it was Amber's food that they ate."

Eleonora passed them each a millet cake from Kelwyn's bag, and they waited. Laurien's head drooped. Three of the guards had slumped against the wall of the building. One paced back and forth.

"He mightn't have eaten with the others," Eleonora said. "Anyway, it's time to go.

They walked toward the building. Moonlight bathed its eerie block walls, and a dank smell emanated from it. The active guard kicked one of the sleeping men, then turned when he saw them approach. He drew a dagger.

"You won't need that," Will said "We're here on official business."

The guard regarded them with suspicion. "State your business."

"We're here to make a delivery for Malory at the lab." Eleonora held up the three full calico bags.

"Let me see that." The guard sliced one open with the tip of his knife and sniffed it.

"You're contaminating it." Eleonora snatched back the bag.

"Why would you come to the keep at this hour of the night, with packages like this?

"We can't waste our time being interrogated." Laurien pushed past him toward the door.

The guard grabbed her. A door nearby swung open, and a girl with close-cropped hair and a brown sack-shaped dress appeared.

"Magnus. Stop. We are expecting these people."

Amber. Will breathed again.

"Malory doesn't like being kept up. You're hours late." Amber beckoned to them to enter the building.

"I don't like the sound of this," the guard called to her. Amber leaned toward him and whispered in his ear. He nodded, and she bustled them inside.

"Don't worry about him, he's on our side. Follow me and do what I say." She led them to a narrow staircase winding down to another floor.

"What's the plan?" Will asked her in a low tone.

"We must restrain Malory, then dismantle and destroy the equipment. It'll be difficult to take Malory captive," she said in a loud whisper. "He prepares his own food in the lab and hardly ever goes upstairs—or outside, for that matter. He's old, but still strong and stubborn. Producing madecia is his life's work, and he's the only one who knows the formula ."

"So if we destroy the lab, no one else can produce it?" Will said.

"That's right."

Dripping water echoed through the walls of the stairwell. "We're getting close now. There's a lot of glass and pottery in the lab, so be careful. Hopefully, it's deep enough underground to muffle any sounds we'll make. But if they get suspicious upstairs about the drowsiness after dinner, then anything could happen."

"Is Malory alone?" Eleonora asked.

"He usually is at this time of night."

"Amber, what will you do after this?"

"I'll cross that bridge when I come to it. One thing I know—this will be the end of my time at Hoarfrost Keep."

Chapter 36

They followed Amber as she unlocked and eased open the hefty door of the lab. Inside, a vast array of glass tubes, retort flasks, and distillation columns glinted. Steam rose from several containers. An old man's angular face and white lab coat shone in the light of a lamp. He stared into a test tube with deep concentration.

Malory.

Laurien tripped on the leg of a bench. Malory's head snapped up, and anger glinted in his eyes.

"You know the rules about entry into the lab, girl. Who are these people?

"Malory, your time is up," Amber said in a sharp tone.

"What do you mean?" Malory lurched from his stool.

Will rushed toward the scientist and wrapped the rope around him. Amber threw her apron over his head. The man shouted and kicked as they pulled him to a heavy metal cabinet on the back wall. They tied him to it, heaving and grunting.

But before the knots were secure, Malory swung a blow at Will. Will ducked but slipped on the floor. Will pulled himself up, the others rushed to help and they all secured Malory to the cabinet.

"You'll be sorry." Malory squirmed against the ropes.

"Keep still. If you move, the cabinet could fall on you," Will said.

Laurien and Eleonora swiped the burners and glass containers off the benches into boxes. Some crashed and splintered over the floor. A pungent chemical smell filled the laboratory. Amber packed bottles of powder and liquids. "I have someone in the castle who'll get rid of this so it can't be used again."

"You think you'll get away with this?" The scientist snorted in derision.

"Now it's time to make amends, Malory," Eleonora said. "Live the rest of your life helping people instead of destroying them."

"If we aren't all poisoned by the fumes," Laurien muttered. They continued to dismantle the lab, crunching around on the broken glass. "Ow!" Blood seeped from a gash on Laurien's leg.

"Do you think this is all I have?" Malory said in a tone of disgust. "What about the other lab? You didn't know about that, did you? It's out of your reach. My little outfit is nothing compared to it."

"There's another lab?" Will stared at Amber.

Amber's forehead creased with uncertainty. "Not that I know of."

"Prove it, Malory," Eleonora demanded.

"Do you think I would tell?" Malory said, then paused and looked at Eleonora through narrowed eyes. "Where did you get that pendant?"

Eleonora clutched it to her chest.

"Why are you wearing it?"

"What's it to you?" she asked.

"Who gave it to you?" His face paled. "You're so like her. Why are you involved in this, of all people?"

They stood frozen, gaping at him.

"Who?" Amber asked with a confused look on her face.

"Isabel." Malory fixed his light green eyes on Eleonora.

"My mother," Eleonora said with a gasp.

"Where is she? Does she know you're here?"

"She's dead."

Malory dropped his head to his chest with a shuddering sigh.

"She drowned when the president filled the Napier Mountains valley for his lake." Eleonora wiped a sleeve over her eyes.

"Not Isabel." Malory shook his head. "She should have been mine, but she chose your father instead. That's why I came here. She was the only one I ever wanted. The one thing in my life I cared for." Every part of Malory's body that wasn't tied with rope slumped. They gathered closer to him.

"Buried myself in the President's work to manufacture the ultimate healing drug. Yes, it has a dark side. I admit it. Lorn promised me power and wealth—but he killed Isabel." His voice was strangled with pain. "Why didn't they tell me?"

"Can you help us, Malory?" Eleonora asked. "This drug you're making is not a panacea. It's harming people all over the island."

Malory clenched his fists and stared at her.

"Tell me your name, and I'll tell you what you need to know," he said.

"Eleonora."

He let out a long breath. She stepped toward him.

"Don't go near him," Laurien said. Will joined Laurien, his hand on his knife.

Malory chanted in a toneless voice.

> "It's far from here,
> But also close.
> In the claws of a bird,
> Who Lorn loves most,
> The path to the prize
> Has no sun for light,
> But leads to the place
> Where you must fight."

They all paused, deep in thought.

"Could the lab be at the Palace?" Amber asked. "But it's not close. It would take over five days to travel there through the Hoarfrost Mountains."

"And we'd never get there before they're alerted about the destruction of this lab," Laurien said. "What do you mean by 'close and dark'?"

"Dumb, dumb, dumb!" Malory said. "Try harder."

"The path to the prize has no sun for light," Will quoted. "Is there a tunnel under the mountains?" He extracted a splinter of glass from his arm.

"It's not far to Nevara as the crow flies." Eleonora said. "But how could the President's pet raven he loves be in charge of a drug lab?"

Malory snickered.

"Does he love anything or anyone but himself?" Will said.

"Right and wrong. You'll see when you get there." Malory's eyes narrowed at the sound of footsteps on the staircase. "The guards are coming. Untie me so I can get the key to the underground passage. It's a five-hour walk to the palace. Faster if you run."

"Don't trust him. It could be a trap." Laurien tied a piece of cloth around her bleeding leg.

"Malory, what's my mother's second name?" Eleonora grasped the locket.

"Elise."

"I trust him," Eleonora said.

Will undid the ropes binding Malory to the cabinet. "Laurien, your leg is bleeding too much for the trip to

Nevara. You and Amber should be tied up so it looks as though Malory's restrained you. That'll free him to make a suitable excuse for all of this." He looked Malory in the eyes. "You'd better come up with a good one."

Malory kicked the broken glass containers out of his path and went to a cabinet. He took a key from it and pointed to a large wooden cupboard on the back wall. "The door to the palace is behind that empty closet."

Will jumped at loud rap at the lab's entrance door.

"It's the guards," Amber said. "Time's up. Hurry."

"Amber, lock the entrance door from the inside to delay them," Malory said. "My allegiance to the rule of Nevara is over." Amber turned the lock and then Malory tied her and Laurien to chairs.

Guards shouted at the door. "Open up."

Malory and Will yanked the closet out from the wall and unlocked the door hidden behind. Will gasped at the dark hole. The passage was high enough for him to stand upright.

Malory grabbed Eleonora's arm before she entered the passageway. "On my life and in memory of Isabel's life, I will tell no one the formula," Malory said, in a fierce low voice. "If you destroy the bottles of green solution at the palace, the madecia will be no more. It's the last of the formula. The trees used to make the solution all died in the last frost."

"All of them?" Will asked.

Malory pointed to a green stain pooling on the floor. "You troublemakers contaminated my last supply. It would have kept us going another three years." The bashing on the lab door became louder and more insistent.

Eleonora patted Malory's shoulder. "If I survive this, I'll tell you about Mom."

"Good. Now go," Malory said in an urgent tone. "There's a lantern and flint-lighter inside."

The lab entrance door splintered as the guards pushed on it. Will's heart hammered. He closed the passageway door and heard the scrape of the cupboard as Malory pushed it against the wall. Blackness surrounded them. Who knew where this place led? He felt for Eleonora's hand as muffled shouts from the guards and screams from Laurien filtered into the passage.

He struggled to get his bearings in the darkness. "We need to find the lantern."

"It's here, I think." Eleonora led his hand with her shaking one, to the lantern. After fumbling with the flint, he lit it. He grabbed her hand, and they sprinted along the passage.

A while later, they slowed to a walk, too breathless to run. Will still gripped her hand.

"I haven't got my head around the shock of finding out about Malory and Mom," Eleonora said.

"He kept us in suspense with his bag of surprises," Will said. "Who do you think is in charge of the palace lab?"

"If it isn't the president, I have no idea."

"Could it be the president's wife?" Will asked.

"Isn't she dead?"

"So they say. But when I was in the throne room at the palace, the curtains parted, and I saw someone. A small bird-like person."

"Sounds far-fetched but possible."

"We might find out if we get that far. I wonder if the news about the destruction of the lab has spread yet." They sprinted for what seemed like an hour. The passageway's even floor made the journey easier. They rested and continued.

"I wonder how deep we are under the mountains? It's so silent. I wouldn't like to be trapped down here."

"Comforting thought." Will grimaced.

Eleonora put her hand on his arm. "Just stop for a minute. To gather my breath." She panted and dropped to the ground.

He sank beside her. "Got any food?"

"Nothing." They sat together, with their backs resting on the stone wall. The lantern bounced reflections on the glistening surface.

"You're going to have a massive black eye." She stroked the side of his face.

He buried his face in her hair for a moment, clasped her hands and pulled her up, and they continued along the passage. A breeze rushed through. The lantern blew out. They stopped mid-track.

A dark dread seeped into Will's mind. "Do you feel something? A presence?"

"You will fail your mission," a guttural voice said in his head.

"Did you hear that?"

"I can't hear anything, but I feel something sinister. The Darkness."

"What'll we do?"

"What we always do." She unwrapped their tightly laced fingers and grasped both of his arms and petitioned the King for protection. The presence faded, and they lit the lantern again.

They were climbing now, and the tunnel smelled foul. The crashing of crockery echoed through the passageway. Reflections from a light ahead bounced around on the stone walls. They paused at the sound of heavy footsteps.

"Great," Will said.

A burly guard barred the way.

"We're on business from the Hoarfrost Keep laboratory. Let us pass."

The guard sniggered. "I haven't been informed of your arrival. We're on the lookout for spies. You two certainly fit the bill."

"We have important information. There's been a break-in at Hoarfrost Keep. I'm sure you would want the President informed," Will said.

"I'll escort you to the Palace. Under guard." The man drew his knife and signaled to them to go ahead.

"Thank you," Will replied, not able to think of anything else. It would give them time to plan.

When they reached a door, one guard turned and grabbed Will's arm, checking it for the raven tattoo.

When he saw the unmarked skin, he gave a satisfied snort. "Drifters. You'll wait here. If you're spies, your blood will run on this ground." He pointed near their feet, then hurried through the door and bolted it on the other side.

An ice-cold chill trickled down Will's spine.

"What should we do now?" Eleonora asked. "We're sitting ducks. He'll come back with reinforcements."

"I'll try to open the door from this side." Will strained without success to push it open.

"Just be ready. The King knows we're trapped," Eleonora said.

The bolt scraped, and the door opened. Four grim-faced guards stood staring at them.

"You are to be interrogated," one said in a stern voice.

Two guards led the way, and the others followed, forcing them into the palace. The reflective white floors and ebony black walls of the corridor were the same as the Nevara entrance hall they'd been dragged through last time. Large square mirrored pots of trees with dark green foliage stood at regular intervals. Their footsteps echoed on the tiles like a measured countdown to catastrophe.

"Not the home-coming welcome we expected," Will said under his breath.

"Stop it," Eleonora muttered.

The guards pushed them into a vast conservatory with a high glass roof. Peculiar plants, many with thick, flat ivory petals and green stamens filled the room. Other fragrant, exotic shrubs with olive-colored leaves and sprays of indigo flowers bordered a central pathway. The guards led them into another light-filled room. Chemicals and glassware packed steel benches. Every sound resonated in the room.

"The other madecia lab," Eleonora murmured to him, mouth open and eyes wide. The room was four times the size of the lab at Hoarfrost Keep.

A tiny woman with a dour expression sat on a giant chair in the middle of a podium at the far end of the room. Will drew in an audible breath. Tall bottles of green liquid, glowing in the light from the glass roof, lined up on a high shelf behind her. Beside her chair, a thick book dwarfed the small table it lay on.

"Michelia, a Craver and a crow," he whispered to Eleonora.

Her weathered skin resembled a decayed, wrinkled peach. Her legs dangled like thin brown branches, and her clawed hands curled on the arm supports. No wonder she'd hidden herself away from prying eyes all these years—the madecia had ravaged her body. Will squashed the feeling of pity.

Chapter 37

"Here you are at last, fugitives," Michelia cackled. "You slipped through my fingers last time, did you not? And now I get to feed you to my birds. Can't you hear them crying for you?" Will lifted his eyes to the glass ceiling. He could make out the circling flocks overhead and hear their distant screeching.

"Take their weapons." Her voice was forceful for such a fragile-looking frame.

"We have the King's sword. You can't take that," Will said.

"I can take what I like," she said in a staccato tone.

"Will I call the President, your honor?" a guard asked.

She bashed the chair arms in impatience. "No, no, no, no. This is my concern, not his."

"Bring the boy. I will give him one concession. He can choose his punishment." She beckoned to Will's guard, who pushed him towards the book on the table. Will glanced at the title 'The Kingdom of Lorn Book of Punishment.' His throat closed in a tight band of misgiving.

"Find the chapter—'Punishment for a Traitor' on page four of the Contents."

Will stood defiant.

"Open the book." Michelia's voice changed to a high-pitched whine ending in a warble. The guard punched him in the stomach and he doubled over. Will lifted the cover and scanned the Table of Contents, handwritten in spidery brown ink.

Punishment for a Liar, Punishment for a Dissenter, Punishment for a Rule-Breaker . . . and finally Punishment for a Traitor, Page 1,400. Will flicked to the page and scanned the various neatly itemized punishments. The brutal and barbaric list resembled what he'd find in a medieval book of torture.

Gorge rose in Will's already constricted throat. He most likely wouldn't survive any of them. Perhaps the kneecapping? But that also included shinbone crushing. A pang hit his legs at the thought. And he certainly wouldn't opt for any sawing and scalping.

He glanced toward Eleonora. He knew her well enough to see she was poised for action. In an instant, he knew what it was. His heart raced at double speed. Eleonora wrenched away from the guard and leaped toward a lab bench. Will stopped breathing. She would try to smash the bottles of green liquid. But they were so high.

She grabbed a glass flask from a bench, swiveled around, and aimed it at the row of bottles. Everyone stood transfixed as she flung the flask through the air. It missed the shelf and smashed into the wall, sending sharp pieces skittering over the floor.

"Terminate that girl. Now," Michelia shouted.

A guard launched toward Eleonora and grappled her to the floor. Will dashed down the podium steps and tackled the guard holding her. But the guard twisted down, stabbed into her waist, and then aimed the knife upwards. Eleonora locked her eyes on Will's. Her mouth formed two words.

"Do it." Then her head hit the ground.

A shock wave launched through Will. He sprinted to the podium and grabbed the punishment book with both hands. He flung it upwards toward the side of the green bottles shelf.

The book clipped the first jar. Tension stretched him to snapping point as the jar teetered against the others with a chinking noise. It unsettled the next bottle and the skinny containers toppled like dominoes, shattering on the hard floor. Bright green liquid splashed in jagged shapes across the white tiles. An acrid odor filled the room. The punishment book lay on the floor open and green-stained.

With a wail, Michelia fell to her knees in the broken glass and emerald liquid. She scooped it up with her hands. "My treasure. My life." Her cries joined with the bird shrieks above.

She staggered to her feet and stabbed her twig finger at Will.

"Do you have any idea what you've done, boy? Don't you know the suffering this will bring?" Her face became as dark as a raven's feathers. "This conspirator deserves to die."

The guards grabbed Will. One hit his stomach with such force that he crumpled to the ground. A knife flashed and a pain stabbed his side, but he ignored it and crawled to Eleonora. A bright red stain had spread into her clothes near her waist. He listened for a breath.

Panic exploded through Will's bloodstream.

"Nevara is doomed," Michelia screeched, still kneeling in the green pool. "There will be three deaths today."

Michelia took a knife from her belt, her lips set firm in an agonized grin. Will turned away as a light thud sounded on the floor. A wind gusted through the room, and the glass equipment on the benches rattled. Footsteps thundered through the room, but Will's sight had become muddled and indistinct.

The distorted faces of Malory and Amber blurred in and out of his vision. Guards dressed in gray, like the guards at Hoarfrost Keep swarmed through the room.

He put his hand to his waist. The clothing was wet and warm. He laid his head on Eleonora's chest, and listened for a heartbeat. He called for help, but no sound came from his throat. His mind no longer felt part of his body. He tried to lift his head, but it was as heavy as a sack of stones.

***

Will woke in a room with granite walls. A distant flute melody mingled with a torrent of rushing water sifted into his consciousness. He pulled himself upright, groaning. His side felt as if he'd been impaled with a stake. He pushed the lavender-scented sheets and a thick cover off his body and lifted his shirt. His whole waist was bandaged.

Rich tapestries of medieval scenes hung on the walls. The room had five tall, narrow windows like a castle. A knock at the door startled him. Before he had time to answer, a young woman with three tight braids around her head and chubby, plum-colored cheeks burst in with a china basin and a towel.

"Welcome to Zenith Peaks." She placed the basin on the table. "For you to wash."

"Eleonora. Where is she?" he asked.

"She's in the healing rooms. They'll call you when the time's right."

"Is she—?"

"Only the King knows. I'm Aldith. Ring the bell if you need anything." She rushed away. Will drew a breath of surprise at the vista from the windows. The place was in the clouds. A waterfall cascaded in a rushing column into a chasm. Aldith returned with a tray of steaming oats and a mug of tea, and then tidied the bed and plumped the cushions. Will ate two mouthfuls of the oats then dropped the spoon back onto the plate.

"How did I get here?"

"The Counselor brought you."

"Do you know what happened to my friends at Hoarfrost Keep?"

"I'll enquire." She bustled out of the room.

He pulled on his coat and ventured into the corridor. He had to see Eleonora. The stone passageway wound around corners, down stairs, through arches and into various halls. Several people dressed in country-style clothes passed him, nodding a greeting. Two imposing angels walked by.

"May the King's grace be with you," they said to him.

A boy carrying a falcon on his arm paused on the stairs when he saw Will.

"Could you direct me to the Healing Rooms?" Will said. The boy had an emblem of a lion and an eagle embroidered a pocket of his coat.

"I'll take you there myself. Come this way." The bird leaned over and tried to peck Will's arm. "I'm Hunter by the way, and I already know who you are. Glad to meet you." They took a right-hand turn to more stairs.

"That's a fine-looking bird you've got," Will said, keeping a safe distance from it.

"This is Oliver. He's been recuperating in my room after a nasty altercation with another bird of prey. He's going back to the forest today." Hunter stared at him. "So you're from the caves near Shannon? I've heard of your bravery."

"Really? Do you live here, Hunter?"

"Yes, but only part of the year. It's a special place for the King's people. I come with my parents, who bring supplies." The falcon nibbled on the emblem of the boy's coat.

"Enough, Oliver. You'll be free soon," Hunter said. "Would you like me to show you around? I can find out where you're staying in the castle and meet you tomorrow morning."

"It depends on Eleonora and this wretched wound in my side."

"You mean Eleonora, the girl you rescued from Nevara?"

"Yes."

"So you are together?" he asked. The falcon gave Will a piercing stare with its shiny marble eyes.

Will swallowed and nodded. "How well-equipped are they here? I mean, medically?"

"Your friend's in expert hands," Hunter said. "Never fear. If her time hasn't come, they'll heal her. If her time has come, then be glad for her." The bird picked at the stitching on the shoulder of his coat. "You'll be together again one day."

They made their way into a room furnished with cushioned leather chairs. A slim woman, with wispy hair around her face, called to them from behind a desk. "Can I help you, young gentlemen?"

"I've come to see Eleonora." Will's heart trembled with a mix of apprehension and desperation.

The woman glared at Hunter. "This is not the place for birds of prey."

"See you later then, Will." The falcon launched from Hunter's arm and flapped out into the corridor.

"I'll check on your friend." The woman left the room. Will waited, twisting the buttons on his coat to distract him from fearful thoughts. After a few minutes, she returned and beckoned to him. "She's in the capable hands of Dr. Anton."

Eleonora lay lifeless on a narrow bed in a large uncluttered room. Will tiptoed closer. A petite, wizened man with a face like a mirren, fussed around her. A pot bubbled over a flame, and the room smelled like the earthy forest floor on a sodden day.

"Is she all right?"

"She's gravely ill," the doctor said. "The knife wound has resulted in severe damage and she has a collapsed lung."

Will dug his nails into his palms, trying to contain his emotions.

Two other patients lay on beds nearby. An angel stood in the corner, watching.

"Can I speak to her?"

"She won't hear you. Perhaps tomorrow. We'll see."

Will sat by her bed all day, holding her hand, and regularly changing the cooling compress on her burning forehead and arms. He watched and waited until evening.

"You must leave now," the doctor said. "And you need rest for that diaphragm injury."

***

Will woke early to a bleak morning. He threw off the covers and dragged himself to the window. Something was wrong. Even the water gushing into the valley was the color of ash. He tried to swallow the dread that stabbed his heart whenever he thought of Eleonora. Why couldn't the Counselor heal her?

Aldith bustled in with an armful of fresh clothes. She passed him a folded piece of paper. "Hunter did some investigating for us."

Jadyn, Laurien and Amber are well.

Your friend,
Hunter.

With a sigh of relief, Will pulled on the clothes Aldith had laid out for him and took a half-hearted bite from the millet bread on the laden breakfast tray. He had to see Eleonora. He'd slept too long. He ran down the stairs, shallow-breathing to ease the pain in his side. But the nurse at the Healing Rooms turned him away.

"The princess is undergoing treatment. We'll call you when it's time."

"But I must see her."

"No. Later."

Will turned back to his room. Barely seeing the stairs and his mind in a haze, he collided with a woman carrying a jug of water. Back in his room and half drenched, he lay on his bed exhausted by trepidation and the pain stabbing his side.

Around mid-afternoon, the doctor knocked and entered with an ashen face. "I'm sorry, Will. She's gone. She's gone to be with the King." His voice cracked as he spoke.

The man's words punctured Will's heart, and grief bled through his body in a surging flood. The doctor stood silently, staring out a window.

Will crumpled onto the bed, his head in his hands.

"Can I see her?" The doctor led him to the Healing Rooms in silence. Will staggered toward her bed. Her translucent face was so peaceful, so angelic. A white throw with yellow daisies covered her body. Will folded up on the floor in a parcel of pain.

He kneeled beside her and took her cold hand. He pressed his lips on her lifeless ones, and his tears poured like the waterfall from the mountain. His life would never be the same.

"It's time to leave her now and I need to change your bandages and give you some pain relief," the doctor said.

That night was the longest he could remember. A black hole of desolation. A hole of no hope, no joy, no escape. He spent the next day floundering through the forest near the castle, crying out to the King and Counselor for comfort. He couldn't bear the thought of never seeing Eleonora again. He couldn't bear the thought of never touching her again. And he couldn't bear that the King had allowed this to happen.

He woke to a damp gray day and driving rain. The Counselor came to him and enfolded him in his arms. Will broke away, dragged himself to the window, and peered into the gloomy gorge.

"You will see her again," the Counselor said.

"But I want her now." Rain sprayed through the window, spattering his tear-streaked face.

"The rule of Lorn is finished and Jadyn is now interim President," the Counselor said. "There's another thing I must tell you. It will cause you more pain."

Will sat on the bed and squeezed his forehead with his hands. He didn't want to hear it.

"It's time to go home," the Counselor said.

"You mean Aporto Bay?"

The Counselor nodded.

Will wrestled with the cruel anguish biting into him with its iron teeth. He didn't want to go anywhere. He would stay here, near Eleonora. To grieve and be close to where she was buried.

The Counselor sat and waited.

A strange thought dropped into Will's mind—a thought he hadn't expected. It was an image of Shadow, his raven, soaring on the breeze. Sleek-feathered and free. Why was he thinking that?

But he knew.

Like Shadow, he'd been trapped in his island cage, crawling around in the grime, lost and broken. But he'd dared to accept help from the Counselor and his friends. He was on the path to wholeness now. The prison door of the iron cage had opened. Opened to freedom.

He could stay grieving for Eleonora. But it was time to be courageous and move out into the big wide world with his new identity. And that big wild world was Aporto Bay.

Eleonora would have wanted that.

PART THREE

THE BAY

Chapter 38

Aporto Bay Hospital: Discharge

Will held out his wavering arm for the blood pressure cuff, trying to smile at his Mom and the nurse instead of grimace. He hadn't expected to wake up in a coma ward at Aporto Bay Hospital, and he'd never felt this sick in his life.

"How's the pain?" The nurse asked.

"I've felt better."

"I'll fetch some pain relief."

It would be good if they could get rid of the fog in his brain. His mind hadn't caught up with the present. He needed more time on the island to grieve for Eleonora, and he longed to get news from Laurien and Jadyn about the overthrow of Lorn.

The nurse made notes on his records. "You're doing fine considering what you've been through. The doctor will be here soon. You might like to ask him about what happens next."

"Yeah," Will said. "I'm fine. I'm hunky-dory." Had she forgotten he was a cripple? "But I'm looking forward to going for a leak on my own."

"Dr. Lindsay's replaced Dr. Cooper. He was your doctor when you were in the coma ward in ICU," the nurse said. "Dr. Cooper's moved to Sandy Bay Private. He wants you to keep in touch with him."

The nurse smoothed the sheet over Will's body, adjusted the white cotton blanket, and looked up as Dr. Lindsay entered with his Mom.

Mom hugged him, beaming. She wouldn't want to know how much that hurt.

"Here's your phone and the other things you wanted." Will turned the phone over in his hands. It was definitely his. Not crushed under a rock in Cawl Desert.

"How's our star patient?" the doctor asked.

Will ran his shaky hands through his hair and gazed around the ward. "Alive. So far. Can't believe I was in a coma for only eight weeks.

"Eight and a half," the doctor said. "We're all extremely pleased with your progress after such serious medical problems. You gave your family and the staff some tense moments."

"It seemed so much longer. I had dreams. I thought it was well over a year. Even more."

"That can happen. I had one patient in a short-term coma who dreamed decades had passed. If all goes to plan, you should be home in two weeks. But you'll need to see the occupational therapist every week for a while. We want to get you back on that surfboard."

"And back to his studies," Susan added.

"And my dozens of late assignments and the exams I just might have missed." The thoughts came back in an unwelcome flood.

"I'm sure they'll make allowances, love."

His mom sat on the bed. "I'm so happy to have you back. I could dance all around the ward."

"You know what I thought while I was having a bit of a dream in the coma?" He couldn't tell her about Eldrad, not yet anyway—it would freak her out. "I missed you so much I decided that if I ever recovered, I'd take you to Rileys Restaurant for dinner, and I'd cook all the meals for a week while you put your feet up. You deserve it."

"We'll think about that when you've recovered." She patted his hand. "I'll see you in the morning, love."

Will stretched out on the bed, staring at the ceiling. He felt as though his bones were hollowed out and he would never have enough energy to do anything again. And he wanted Eleonora. She couldn't be dead. The King wouldn't have let it happen. And where was the Counselor? Where were Jadyn and Laurien? Torn in half with pain and longing, he pounded the mattress.

***

The next morning, Jade the physiotherapist pulled a walker toward Will's bed. "Let's see if you can get to the bathroom on your own, Will. It's not far to walk. And we need to check that bedsore."

"Is that walker for me?" he asked.

"It is."

"I'm not using that contraption."

"You haven't been on your feet for a long time."

"And my limbs have atrophied. As they've told me a million times." He squeezed at the non-existent muscles on one of his arms. "How about crutches?"

"We could try," she said. "First, let's see how you go sitting up. I'll elevate the bed to make it easier."

A haze of nauseating dizziness swirled around his head as he pulled himself up. He plonked his body back on the mattress. "Feel as if I've been squashed under a steamroller."

"No bathroom visit for you today. I'll get a urinal."

When Jade rushed away, a guy with a crop of brown curls and face in a mess of peeling skin bounded into the room, with a packet of Oreos under one arm. "Hey, man. Never thought I'd see you with your eyes open again."

Mitch. "Yeah, had a bit of a sleep-in. They've decided it's time for me to get out of bed. Never a moment's peace in this place."

Mitch threw the Oreos onto the bed. "You'll need to put some meat on those bones before Ben sees you."

"What happened to your face?"

"Surf comp." Mitch's chapped lips stretched into a smile. "Aced it."

"Awesome."

"Did they tell you we lost . . . Lenny in the stadium accident?" Mitch's voice faltered.

Will bit his lip. "Mom told me. I still can't believe it."

Susan arrived and arranged Will's toiletries in the drawer beside his bed. Her phone rang, she checked the caller and passed it to him. "It's your father."

Anger streaked through Will. His emotions were as raw as uncooked steak.

"Later." He couldn't handle it now.

After his Mom and Mitch left, the physiotherapist returned with crutches and a urinal.

"We'll start our exercise program first thing in the morning."

"I hear Nurse Baxter looked after me in ICU. When you see her next could you thank her for me? She did an amazing job. Maybe I could get her a coffee and flowers or something."

When everyone left, Will pulled himself up off his pillows. The wave of dizziness gripped him again. He swallowed and swung his pale, bony legs over the edge of the bed, wedging the crutches firmly under his armpits.

Then crashed to the floor.

***

The hospital discharged Will two weeks later. The ICU staff came to farewell him. Susan and Jess picked him up in the car, decorated with shiny streamers and balloons. Halfway along Sanderson Street, Jess pointed at a painted cardboard sign nailed to a power pole:

WELCOME HOME WILL

YOU TOOK YOUR TIME!

They all laughed.

The guys, Rob and old school friends waited in the front garden with his favorite party food and more balloons. They cheered as he arrived, giving him hugs and high fives. Will hobbled around on his crutches.

After his friends left, he tottered through the house. The evocative mix of furniture polish and yesterday's meals had been distant in his memory for so long, but now poignantly familiar. It was as if he was dreaming and needed to wake up.

Every cell in his body begged for rest. He limped into his bedroom and slumped on the quilt. The old school photos and the Ryder posters were still on the wall. The chest of drawers he'd painted with Dad was there, plastered with his favorite hero stickers and crammed with past trophies. He longed for Eleonora. He wanted to talk to Jadyn and the Counselor. Was the island an actual place, or in his imagination? If it hadn't been real, why did he feel different now? Why did he feel right about talking to the Counselor as though he was still with him? And why did he feel his brain was rewired, in a good way?

***

Three weeks later, Will woke as usual to the sound of birds squawking in the tree outside the bedroom. The annoying and familiar wave of dizziness overwhelmed him as he sat up. He collapsed back on his bed and pictured Eleonora lying under the daisy cover at Zenith Peaks, her honey hair matted with blood, dark circles under her eyes and impossibly beautiful—even in death. Loss slashed at his thoughts. He crushed the pillow over his face, trying to squeeze out the desolation.

He checked his watch and fumbled for jeans and a clean shirt. Today he had an appointment with the Year Adviser at college and a reunion with his tutorial group. He didn't know how he would catch up and finish his degree. He could barely get through the day. He'd leave the crutches behind this once. Crutches could be lethal on a bus. But once he lurched up the stairs and into the crush of people, he wasn't so sure. There were no seats left. He tripped over a stroller and sweated with the effort of staying upright all the way.

An expanse of summer-crisp lawn stretched out in front of the familiar red brick buildings. He tried to ignore the weakness wracking his limbs as he walked through the wrought-iron gates. Some students rushed to their next lecture, arms loaded with laptops, folders, and books. Others sat or lay on the grass in the sun, chatting.

It seemed like months since he'd been at college. This time was so different. Every step was an effort. He wasn't even sure he'd make it to the lecture rooms without a frantic search for a bench. Not that he'd tell anyone. The weakness was most likely just a temporary symptom. That's what Dr. Lindsay had told him. It was the "most likely" that concerned him.

A lanky college student with close-clipped hair hurried toward him. It was Rob, his tutorial partner.

"Hey, Sutho. Hope you're feeling better than the last time I saw you. We're all meeting in the usual tutorial room. Having a bit of a party for you."

"Wow. That's great." Will's knees were threatening to buckle. "How did you manage that massive psychology assignment without me?"

"They paired me up with Mia."

"How d'you go?" Will's knees knocked.

"A bit challenging. She's not up to your standard when it comes to essay writing. Are you working at the café again yet?"

"Yeah, but not until next weekend. Sally, our neighbor, works there and organized a two-hour shift to start me off. The manager wants to make sure I won't attack or poison the customers."

"Ha. And back to college full-time?"

"Part-time till I get the OK from the neurologist." Will staggered to a bench. "I'll just sit down for a moment.

"So the old body and brain took a real bashing?"

"Just a bit." They walked into the building. It reeked of sweaty sneakers and stale deodorant. Perhaps he should go back and lie on the lawn for a while.

"Are you free one night next week?" Rob asked. "Mom wants to have you over for dinner. Dad's always asking about you."

"Love to, but I'm not allowed to drive yet. Might have a seizure at the wheel." His laugh had a bitter edge.

***

A week later, Will waited outside his house for Rob to pick him up. They drove to Ainsley Crescent with its well-kept houses and neatly trimmed lawns. Solar lights lit a path bordered with a box hedge. Tom and Libby Vincent rushed to the door to greet him.

"Come in, come in." Mrs. Vincent ushered Will inside. The nostalgia evoked from the smell of the baked dinner and unexpected thankfulness that he could actually be there, overwhelmed him for a moment.

"It is so good to have you back with us. Our prayers are answered," Tom Vincent said.

Libby Vincent welcomed him with a cushiony hug. "We have a roast lamb dinner and key lime pie."

After dessert, Rob and Will sat in the study and Rob passed him a bowl of chocolates. "Do you need to unload about anything?"

Will peeled the foil wrapper from a chocolate. If he were to confide in anyone, Rob would be the one. "Yeah, but brace yourself. You won't believe what I'm about to tell you, so keep it off the record. I've told no one else. It's just too mystifying."

Rob's face changed from attentive to super-excited as Will unfolded the Eldrad saga. Every few minutes, he leaped off his chair and paced the room.

"The King has given you an astonishing experience." Rob said. "It must be for a reason. There's a bigger picture to this, and it may not make sense until you find out what it is." He took a book from a shelf and gave it to him. "This is your treasure box. The King's Word. We read it daily at our house. Take it, it's yours. We have more."

On the way home, Will's thoughts twisted and turned. The Vincent's were King followers. He wanted to meet more of them. What was the big picture? Did it involve his life now back at Aporto Bay? He gripped the book Rob had given him. A feeling of connection with Eldrad and the King filled him with good feelings, despite his pining for Eleonora.

Chapter 39

Will woke late on Sunday morning. The low hum of distant lawnmowers and passing cars reminded him he wasn't in his island cave. His body hurt as if he'd been in the worst dumper. But he hadn't been surfing, he'd only just survived his first Saturday shift at the café the day before. At least the crutches were ditched. Stumbling out of bed, he limped to his laptop.

He had three more assignments to finish before the end of the month. He'd be working all day. He wished he had the Counselor with him like he did on Eldrad. He missed Eleonora as much as ever and he needed to talk to Rob again.

After a marathon of typing, he wandered into the kitchen, hungry. It was already almost dinnertime.

"There's lasagna in the fridge if you want it," Mom called. The echo of high heels on the wooden floor reverberated through the lounge room. How many years had it been since she'd worn stilettos?

He stuck his head out of the kitchen door. Perfume wafted through the house. She had a newly styled bob and an orange dress that hugged her curves too tightly.

"Going out?"

"Won't be late."

"Very swish. On a date?"

"Not really."

"Then what?"

"Just out for dinner."

"Who with?" Will's thoughts back-flipped at the idea forming in his head. It didn't seem right somehow.

"Just touching base with Dad."

A streak of anger sizzled in Will's brain. "Looks as if you are more than touching base in that outfit."

"Don't be silly."

"Can I borrow the car again?" he asked. "I need it tomorrow."

"But you can't drive."

"I'm fine, Mom. Dr. Lindsay's given me the all clear."

"Okay." Her expression was uncertain. "By the way, Dad said he's coming up to see you and Jess next weekend."

Will nodded. He was ready to see him.

***

Will met Rob at the college canteen in its post-lunchtime lull. A few students hunched over their laptops or phones, cramming in fast food before the next lecture.

Rob swept the crumbs off a table with a serviette before he threw down his folders. "I'll get some fries and drinks."

Will opened his laptop. "I'll have a look at our next assignment."

Rob pushed the fries into the center of the table, leaned over and shut the laptop. "Firstly, how are you after our talk the other night?"

Will screwed up his face. "I'm still missing Eleonora and the others. I don't have the Counselor—or should I say the King, dropping into my life like I did before. I miss that."

Rob nodded. "We all go through seasons in our lives. This is a testing time for you. But it's all part of the plan. Just don't ask me what it is. I know no more than you do."

Testing. Will was back in Cadwyn's forge. He was the sword in the flame, red hot and burning.

"When I need help, I always turn to the King's word and I ask him things," Rob said. "And as you trust him more, you'll find you'll be less in need of answers from him and more interested in connecting with him."

As they munched on the fries, Mia strode to their table dressed in a pleated tartan skirt and black leggings, her arms loaded with folders. She took a chip and tossed thick red hair from her face. Will smirked—she was so like *Brave's* Princess Merida.

"Looks as if I've lost my tutorial partner," Mia said. "But it's good you're back, Will." She plonked her folders on the table. "Rob, I was wondering if you'd come bowling with me on Friday night." A bright spot of pink tinted each of her cheeks. "There's a few of us, but Mom won't let me go on my own, and you have a car."

"Sure. Message me the details. Why don't you join Will and me on the next assignment? We're allowed to choose who we work with."

"Will do." She grabbed her books and bounced away.

"A date?" Will asked.

"Who knows?"

"Do you mind?"

"Mia's pretty awesome once you get to know her. Anyway, let's go back to our conversation. I was thinking about Eleonora. She and everything else could have pre-occupied your mind to such a degree you've lost the way the King's planned for you. Work through it with him. Not on your own. You won't be disappointed."

"I'll guess I can try." Will paused for a moment. "Have you ever been through hard times, Rob?"

"Yes, but nothing like you. Remember when Ellie dropped me? It was tough, but I asked the King for help. His plans for us are good, and it's all about transformation."

"Do you think he'll ever show me why I was in the stadium accident and how I ended up in that weird coma dream?"

"Most likely—when the time's right." Rob picked up his folders. "Why don't you come to Lifespring one

Sunday night? You may find answers to your questions. I'll be there."

***

It was late Sunday afternoon. Will paced the floor of his bedroom, then sat at his desk and checked his phone for Lifespring's address. He did some breathing exercises Dr. Lindsay had suggested for anxiety, crunched his weights, and made a coffee as a distraction from his churning doubts. Mom was having dinner with Sally next door. The car was free, so he grabbed the keys.

When he arrived at Lifespring's auditorium, the parking lot was three-quarters full. People wandered to the entrance, chatting and shouting greetings. He wiped his sweaty palms on his jeans.

Leave this place. You don't belong here.

He recognized the voice in his head, and it wasn't the voice of the King. He took a breath through his clenched teeth, and headed toward a girl with a ponytail, giving out leaflets at the door. Inside, a band boomed a song, and three singers swayed with the music. The audience joined in with abandon. A woman dressed in a pants suit and white sneakers climbed onto the stage and read verses in a lilting accent from The King's Book. '*He has sent me to bind up the brokenhearted, to proclaim freedom for the captives, and release from darkness for the prisoners.*'

Will closed his eyes, the words transported him back to the time Roland read the same words. After a few more songs, a man bounded to the microphone.

"We need volunteers to help with our new youth group initiative on Thursday nights. It's for kids who've been in trouble with the law or are having a drug problem."

Will couldn't see Rob anywhere, but a girl dressed in a cream blouse sitting in the western gallery caught his attention. The speaker's voice faded into the background. The room spun like a merry-go-round. Surely his mind was playing tricks on him.

It was her.

No. It couldn't be

But it was her.

Shock hit Will's chest in an explosion. He doubled over, gasping for breath, his face as hot as a Caves Hill fire.

It was Eleonora. The blood from his drumming heartbeat roared in his head. He'd forgotten how to blink.

But she was dead. Dead at Zenith Peaks. Only alive in his dreams.

He staggered to an empty seat nearby to see the girl more clearly. The man behind him tapped him on the shoulder. "Are you all right?"

Will nodded. But he wasn't. He was hyperventilating.

The girl sat with a guy around her age with blond hair and an aqua checked shirt. She spoke to him, and the guy grinned. Will gritted his teeth.

It had to be her. But how could she be here, in the bay?

The checked-shirt guy casually put his arm around her. She was with someone else. Disappointment sank through his body in a lead weight. The service finished with another song, and a woman dressed in jeans leaned toward him.

"I'm Lena. What's your name?"

"Got to go." He sprang out of his seat and pushed through the crowd. Where was she? He hurried out of the building into the car park. Cars sounded their horns as he wove back and forth like a madman on a mission. Then he caught sight of her toward the rear of the car park. She even walked like Eleanora—so graceful. He half-sprinted and half-limped toward her. The blond guy opened the door of a blue hatchback and she climbed inside.

"Eleonora!" he shouted uselessly as they drove away.

That night Will thrashed his sheets into a tangle of knots. If it was her, what was she doing in the bay? Who was the guy with her, and what would he say to her if they met face to face? Hello, Princess. Do you remember me? We were together on the Island of Eldrad. He gave a how-stupid-is-that snigger.

Anyway, it couldn't be her. It couldn't.

***

Will had three assignments to finish and an exam to study for, but he had problems focusing. The next few days disappeared in a haze. He stared at every girl he met in the street, every customer he served at the cafe, every girl who passed him in the college library. He worked late into the night, but the distraction turned his motivation into a slow-motion failure.

Two more assignments to complete and an upcoming exam. He'd never get them done.

The next morning, Mom wrapped cheese and pickle sandwiches at the kitchen counter.

"You look under the weather, love. I hope you didn't go back to college too soon. There's leftover satay chicken in the fridge if you and Jess want it. Have to leave. Running late. By the way, how was your doctor's appointment last Friday?"

"Had to cancel, Mom. Too many assignments."

"Make sure you go next week. You still need the check-ups. It takes a long time to recover from what you've been through."

Will bit into a piece of raisin toast and chewed without tasting it. He was back on the island with Eleonora, sitting outside Roland's cave, in front of the fire, with the dancing flames reflected in her eyes, talking about the day's events. He wanted to be there, just the way it used to be.

***

It was Saturday. Will had one more assignment to finish before his shift at the café. He'd have an early breakfast and work solidly all morning. The doorbell rang, but he continued to type. Mom or Jess could get the door. Plates stopped clinking in the kitchen sink. His mother and a girl were talking.

"Will, you have a visitor." There was something strange in the tone of his mother's voice. He saved his work and headed to the lounge room.

The girl stood in the doorway.

A hot tide of emotion tore through his body, from his head to his feet.

She stared at him with her ocean eyes. "Hi, Will." A forest garden fragrance wafted into the room. She gave a half-smile, with that hint of uncertainty.

Eleonora.

He knew every soft curve of her face. Every gorgeous curve of her body.

He tried to speak, but his throat was as rough as sandpaper. He gripped the sideboard, swayed, then slumped to the floor.

Chapter 40

Will opened his eyes, and two faces came into focus, their foreheads creased with concern.

"He's still not well. I'd better call Dr. Lindsay."

He propped himself up on his elbow. "No, I'm fine." He tried not to gawk at Eleonora. "So sorry. I don't normally faint like that."

The girl stroked his forehead. What was she doing? "Who are you?" he asked.

"Sorry. I know you don't know me," she said. "But I know you." She and his Mom helped him onto the couch.

Goosebumps rippled over his body at her touch and the sound of her voice.

"She actually knows you very well." Mom laughed.

"What do you mean?" It was too weird for words.

Eleonora sat on the lounge chair opposite him and arranged her pink gathered skirt around her knees.

Her clothes were different, but her fragrance was the same, and her soft pink lips and azure eyes were the same.

"Let me introduce Erin O'Connell," Mom said, smiling. Jess entered the room, threw down her bag, and rushed to hug Erin.

He sat, speechless.

"It's so good to see you up and about, Will," Erin said. She kept gazing at him without blinking.

A hot crimson tide crept up his neck. He could scarcely breathe. He pulled at his collar.

"I would have been over sooner but I've been down the coast with my parents," she said.

"Sooner?" he said in a tight voice.

"You don't look well, Will. Do you want Erin to come another time?"

"No." You've got to be kidding.

"Do you remember anything about the accident?" Erin asked.

"Yes, some of it. I fell between the seats. A bar hit my head."

"Did you know I was sitting in a row near you?"

"You look familiar."

"Really?"

"And I saw you at Lifespring last Sunday," he said. He couldn't tell her the truth.

The doorbell rang. Erin looked at her watch. "It's Tim. I have to go. He has soccer practice. Could you send me your number Will?"

"I'll fill Will in about the connection," Susan said to her as she left.

He wished she could stay.

Mom sat beside him. "You look as though you've seen a ghost."

"Tell me about that girl," he said in a tense tone.

"She was lying on the ground near you, under the stadium. You tried to protect her from the metal bar falling toward her. It hit the side of your head. You were unconscious the whole time the paramedics worked on you." Susan paused, as if lost in thought. "If it had fallen any closer, you wouldn't have survived."

"Was Erin injured?"

"She broke both legs and was unconscious but came around in the ambulance. I'm sorry I haven't told you everything yet. The memory's still raw, and we didn't want you any more traumatized at this stage of your recovery. The doctor warned us you might suffer from post traumatic stress disorder." She pulled him towards her and buried her head in his shoulder. "I'm so glad to have you home."

"But you haven't told me why I would find Erin familiar."

"I don't know. Could you have met before the accident? You said you saw her last weekend. By the way, what were you doing at Lifespring?"

"Rob invited me."

***

The sun was sinking over the bay when Will returned from his lectures, bursting with questions. Mom was outside, watering the side garden shrubs.

He opened the gate and took the hose "Let me do that."

"How did you get on with your father?" she asked.

"As well as can be expected. I know I have to move on and accept what happened. It's just hard. I spilled coffee all over his trousers. He probably thinks I did it on purpose. I didn't . . . well, maybe I did." Will hosed the hydrangeas. "Tell me more about Erin, the girl who came around yesterday—and who's Tim?"

"I don't know Tim. He picked up Erin at the hospital sometimes. Jess might know." Mom looked at her watch. "I'm late for an appointment. We can talk tonight."

"I won't be home till late. Going out with Mitch and the others."

His phone pinged. Erin. He dropped the hose, bounded up the steps to the house as he read the message, overturning the potted cactus.

"Are you free Saturday afternoon?" Erin.

He messaged back. "Shift at White Sands Cafe finishes at four. Can you meet me there?"

***

Will spent the entire shift with his heart pumping double speed at the thought of seeing Erin. She arrived as he was clearing the last table, with her hair French-braided and in denim shorts. She waved to him and sat at a table.

"What can I get you?" he called.

"An iced coffee would be great."

He made the drink and took it to her, hoping she wouldn't notice his trembling hands. "I'll load the dishwasher, wipe down the benches, and be with you."

It was a dream come true, having her in the café. He carried the last tray of glasses to the sink. But a car exhaust pulsed in Ocean Parade. A red Ferrari. The tray tipped and glasses slid and smashed on the concrete floor.

A few minutes later, Ben Maddock swaggered into the cafe with three others. Great, just what he'd always wanted—his favorite gang: JB the bully, Steroid Seb, and Cocaine Col. All topped off with a Maddock.

Ben's Armani aftershave overpowered the Windex. Ben made a rude gesture at Will, and when they caught sight of Erin, they sat near her table.

"Hey, waiter," Ben shouted across the cafe. "We'll have four double-malted chocolate milkshakes with five scoops of ice cream in each. We all know how stingy you are."

"Can't you see we're closed?" Will swept up the broken glass and slammed the last plate in the dishwasher. It was the worst timing in his life.

"Terrible service, as always. I'll have to speak to the manager. Again." Ben strolled to Erin's table, flashing his perfect white teeth. He flipped the black hair out of his eyes and leaned over the chair next to hers. Erin looked up, smiling.

Will's temperature ratcheted up to a furnace heat. Don't do it. Don't smile at him like that.

"Want to go out with me for dinner tonight?"

Erin laughed. "Sorry, I can't."

"What's wrong with the service around here?" Ben asked.

"The cafe closes at four." Will was ready to explode.

"What's an attractive girl like you doing here on your own?" Ben asked. He turned toward Will. "Surely you're not waiting for a Sutherland loser?"

Will fumbled off his apron and walked to the entrance door, trying not to stumble.

"Let's go," he said to Erin. He swiveled the entrance door sign to 'Closed'. "I'm locking up." Erin picked up her bag. Will pulled the café keys out of his pocket. The four boys scraped out their metal chairs. Ben knocked his over with a crash as they left.

Will led Erin out of the cafe, his entire body buzzing with rage as he locked the door behind them. "Let's walk down to Driftwood Beach. It's nice this time of day." Ben would be unlikely to follow them onto the beach. He might get his designer jeans sandy.

"You okay?" she asked.

"Sure." His throat was as tight as a guitar string. "How long do you have to chat?" He avoided her eyes so she wouldn't see the fury in them.

"Tim's picking me up from the café just before six."

They strolled along Cowrie Street and turned left into Pearl Avenue, past the beach rentals and then along the narrow sandy path lined with spinifex grass. Will breathed in the sea breeze. It was calming and reminded him of Caves Hill. He couldn't believe she was here, walking beside him. It was a miracle. She limped slightly—she must have had a hard recovery as well. His gut panged at the thought.

They reached the beach and took off their sneakers. Their feet made a squeaky sound in the warm, dry sand and they found a spot to sit just above the high-tide line. Seagulls sailed on the air currents, and their cries joined in with the sound of children squealing at the water's edge.

"I owe you a big thank you for visiting me in hospital." Will dug his heels into the sand.

"I'm the one who should thank you. What you did was—"

"What anyone would have done." He grinned at her.

She put her hand on his arm and squeezed it. Her touch scorched him, and he jolted his arm away.

"Sorry." Her face reddened. "I guess I know you, but you don't know me."

If she only knew. That would be quite a conversation— if he could ever bring himself to tell her.

Erin arranged shells into a circle on the sand. "I had a lot of time on my hands, so I'd visit you. My physio was at the hospital, and I had two appointments a week, plus other specialist appointments." After the wheelchair, I hobbled around on crutches. I always had trouble on the stairs and the physio would say 'good leg to heaven and bad leg to hell' so I'd remember to step with my best leg first. But the trouble was both legs were as bad as each other.

"How are you now?" Will stole a long glance at her as she gazed out toward the hazy horizon. There were thin white scars on her legs.

"Great, considering. The doctors worried the bones weren't knitting at first. I still go to physio and have discomfort, but nothing like you. One priority is to do well in my occupational therapy course."

"Great. Have you lived at the bay for long?"

"We moved down here from Sunshine Beach eight months ago."

He gazed out to sea as the sun sank and the sky dissolved into a misty gold. How could he tell her she was inextricably bound to him because of the past? And how did it happen? Perhaps he opened his eyes in the hospital and imprinted her face into his coma dreams. But that didn't explain how he could dream about things he had no knowledge of, and how could he have changed so dramatically? It didn't make sense.

Erin's phone pinged.

"It's Tim. He's picking me up at the cafe in eight minutes. I'll have to go."

As they strolled back, they chatted about the coma ward, the doctors, the accident, and how it had affected the entire town. But he had questions, questions he couldn't verbalize. Not yet. He stared at her soft lips. If only he could touch her like he had before, hold her and pour out his feelings.

"Can I call you next week?" he asked. His knees suddenly went to jelly. What if she said no?

"Yes, sure."

Her face brightened when she caught sight of Tim waiting for her. Will held out his hand to Tim. His grip was overly firm.

"So you're the one who made the surprise recovery?" Only Tim's mouth smiled.

"Ah. Sort of." Will walked to his bike at the back of the cafe. Uneasy feelings and thoughts dragged at him like a rip in the surf.

***

Will sat at his desk, laboring over the last assignment of the week. He closed the lid of the laptop and picked up his Rubik's cube. With a few quick twists, he aligned every row into the solution. He'd always been a whiz with the cube.

He wished his life was as simple. The riddle of his life wasn't a one-dimensional jigsaw puzzle anymore. The enigmas were multi-layered. Why did he end up on the island? How could Erin be the princess? What was the truth? He was on his way to a solution thanks to his journeys on Eldrad, but it would need another miracle to get all the puzzle layers of his life to align perfectly.

The guys were meeting at White Sands Beach in the afternoon. Will lugged his surfboard down Cowrie Street and then turned into Ashton Road. His limbs burned with the exertion, and he panted like he'd been working out for hours. The welcome strip of ocean spread its blue splendor to the horizon as he rounded the bend. The smell of charred sausages and onions wafted in the breeze from the grills in the park. Families strolled to the beach with beach bags, stripy towels, and flip-flops.

Someone slapped him on the back. "Race you to the surf."

"Mitch! Hey, that's not fair."

"I'll give you a minute's head start."

Will hobbled toward the beach, his body straining with the weight of the surfboard. Mitch streaked ahead. Will finally reached the surf and collapsed into the cool water, letting it bubble and wash over his body. He came up for air and flicked back his hair. It had been too long.

Chapter 41

Later that night, Will sat with Mitch, Phil, Chen, Spud and Jordan in a circle on the beach around a blazing fire.

"Hear you hit the surf this afternoon Will," Spud said.

"Yeah. It was pretty lame. Caught an ankle buster and had to bail out." They laughed, and Phil passed him a packet of cigarettes. Will took one and held it out for Phil to light. He could do with a smoke. He waited for a moment and then stubbed it out in the sand.

"What's up?" Phil asked.

"Just don't want to smoke."

"Come on. One won't hurt you. Have it for Lenny."

"Can't afford the habit, anyway."

"New girlfriend expensive?" Jordan asked.

Will laughed. "Erin's not my girlfriend."

"I've seen her at the hospital," Mitch said. "She was stalking you way back when she was in a wheelchair. A bit of all right."

Spud pulled a bottle of vodka from his pack.

"No way, dude," Phil said. "Thought you were out of cash."

"I have my ways and means, and I'm serving at Corellas Restaurant now. Bow tie. The works."

The fire died down, and the ocean surged rhythmically back and forth. Fronds of seaweed washed onto the beach as a watery moon peered through the mist.

"There's something I'd like to do," Will said, breaking the silence.

"Give Ben Maddock a run for his money?" Jordan asked.

Will chuckled and shook his head. "You remember the windows we broke at old Holsworth's factory."

"You broke, you mean."

"Will and I did it," Mitch said. "I did a couple. He did the rest."

"I think an apology's in order." Will passed around the potato chips.

"You've got to be kidding," Spud said. "You know what he's like. Old dog-face will call the cops."

"Don't count me in." Mitch buried his feet in the sand. "Remember, he ripped off my dad with that dud boat engine."

"The hospital's addled your brain, mate." Chen pulled on his hoodie against a sudden gust of wind. "We all know Holsworth deserves everything he gets."

"Everyone at Belmont Martial Arts is asking when you're coming back," Jordan said.

"Can you imagine me doing a sidekick?" Will stuffed a handful of chips in his mouth, trying not to think about the vodka. "I'd fall flat on my face."

"Time to practice then." Jordan and Mitch wrestled him onto the sand.

Will threw them off and shook the sand out of his clothes.

Phil took a long swig from the bottle of vodka and passed it around. Will handed it on to Jordan. He wasn't ready to trust himself with alcohol.

They sat without talking, as they often did, listening to the crash of the breakers and the crackling and spitting of the fire. One day he would tell them about Eldrad. One day. Or maybe never. He could just imagine the looks on their faces.

"It's Lenny's nineteenth birthday soon. Why don't we have a memorial next time we meet?" Mitch said.

***

That night, Will tossed and turned until his sheets wound around the cord on his bed lamp, which then crashed on the timber floor. He dreamed he went to Mr. Holsworth's factory. Guards in brown uniforms arrested and hand-cuffed him and threw him into prison. A demon-faced President Lorn glared at him through a glass window, arranging piles of gold coins in a pyramid on a table.

The next morning, he splashed his face with water, dressed, grabbed a piece of toast, and then threw it in the bin after one bite. He'd lost his appetite since Erin had come into his life, and now he had to follow through with the broken windows saga.

The phone buzzed in his pocket as he walked through the front garden.

Mitch.

"You're a dork," Mitch said, "but I'm coming with you to Holsworth's. Can't let you get nailed all on your own. Meet me at my place in an hour. We can walk—it's not that far."

Will sighed in relief. "Radical. I owe you one!"

***

They walked past the derelict shopfronts along Quay Road and then turned right. Rusty burned-out cars lined the roads of the industrial area, with rows of rundown factories, a display of peeling paint and busted dreams.

"Here it is. Holsworth's palace," Mitch announced. "New windows, but the same old stinking factory." They picked their way along the entry path of cracked concrete pavers bordered with thistles and pulled open the scratched wooden door. Will grimaced as he entered. This was the door to the journey of making amends, and he wasn't looking forward to it.

The dimly lit counter was unattended. An electric drill from the rear of the factory pierced the silence. Will squashed a sudden urge to run. He rang the bell on the faded bench, half hoping no one would come.

A bent, unshaven man with a receding chin shuffled from the shelves on the right. He peered at them through slitted, bloodshot eyes. "What do you troublemakers want? Get out before I call the police."

Mitch stepped back.

"Mr. Holsworth." Will drew an audible breath. "We're here to apologize for something we did. A while ago. A stupid thing. We're sorry and would like to make amends."

"What was that?" The man asked in a scornful tone.

"I broke your front windows."

"I broke a couple as well," Mitch said.

The veins in the old man's neck bulged as his face flooded purple-gray. He bashed his fist on the counter. "You kids are nothing but vermin. I bet you've never seen a day's hard work in your life. They should lock you up and throw away the key."

"We don't have money, but we could work to make up for it," Will said. "We can come in on Saturday mornings."

"I'm calling the police." Saliva sprayed from old Holsworth's mouth onto the counter. He grabbed his phone.

"Please don't, Mr. Holsworth. We can start today if you like. We can work from six-thirty until ten on Saturday mornings."

A woman bustled in, her face as plump as a ripe pumpkin. She dragged off her apron. "What's going on?"

"We're here to apologize and make up for breaking your windows, Mrs. Holsworth."

"You took your time." Her face twisted with disapproval. "But you should give them a chance, Bert." She gave him an I-always-know-best-and-you-know-it look.

Mr. Holsworth poised his finger over the phone and glared at them. "You good-for-nothings can start on the weeds at the back, then sweep the factory floor and unpack my boxes of spare parts." He wiped saliva from his chin with a stained handkerchief. "If anything goes missing or you cause one iota of trouble, we'll have the police up here in a shot. You'll come every Saturday morning for six weeks."

Mitch gaped.

"Thanks, Mr. and Mrs. Holsworth," Will said.

Mrs. Holsworth led them into the backyard, tying the bow on her apron with a snap.

"You boys should know better. I don't know what the world's coming to."

They yanked on the towering weeds in silence. After an hour, Will stopped to pick seedpods out of his hair. "This is like working on a planet with attacking alien plants."

"Tell me about it." Mitch picked spikes out of his jeans.

After two hours, Mrs. Holsworth brought them hot tea and cookies.

They worked until Mr. Holsworth came out and shouted at them. "Off you go now, you layabouts. Next Saturday, or I call the cops."

Will and Mitch walked back home as the midday sun gilded the corrugated roofs of the factories. Will's arms and hands ached, and his skin itched, but overall, his strongest emotion was relief. Best of all, he was seeing Erin after his shift at the café on Sunday. He couldn't wait to see her again.

***

The next afternoon, Erin came into the café, sat at one of the tables and waved to him.

"Nearly finished," he called from the counter. Will's hand froze mid-plate at the dishwasher. Ben was back.

Ben sauntered to Erin's table, chewing gum. "Thought I'd find you here. Why don't you come to the movies with me?"

Erin smiled at him and smoothed back her hair with a shining face. Will clenched his fists. *Don't encourage him, Erin.*

"What are you going to see?"

"*Alien Forces* or *Superball Three*—your choice. Did you know you're the most beautiful girl in Aporto Bay?"

Will's blood pumped iced fury through his veins. But he'd forgiven this guy. He needed to get a grip on himself.

"What about that new French restaurant in Main Street?"

"Sounds great," Erin said. "But I'm busy."

"Erin, someone should tell you the Sutherlands are bad news. You'll thank me one day for warning you."

"Help me before I punch him," Will said under his breath.

As Ben left the café, he elbowed Will in the shoulder. Will ground his teeth and slammed a tray on the table. At this rate, his teeth would be ground to powder.

Will walked over to Erin. "You aren't really thinking of going out with him, are you?"

"Of course not, silly. Tim would be furious. Anyway, it's best to be in their good books."

He sat with her, gulping his smoothie. It was as chilled as his thoughts. Tim came back to pick her up. He was half an hour early.

***

Will slumped on the couch in the lounge room with an overflowing plate of pasta. He'd spent the day in lectures and still had one assignment to finish by nine the next morning. He flicked on a news channel.

Five people were killed when a gunman opened fire in the street at Smithson. The gunman was arrested and taken for questioning and drug testing.

A bridge collapsed near Tahmoor, sending several cars into the water. It was a miracle no one lost their lives.

There is still no sign of two-year-old toddler Micky, who went missing five weeks ago. The parents and community are all hoping and praying for a breakthrough.

The drug trade in Belmore is making it unsafe to walk the streets even during daylight hours.

Will sprinkled more parmesan cheese onto his pasta. He still hadn't taken a mouthful.

Suicide statistics are on the rise: on average, 123 every day.

There have been 50,000 deaths in the past twelve months due to drug overdoses.

And now in overseas news: three tourists were discovered in a basement. They had been kidnapped for the human slave trade.

Will pressed the off button. The news weighed him down. He gulped a mouthful of pasta, and settled the laptop on his knees, opened it, then closed it down. A sudden spark of resolve flashed through him. He could make a difference in the world. His experiences hadn't been for nothing. He may not be fighting an all-out conflict on Eldrad, but there were people in desperate need because of the forces of evil and mayhem. Just because he was back at Aporto Bay didn't mean his responsibilities as an ambassador of the King had lessened in any way. He now had the power to change the world for good.

Will called Lifespring the next day and volunteered to help with the youth group.

***

It was Will and Mitch's fifth week at the Holsworth factory. It had gone more quickly than Will had expected. Although the work was tedious, Mrs. Holsworth's strong tea and homemade shortbread eased the ordeal. She always held her finger to her lips when she set down the tray. They had filled two dumpsters with weeds, cleaned at least five layers of grease from the shelves in the workshop—or that's what Mitch claimed. They also learned about the intricacies of boat engines, and Will told Mitch all about his experiences on the Island of Eldrad. Mitch said he couldn't hear enough about it.

Mr Holsworth glared at them as they said their final goodbyes. He took two envelopes from Mrs Holsworth and gave one to each of them. They tore the envelopes open on the way home to find $200 cash, in each.

Chapter 42

It was Lenny's memorial. The sun sank below the horizon, and a salty chill settled on Will and the huddle of figures around the beach campfire. The acrid smell of smoke from the crackling logs reminded Will of Eldrad and it flooded his thoughts with memories. He longed to sit and chat with Roland and the Counselor again, but he had the Counselor with him. Right now. The Counselor had promised.

"Where's Phil?" he asked.

"He's busy." Chen passed around cans of drink.

"What do you mean—busy?"

"Got a new game, Zombie Dereliction. Has to finish it."

"Once you start, you don't stop," Jordan said.

"Haven't seen him since our last get-together." Spud threw more sticks on the fire.

"Hasn't been surfing either," Mitch said.

"Here's to Lenny, one of Aporto Bay's best," Will said, raising his can. "Forever in our hearts."

"A life lived well," Mitch added. "Till we meet again."

"Hear, hear." They all held up their cans with solemn faces.

"I'll never forget it, the crowds streaming off the stadiums, screaming, and the ear-piercing sirens and the flashing lights. Like a horror movie," Spud said. "When they carried Lenny away on the stretcher. I couldn't look."

"Wonder if he was conscious enough to know about it?" Jordan took a final drag on his cigarette and tossed the stub into the fire. "They said he carked it in the ambulance on the way to the hospital."

"What happens after we die?" Jordan stared at Will. "I hear you've gone all religious."

"Who told you that?"

"Hard not to notice."

Spud scratched the anchor tattoo on his arm. "When you're dead, you're dead."

"Death is not the end. It's not the end for anyone," Will said. "There's a forever."

"So we all go to that heavenly place in the sky?" Chen raised his can. "Here's to forever."

Will's mind raced. How would he tell them the truth? "It's our choice where we go. We either end up with the King in his realm, or we end up with the evil guy in his."

"The evil guy." Spud sniggered.

"That's Satan," Mitch said.

"Anyway, who would choose him?" Chen threw more sticks on the fire. "We don't have seances and call on spirits."

"I haven't chosen him. So I'm safe," Jordan said.

"He owns you if you don't belong to the King. You're fair game," Will said.

"Now you're freaking me out." Jordan lit another cigarette.

"Yeah, man," Spud said.

"It's all too far-fetched." Chen choked on his drink.

"You're entitled to your opinion. But be sure about it." Will stabbed a marshmallow on a stick and twisted it round in the flames.

A wave washed onto the sand, quenching the fire and drenching them.

"Time to pack up," Jordan said, shivering.

***

It was Will's Saturday afternoon café shift. The place resonated with the gurgle of the coffee machine, sizzle of bacon, and the buzz of conversation. Tim sometimes dropped Erin at the cafe after Will's shift, and they wandered to the beach together. It was always the highlight of his week. Being with her was incredible. Will wanted to see her more and take the friendship further. They held hands and sometimes hugged, but he should be kissing her by now. He needed to face the reality there was a barrier. He had to find out how serious Erin's relationship with Tim was, and perhaps face the raw fact that she only wanted friendship and nothing more.

"Everything OK?" she asked as he closed up the café and made two coffees to drink before their beach walk.

"Seen better shifts." What else could he say? He was anything but chilled and relaxed. It was time to ask the question eating at him like a dog with a bone.

"How long have you known Tim?" Will choked on a too-hot mouthful of coffee.

"Let me see." She flicked the hair from her shoulders. "He's been in my life for three years. It's been awesome."

A barb twisted into Will's heart.

"That's nice."

"Could we meet tomorrow?" she asked. "We could go for a swim."

"Would Tim mind?" He downed the rest of the coffee in a couple of gulps, not caring about the burning in his throat.

"He'll be fine about it, although I think he gets a bit jealous about the time I spend with you."

Will scanned the strip of blue ocean through the windows of the café, hoping it would distract him from the pain stabbing holes in his heart. He clenched his teeth. He had to make the break. Before he bled all over the floor.

"Look, Erin. You have your life, and I have mine. I need to get back on track. The accident and the coma took more of a toll than I thought, and I'm having a rough time with my courses this semester."

"Of course."

She didn't get it. "What I'm saying is—it would be better if we didn't meet anymore." The coffee in his stomach scorched a track all the way up to his throat.

"I . . . we . . . I don't know what to say." Erin's forehead scrunched into a frown, and the sparkle died in her ocean-blue eyes.

They sat in silence for a moment. She pressed her hand on his for a second and walked out of the cafe without looking back. His heart wrenched at her last touch. Completely gutted, he dragged his feet to the kitchen, his heart as empty as the coffee mugs. If he managed to get home without breaking down, it would be a miracle.

***

The next few weeks passed in a tumult of lengthy assignments, constant medical appointments, gatherings on the beach with the guys, and an aching loss. He avoided going to any place where Erin might be. But he read The King's Word every day. If he didn't understand what he read, he researched. He listened to music written for and to the King. It helped him feel whole again. It helped him forget the bone-deep longing for Erin. Erin had been a short and sweet part of his life, but the King was part of his life forever. And the King wanted what was best for him. He needed to have confidence in that.

It was around four that afternoon. Will closed his bedroom door, sat on his bed, closed his eyes, and called to the Counselor. The Counselor arrived, beaming, dressed in safari gear and sandals. Will smiled. Maybe he had an overactive imagination. Granny Meg always said he did.

"I've been missing your company," Will said. "Come outside and sit with me on the veranda, just like we used to." Will took him through the back door to the plastic chairs overlooking the straggly grandiflora rose garden near Granny Meg's flat in the backyard. The garden hummed with bees and insects. It was as close as he could get to the gardens at the House of Wisdom.

"You have access to the spiritual world as a follower of the King," the Counselor said, as if he'd read Will's mind. "Your thoughts can be in the supernatural. Now tell me everything."

"It'll take a while."

"You know I have all the time in the world."

Will stretched out his legs and poured out one thing after another—his worries about his health problems, his disappointment about losing Erin, and his simmering anger toward Ben and Tim. He paused and turned to the Counselor. "And there's no way I'll get my psychology assignment finished by tomorrow. But you know all this already, don't you?"

The Counselor nodded. "But it's good to unload your worries to me. A trouble shared with me is a trouble unburdened. Why didn't you give me your problems before?"

"I forgot."

"Have a chat with your psychology lecturer about your assignment."

"Mr. Drake never gives extensions," Will said. "Not in a hundred years."

"Call the lecturer in the morning and see what happens. I know how hard you've been working." They sat in silence, comfortable in each other's company, and watched the sparrows flitting in the willow. Will soaked in the peace.

The following morning, he called Mr. Drake's office at just before nine.

A woman answered the phone. "Sorry, he's not available."

"It's Will Sutherland. I needed to talk to him about an extension to the assignment due today."

"I'm taking his classes while he's on extended leave," she said. "You're on the list as one of the students injured in the stadium collapse. Mr. Drake's left a message to give you any extensions you need."

Will punched the air. Yes, he needed to be more trusting.

***

One month passed. Will caught up with his course and could surf again. The oceans of tears he thought he would shed for Erin became oceans of exhilaration as he got to know the King better.

"Mrs. Holsworth is on the phone, Will," Susan called to him.

A flicker of anxiety crossed Will's mind. Why would she be calling him?

"Will," Mrs. Holsworth sobbed into the phone, "Fred's sick. I felt something was wrong, but you know how stubborn he is. He refused to go to the doctor. Last week he couldn't get out of bed."

Will dropped onto the couch.

"I called Dr. Mann's, and he did tests. Fred's dying Will. Just like that. He doesn't have very long."

"I'm so sorry, Mrs. Holsworth."

"Fred's sent for you."

Will paced the room. It wasn't long ago that Mr. Holsworth had said never to darken his door again.

"Can you come tonight at around seven?"

"Sure." The flicker of anxiety became a scorch.

***

Will made his way to the Holsworth's house in Rawson Street. His heart wasn't in this visit. He stepped along the concrete path bordered with a bed of straggly azaleas and pressed a gnome-shaped doorbell. Mrs. Holsworth peered through the door. Her ample chins trembled. He entered the dimly lit hall, breathing in a mix of boiled vegetables and a faint moldy smell.

"Come." She led him past a wooden console with a faded, dried leaf arrangement in a vase, and into a bedroom off the hall. Will paused and entered.

He tried to hide his surprise at the old man's deterioration and held his breath for a moment against the stale odor in the room. "How are you, Mr. Holsworth?"

"No good. It's terminal, this confounded thing." He pulled back the sheet and pointed to a large bandage covering his right leg. "Melanoma. It's spread. I'm just rotting away."

Will's chest tightened.

"Well, let's get down to business. Pull up a chair." Mr. Holsworth wheezed and beads of sweat covered the man's swollen face. "I heard you talking to that Mitchell friend of yours. You know what I'm talking about. The journey you went on when you were in a coma. You didn't know I listened, did you?"

Will shook his head.

A laugh gurgled in the man's throat. "I need to make peace with that King of yours." He struggled to pull himself higher onto the pillows. "I know I've done a lot of things. Wrong things. I've ripped people off."

Will rearranged his pillows. The discomfort he'd always felt in Mr. Holsworth's presence had vanished. This man was asking him to save his life and change his destiny. And he knew how. "Have you got The King's Word in the house?" Will asked.

"Over there on the shelf. My great grandfather's." The man's chest rattled, and he coughed. "I don't want to go to the other place. It's not too late, is it?"

Will gave Fred a sip of water. The King's word. The King's sword. He held the sword of life. He'd give Mr. Holsworth the key to the kingdom.

"It's not too late, Mr. Holsworth." Will wiped the dust from the cover with his hand, opened it, and read. The old man's breath rasped in his throat, and he closed his eyes. An old bronze clock on the wall ticked.

Will thought the man was sleeping, but he reached out and grabbed at his wrist with a moist hand. "Don't you waste your life like I did, boy."

Mrs. Holsworth hurried in with a rattling tray of pills.

"It's not too late, Lilian," Mr Holsworth said in a thick and slurred voice.

His face sagged into the pillow and his mouth hung open. But his eyes shone.

Chapter 43

Will poured milk onto the cereal in his bowl and chewed as he typed on his laptop. It was already Friday. His next essay was due on Monday. Jess sat at the table and spread a thick layer of peanut butter on her toast.

"Stella was asking about you," she said. "Reading between the lines, I think she wants you back."

"I'm not interested in getting back with her."

"And I saw Tim yesterday at the shops with Erin's mom. He's hot. You must introduce me."

"I wonder why he was shopping with her," Will said, still typing. Then something in his head did a backflip. "What did you say?"

"You need to introduce me to Tim—Erin's stepbrother." Jess drizzled honey over the peanut butter and licked her fingers. "By the way, I haven't seen you with Erin lately. I thought you two had something going."

His cereal turned into a plate of lumpy cardboard. He rushed to the sink and hung over it, choking. Erin's stepbrother? The words were a dumbbell, crashing into his thoughts. An embarrassed tide spread through his body.

"Is Erin adopted?" He still hung over the sink.

"Hasn't she told you?"

"Told me what?"

"Their parents married after their previous divorces."

Will rushed back to the table, slammed his laptop closed with a snap, dashed to his bedroom, and punched his pillow. Mortified. Mad. Ecstatic. He sent Erin a text. "Can you meet me at the café after 4? Something important."

He paced the floor for half an hour, panting and waiting for a reply.

The phone dinged.

"Can meet after your shift for 20 minutes. Have Zumba."

"Great." He messaged, adding two smiley emojis.

Will wrote the first half of his next assignment and then deleted it by mistake. At ten he rode his bike to the café for his shift, his emotions in a chaotic turmoil. What if it was too late? What if she was with Ben now? He hadn't seen Ben for a while. He could imagine Erin on Ben's arm. His trophy girlfriend. Nothing but the best.

He hurried into the crowded café. Sally passed a list of orders to him. He scanned it and like a robot, threw six rashers of bacon, four eggs, and sliced halloumi onto the hotplate and then he made five cappuccinos. He carried a tray of metal milkshake cups to the dishwasher but the tray slid out of his greasy hands. The cups crashed on the concrete floor, splashing his jeans and sneakers with the dregs. A customer gave him a you-clumsy-incompetent glare.

Another surly customer plonked his plate on the counter. "This isn't what I ordered. I didn't want egg." The air-con failed. Will sweated like a pig in hell. Not only his hands, but all of his body shook. He never used to be like this. More customers streamed in, searching for a table. There was no way he'd finish by four.

Erin arrived early. Will sensed she was at the counter before he turned around from the sink. His heart pumped so hard in his chest and throat, he didn't think he could speak. She looked at him, her eyes cool. Hurt.

"You look busy, Will."

Her golden skin contrasted with her white dress, and she was more gorgeous than ever. He tried to smile, but his lips were as stiff as the china mug he gripped.

"It's been one of those days." His voice sounded through his ventriloquist lips. "Won't be long. Let me get you a drink. A smoothie?"

"Mango and banana." She sat with her back to him, looking at her phone.

He finally hung the CLOSED sign and joined her. He'd clean up later, and then it would be an all-night job on the assignment.

The paralysis of his lips had eased. "Great to catch up again." He pulled out the hem of his t-shirt, trying to dry the slick of sweat dripping down the center of his chest.

She sat, looking out the window, with a furrow between her eyebrows.

The perspiration kept pouring. "Erin." He paused and rubbed his sweaty hands on his jeans.

"Is everything all right?" She crossed her legs.

Will couldn't stop staring at them.

"Not really," he said. "I've just discovered I'm the biggest fool in the universe."

"What have you done?" She leaned toward him with a puzzled look.

"I don't know how to tell you."

She pulled at the frill on her dress. "What."

"I thought Tim and you w-were an item."

Erin's jaw dropped. "Tim and I?" Shock turned to disbelief, and then amusement played around her deep-ocean eyes. "He's my step-brother. That's all. I thought you knew. Is that why you wouldn't see me anymore?"

"It was stupid of me. I should have spent more time talking to you about your family. I was so absorbed with my own world." He'd been jealous, blind, and besotted.

"I'm gobsmacked." Erin stabbed the straw into her smoothie.

"What about Ben? Has he been hassling you?"

"That's another story." She sucked up the last of the smoothie with a gurgle. "He doesn't like taking no for an answer."

A slow constriction of unease wrapped itself around Will's lungs, but he reached out and put his hand on hers. "Is it too late for us to see each other again?"

She clasped his hand in hers. The coil around his lungs loosened.

"Do you want to go to the beach tomorrow?" he asked. "I'm free after four. We'll have more time to talk then."

She checked the time, leaped up, and gave him a quick hug, her hair brushing his face. "Okay."

"I'll pick you up at four-thirty," he said. "The car's free." She nodded and left. He bounded to the kitchen, and all the tension poured out as he sloshed the left-over drinks down the sink.

"Why don't I trust you more?" he said to the King. He cleared the tables, wiped the floor until it gleamed, packed the dishwasher without fumbling a single glass, locked up and was home in record time. The essay would be a snack.

Mom came to the front door when he arrived home. "I got a call this morning from Mrs. Holsworth while you were out. Her husband died last night in his sleep. She wants you to speak at his funeral." She shook her head with a puzzled expression. "I thought you two were enemies."

"It's all good. I'll call her and organize the speech."

***

Will and Erin wandered to the rock platform near White Sands Beach. The sun sank to the horizon, flinging its last flashes of orange and crimson into the heaving ocean. Erin swished her feet around in a rock pool, pulling her toes away from the delicate sea anemone tentacles.

He wanted to hold her. He wanted to tell her how much he needed her. He ached with desire for her.

"I was wondering if you were free next Saturday night?" He tried to sound casual. "Would you like to go for dinner at Sandy Bay Italian? I can pick you up around seven."

She checked her phone and frowned. Will held his breath. Would she agree to their first actual date?

"Yes, I'm free," she said.

He let out a long breath and grinned. "I've something to show you when I pick you up."

"Tell me. Now." She threw a handful of wet seaweed at his chest.

"No, and you'll never guess what it is," he shouted as he chased her across the rock platform.

When he arrived home, his Mom was sitting on the couch waiting for him. She patted the seat beside him. "Isn't it time we had a chat? I hear you're back with Erin, and you haven't told me about Mr. Holsworth's funeral."

He flopped down beside her. "Yeah, maybe it's time to tell you everything. Do you want a coffee? This is going to take a while." She walked with him into the kitchen with a bewildered face.

Will spent the evening unloading how well Mr. Holsworth's funeral went—for a funeral anyway—except when the casket didn't fit into the grave and someone called out that it was because of Mrs. Holsworth's cookies. It took an hour to dig the hole bigger.

Then he told her about Eldrad. She shed floods of tears until he'd finished.

"You have to tell Erin," she said, at least a dozen times.

***

Will cruised along Vernon Street with his Audi sports car surprise. He'd spent the morning waxing and polishing the silver paint to a mirror shine. Erin lived in a rented house in an established part of Aporto Bay. Most of the houses were weatherboard. Wind chimes hanging near her front door tinkled in the breeze.

He ran his hands through his hair, adjusted his collar, tucked in his shirt, and then clanged the dull brass knocker. The door sprang open, and Erin curtseyed in a floral sundress. His heart did an acrobat flip.

"Is that what you were going to show me?" she asked, when she saw the car parked outside.

"Come and have a look."

Erin ran her hand over the surface. "It's in great condition. How did you manage to get it?"

"Dad organized it for me, and I used the insurance payout. It's only three years old. Andy, my uncle, sold it to him for peanuts because Dad helped him with his house extension and Andy's bought the latest model." Will opened the car door for her, and they headed to the restaurant.

He maneuvered the car into a space in the parking lot. "It's good to have a car again. I'm beginning to feel normal at last. Let's go. I've booked a table." Fairy lights twinkled on the potted ficus on either side of the entrance of Sandy Bay Italian. Tables spilled out onto the pavement. The smell of garlic and grilled seafood wafted through the air. A waiter led them inside to an upholstered booth next to potted golden palms and handed them a menu.

Will poured them both a glass of water. "Erin, I want to ask you something."

"Fire away."

"As a follower of the King. How well do you know him?"

"I'm working on it. He helps me get through the day. I don't know how people manage without him in their lives."

"Do you think he gives us dreams or visions to show us things, to point us in the right direction?"

"I'm sure he does." She passed him the garlic bread.

"How can you know what the King wants you to do?" He longed to tell her about Eldrad, Eleonora, and his journeys, but it wasn't the right time. What if she decided he was too weird and didn't go out with him again? He couldn't risk it.

"He uses different ways, like his voice, his word, and our dreams. Sometimes he'll open or close doors." She heaped spaghetti marinara onto his plate. "He'll also give us skills, even a passion for something. What are you passionate about, Will?"

He leaned toward her and took her hand. "There's a girl I'd like to get to know better." But touching her suddenly took away his appetite.

She smiled.

"But seriously, I want to be useful," he said. "Give back, especially after the accident and coma. I'm helping at the Lifespring youth group on Thursday nights. Mitch and Chen said they want to come along as well."

***

After tiramisu, Will drove to the Driftwood Beach parking lot, which overlooked the rock platform. "I promised Nurse Baxter a coffee. Mom said she was the nurse in charge of me while I was in a coma. It turns out her sister works with Mom. I owe her a lot. She's not at the hospital anymore though, and I'm not sure where she is now. Mom's finding out."

"I found her quite rude and cranky at times," Erin said. "There was something strange about her. I saw her taking packets of medication and swallowing pills from the hospital store. I think she was addicted and was busted."

He opened the window to let in the sea breeze. "Even so, I'd like to thank her. She was fine with me—when I first woke up in the coma ward, anyway." He slipped his arm around her shoulder.

She snuggled closer to him. "You're right. No sense in being negative. Who knows what happened in her past that caused her problems. I'd love to know what was going on between her and Dr. Cooper. Perhaps we can squeeze it out of her."

"Why don't we take her for a coffee at Ridges, that trendy place in town?" It would be another excuse for him to see Erin. "I should buy her flowers."

"Something with lots of thorns!" she said.

"Ha."

He drew his hand through her hair, longing to feel her lips on his, but couldn't afford to make any mistakes. He'd never hesitated like this when he'd been with a girl from the bay before. He squirmed as he remembered.

If only he could kiss her the way they had on Eldrad and more. But this was a different time, a different place. He couldn't believe how nervous he was, but when she lifted her face toward his, he couldn't hold back. His lips melted into hers. Like they were meant for each other. His heart pounded like the waves on the rocks. How could this feel so right, so perfect? The beach, the bay, and everything dissolved away except for the enthralling sensation of her.

After Will dropped Erin home, he collapsed into bed, emotionally exhausted, but pleased about his date with Erin. He woke in the early hours of the morning. A dark shape stood at the end of his bed. It was the Darkness again. Fingers of fear spread down his body. He struggled to sit, but his limbs had frozen.

Eleonora, the fake Princess She belongs to Ben Maddock. She always has. She always will.

Wide awake now, Will grabbed his phone from the bedside table. He read from his King's Word You Version app until he felt safe again. But doubts about Erin continued to pool in the pit of his stomach.

Chapter 44

The next day, when Will and Erin arrived at Ridge's Cafe, Nurse Baxter was sitting, tense, at an outside table. She'd crushed her serviette into a ball. They gave her a light hug, and Will handed her the bunch of lavender.

"It's good to see you, Nurse Baxter," Will said. "Order whatever you like—this is our treat. I want to thank you for looking after me for so long while I was in the coma. Although I'm sure this doesn't make up for those awful daily procedures you had to do to keep me alive." Will scrunched up his face. "My mind boggles at the thought."

She laughed. "All part of the job—and call me Skye."

"Do you have many of your family in the bay?" Erin asked.

"Just my sister Laura, who works with Will's Mom. We don't exactly get on."

"That's a shame," Erin said.

They sat in silence.

"The coffee's good." Will stirred the chocolate into the foam, but his attention was fixed on Erin in her stylish ivory blouse.

Skye stared at Erin. "Why did you spend all that time with Will when you didn't know if he'd ever recover?"

"I was grateful that he saved me in the accident. I-I guess I cared about him."

Skye scrunched her serviette into a tighter ball.

"You must miss Dr. Cooper now he's moved hospitals," Erin said.

"Yes." She stared at them with widened eyes. "But I'm seeing him."

"You mean you're going out with him?"

"Yes. He wanted me to go out with him. That's why he took another position. I don't know what he sees in me."

"I hope it works out for you," Will said.

"I want to apologize to you guys," Skye said. "I wasn't always as cooperative as I could have been. I've been going through a tough time recently." She looked at Erin, discomfort clouding her face. "I know you saw me taking the pills. I have chronic back pain and ended up with a dependence on opiates." She took a sip of coffee and gave a choking cough before she continued. "I needed them so badly, I didn't care. Max's been very supportive. I've taken leave, and I'm getting help."

Will stared at her, speechless. Erin reached out and put her hand on the woman's arm.

"Unfortunately, I needed increased doses to get the same effect and I had problems keeping up the supply." She stuffed the sweaty ball of serviette fragments into her bag. "The drug reprogrammed my brain. Please keep what I've told you confidential."

Erin squeezed her arm. "Of course we will. We hope you have a speedy recovery and call us if you need to unload. We've all been through a lot together."

"Thanks." Skye put her nose to the lavender and breathed in the perfume. "You've made my day." She smiled at them and left.

They sat, silent, processing what she'd told them. "That answers some questions." Erin let out a long breath. "I hope she keeps in touch. It won't be easy for her."

***

On Tuesday, late afternoon, Will picked up Erin after his last lecture, bought dinner from the Chargrilled Chicken shop, and then drove to the bay lookout. They sat in the car, watching the waves churning and foaming at the base of the cliff. A silver moon stretched its carpet across the ocean to the dark horizon.

"Has Ben been calling you?" Ben had been coming to the café more than usual, and that negative nightmare voice kept playing in his head. *She belongs to Ben Maddock. She always has. She always will.*

"He called last night."

"Why would he do that? You wouldn't go on a date with him, would you?"

"You're upset."

"I have an issue with him." Will stared at her with a mix of longing and misgiving. His resolve to trust in the King's way sometimes vanished when he thought of the Maddocks. "The Maddocks and the Sutherlands don't get on. It goes back generations." His voice came out as though his throat had been scraped with a cheese grater.

"Why hold a grudge for something that happened so long ago?" Erin pulled the lid of the box open. The aroma of roast chicken and fries filled the car.

"We've always hated one another. I know I have to forgive. I have." But he may need to again. He tore open the salt packet and sprinkled the contents on the fries. "That doesn't mean they have my trust."

"So why all the conflict?"

He paused as a fishing boat chugged to the nearby bay over dark satin ripples. "Many years ago, Vivien Larson jilted Max Maddock, who was Ben's great uncle. She ran away with Karl Sutherland, my great uncle."

"So? These things happen." Erin took a chip and munched on it.

"Max Maddock took his life a week later. He was an only son."

"They blamed your great-uncle? I can understand that." She picked up a chicken drumstick.

"After the suicide, another awful thing happened, one month later. Karl didn't come home one night." Will wiped the now foggy windscreen. "Someone noticed a smell in a reserve behind the local park." The police found Karl lying under a pile of branches.

"Ew." She dropped the chicken back into the takeaway box. "Dead?"

"As a doornail. And they had two suspects, Max Maddock's father and his cousin. The police said they didn't have enough evidence. When you hear the story, there was plenty. You can never be sure how a court case will end. Without a resolution, the saga has continued ever since."

Erin picked at the skin on the chicken and shivered.

"Anyway," he said, "I'll be honest. I don't want you to go out with Ben. I want you to be with me." The look she gave him melted something inside him as big as a boulder. He picked up a drumstick and bit into it.

She wiped her fingers with a serviette and turned to him. "Would you like to come over next Saturday after your shift and meet my parents?" Will nodded, his mouth and heart too full to speak.

***

A few days later, he parked outside Erin's house and bounded up to her front door, full of nerves. He straightened his jacket and clanged the brass knocker.

Erin greeted him in a floral apron. "Come in. I've made an apple cake. Sorry about the boxes piled in the corridor. We're renting at the moment."

"It's fine." But Will did a double take. It wasn't fine. Apple cake? Of all the cakes in the world, why did she make apple cake, just like Eleonora? It did not make sense.

He followed her down the hall. Will chatted to Erin's mother and stepfather, Deb and Scott, in the living room while he demolished three slices of the cake.

"The accident at the arena was an enormous shock to all of us," Deb said. "We're so grateful Erin came through reasonably unscathed. All thanks to you, Will."

Scott checked his watch. "We have to pick Tim up from his soccer game. It's been great to meet you at last." Scott shook Will's hand, and they left.

"This apple cake is the best." Will picked up the last few crumbs from the plate. It transported him back to the time when they sheltered from a storm in a cave and ate apple cake. Perhaps this was the right time to tell her about his coma dream.

An unmistakable throbbing from a car muffler pulsed through the front screen door. "A neighbor?" But he didn't need to ask. He'd recognize that sound anywhere. A car door slammed, and the door knocker clanked.

Erin frowned. "I'll get it." She leaped up and walked to the front door. Will waited, his knees bouncing in overdrive and his ears hyper-alert.

"Hi, Ben. What are you doing here?" she asked.

Will clenched his fists. Yes, why was Ben visiting Erin?

"Just came to see you. I've been thinking about you all week."

Will cringed at the ooze of charm in Ben's voice.

"Really?"

"Look, I'd love to take you out again. How about tonight if you're free?"

Again? Had he heard that right? The trickle of concern became a wave of thunder.

"I'm not available, Ben."

"Look, you know I'm the most eligible guy in town with the fastest car and the best means to give you a first-class experience. Our last date was a disappointment. We both know it was. It's time I made it up to you."

Will's tolerance shattered. What was he doing with a two-timing girl who kept breaking his heart? His heart shredded like meat in a grinder. Nothing would mend it now.

"Only the best will do, and you are the best," Ben said. "I have it all planned. We'll go to the movies and then to The Reef for a candlelit dinner. You know it's the finest restaurant. Wear that red sequined dress I like. The next day, we'll go for a helicopter ride over the national park."

Will's nails cut into the flesh on his palm. How could he match that? It would take his entire wage for the month. His heart was no longer shredded. It was pulverized.

"Sorry, Ben."

"What do you want, then? Not that idiot . . .

Will strained his ears to hear her reply. A car sped past, muffling their conversation, and the screen door slammed.

He sat, stiff in the wicker chair, as rattled as a snake stuffed in a basket. He glared at her as she walked back into the room.

"I heard the conversation. I can't believe you didn't tell me you went out with him." He lurched out of the chair, brushed past her, and left before she could reply. He didn't want to hear her excuses. He sped down Main Street, narrowly missing a red light, and headed toward the Bar Room on Strand Street to get a drink—if he could wangle his way in.

But he heard the Counselor's voice. *Give me that heavy load of worries you carry.* Will slowed the car and took a deep breath, lightened at the thought. He would do that and let the Counselor sort it out. He passed the bar and headed toward the Belmont Martial Arts and Fitness Center instead.

***

Will finished cleaning up at White Sands Cafe on automatic. His thoughts were a long way from scraping down the plates and throwing out coffee grounds. Erin had messaged three times during the week. He'd ignored them. He was fed up with the jealousy in his heart. He was fed up with Ben's interference. And he was fed up with the unending uncertainty. It was time to get on with life. Girls would be a low priority from now on.

But Erin had left a message on his phone that morning—one he couldn't ignore. His throat closed every time he read it.

"Moving to Mornington Valley. Can I see you after your shift before I leave? Erin."

He slammed the mugs into the dishwasher. Mornington Valley. Two hours away.

He sent a message in agreement. It would have been pigheaded not to.

***

She sat at a table, arms folded, watching him. He closed the café and joined her.

"Anything to drink?" He sweated, but not from the heat.

She shook her head. "Will, I'm leaving this week. I was going to tell you last week, but you left before I had a chance." She pressed her chin into her fist. "I want to say goodbye and explain about Ben."

"There's nothing to explain."

"I would never go out with him."

"So he was lying?"

"No."

Will gasped with exasperation.

"What then?"

"When you were in the coma, a group of my girlfriends, including Jess, were leaving the Main Street Movie Theatre. Ben and a few other guys from his old private school came out at the same time. They asked us to go to Roma Pizza down the road and said they'd pay. My friends wanted to go, so I went along. I ended up sitting with Ben. And I was wearing that red dress."

Will fiddled with the salt and pepper shakers. That would be right. Ben Maddock, the troublemaker. "So you didn't go out with him any other time?"

"No, and it wasn't a date. I was with a group. What do you take me for?" Her eyes flashed like lightning on the ocean. "I'm sure he knew you were at my house that day you came over. He likes to drag race down our street to get my attention. He would have seen your car at the front of the house. Did you think of that? It was his pathetic attempt to break us up." Her eyes brimmed.

Will went into the kitchen and poured two waters. He filled them to the top with ice. He needed to think.

"You can come down on weekends to visit me at the valley when you don't have a shift," she called. "We have a sprawling house with pear trees and a camellia grove. Mom said it's the home she's always wanted."

"Sounds nice," he said in a dull tone, swirling the ice in his glass, trying to distract himself from the turmoil of indecision.

"I was hoping to see you at the Hospital Charity Ball in September." Her voice faltered. "My family's coming up to the bay. We've already booked an apartment at The Waterfront Hotel."

He swallowed the lump in his throat. "Maybe. I'll see." He needed to ask the King first which way to go.

Chapter 45

The next few months went in a blur. Final assessments and exams at college kept Will busy. The cafe manager promoted him, and he worked extra shifts. He was seeing Erin again, and drove to Mornington Valley for precious hours with her when he could. He had a new confidence in the relationship. Somehow, all their problems had cemented their bond.

"I'm driving down to see Erin, Mom. It's her birthday," Will called.

"When will you be back?"

"Tonight. Not until late. I'm having dinner." He put the velvet box with the silver bracelet he'd bought her into the side pocket of his jacket. Elation surged through him at the thought of being with her again. He cruised along Bannock Street into Portland Highway and picked up speed. The weather was fine and the traffic light.

A siren behind pierced his ears. He glanced at the speedometer to check his speed and looked in the rear-vision mirror. A police car raced up from behind and overtook him. More sirens. His body tensed. Two more police cars and three ambulances streaked past and sped south. There was no oncoming traffic. Strange.

Cars ahead slowed to a stop. Fire engines and emergency vehicles raced past. He tapped his fingers on the steering wheel, fidgeting and squirming in his seat as his gut twisted into a knot. He parked at the side of the road and walked south until he rounded a bend.

The stench of burned rubber, petrol, and fear filled his nostrils. Colored lights flashed and pulsed their warning in time with the pounding of his heart. Crumpled vehicles and debris spread out as though a semitrailer had lost its load. Five mangled cars scattered across both sides of the road.

"Stay back!" A crimson-faced police officer motioned to him. Two more ambulances arrived. The place was lit up like a laser light show. Paramedics checked inside cars. Will strained to see what was happening in the carnage.

An SUV had flipped onto its roof. Another had the side peeled off. There was a red car. The bonnet was crushed up to the broken windscreen, and two people sat in the front seats. Will's adrenaline-fueled pulse accelerated. A number plate lay on the road, bent and twisted. His knotted stomach rolled over, clenched and cramped.

He knew that car. He knew that number plate. He knew that driver. Fear slicked down his back to his feet. He closed his fist on the velvet box in his pocket.

It was him.

Ben sat in the driver's seat of the crumpled Ferrari. White as his shirt. Where it wasn't stained red. A girl sat crookedly next to him like a plaster statue, with black glassy eyes, staring.

"We'll have to cut him out," a paramedic said. "The dash has pinned his legs."

The paramedics and the police moved from car to car, taking photos and checking passengers. Two emergency workers removed a woman from a white car and carefully placed her on a stretcher. She flopped like a doll. A paramedic gave a man CPR on a blanket on the road.

Will strode to a police officer, his knees quaking.

"I'm a friend of the guy in the red Ferrari. Can I talk to him?"

"By all means, but don't impede the emergency workers."

Will crouched next to the window of Ben's car. "So sorry, mate. Can I help you with anything?"

Ben swiveled bloodshot eyes toward him without moving his head and let out a long groan. "And I didn't think it could get any worse. Get lost." His voice sounded croaky.

"Let's cut through the niceties. Just this once."

"What can you do to help?" Ben shifted his upper body and then flinched in pain. "Bring Candice back to life? She's dead. Look at her. I killed her."

Will choked at the vapor of spirits on his breath.

A paramedic approached with a bag of equipment. "Hello, my name's Maggie. I'm just going to check your passenger. What's her name?"

"Candice." Ben's chest heaved. "Candice-no-more."

Maggie wrenched at the jammed passenger door handle. She leaned into the car window.

"Tell me," Ben said, his voice tight. He stared straight ahead with a clenched jaw.

"Sorry, love, your passenger didn't make it."

"I know. I know already." His breath came out harsh and shallow.

"Unfortunately, we can't move her until after we get you out. I need to take your pulse, love." Will stood aside.

"Is there any pain in your legs?" she asked.

"Nothing. A bad sign, isn't it?"

"Too early to tell. Just rest and wait. I'll be back as soon as I can." She walked to another patient, sprawled on the ground.

"Get me my phone off the dash. I can't reach it." Ben grabbed Will's wrist, smearing blood on his jacket sleeve. "Call Mom. I need to talk to her before the cops." Something in his throat gurgled. "Password: 1263."

Will dialed the number. "There's no answer."

"Give it to me. I'll leave a message." He took the phone. It slipped out of his hands onto the floor under the dashboard. Ben cursed and shut his red eyes for a moment. "I'll be dead for sure by the time the cops get me out of here. Remember Leo, that guy in my year? His legs were pinned. When they cut him out, he died, just like that. No warning."

"That's bad." Not something Will wanted to think about.

Ben fumbled a box of cigarettes from the side pocket of the car. "Get me a light."

"I can't."

"Why not?"

"There's petrol." Will pointed under the car. A seepage oozed out onto the road.

"So what. I'm as good as dead anyway."

"I'm here to help you, Ben."

"Well, now's your chance," Ben said. "You think you're so cool with your miracle recovery. You don't know the half of it." Ben choked on a laugh. "I smashed up your car. May as well tell you all of it."

"I knew about the car, so what else?"

"Why do you think your cheating father left you?"

"What do you mean?"

"Arty farty Maureen is my aunt. You didn't know that, did you?"

Will crushed the velvet box in his pocket with his fist until the clasp broke.

"None of you had a clue we set him up." Ben's words slurred. "The Maddocks know how to get revenge. Now you can get yours. I'm giving you the key. Revenge is the name of the game."

A streak of hot anger fried Will's brain. He wanted to pound Ben, pound him for what he'd done. He pressed a hand over his mouth, rushed behind the car, and threw up. He wiped his mouth and headed back. He had to find out.

Ben had a smirk on his now blue-tinged lips. "Back again?"

"So she doesn't really care for my father?"

Ben spat fresh blood on his sleeve. "She fell for him. Wasn't supposed to do that." He wheezed.

Shouts came from behind them. "Ben. Ben." Will swung around. Mr. Maddock shoved a paramedic out of the way. His lips tightened when he saw Will.

"What are you doing here, you little swine? So you were the cause of all this?"

"Leave it, Dad. He wasn't doing any harm."

"Ben's waiting for the paramedics to get him out," Will said. "It should be soon." Every cell in his body shook as if he'd been jackhammering for a week.

Two police officers approached Bruce. "We're going to breathalyze your son."

"Can't you see he's not in a fit state?" The man's face was boiling red.

Will crouched next to Ben's car window. Ben's eyes were full of darkness and fear. A surge of pity wrenched Will. He reached in and held Ben's clammy arm. "I'm going now, but let me know if you need anything. I'm here for you, Ben," he said.

Will left the wrecked-car prison and staggered away. He sat for a while until his hands were steadier and then took the detour the police had set up and continued down the highway. The timing of his arrival at the accident had to be more than a coincidence. What if there was no such thing as a coincidence?

After a few minutes, he parked his car to call his father. He'd touch base but wasn't ready to let him know what Ben had said about Maureen. But it had to be soon.

***

Four weeks later, Will strode toward Aporto Bay Hospital, clutching a box of chocolates. With a mix of hesitation and resolve, he took the lift to Level One, squashing in with a nurse and a pale-faced patient on a stretcher bed.

"I'm here to see Ben Maddock," he said to a nurse at the main desk of Ward 5B.

"Room four, to the left." She pointed along the gleaming corridor crowded with trolleys of equipment. He paused at the door. The whiff of disinfectant brought back too many memories. What would he talk about? He wasn't sure.

Ben lay back on a pillow with his hair sticking up in uncharacteristic tufts and plaster encased his left arm, right leg and foot. He stared at his phone.

Will put the chocolates on his bed.

Ben looked up, then back to his phone. "Still hanging around like a bad smell? Talking of bad smells, don't kick over the bottle of apple juice." He pointed with the phone to the urinal next to his bed. "My visitors are making a sport of it."

"You have more broken bones than I expected," Will said.

"I've been here too long. Still, it's better than the clink. You should've lit that match."

"You don't look that sick."

"You know what I'm talking about." Ben put his phone on the cabinet next to the bed.

"You nearly knocked me out that day with the alcohol on your breath," Will said.

"We all have a vice, don't we? What's yours, Will Sutherland? What's taken the place of nicotine and alcohol in your life?" Ben elevated the bedhead with the bed control and recoiled in pain. "Sex? Gambling? Your grandfather squandered the family fortune, didn't he? Spent it all on the horses and the slot machines."

Will clenched his fists. A red tide of anger washed through his body. Payback or peace? Which one would he choose? He took a deep breath. "Yeah, I know. But that's history now. We move on and learn our lessons."

"So, what is it?" Ben leaned forward and grunted. "This bed will be the death of me. Wonder how long it takes to get bedsores?"

"Not long—if you don't move around." Will pulled up a nearby chair.

"Everyone has their secret little pleasure." Ben turned over the box of chocolates to check the fillings on the back. "I suppose it's Erin. What she sees in you, I'll never know."

"She's important to me but—"

A nurse bustled in. "The doctor's here to see you, Ben." The doctor walked in with a haven't-slept-for-two-days zombie face.

Will patted Ben's plastered leg and left.

Chapter 46

The Hospital Charity Ball started at seven. Will waited for Erin near the front entrance, festooned with an arch of black and gold balloons. Her family was traveling straight from Mornington Valley.

His heart missed a beat when he saw the O'Connells drive into the drop-off zone. Tim opened the rear door for Erin, and she stepped out. Will drew in a sharp breath. Her spun-gold hair cascaded over her shoulders, and her lilac chiffon dress reminded him of the Eldrad skies. No princess in the entire world could be as elegant as her.

Her face lit up when she saw him, and she hooked her arm into his as they entered the hall. Streamers crisscrossed the ceiling and waiters glided through the crowd, offering drinks on trays. The hospital staff and public circulated with a buzz of conversation and the clinking of glasses. Trays of roast meats and pasta, dishes of vegetables, and bowls bulging with salads lay on tables at one end of the room.

After the meal, the lights dimmed, music blared, and couples crowded on the dance floor, gyrating and jiving to an eighties play-mix. Will led Erin onto the floor. Everything about her was dazzling. He couldn't help thinking of the ballroom with its chandeliers back at the House of Wisdom. To dance with her in the flesh was a dream come true. The only thing missing was Ben. But he could manage without Ben.

"Look over there, near the drinks table," Erin said.

"Dr. Cooper and Skye."

The doctor danced with Skye, their faces elated. Skye's navy blue dress swirled, and her tightly coiffed hair sprang undone.

"We must talk to them later," Erin said.

Will wrapped his arms around her waist, loving having her close. He swung her into a Viennese waltz, trying not to tread on her toes. "Have your parents told you I'm taking you to a mystery destination tomorrow?"

"You asked my parents, but not me?"

Doubt dropped into his gut. He should have asked her first. "It'll take all day, so I thought I should ask your parents first. I'm picking you up from your motel early. At seven."

"Sounds intriguing."

Will breathed a quiet sigh of relief. His nerves were already on edge, thinking about what he'd planned. Tomorrow would be crunch time for them.

"Another thing," she said, "Your parents are dancing together, and it looks cozy."

"That doesn't surprise me." He smiled. He could handle having Dad back now. It was the icing on the miracle cake.

Will's parents waltzed toward them. "You make a great couple," Dad said.

Susan nodded. "Oh, and before I forget, were you expecting a delivery, Will?"

"No."

"A parcel came to the house just after you left for the ball. We put it in the hallway. It's something unusual."

Will and Erin left the ball early and dropped by the house. A long shape wrapped in patterned paper leaned against the wall. It reached to just below the ceiling.

"I know what that is," he said. "There must be some mistake."

"Check the envelope."

He took the envelope hanging from a string around the object, tore it open and stared at the neat writing on the plain card, which was signed with a flourish.

"It's from Ben."

Erin shook her head, her eyes wide, as she looked over his shoulder and read the card out aloud. "I'm sorry. Ben."

Will ripped off the wrapping.

"It's the most expensive surfboard you can buy." He smoothed his hand down the surface.

"Do you think there's an explosive device in it?" she asked. They chuckled.

"Unusual present," she said.

"But a good one."

***

Will picked up Erin at Dolphin Shores Motel at seven the next morning. They traveled up the coast for an hour. He couldn't help stealing glances at her, beautiful in her cream safari-style dress. He slowed at a sign, 'The Wilderness Lodge', and turned into a gravel driveway lined with poplars. It led to a sprawling sandstone building with a verandah.

"My parents brought me here when I was in my mid-teens. We'll have breakfast, and then I'm taking you to the mystery location."

He'd tell her about Eldrad. No more procrastinating. Will found a table in the terrace room while Erin fetched the menu and the weekend paper.

"I could sit here and admire you all day," he said when she returned.

She reached out and laid her fingers on his. "But look at this." She pointed to an article in the newspaper. "It's about the Maddocks."

"What does it say?"

"Ben's had some serious charges laid against him. He won't be driving for a long time, and Maddock Construction's court case has been extended."

"It wouldn't hurt to spend some time with Ben," Will said. "Might give me a chance to get to know him better. He must feel pretty low."

"You're awesome. Did you know that?" she said.

And now it was time to tell her about Eldrad. He wasn't sure how—especially the bit about the princess. And his leg was touching hers under the table. It was messing with his head.

Her voice broke into his thoughts. "I know you have a surprise for me, but I have one for you as well. You don't know how hard it's been, not spilling the beans." She pulled her leg away from his, reached into her backpack, and dragged out a thick wad of paper clipped at the top. She placed it on the table in front of him with an expectant look on her face. "Can you guess what it is?"

"I've no idea," he said. "Your occupational therapy assignment? A list of my medications? Times and dates of my catheter attachments?"

She let out a long breath. "Ha. No. This is the print-out of what I was writing on my laptop while I visited you in hospital—and after they discharged you. I've actually read two-thirds of it to you already."

Will took the wad of paper and flicked through the pages, then gasped. He couldn't believe his eyes. It was mind-blowing. He turned to her roughly drawn map of Eldrad. He knew it so well he could have drawn it himself. Words and sentences flashed in front of him—Jadyn, Eleonora, Roland . . . Nevara.

He set the pages down on the table and stared at her, his mouth open, trying to gather his thoughts. "I-I don't know what to say."

The waiter came for their order and described the specials, but Will didn't hear a word. His brain was numb. He couldn't think.

"What's your order, sir?" The menu was a haze of words. Food was the last thing he needed. "Same as . . . her."

"Would you like to read the story sometime?" Her voice wavered, and her eyes reddened.

The shock and haze in his mind cleared. The pieces of his life's puzzle, which had sat in a confused Rubik jumble for so long, now twisted back and forth—turning like clockwork.

How could he tell her he already knew the story? He glanced at the pages, starting at the first chapter, then flicking to the end. "Did a scientist called Malory run the lab?"

Erin gave him a quizzical look. "Yes, that's right."

He took his coffee and slurped it, but his taste buds had shut down. "Is there a place called the House of Wisdom where Will goes through six doors to find the truth?"

"Yes." She bit her bottom lip. "Are you a speed reader?"

"I'm a fast reader, but not that speedy."

"Does the princess die?"

"No."

"Is Ben mentioned in the story?"

"Of course not."

"Is there a place called the Alley?"

She shook her head.

"Do Jadyn and Laurien end up together?"

Erin's forehead creased into a network of puzzled lines. "How can you ask these questions when you haven't even read the story?"

Will threw the wad of paper on the table, leaped up, and paced the room. All the puzzle pieces lined up. They had rotated into the only possible staggering conclusion. This story was his coma dream, and a warrior princess called Erin imagined it. But the story had also melded with events and imaginings of his own private life.

Two worlds and two stories had collided into a life-changing experience that was way beyond anything he could ever have imagined.

She twisted and pulled the ends of her hair and gaped at him.

He gripped the notes with both hands. "This is a mind-boggling." He had a thousand goosebumps. "Brace yourself. You won't believe what I'm going to tell you."

"What." Her eyes overflowed now.

"I dreamed this story while you read it to me," he said. "I lived and breathed the world you created. I fell in love with the characters. Especially Eleanora. I went on the journey."

She shook her head, her eyes and face as wet and wild as a Caves Hill storm. "Why didn't you tell me?"

"I didn't know how it happened." He flicked to the chapter about his visit to Idella, then back to the Fernhill Gully scene. He was a wound-up spring. He stretched back in his chair, trying to release the tension before he bounced all over the room.

He reached over and grabbed both her hands and they stared at one another, silent for a moment.

"This certainly ups the action for the surprise I had for you." Will chuckled in disbelief. "But it's not really a surprise anymore. You know it as well as I do."

"Does it have anything to do with this story?" Erin asked in a breathless voice, with a flushed blotch on each cheek.

"You'll have to wait and see. And I can't wait to read every single word you've written." He still had goosebumps.

***

Later that morning, Will drove along a winding dirt road toward Green Point Forest. "So did the princess and Will end up together in the end?" he asked.

"Of course," she said, "and Jadyn and Laurien also end up together. The people on the island live happily for many years under Jadyn's presidency."

He let out a long and satisfied breath. He pulled into a clearing. It was as if the day had already been a week. He sat quietly with her, admiring the view across the valley. He inhaled the scent of her. It was like Silver Book's garden, mingled with the smoldering smell of the Wilderness Lodge log fire.

He stroked her arm and then pulled her close. He ran his fingers through her hair and leaned down to find her soft lips. They were hot, inviting. Warm honey poured through his bloodstream. He longed to lose himself, give in to the emotions coursing through his body, held back for so long.

He pulled away, breathing fast, and cupped her face with his burning hands and dragged his gaze from her lips to her deep-as-the-ocean eyes. The alchemy of emotion from the revelations that morning and the kiss melded them and bound them into something new. A promise of good things to come.

His heart pounded in his body at the wild waves of emotion, but he let her go. "We have plenty of time for this, in the future."

She nodded and hauled back her unruly hair with unsteady hands.

***

"Now, for the surprise I have for you," he said.

He led the way into a rainforest jungle of towering ancient beeches and tree ferns. Buttress roots dug into the moss. A myriad of birds twittered and shrieked through the valley. He turned and helped her to climb down the rough earth steps. "Do you know why I brought you here?"

"It's Fernhill Gully." Her eyes burst with wonder.

"It's like the first place I saw you. I think it was love at first sight." He wiped the moisture dripping from the leaves above from his face.

Strongly scented orchids spilled over the descending track. A gushing waterfall splashed into an azure pool below. A dog barked in the distance.

Will paused. "Wolfie?"

"If only." Erin stepped down the steep embankment to the sandy shore and scooped the fresh water to her mouth.

He joined her. Dragonflies flitted over the surface of the pool. The quiver of their wings matched the tremors in his body, which still reeled with sensation from their kiss. How could the worst day of his life have turned into the best day of his life?

"If you were given a genie in a bottle with three wishes, what would they be?" she asked.

He glanced at her. *To be with you. To be with you. To be with you.* "Let me see, maybe unlimited wine, women and gaming."

She punched his arm.

"Seriously, if I had all those things, they'd never satisfy me," he said. "No matter what happens, even if our lives don't work out the way we expect, we still have the most important thing."

"What's that?" Erin edged closer to him and laid her head on his shoulder.

He pressed his lips to her hair for a moment. "We have the King in our lives. And that's forever."

The mingled fragrance of the mossy tree trunks and flowering vines transported him. Back to Eldrad, the island of tragedy, truth and hope. Back to the desert, the emerald woodlands, and ice-capped peaks.

Back to where it all began.

Thank you for purchasing this book. If you enjoyed reading it please leave a review, and tell your friends.

https://www.amazon.com/review/create-review?&asin=0645187615

Book Club Questions:
https://jeansaxby.com.au/book-club/

Get a free short story at:
https://jeansaxby.com.au/free-offer/

Acknowledgements:

I would like to thank my wonderful beta readers: Carol Green, Deborah Daniels, Dr. Elizabeth Babich, Judy Malone, Penny Ovens, Alison Kilford, Barbara Smith, Sarah Hutt, Judy Taylor, and Sally and Victoria Pengilly. I'm so grateful for the time you spent reading the book and giving feedback. A special mention should be made of Lindsay Kemmis for his dedication and help with three drafts of the book.

For medical advice about head injury and coma, I thank Dr. Elizabeth Babich, and Tammy Ho. I'm grateful to Ian, Angela and John Hayles who were so generous with their sharing about the ordeal of having a family member in a coma. Big thanks to Maggie Sinden, paramedic, for her guidance about serious car accident events.

I must give credit to Norma Cody and Samuel Robinson. I may never have finished the book without your vision and insight at the 2017 Eagle Summit in Kelowna, Canada.

Mention must be made of my friends and colleagues in the Omega Writers' Group, the Children's Book Council of Australia, NSW branches, and my St Philip's family. Your support during the writing of this book made a huge difference.

I also wish to offer my profound gratitude to the author of my life story and the author of best story of all stories. He is portrayed as the King in this book.

I extend my gratitude to Margie Lawson for her mentoring and Iola Goulton, my editor, for her expertise and hard work. I give my thanks to all the 2020 CALEB Award judges. You are anonymous, but your wise suggestions and encouraging comments were invaluable.

A special thanks must go to my family for their assistance. I'm indebted to Carol Green, my sister, for 'holding the fort' during the writing, and for her understanding. Thanks to my children Cathy and Scott for their help, and special mention must be made of Stuart for giving so liberally of his time. I wish to express my heartfelt appreciation to William, my husband, for his constant cooperation, advice, and encouragement.

Other:
I thank Selwyn Hughes, (1928-2006), for the idea of the Sea King story and for his inspirational writings.

Humility quote, page 194. Warren, Rick. 2012. *The Purpose Driven Life: What on Earth Am I Here For?* Michigan: Zondervan.

Note from the author:

This book has taken years to write. I hope you enjoyed Will Sutherland's journeys on the Island of Eldrad, and his unfolding romance with Erin. The story explores themes such as—what are we seeking in life and where and how do we find happiness? I hope that this book has been an adventure and unfolding of discovery for you.

If you would like more information I have an author website at https://www.jeansaxby.com.au/. Please subscribe at my website to get free resources and useful links. If you are looking for a better life or need help for addiction and habit changes, check out my website at https:// towardsrecovery.com.au/. I can also be found at:

 https://www.instagram.com/jeansaxby1

 https://www.pinterest.com.au/jeanfsaxby/

If you would like to explore the spiritual themes in this book further, here are some links to start with. There are many more:
https://www.christianityexplored.org/
https://www.biblegateway.com/

About the author

Jean Saxby BSc DipEd is an award-winning #1Best-Selling author, teacher and blogger. She writes what inspires her and to make life better. She thrives on books, beach walks, being thankful and loves family, furbabies, and fun.

https://jeansaxby.com.au/